AN AMISH KISS

When she started walking again, he noticed she was struggling in the deep sections of snow. "Let me help you." He reached out to her, and she took his hand, but as she continued she slipped and started going down.

"Whoa." He stepped closer and slipped an arm around her waist, bracing her against his body for support.

Suddenly, he was holding her in his arms, and his body thrummed with joy.

"I'm so awkward," she sputtered.

"It's not you. The snow is slippery. Icy."

"Well, you saved me." She tipped her head back, and suddenly her face was inches from his.

He tipped his face down and their gazes locked. Her eyes, green with golden bits of sparkle, didn't hold the hesitancy or apathy he expected.

Instead, he saw a tender curiosity. A longing?

The next thing that happened wasn't planned or even wise, but he couldn't help letting his face drop gently, his nose brushing hers, his lips grazing hers . . .

Books by Rosalind Lauer

AN AMISH HOMECOMING

AN AMISH BRIDE

Published by Kensington Publishing Corp.

An Amish Bride

ROSALIND LAUER

ZEBRA BOOKS
KENSINGTON PUBLISHING CORP.
www.kensingtonbooks.com

First Printing: March 2022
ISBN-13: 978-1-4201-5212-8
ISBN-13: 978-1-4201-5215-9 (eBook)

10 9 8 7 6 5 4 3 2 1

Printed in the United States of America

Chapter 1

That morning, the day of her oldest daughter's wedding, Miriam Lapp was up with the mice, as her grandfather used to say. There were cows to be milked and children to be fed before anyone arrived. And although most of the duties of today's festivities fell on the shoulders of volunteers, Miriam could hardly stay in bed while others were up and about tending fires, cooking, and setting up. She stepped into her bedside slippers and felt her way to the dresser.

A match flared in the darkness as she lit the kerosene lamp and glanced back at the bed, not wanting to wake her husband too soon. Lo and behold, his side of the bed was empty. He must have slipped out before she even stirred, that man of hers. A hard worker if ever there was one.

Miriam went to the window, opened the shade, and peered through the chilly glass. Two lights bounced in the dim shadows of the near meadow. Headlamps. Someone was bringing the cows in for milking. As her eyes adjusted to the darkness, she noticed a third light and recognized her husband calling to the cows as he guided them toward the milking barn. The tall, lean figure opening the barn door was no doubt their oldest son, Sam. By all rights, twenty-one-year-old Sam should have been married and on his own by now. She knew it bothered him to see his sister marry first, and she suspected that Sam had held a young woman in his heart for some time now. But that wasn't something a young man wanted to talk about with his curious mem. Still, she wondered. What was the holdup?

She closed her eyes and prayed for patience. Gott made everything happen in its right time! Sometimes it was hard to accept that when you were a mother waiting for love to come to one of your children.

The low croon of a cow brought her attention back to the yard below. The girl in a swinging skirt dress and high black boots was sixteen-year-old Annie. Their second daughter had never met an animal she didn't love and respect, and her contributions in the barn helped to offset the girl's dislike of women's work in the house. That girl would spend all night in the barn nursing a sick horse, but good luck to anyone trying to get her to spend ten minutes making a bed!

Which reminded Miriam . . . there would be hundreds of guests in the house today. Well, they were as ready as they'd ever be. In the past two days most of the furniture had been cleared away from the downstairs rooms, and last night they'd finished setting up benches from the church wagon. After the ceremony was held in their house, the crew of volunteers would move the benches to the buggy barn, where tables for the wedding dinner were covered with red and green tablecloths and set with table settings and china from the wedding wagon.

Thank you, Gott, for this fine day, she prayed silently

as she quickly made her bed and washed up. *Thank you for our loving family and friends . . . so much love! And thank you for the marriage vows you will bless today.*

On the way back from the bathroom, she stopped at the boys' room and peeked inside to find the twelve-year-old twins, Pete and Paul, still sleeping lumps in their bunks. She let them be for now.

The girls' room was full these days, since the arrival of her Englisch nieces last summer. Miriam lowered the lantern light and stepped inside to the sound of sweet breathing, a symphony of life. The eighteen-year-old twins, Serena and Megan, were asleep in their bunks, as was their sixteen-year-old sister, Grace. Good girls, the three of them, but so wounded by the death of their mother from that terrible disease, cancer. Over the past few months Miriam had seen sure signs of healing, as well as growth. At times she'd caught glimpses of her younger sister Sarah in their demeanor—stubborn, spirited Sarah—moments of memory that had taken her breath away. Miriam missed her sister, but in many ways she'd lost her years ago when Sarah had left the plain life behind.

Essie was turned to the wall. The covers had been thrown back on Annie's empty bunk when she went out. Two dark heads popped above the comforter in eleven-year-old Lizzie's bed. On closer inspection, Miriam saw that the second sleeping girl was five-year-old Sarah Rose, who must have crept out of the nursery and slipped into the comfort of her sister's bed during the night. She folded back the comforter covering Sarah Rose's face and marveled at both girls' perfect lips, pink as spring rosebuds. She kissed them each on the forehead.

Her heart was full of love for these children and young people. How she cherished having a houseful!

"Mem?" whispered a voice from behind her.

Miriam turned and saw Essie sitting up in bed, her dark hair falling in a braid over one shoulder. This would be the last night Miriam would find her eighteen-year-old daughter waking up in a bunk in the girls' room. Their lives would be changing with the prospects of future celebrations, different households, and grandchildren. Oh, but wonderful changes.

"Is it time to get up?" Essie asked.

"You can sleep a bit more," Miriam whispered, sitting at her daughter's bedside. "It's just after four, but I wanted to get some coffee going and check on the cooks in the wedding wagon."

Essie rubbed at one eye. "I can get up . . ."

"No. Stay." She squeezed her daughter's hand. "Such a big day ahead."

"I'm so excited. Our dresses turned out so well. All the girls will be beautiful, and did you see the buggy barn last night?" Dozens of volunteers had cleared out the extra farm tools and buggies to set up a dining hall for the wedding. "It looks so Christmassy with the red and green tablecloths."

"I did take a peek, and it reminds me of the season of Christ's birth. It was a good choice, Essie. I'm sure the wedding will go well."

Essie gave a knowing smile and lifted her mother's hand. "And . . . what else? I can tell you have something important to say."

"Just that the most important part of the day will come this morning. Your sacred vows."

"I know that." Essie squeezed her mother's hand. "It might seem that I'm all caught up in the trappings of the wedding, but I know what matters, Mem. Gott's blessing on our marriage will start our lives together as a couple. That's what's important. That's what warms my heart, and scares me a little, too."

"Now, what do you have to be afraid of?"

"Being a wife. I love Harlan, but what do I know about being a wife and running a household?"

"Essie, you just helped clean this house from top to bottom, and you're a wonderful cook. There's not much more than that to running a household."

Essie shook her head. "You've always managed everything, Mem. You make it look so easy, so effortless. You never make mistakes."

"Ach! I goof things up all the time, and you know it."

"I never noticed."

"Because I make the most of each situation. If I make the pancake batter too thin, I call it a breakfast crepe. When I make a mistake and cut fabric for Sarah Rose's dress too small, I turn the cloth into squares for a quilt."

"Sewing has never been your specialty," Essie admitted.

Miriam chuckled. She was a terrible seamstress. "That's right, but I've found that a smile and a positive outlook can cover mistakes like icing on a cake. We do our best and ask for forgiveness, and with Gott's grace the people who love us learn to accept our faults."

Essie nodded, her gaze steadfast in the lantern light. "I'll do my best."

"And I'll be here if you ever need help."

"I love you, Mem."

Miriam reached down to wrap her daughter in a hug.

"You know I love you, my girl." If she could stop time, Miriam would have hugged Essie for hours, breathing in the flowery scent of shampoo mixed with lemon from the recently waxed furniture. But the morning was tick-ticking away. "Now close your eyes for a spell and pray for Gott's blessings upon your marriage."

"I will. Denki, Mem."

Moving silently from the room, Miriam felt a mixture of sadness and joy for Essie. There was a tinge of regret that her oldest daughter would be leaving them, but it was tempered by joy for the new phase of Essie's life. The Bible said to everything, there was a season. For Essie, childhood was moving behind her and the season of marriage and motherhood had arrived. How wondrous it would be to see what life brought Harlan and Essie as a couple!

Back in her room, Miriam pinned up her hair and covered the brunette twist with a white prayer kapp. Then she dressed in her church clothes, the dress a deep blue hue that made her think of summer skies. No one would be noticing her dress today, with Essie and her attendants wearing new dresses sewn with loving hands in the past few weeks. What a whirlwind it had been, preparing for this December wedding, the last of the season! Cleaning and painting the house. Lining up volunteers to cook and serve. Organizing bakers and getting to market for the food, which included one hundred and fifty pounds of chicken and two fifty-pound sacks of potatoes. Fortunately the cook wagon and bench wagon had arrived on time, and setup had commenced two days ago so that the cooks could get started cutting up the chicken and potatoes, chopping celery and toasting endless loaves of bread to make the stuffing for the traditional roasht, a casserole of chicken, bread cubes, celery and egg. Yesterday cousin Ginny and her husband Floyd had started roasting the chicken on a huge outdoor grill, and their helpers had made good use of the three stoves and ovens in the rented wagon. Such a wonderful team!

Seeing all the preparations firsthand, Miriam marveled at how families pulled it off these days. The invite list for Amish weddings needed to include distant family as well as everyone in the church community. For Essie and Harlan's wedding, that entailed over three hundred guests! Late last night, when they realized they needed to add portable heaters to the buggy shed, they'd had to take down a row of tables and switch the dinner plan to accommodate two separate seatings. If she'd been hosting this on her own, Miriam might have fretted, but she was blessed to have organizers and cooks who had pulled off a dozen weddings, and they weren't worried at all! Amish weddings brought the church community together, and it was only because of the many helpers that Miriam could feel free to move down the stairs, light as a feather, on this special day.

Down in the kitchen, Miriam started a large pot of coffee and put paper cups, milk, and sugar on the kitchen table so that anyone passing through could help themselves. Most likely the volunteers already had an urn of coffee made in the wedding wagon, but on a day like this, you could never get enough! She was fetching a spoon for stirring when she noticed the wooden plaque hanging over the calendar. Funny how you can see something so frequently in your daily life that it stops registering.

As a newlywed, Miriam had seen the motto in a gift shop and had asked Alvie to carve it onto a wood placard.

He'd done a wonderful good job. It read: "Marriage may be made in heaven, but man is responsible for the upkeep."

"Amen!" she said aloud. After weeks spent trying to think of a wedding gift for Essie and Harlan, she'd found the perfect solution. She took the sign down, blew at a duster feather clinging to its edge, and set it on the table to wrap. Not yet dawn, and already one problem was solved!

Chapter 2

Sam Lapp pulled on his hat as he wove through the gaggle of wedding guests that had spilled out of the heated barn and house. Most of the younger guests had eaten and were consequently gathering outside on the crushed stone path and frozen lawn near the paddock. Although he was an attendant in his sister Essie's wedding, the ceremony had been over for hours, the first seating of lunch was complete, and Sam figured he was nearly done with his official duties as brother of the bride. Now he could take a moment to pursue his own crazy idea. Although women were wrapping themselves in shawls and many had coats, mufflers, and mittens, Sam wore no jacket over his black Sunday clothes. The cold air was refreshing, and he needed a pick-me-up as he searched for the young woman with glimmering green eyes and a heart-shaped face.

Where was she? One minute, he'd been called away from the eck, the corner table where the bride, groom, and their attendants sat, to help one of the servers transport a heavy tray of dishes. The next minute, he'd turned back to the eck to find Sadie gone—disappeared—along with the bride and groom. And here he'd barely finished his roasht, a traditional casserole of moist bread stuffing and chicken. He'd grabbed two more buttery bites before leaving the barn in search of Sadie.

His gaze lingered on each young woman who wore the emerald green dress of his sister's side-sitters, the wedding attendants who doted on Essie as if she were a queen bee. Where was she? Since he'd been paired up with her for the day, he figured this might be his last chance to let her know how he really felt.

A hand clamped on his shoulder, stopping him in his path. He paused, caught by his Englisch cousin Meg, a solid young woman with wise brown eyes and toffee-brown hair cut shorter than that of most Amish boys. Megan wasn't the girl he'd been looking for, but in the past few months they'd become unlikely friends, and Sam felt more comfortable talking with her than with any of his sisters.

"Are you looking for Essie?" she asked. "I think she's over by the cook wagon."

"Is that so?" He glanced off the question, not wanting to admit it wasn't Essie he was looking for. Sam skimmed the crowd, which mostly consisted of young folks who had eaten lunch in the first sitting and were now roaming outside. All around him young people gathered in friend groups to talk and joke, undaunted by the cool nip in the December air and the dusting of snow that still clung to the distant rolling hills. Everyone loved an Amish wedding. Sam wished he shared their joy in his heart. The small puffs that burst into the air as they laughed aloud. The smiles that lit their faces. He was happy for his sister, but joy rang hollow in an empty heart.

* * *

"I saw her head in that direction with Harlan," Meg said. "They seem really happy. Essie's bubbling over like a pot of jam on the stove. I've never seen her so pleased."

"I guess that's what marriage will do when you've met the right one." Sam couldn't help the cool note in his tone as the words slipped out. Sour grapes? Probably.

He kept his eyes on the young people filing out of the barn, not wanting his cousin to see the raw emotions that had been churning inside him today. Bad enough that he'd had to keep a stiff upper lip and force a smile these past few weeks when wedding preparations for his younger sister had turned the whole household upside down. He wished Essie well. He really did. But couldn't she have waited another year to marry Harlan? Although there was no hard and fast rule, it was traditional for the oldest sibling to be married first. Sam should have been first, but since it didn't happen that way, he was now left to fend off the jokes from his friends and the sympathetic looks from relatives who'd traveled to Lancaster County from far and wide to celebrate the marriage of Harlan and Essie Yoder.

If that humiliation wasn't enough, Sam had to contend with his sister's cluelessness when it came to his feelings for Essie's best friend, Sadie Beiler. "You two have known each other since grade school, and there's nothing there," Essie had told Sam.

Nothing there? Maybe back when they were children, ten or eleven, and Sadie had spent every summer day and night at the Lapp farm, helping with the milking and chores, eating at the table elbow to elbow with Sam, splashing him as the children walked through the shallows of the river or splattering him with a water balloon on a hot summer day.

Back then, when they were young, they'd been like siblings. But recently, the ease between them had fled.

Last summer, when the family had been engaged in a water balloon battle, Sam had taken aim at Sadie and paused, his arm cranked back in midair, as he took in the sight of her: black apron cinched around her slender waist and full curves; round green eyes; skin tanned lightly from the summer sun.

A beautiful woman.

When had Essie's scrawny, quiet friend grown up to be a bright, graceful flower?

That sunny summer afternoon, he had seen the woman Sadie had become.

Hesitating with a cold, slippery balloon in one hand, Sam had been caught staring by Sadie, who had tilted her head, a look of curiosity in her moss-green eyes. Had she realized Sam's new awareness of her as a woman? Not just the quiet girl who'd always shadowed his sister, but a flesh-and-blood woman?

He couldn't tell. Who could know the mind of a woman?

But one thing was for sure as her brows rose and her arm lifted to take aim at him. Little Sadie Beiler had grown into a fine young woman. And when nineteen-year-old Sadie launched the balloon and sent an explosion of water running down the front of his shirt, Sam's heart was lost forever.

But somehow, sister Essie hadn't noticed any of this. And so she had matched Sam up as if he were a trusted gelding hitched up to pull her bridal party along.

"I paired you with Sadie for the day, since Sadie's beau gets jealous easily and everyone knows you and Sadie are like brother and sister. I was going to put you with Laura, but she's interested in Saul Esh, Harlan's friend from the

Amish furniture factory, and Annie will be paired with a boy she's fond of. So anyway, you'll be with Sadie for the day. Sorry I couldn't find a real match for you."

Sam had nodded, even as he'd tried to swallow back the multitude of feelings that had tangled within. The joy he felt in Sadie's presence. The flare of annoyance and distrust for her beau, Mark Miller. The embarrassment and annoyance with himself for having waited too long to make a move and letting her slip through his fingers.

As if she'd ever been his to hold.

And now here he was at the celebration of his younger sister's wedding, still smarting over the jokes about how he'd better find a wife soon before all his siblings married and put him to shame.

"Penny for your thoughts, Sam." Megan's expectant look brought him back to the present.

Sam knew he could trust Megan. Having spent many hours walking the fence line with his cousin and teaching her how to coax and spur the dairy cows along, Sam had learned that not much escaped the scrutiny of Megan's big brown eyes. Everyone said that she looked exactly like her twin sister, Serena—save for her toffee-brown hair, which had been cropped short, just covering her ears in slight curls. But Sam knew better. While Serena had her head in the clouds, her constant chatter floating in the air like soap bubbles, Megan was rock-solid, strong, swift as the wind, and observant. If Serena was the sugar in a pie, Megan was the salt in a stew.

"You're a million miles away," Megan went on.

Sam looked down and tapped his chest with both hands. "Feels to me like I'm right here."

"So literal," Megan said. "I can tell when I'm getting the brush-off."

"Don't be that way." Sam felt his resolve soften. He knew Megan was a fish out of water here, and it was up to him to let her know she belonged. He looked around for eager ears and was glad to see most of the guys and girls his age were gathered by the paddock. "Truth is, I was looking for Sadie."

Her eyes flashed with recognition as she nodded. "Your partner for the day."

"Yah. Because Essie didn't want to burden any other poor girl with me."

"That's so not true." Megan lowered her voice. "Have you had a chance to talk with Sadie?"

Sam shook his head. "That's why I was looking for her. Not a lot going on until after all the lunches have been served. I thought it might be a good time to talk."

"I'll let you know if I see her," Megan promised, looking to her right to scan the young people passing by. It was her first Amish wedding, and she had admitted earlier that she didn't know what to expect. "So what comes up after they finish serving lunch?"

"The servers will cut the cakes and pass around sweets."

"More food, the staple of Amish love." Megan cocked her head to one side. "Why am I not surprised?"

"And then we'll take a break before dinner. There'll be youth singing in the afternoon, and some time for games if the weather holds. Volleyball, or maybe some of us will get out on the ice."

"Now we're talking. I'm finally getting used to skating on ice that hasn't been smoothed by a Zamboni."

He wasn't sure what that meant, but he had noticed Megan's quick improvement at skating. Just last week, when the pond had frozen through and everyone had wanted to be outside, Megan had laced up a pair of Essie's old skates and hit the ice. After a slow start, she was skating circles around most girls out there. Swift and controlled and agile as a cat, Megan had proven herself as an all-around athlete. "That's my cousin," Sam had reminded the other guys, young Amish men who'd never seen a girl command the ice that way.

"Promise me you'll let me know if you're doing a pickup hockey game," Megan said.

"You'd best stick with volleyball or field hockey," he advised. "Round here, Amish girls don't play ice hockey."

Megan shrugged. "No skin off my teeth. You keep forgetting I'm not Amish."

Loud voices and laughter rose from the area near the paddock. Both Sam and Meg turned to take a look at the young Amish folks starting to gather there.

"What's the commotion about?" Meg asked.

"I'm not sure." Sam rubbed his knuckles against his clean-shaven jaw as he squinted over at the group. A couple of the guys were grabbing at Joe Fisher, who dodged them, pushing them off and escaping to the perimeter of the crowd.

"We'll get you, Joe," someone called after him. "Before the day is up, you'll be going over."

"Not if I'm quick," Joe shouted as he continued to back away.

Sam gave a chuckle as he nodded toward the group. Antics like this were the best part of a wedding. "Come. You'll want to see this."

"See what?"

"A prank, sort of. A wedding tradition for the groom." The crowd shifted suddenly as the young men pounced on someone else. Ephraim Kraybill, who had been a groom just last month when he married Suvilla.

Sam chuckled. "Looks like Ephraim is the first to go." Sam and Megan cut around groups of chatting girls as they headed toward the paddock. "It's perfect for today, since this is probably the last wedding of the season. Time to send the newly married men over the fence."

"Over the fence to where?" Megan asked, scrambling to catch up with Sam's quick strides.

Sam shrugged. "To the other side!" he said abruptly before pressing into the group of young men.

"You don't have to do this!" Ephraim was complaining, but there was a smile on his face.

"Yah, we do!" Sam reached down into the fray of men and managed to grab hold of Ephraim's left calf.

On someone's count of three, they worked together and lifted Ephraim up until he seemed to be floating at eye level amid laughter and some groans.

"You know what they say," Sam's friend Isaac called out. "You're not really married till you're tossed over the fence."

"Okay, then." Ephraim turned his head toward the wooden post-and-rail fence, and the motion knocked his hat to the ground. "Give me the old heave-ho!"

Moving like a giant centipede, the cluster of men held Ephraim high as they struggled closer to the fence. All around them girls were gasping and squealing and folks were laughing and cheering.

"Go easy on me, fellas!" Ephraim pleaded in a giddy voice. "Think of me as your mammi's favorite hen!"

Sam could barely keep from laughing at the silliness of it all.

"Ach! Don't be so chickenhearted," someone answered.

"Here we go!" On the count of three, Sam put his weight into the toss as they sent Ephraim sailing over the fence.

For a brief, satisfying moment, the young man's body floated through the air like a football.

Fortunately, there was a substantial group of bearded Amish men standing on the other side of the fence with their arms open to catch him. Once over the fence, the young man landed in their arms, no worse for the wear. The crowd let out a roar of approval, a big "Yeah!" as the catchers tipped the man and righted him inside the paddock, feet on the ground, and finished his voyage with a few hearty claps on the back.

That done, Sam clapped his hands together and scanned the crowd of young people in search of other recently married men. He checked the faces under the brims of dark hats, knowing there had to be more grooms among the party guests. "Next?" If he couldn't spend time with Sadie, tossing guys over the fence was the next best thing.

Chapter 3

"The green of that dress truly brings out the green in your eyes," Amy Troyer told Sadie as they walked together down the lane.

Sadie Beiler cast a curious look at Amy, not quite sure how to handle a compliment from the bishop's daughter. It was wrong to be prideful about beauty or physical appearances, but Sadie couldn't help but feel warmed by the compliments she'd received from various wedding guests today. Yah, pride was wrong, but it felt good to be noticed. Gott had given her these green eyes, this bountiful shiny brown hair, and a strong body, and she was grateful for that.

"Denki," Sadie said with a modest smile. "But you know that Essie chose the color as a celebration of Christmas. It's only a few weeks away."

"And everyone loves Christmas. Do you think it will snow?" Amy asked.

"It's sure cold enough." Sadie pulled her bulky hand-me-down coat closed at the neck as she kept stride with Amy on the uneven gravel drive. She hated to cover up the pretty emerald dress, one of a handful that had been sewn for Essie's attendants to wear, but her throat was throbbing, and she couldn't shake these shivers. The December afternoon had grown cold, and Sadie knew it would be a long trek to the parked buggies, where Amy had left the cupcakes she'd made for dessert. "I'm so happy for Harlan and Essie. They're such a good couple," Sadie added. "Their ceremony was so moving, wasn't it? I cried a little when they took their sacred vows."

It was Sadie's first time as a side-sitter, and she had found the weeks of preparation energizing. Each and every task, whether hemming dresses or addressing invitations, had been a labor of love for all involved. Today, in the culmination of all the planning, she felt overjoyed to be part of the circle of folks Essie and Harlan loved.

"How long has Harlan courted Essie?" Amy asked.

"Years, and I know Essie has prayed to be married to Harlan for a long time."

"And Gott answered her prayers," Amy said quietly. "I'm beginning to think he can't hear mine."

"You shouldn't say that!" Sadie looped her arm through Amy's. "Gott hears all prayers, and he doesn't make mistakes. As the bishop's daughter, you must know that."

"I'm tired of being the bishop's daughter." Amy's words puffed out in cold, white breaths. "Especially if it means no young man will come near me, for fear of getting a finger-wagging lecture on the Ordnung."

"Come now, Amy, it can't be that bad," Sadie reassured her.

"It is." As they walked to the farm field where the Troyer buggy was parked amid dozens of gray Amish buggies, Amy Troyer, the bishop's daughter, told Sadie about the handful of times the bishop had scared young suitors away from their home.

In Sadie's opinion, the stories were a sweet distraction from the pain in her throat. Some even made her smile. Bishop Aaron was a protective father who loved his daughter—a stark contrast to Sadie's own dat, who had frightened all her friends away over the years when his dark side had been revealed. Reuben Beiler's moods were similar to the phases of the moon. Sometimes you could bask in the golden warm glow of Dat's good nature, but you could never rely on that. Sometimes, just as the sky was dark and void of light, the house was a frightening place where anger could lash out without warning and arguments and criticism buzzed in the air like a swarm of irate bees. Sadie shivered, haunted by the dark memories, worn down by the pain that was now spreading to her head.

"But you don't have worries like that," Amy said, drawing Sadie back into the moment. "Your dat isn't a church leader, and you already have a beau. You're so lucky to have Mark!"

"I'm grateful that Mark and I are together," Sadie said. On the topic of her father, she decided to keep mum. Most likely Amy hadn't heard the whispered accounts of the angry outbursts overheard coming from the Beiler home or the occasions when Reuben Beiler had been found passed out along the roadside. Amy was one of the few who thought Reuben Beiler had a happy family and a home in which peace lingered in the air like the aroma of cinnamon spice cookies. In reality the Beiler house was often shadowed with tension, blame snapping in the air like a whip.

"I have to admit," Amy confided, "I figured the two of you would be hitched by the end of wedding season."

Sadie bit her lower lip, unwilling to admit that she'd been counting on that, too. It had been one of many disappointments from Mark, but Sadie had tamped down her sorrows, praying to Gott for humility and acceptance. And grace had come when Essie and Harlan announced their plans to marry. After that day, every moment of Sadie's spare time had been taken up by joyous wedding preparations for her friend.

"Do you think you'll get married next fall?" Amy asked as they approached the gray buggies that had been pulled off into the field in neat rows.

The question was kind of personal—rude, even—but from the dewy innocence in Amy's round brown eyes, Sadie sensed that she meant no harm. "We're thinking on it," Sadie said. "We're moving in that direction, but next fall sure seems a long way off to be making plans, doesn't it?"

"I guess," Amy admitted. "Am I being too nosy? I probably am. I'm sorry, Sadie. It's just that I'm wondering how those things work. I mean, when you're seeing a guy and thinking about getting married. I've got no experience to gauge anything."

Sympathy warmed Sadie's heart. "I never realized how tricky it can be to do rumspringa when your dat is a bishop."

"It would be different if Mem was here. She always smoothed things over with Dat. She would have made the boys feel more comfortable. She was good at calming things down."

How wonderful it would be to have a mother with a gentle touch who smoothed things over. Sadie remembered a time long ago when Mem would rock Sadie and the other children in her arms and dry their tears. So long ago, it seemed like a dream.

"Here's our buggy." Amy cut in between two parked vehicles and went to the back of the buggy. Reaching in, she lifted a rectangular Tupperware container and handed it to Sadie. "Thanks for coming along to help," she said, removing a second large bin of cupcakes. Both containers were labeled "A. Troyer" in black marker. "If I had to carry both, the frosting would have smudged."

"It was good to walk with you. I needed some fresh air," Sadie insisted as they returned to the gravel road and headed back toward the main house and barn. As they walked briskly under a pale winter sky that threatened snow, they chatted about other weddings they'd attended that season and about Amy's recipe for chocolate chip cupcakes. It would have been a glum winter day if not for the wedding. The sound of conversation and merry laughter traveled down over the garden, outhouses, and open fields on this side of the farm. It was a place that Sadie knew like the backs of her hands, having spent many summer days and winter nights in the farmhouse. As children, Sadie and Essie had been inseparable—two peas in a pod—and when things were bad at home, Sadie had always felt welcomed here.

They approached an outbuilding that had once been used as a toolshed and woodshop. Sadie had heard that Essie's cousin Serena had begun using the cabin to restore furniture, which had become a hobby for her. As they passed by, a movement on the far side of the building caught her attention.

Someone was there. A couple.

The young woman had her back to the shingled wall of the building, and a young man had his hands on the wall on either side of her face. It was as if he had her pinned there, and they seemed about to kiss.

It was clearly a highly romantic moment, though neither she nor Amy looked away.

"That's June Hostetler," Amy whispered, though it wasn't necessary. They were probably too far away to be overheard.

"Really? I didn't know she had a fella," Sadie said.

June put her hand on the shoulder of the man's jacket and unwound his muffler. Her laughter tinkled in the cold air like a spoon falling into a glass dish—not unpleasant, but a sound that made a person wary. The young man laughed along as he took the scarf and wrapped it around her neck and dipped in closer. He tipped back his broad-brimmed hat . . .

And that was when Sadie saw it.

The black birthmark at the base of his ear. The dark wool coat, newer and finer than most Amish could afford. The way he bent his knees as he spoke, as if he were too overcome with emotion to stand straight and tall.

That was Mark swooping in on June, trying to kiss her.

Her beau, her love.

Blood pulsed in Sadie's ears, and she felt the sting of embarrassment and betrayal on her cheeks. What was the man she planned to marry doing there, alone with a young woman?

"We shouldn't stare," Sadie whispered, grasping the Tupperware with one arm so that she could guide Amy ahead on the path. "It's wrong to spy." Had Amy recognized Mark in that embrace? A quick glance revealed that Amy seemed intrigued but not alarmed.

"It's not spying if they weren't really hiding," Amy said. "Did you see who it was? Who was the fella?"

So Amy hadn't recognized him. A small relief. "It's hard to say," Sadie answered, thinking it was mostly the truth. It would tear at her heart to admit that she'd just seen Mark with another girl.

Sadie swallowed hard, wanting to cry out in pain. She'd woken up with a scratchy throat this morning, and now it was worse; that thick feeling of lumped-up emotion seemed to be choking her. She couldn't cry, and she couldn't make a scene. Not here, at her best friend's wedding!

But she couldn't let Mark leave today without explaining himself. As if there were an explanation she could bear to hear. So often his actions led back to the one thing that rocked her to the core:

What if Mark didn't love her?

That would explain some of the ways he'd disappointed her. How she'd caught him, more than once, whispering in the ear of a pretty Amish girl at the auction house his father owned. How he lacked generosity when it came to pitching in to help needy families in their church community. How he took the secrets she'd told him and turned them around to hurt her. On a bad day, there was a shadow in his eyes, a stern set to his jaw, and an appetite to argue that frustrated Sadie to no end.

When Mark was in a mood, he always had a reason, an excuse, a way to explain his behavior so that it made Sadie seem like a squealing pig, complaining over nothing. A few times Sadie had resolved to end their relationship. But by the time she spoke to him, he had turned back into the man she loved, charming and social and quick to smile. This was the man she had fallen in love with, outgoing and cordial, able to strike up a conversation with any of the hundreds of folks who passed through the auction house.

"Smiling Mark" had wooed many a girl in rumspringa. But these days, Smiling Mark was hard to find.

When she pushed him, Mark promised to be more considerate of her "delicate feelings." She had long believed that his behavior would change; that he would learn kindness once he saw it. That his affection for her would soften the hard shell around his heart. That baptism would fill him with Gott's love and generosity.

But baptism hadn't changed Mark except for the increased pressure he seemed to feel from his father to marry.

And now, here today at the wedding, for Mark to be romancing another girl for anyone to see . . . it was so humiliating, so crushing that she wished she could go home and find a place to cry alone in the shadows of the buggy garage.

But she couldn't leave her best friend on her wedding day.

Drawing in a deep breath, Sadie focused on the path ahead and resolved not to spoil things for Essie. For now, she would keep mum, say nothing, and suffer in silence.

Chapter 4

"Yeah!"

Megan Sullivan joined in with the cheering crowd as she watched yet another young Amish man fly through the air.

Tossed like a human Frisbee.

All part of an Amish wedding, apparently. Megan was surprised but not shocked. Last year, when she and her sister had been out clubbing with their fake IDs in Philadelphia, Megan had seen performers dive into the audience, trusting that they would be held up and passed around by the audience. This was sort of the same deal, just not what she'd expected at a wedding in the Amish community where she and her sisters had spent the past few months. After hearing her aunt Miriam mention the "sacred vows" so many times, Megan had expected the entire day to be somber and serious.

But this was crazy fun. Something to tease Sam about. But he was still ensconced in the crowd, which was building volume as a new victim seemed to be snagged. The crowd of young men was growing, and she realized that they were dividing themselves, with all the clean-shaven guys on this side of the fence and the bearded men beyond. Enthusiasm was building as newcomers arrived and greeted one another with handshakes or friendly claps on the back. Dressed in colorful shirts—blues and burgundies and beiges—the men were a lively group that was, at the moment, closing in around a young man with sandy brown hair and a thin, wiry appearance.

"Come, Don. You're going over the fence!" someone hollered, and the crowd laughed and cheered in response.

Megan grinned as the guys lifted Don into the air and moved toward the rough-hewn post fence. Her nervousness about fitting in at an Amish wedding began to fade as she chuckled along with the group gathered by the paddock.

Last night, as they'd grabbed a quick supper in between setting up tables and benches for the wedding hall, Megan had confided to Sam that she felt awkward about the big event.

"I'm going to stick out like a sore thumb," she had told Sam.

"Don't worry, Megs," Sam had assured her, using the nickname he'd coined for her during their long walks. Megs-with-the-fast-legs. "You girls are family. You've got to be there."

As one of the few Englisch people in attendance, Megan didn't know what to expect. Watching the Amish wedding preparations, Megan had once again been reminded of how different Amish life was from the world the Sullivan sisters had left behind in Philadelphia.

Instead of calling a caterer and booking a hall, Essie and Harlan had booked these portable trailers—a bench wagon and a wedding trailer that contained ovens, stoves, and multiple sinks. To make the celebration go smoothly, friends and relatives had cheerfully signed up for various tasks. Hundreds of chickens were roasted by experienced cooks, the succulent meat cut into small pieces. Other workers cubed pounds of bread and diced celery to combine it all in a chicken casserole known as "roasht," a specialty of Lancaster County and the main dish served at the wedding. There were ladies to make cream of celery soup and volunteers to make desserts. A crew of helpers had loaded benches out of the wagon to seat the guests for dinner. The farmhouse that Megan and her sisters had called home since their father brought them here this past summer had been scrubbed clean and painted, the ground floor cleared of furniture to accommodate the benches that had been loaded in to transform the living room for the wedding vows.

There was something wonderful about the way everyone had pitched in, making the wedding a community event instead of just a big party. Megan herself had worked on the bridesmaids' dresses, cutting out patterns and running stitches on the old-fashioned sewing machine powered by a foot pedal. The hours of close work with thread and needle had bonded Meg with Essie's close friends Laura and Sadie, even as Megan had observed the tender love between mother and daughter as Aunt Miriam helped Essie with her boldly colored bridal gown. It wasn't easy to organize a wedding in a matter of weeks, but Megan had been happy to be a part of it.

The latest groom was tossed over the fence, and Megan joined in the raucous cheer of the crowd. Beyond the group of Amish young people, beyond the paddock, was a patchwork of fields dusted with snow, some of them bordered by bare trees that looked like standing guards holding up the pearl-white winter sky. Just beyond some of the farm buildings sat the pond, now a frosty white lane that was probably bigger than a football field. It was perfect for ice hockey, one of her new passions, thanks to Sam and her twin cousins Paul and Pete, who had gotten past treating her like a girl once she ran circles around them on the ice.

Hockey with the cousins was a blast, but it was yet another reminder of the athletic life she'd left behind last summer when she'd been dumped here by Dad. She still missed soccer—the passion that had gotten her through junior high and most of high school. But it wasn't Dad's fault that she'd injured her knee. And it wasn't Megan's fault that she'd become addicted to the pain pills the doctors had prescribed. The pills had blocked out the pain in her knee, as well as the ache and doubt she'd felt deep down in her soul. Amazing how little white pills could wipe all the bad stuff away—at least temporarily. But the drugs got their hooks in people, taking over their emotions and lives.

This time last year, she believed she couldn't live without those pills.

Now, finally, she knew better.

She'd been sober and drug-free for months now. Dad's solution had worked. By removing the girls from their old stomping grounds in Philly, he had helped them get a clean break from their bad behaviors.

Surrounded by her Amish family, Megan had learned how to channel her stress into long walks and exercise. Living in Pennsylvania Dutch country, she had no problem staying away from drugs and alcohol, putting her energies into school instead.

Her twin sister, Serena, an itinerant party girl, had been plucked from Philadelphia's party scene. She'd found a therapeutic hobby refinishing furniture, and she'd made friends with a local guy. Close friends. Scout Tanner was crazy about Serena, though Megan saw that he had the common sense to stand up to her sister when Serena went overboard.

Their youngest sister Grace hadn't really changed all that much. She missed Philly and still talked about moving back, though Megan didn't see that happening anytime soon. Dad had brought them to live here because he couldn't keep them safe back in the city. Since Dad needed to stay on the job, which required working odd hours round the clock, he couldn't be there for his three daughters.

Megan realized that she and her sisters were better off here. She had come to love her rambunctious, hardworking Amish family, but that didn't make her stop craving an escape back to the world of electricity, central AC and heat, and a wireless connection. She'd been working hard in school, keeping her grades up so that she could head off to college in the fall.

"What's going on over here?" asked a bright, girlish voice from nearby.

Megan turned to see her younger sister, Grace, walking with a girl in a black Amish bonnet and an emerald green dress—Essie's friend Laura.

"They're throwing grooms over the fence," Megan said.

"Wait. What?" Grace squinted, perplexed. Dressed up for the wedding in her black dress and coat, she almost fit in with the Amish women. Almost. None of the Amish sported the nose ring and bright green streaks that stood out in Grace's hair. "Did you say brooms, or grooms?"

"Grooms, as in young men who were recently married," Megan said.

"Are you kidding me?" Grace grabbed Megan's sleeve. "They're tossing guys over the fence?"

The Amish girl with pale blond hair and an upturned nose gave a sweet smile. "It's a wedding tradition. Has Harlan been tossed over yet?" Laura asked.

"Not yet," Megan said. "I heard his name come up, but no one seems to know where he is at the moment."

"So they throw them over?" Grace was still in disbelief. "Like a body toss?"

"Sort of. But there's someone on the other side to catch them."

"The married guys," Laura said. "They catch them on the other side. It's their way to welcome the groom to married life."

"That is hilarious." Megan pointed into the crowd, where the young men were pulling someone closer to the fence. "Look there! They're going after Harlan."

Grace folded her thin arms across her chest and turned toward the crowd. "This I got to see."

"You fellas don't need to do this," Harlan said, trying to reason with the mob of young men. "You sent plenty of grooms over already. And we're setting up for ice skating and some Ping-Pong in the barn. You don't want to miss out on that."

"We won't miss out," one of the guys said. "This will only take a minute."

"You're killing me," Harlan said with a grin.

"We wouldn't dare," Isaac said. "Essie would never let us forget it."

"All right," Harlan said, holding his arms out. "Just take it easy on my church clothes."

"Stop making excuses and go over!" Essie called as she hurried over to join the girls, a huge smile on her face. The tension and hard work of wedding planning was over, and Essie seemed to be enjoying her big day.

The guys cheered at Essie's comment, and her new husband was hoisted in the air. Megan touched Essie's arm lightly as they watched together, laughing as Harlan called out, "See you on the other side!"

Over he went, into the capable arms of the married men, accompanied by a hearty roar of approval. "Yeah!"

"You're a heavy one," one of the men told Harlan as his feet were lowered to the ground. "You must have put on weight."

"It's that delicious roasht." Harlan patted his belly as he straightened his jacket. "Maybe I ate too much, but it was worth it!"

Everyone was in high spirits as the crowd began to disperse. Laura and Essie were telling everyone that dessert was going to be served soon, and then people would have time for some other activities before the singing.

Megan gave a thumbs-up. "That means ice skating."

"It's too cold," Grace said, turning to Megan. "Let's go to the barn. We can play that beanbag toss game."

Megan shook her head, pointing to the spring house out near the pond. "I've got my skates stashed so I can be ready to hit the ice."

Grace rolled her eyes. "I think you have ice in your blood."

"Once you get moving, you'll warm up," Megan said.

"Not me. But maybe Serena and Scout will join you. They're both a little bit wacky."

Laura chuckled. She seemed amused by the verbal tug-of-war. "I'll play cornhole with you," she offered. "I won't chance skating in my new dress."

"I don't blame you," Megan agreed. Even with their capes and aprons, the polyester dresses worn by the Lancaster Amish women provided little warmth. And dresses were lousy for sports. "I don't know how you do it. Skating and volleyball and Frisbee in a dress."

Laura smiled. "Wearing a dress doesn't stop you from using your legs."

"Trust me—if I had to wear a dress, I would lose all my athletic abilities." Megan saw that Sam was motioning for them to head back to the buggy barn, and they fell in step with the line of people headed back for dessert.

Earlier in the day Megan had seen the beautiful four-tiered cake with pink frosting flowers. In pink icing, some-one had written "Mr. & Mrs. Harlan Yoder" in amazingly perfect cursive. Now the cake had been cut into pieces and was being served along with other baked goods. Cupcakes, bar cookies, and smaller cakes gave plenty of options. Megan chose a piece of coconut cake and joined Sam and his friends—his "buddy bunch," as Sam called it. Jacob Kraybill had straw-blond hair and was so tall and thin his friends used to call him "Scarecrow." Isaac Lapp was also Sam's cousin, his uncle Vernon's son, so the two boys had grown up together. Though his father owned a small dairy farm, Isaac eschewed farmwork and was always cobbling together other small jobs to make money. He volunteered for the local fire and rescue corps, plus he was going to school—community college.

Megan had seen Isaac in the public library when she'd been there with her sisters, using the computers and books for their schoolwork. While it was inconvenient to have to hit the library every time they wanted a reliable Internet connection, Megan had gotten used to organiz-ing her homework so that she could maximize computer time in the two-story building that was packed from floor to ceiling with books.

Megan had learned that the Amish not only enjoyed

borrowing books from the library but that they often came in to make use of the computers and printers. At first it had seemed incongruous to see Amish people staring at monitors and pecking away on keyboards—especially the men, with hats on their laps, long beards, and spectacles. "Why are all those Amish people on the library computers?" Megan had asked her uncle when he'd picked her up from the library last summer. "I thought you weren't allowed to use electricity."

Alvin had pushed the brim of his straw hat up as he'd flashed a glance at Megan. "We can use it. We're just not allowed to have it in our homes." He had explained that some Amish houses actually had electrical wires running to the house, as well as outlets. "But an Amish family would not contact the electric company to turn the service on."

It was one of many lessons learned over the past few months. Another lesson had been that not all Amish youth planned to follow in their parents' footsteps. Isaac was one of those who heard a different drummer.

"He's going to school—community college," Sam had explained when Megan had asked about his friend. "All of his classes come over the Internet. I don't understand how it works, but he needs a computer to do schoolwork."

"Online classes." Megan had never done that, but she was intrigued by Isaac, who was no ordinary Amish guy. She was curious about why he was attending school beyond the time most Amish finished, but since he tended to be the quiet one in Sam's group, she didn't feel comfortable approaching him with questions.

The clamor in the crowd brought Megan's attention back to the present. At the moment, Sam and his friends were recounting Harlan's flight over the fence.

"So which one of you fellows will be going next?" Laura asked. She held a paper cup of coffee in one hand and a mint brownie in the other. "You're all of age. You'll need to marry soon if you don't want people to talk."

Megan found the question insulting, but the guys simply shrugged good-naturedly.

"None of us got baptized yet," Sam said, "so we'd have to start with that before any of us can get hitched."

"The next baptism is in the spring," Laura said. "You three had better arrange classes with the deacon."

Jacob nodded, his mouth pressed into a stern line. "We should talk to the bishop about starting instruction," he said, looking from Laura to his friends. "The time has come, my friends. Time to be men about it and take brides."

"Speak for yourself," Isaac said.

"Don't be bashful, Isaac," Jacob said. "We might as well do this together, like we've done most other big things."

"Getting baptized together is one thing," Sam said, a wry glint in his eyes. "But no matter what you say, I'm not going to marry you, Jacob."

Everyone laughed at that—even Jacob.

"You got me there," Jacob said, lifting a fork of cake. "Henrietta will be relieved you turned me down, Sam. But I still think the three of us should get baptized together in the spring."

Megan stayed quiet, happy to observe the dynamics among the three young men. Close, honest with one another, yet quick to cajole their friends. As a tomboy, she'd played soccer and baseball with boys in her grade school years, and she recognized the way these guys treated each other. She was so there.

"So we'll do it all together," Jacob said. "Next time I see the deacon, I'm going to tell him we want to get baptized."

"Hold on, there. Maybe some of us aren't ready for it yet," Isaac said. His hazel eyes, framed by dark, square glasses, seemed serious. "It's not like bringing in the hay or going to a singing. Joining the church is a big decision. A commitment for life."

"You've got reason to get going, Jacob," Sam said. "You've been seeing Henrietta for a hundred years."

Jacob grinned. "More like three years."

"It's probably time, then." Sam tossed the last bite of cupcake in his mouth. "Don't keep her waiting around too long. You don't want to lose her."

"I don't," Jacob said earnestly. "She's getting eager, and my parents are pushing me, too."

Megan knew that the Amish married young, but she hadn't realized they were under this sort of pressure. Had Aunt Miriam and Uncle Alvin pressured Sam and Essie? She had never noticed one way or the other.

"I'll talk to the bishop about starting lessons for baptism. But it would be great to have you guys along . . ."

Isaac waved a hand in the air. "I pass, buddy."

"I'll let you know," Sam said.

"Aw, you two know you're going to be baptized eventually," Jacob said. "I know you're not leaving Joyful River or your families. I know you'd never leave me, sweet Isaac," he joked.

"Never say never." Isaac patted Jacob's cheek affectionately as the group chuckled.

Megan laughed along, amused by the camaraderie of the three friends and the choice ahead of them. How interesting that Amish young people were compelled to choose whether to commit to a way of life or become removed from it.

Given the choice, Megan wondered what she would do. Watching these three young men, she couldn't imagine any of them making a choice that would draw them away from this friendship. What had Sam called it? His buddy bunch. Buds for life.

Chapter 5

On the walk back, Sadie managed to distract Amy and steer the conversation away to avoid the terrible revelation that ached inside her. She hid the heartbreak, along with the agonizing feeling that seized her every time she swallowed. The pain in her throat was sharp and relentless, as if she'd eaten a thornbush. She focused on the physical pain as a distraction and kept plodding ahead, one foot in front of the other.

Once they reached the buggy barn that was being used as a dining hall, the warmth of the big room was a relief, but the sudden change made her cheeks flush with heat.

"Oh, no! They've already served dessert," Amy said, noticing the paper plates of sliced cake laid out on the table.

"We've got plenty of folks coming back for seconds," one woman said. "It won't go to waste." They placed the cupcakes on the dessert table, where one of the eck-tenders whisked them away to be served with the other homemade goodies. Amy thanked her and hurried off to find her sister.

That left Sadie, weary and hurting, in the large space warmed by hundreds of animated wedding guests. She loosened her coat and glanced over the many tables of dining guests—mostly parents and elders in this sitting. She couldn't find her own parents among the guests, but she did see Amy's father, Aaron Troyer, their bishop, as well as Essie's mother, Miriam.

How she longed to pull Miriam aside to a quiet place and tell her about Mark. Essie's mother always seemed to have the time to listen to a story and give advice. In many ways, Miriam had taught Sadie more about life than either of her parents, who seemed to believe that their children had been brought into the world to make orchard chores and housework lighter. Miriam had a way of pointing people on the right road and showing you what you might learn from a hardship.

But right now Essie's mother was talking with some friends—older women. The whole cluster of women laughed as if they didn't have a care in the world. It would be wrong to spoil their good time with her worries.

Best to focus on the purpose of the day—Harlan and Essie's wedding. She needed to find her friend and see if she needed help with anything. Spending time helping dear Essie would chase this dark cloud of misery from her heart, at least for now. She turned toward the eck, where, little more than an hour ago, Sadie had enjoyed her dinner alongside Essie, Harlan, and the other attendants. Now there were bowls of sweets and candied fruits there, but the bridal couple had moved on.

She walked along the lane by the portable heaters and scanned the large barn, not feeling the strength to push through the tables in search of the bride. A foray into the crowd of older Amish would surely bring countless questions about her family, her parents, and her job at the pretzel factory. She was in no mood to pretend that everything was fine and her life was merry.

"Sadie!" Sam Lapp approached, his black vest flapping open with each quick stride.

Relief seeped through her to know it was just Sam. He wouldn't expect polite and silly conversation. Sam was just Sam.

"Come join us," he said. "We're all hanging out at that table in the back. Some of my cousins are there, and Laura, too. She says you should come over."

"Is Essie with you?" Sadie asked, trying to make out the people at the back tables. The heaters seemed to be going full blast, making the air dry and hot. She slid off her coat. "I've been trying to find her."

"She was just here. I don't know where she went off to, but Harlan's planning to play hockey for a bit, so she'll probably come out to the pond. I'm sure you could borrow skates if you want."

"Nay, not today." She shook her head no, feeling a wave of weariness at Mark's refusal to go on the ice. He couldn't skate, and he would simmer with annoyance if Sadie went skating without him. Even if she had reason to be angrier than a poked bear, she couldn't go to the pond. She would never do anything to hurt him.

"Did you get dessert yet? The chocolate peanut butter bars are the best. We took a vote," Sam said with a grin that softened his square face.

Peering up at him, Sadie felt undeserving of his kindness. "I can't eat."

"Come on, I've never known you to pass up a sweet."

Essie's older brother usually wasn't so talkative. When they were children Sam often seemed to tolerate Essie and

Sadie as they played and did chores together. They made old boxes in the shed into a village for their dolls. They collected weeds from the garden, pretending they were vegetables to take to market. They played with the hose in the summer, crackled leaves underfoot in the fall, and built snowmen in the winter. Sam was like the brother she'd never had, the brother who might have protected her if things had been different.

But that wasn't Gott's way. She was on her own at home. She had no brothers, and her two sisters had married and moved off years ago, one across town and the other to a settlement in York that was nearly an hour away.

"I . . . I'd better find Essie," she said, finding it hard to focus. The noise of conversation and clanging dishes rose like a bubble of sound closing around her.

"Hold on, Sadie." Concern washed over his handsome face. "You seem a little shaky. Are you feeling okay?" He touched her arm, his fingers grazing the green fabric of her sleeve.

For a moment Sam's touch was the only thing that got through the heat of the room, the noise, the raw pain in her throat, the tension thrumming in her head. Sam was helpful. Sam could be trusted.

"I don't know. It's so hot in here, and . . . it hurts to swallow."

"Are you sick? Come back to the table and sit down."

"I can't—" The rest of the words stuck in her throat as her knees folded suddenly and she felt herself collapsing. It would feel good to be on the ground, good to close her eyes and rest. Escape the pain. Just let go.

* * *

Later she learned that Sam had caught her in his arms before she hit the floor. With the help of his cousin Isaac, who had some medical training, he managed to get Sadie to a bench, where she woke with her feet propped up. Her head was leaning against someone warm and soft.

"She's waking up," Sam said. Her first vision was of Sam, his big brown eyes full of concern as he bent over peering at her. "Are you okay?" he asked. "Do you want some water?"

She managed only a blink of the eyes, and even that took some effort.

Essie's cousin Isaac was there, studying her as if she had a very important answer.

"She's pinking up," Isaac said. "That's a good sign."

"How did you know to elevate her feet?" Sam asked.

"From paramedic training," Isaac answered. "But there's an easy way to remember it. If the face is pale, lift up the tail. If the face is red, lift up the head. She was white as snow."

"I'll remember that," Sam said. "Good thing you were close by."

"Get her a drink, Sam," said the voice beside her. Sadie turned her head just enough to see that it was Essie's mother cradling her head in her lap. "How are you feeling, dear Sadie? You gave us quite a scare."

"Not so good. My throat hurts."

"And you're burning with fever. Poor thing, on this big day." Miriam clucked sympathetically as she rubbed Sadie's shoulder. "And here I thought maybe you just hadn't gotten sleep or food in your stomach." She smoothed a cool hand over Sadie's forehead and clucked again. "I don't know what to do but to send you home," she said. "Rest and lots of fluids are what you need. Maybe a visit to the doctor."

Sadie started to cry. Doctor visits cost money, and besides that, she didn't want to leave. "I can't go. I promised Essie I'd be here for her."

"Now, now, you were by her side when it mattered, for the sacred vows. That's the important part. I know Essie appreciates your help and love and support. Could she have made it this far without you? Nay. A childhood friend is one of Gott's treasured gifts."

"I love Essie," Sadie said, sniffing.

"And we all love you," Miriam said sympathetically as Sam returned with a cup of water. "Here. Drink as much as you can."

Sadie felt Sam's expectant gaze upon her as she took a small sip and winced. Instantly her throat flared with the movement. She was so thirsty, but swallowing was torture.

"Do you want something different?" Sam asked. "Maybe tea with lemon and honey."

Sadie shook her head. "It hurts too much. But I'm glad you were there when I fainted."

"Yah. Sure." Sam nodded, staring at her as if she were a sad, broken doll.

Meanwhile, Miriam was organizing the young people. She dispatched Laura to find Sadie's parents and sent Megan hunting for Essie.

"I know she'll want to say goodbye." Miriam's arm around her shoulder was so comforting that Sadie wished she didn't have to leave. It was a wish she'd held since girlhood. If only this were her home. If only she were Essie's real sister instead of her best friend. Her life would be so different, so much better. But all the prayers in the heavens weren't going to make that so.

Miriam squeezed her arm gently. "When you get home, fill the tub with warm water and apple cider vinegar and have a good soak. Tylenol for the fever. And do you have liquid vitamin C and Unkers?"

"Unkers?" Sadie was confused.

"It's a healing salve to put on the skin. I'll get some things from my medicine chest to send home with you."

Sadie closed her eyes for what seemed like a few seconds. When she looked up again, Essie was there in her lovely purple dress. Her face was radiant, probably because her new husband Harlan was standing behind her, squeezing the brim of his black hat in concern.

"Oh, Sadie, I feel so bad for you." Essie leaned down before her, resting her palms on Sadie's knees. "You should have told me you felt sick!"

"But I was having a good time, and I wanted to be here for you." Sadie frowned at her friend. "I'm sorry. It's your wedding day, and I don't want to spoil it."

"Don't think of it. You were here for me, suffering though you were. I'll always remember that. And most of the big day is over." Essie tapped her knee. "You go home and rest up."

"But I want to help," Sadie pleaded.

"Come back tomorrow if you feel better. There'll be plenty of cleanup to do."

Sadie's mother arrived, a bit breathless and concerned over the news that her daughter had fainted. Miriam chatted with Joan Beiler about home remedies for sore throat and viruses. Listening to the women, Sadie felt relief that her father had gone directly to the edge of the property to have the hostlers hitch up their buggy. Sadie knew that celebrations like this sometimes included wine for those who wanted to imbibe, and Reuben Beiler was known to find his way to a drink or two or three if given a chance. To see him stumbling here, in front of her good friends, would only add to Sadie's current misery and humiliation.

"Okay," Mem said after a time. "Here we go, Sadie girl."

Before she realized what was happening, Sadie was helped to her feet with her mem supporting her on one side, Miriam on the other. People standing near the door of the buggy barn stepped aside, making a path for them in response to Miriam's firm instruction.

Watching their faces, Sadie sensed their sympathy and curiosity. When an old friend, Bridget Yoder, called to her, she said she was fine and continued taking careful steps out into the cold afternoon air.

Once they got going on the path, Sadie fell into a steady, easier rhythm. "I think I can do it," Sadie said.

"Just to be safe, hold on to your mem," Miriam said. "I'm going to stop off at the house to fetch those home remedies I mentioned, then I'll bring them to the buggy parking area for you."

Mem thanked her, and they moved ahead into the waning afternoon.

"Such a nice wedding," Mem said as they made their way down the gravel road. "Essie and Harlan seem very happy."

"They're a good couple," Sadie said.

"Everyone was so worried when they heard what happened to you," Mem said. "That Laura fairly rushed me over to you. It's a shame it had to happen during the wedding celebration."

"Yah."

They were passing the woodshop now, the shadows long, and Sadie thought back to earlier in the day when she'd seen Mark there with another girl. The side of the building was empty and shadowed now, but she could still see him there, leaning in close to her. She could hear her tinkling laughter. Funny how her friends had gone out of the way to help when she fell sick, but Mark had been nowhere to be found. Where was Mark when Sadie needed him?

Probably off lollygagging with the likes of June Hostetler. Today, he had shown his true colors.

She longed to tell her mother what had happened, but she was in no mood for conversation, and Mem would be disappointed by the news, as she thought Mark was Sadie's ticket to a successful marriage. Everyone thought that. Money had nothing to do with the reasons Sadie had fallen in love with him, but it had a lot to do with Mem and Dat's approval of Mark. Once a girl married into a wealthy family like the Millers, there would be no worries about having enough money to buy coal for the furnace in winter or to pay an emergency hospital bill. Such financial security would be a blessing, for sure, but that, like so many other things, now hung in the balance.

When they reached the Dawdi House, the small, private house built on many Amish farms for the older grand-parent residents, Mem suggested that Sadie wait while she went ahead to check on whether Dat had the buggy ready. "Have a seat here while I go on ahead," Mem said, helping Sadie onto the bench at the edge of the garden.

"We'll bring the buggy back to pick you up so you don't have to do so much walking." Mem took off her shawl and tucked it around Sadie's lap before hurrying off.

Sadie was exhausted, but the cold made her body tense up and stiffen. She was a mess. Sweating and shivering at the same time, she fixed her gaze on the winter garden for distraction. There were a few dried stalks here and there, but in a few months buds and green shoots would be pushing through the rich soil.

So many hours spent weeding here alongside Essie and her brothers and sisters! So many games of tag and hide-and-seek; Easter egg hunts and water-balloon games. Now that Essie was married, there would be fewer occasions like that. Once Essie and Harlan found a place of their own, she might not be back here on the farm at all.

Things were changing. Sadie tried to tell herself it was all for the best, but she wasn't entirely convinced.

Dusk began to fall as she stared out at the gray garden, and someone called her name.

"Sadie?"

She turned away from the garden and saw him approaching from the road.

Mark.

Her skin was hot with fever and her muscles ached, but all that hardly compared to the pain twisting in her heart.

She turned back toward the garden, but he kept coming.

"Sadie! I heard what happened." He came around the bench and sat down beside her. "Are you all right?" He touched her arm, but she pulled away.

"Best keep away. I have a sore throat, and it might be contagious."

He leaned back. "And you're in a cross mood, I see. What are you doing sitting out here in the cold?"

"Waiting for my parents to bring the buggy around. I'm going home. And I have reason to be cross with you."

"Nay, not with me. The fever must be getting to your brain, confusing you."

"Where have you been all afternoon?"

"Here at the wedding, and you know I came out of courtesy to you. Harlan and Essie are not my friends. I came because it mattered to you."

He made it sound like it was a punishment, coming to a wedding. She folded her arms, staring down at the patches of dead grass. "I saw you with her, Mark. I saw you with June Hostetler."

"Did you? Well, I spoke to a lot of girls today. Guys, too. I had hours to fill while you were off attending to the bride."

"It was more than talking. You were . . . touching her. Wrapping your scarf around her. Did you kiss her, too?" Sadie asked.

"What do you think?" The grit of ire in his voice made it seem like she was at fault.

Sadie shook her head. "I think you need to answer me." She lifted her head and faced him, and for a moment she was taken aback by his handsomeness—his strong jaw, broad mouth, and glimmering dark eyes. Somehow, after what she'd seen today, she hadn't expected him to look quite so good.

He let out a breath. "Look here, I loaned my scarf to someone who was cold. Isn't that what Gott tells us to do? Love our neighbors as ourselves?"

"It was more than that, Mark. I saw it with my own eyes,

and after all this time . . . I need some answers. I need to know, do you favor June Hostetler?"

"I told you, it was nothing."

She so wanted to believe that. She truly did. But the image of the two of them was branded in her mind, two twittering lovebirds.

"Why are you judging me?" he asked. "Blaming me for an innocent gesture? The girl was cold. I gave her my muffler. What's wrong with that?"

"It didn't look that way."

"To you. But you're wrong. When was the last time you had your eyes checked? I'll bet you need glasses."

"Glasses?" It was just like Mark to change the subject. Sadie lowered her head to her hands, her mind too muddled, her thoughts too confused to sort through this now. He wasn't being truthful. Didn't he see how she was hurting? Didn't he care?

Her mind swirled with images of the day. Her best friend standing before the deacon, professing her love to Harlan. Mark leaning in close to June. The spinning dining area, hot and full of noise. Sam reaching out to her as she sank to the floor. Had it been a sad wedding day?

Lifting her head, she realized her cheeks seemed frozen, but her forehead was burning hot. "I'm so sick," she muttered.

"You'd better go to the doctor," Mark said. "And while you're there, get an eye exam. That must be your problem."

His words stung like vinegar on an open sore. Sadie bit her lips together, trying to hold back the tears that threatened. Crying would only make things with Mark worse. She knew that from experience. "You'd better go."

"Why? Because you can't bear to hear what I have to

say?" He lifted his hat to scrape back his dark hair, his face stern and grim. "You'd be wise not to blame me for all your problems. You got sick, and now you're making up things that never happened. It's a craziness, that's what it is. Maybe it's the fever. Or maybe it's just you being crazy."

"I'm not!" she cried, her hoarse voice cracking.

But Mark was on his feet and walking away. Finished with her, at least for now.

Chapter 6

Sam ground his teeth, a sour taste stinging the back of his tongue. Sickened by what he'd seen, he pressed back into the shadows of the Dawdi House porch and watched in silence as Mark Miller strode back toward the wedding festivities.

He hadn't meant to eavesdrop. Mem had sent him with a basket of sore throat remedies. "Run down toward the buggy parking and see if you can catch Sadie before she goes," Mem had told him. "These things should ease her pain through the night."

He had jogged down the lane on a mission, determined to hand the basket off and wish her well, until he passed the Dawdi House and saw the two of them in the garden, Sadie and Mark, their heads and shoulders silhouetted over the bench in the waning light.

At first he thought he would just cut in, interrupt their conversation, and hand over the basket. But once he had caught a few grains of their conversation, he'd had to hear it all. He knew the Dawdi House was empty at the moment, as its current residents, Harlan, Collette and Suzie, were all at the wedding. So he'd crept over to the porch of the house and pressed against the wall, close enough to hear what they were saying.

Close enough to pick up on Mark's cruelty and Sadie's frail attempt to set things right between them.

Maybe it was none of his business. Sam had never been serious with a girl before, and he supposed that what went on between two people was meant to be personal. But a few times as he'd listened in, he'd had to hold back. Every bone in his body had ached to leap forward and confront Mark for treating Sadie that way, twisting things around and blaming her. Even cheating on her.

That was no way to treat the girl you loved. That was no way to treat anyone.

Mark's cruelty toward Sadie bothered him the most. Sadie was sick, and yet there was Mark, arguing with her, twisting things around, trying to blame her for his bad behavior, calling her crazy.

He wondered what had gone on with June Hostetler. He wished Mark would take up with June and leave Sadie alone, though that would probably break Sadie's heart.

Which would leave Sam in a very bad place.

This morning, as he'd helped his dat milk the cows, he'd thought of the road ahead as the stainless steel milking machine had click-clicked away in the predawn. Although his friend Isaac was making noises about leaving the plain life, Sam had a solid view of what he wanted to do. He would get baptized, join the church, and live his life with the people he loved. He'd had his fun with a cell phone, the Internet, and a beer blast out in a friend's cornfield. But those things were fleeting; dust in the wind. He'd come to see what mattered in life. Like the Bible said, there were only three things that lasted: faith, hope and love.

"And the greatest of these is love."

Sam loved his family, and he could see a good life ahead of him working in the Lapp Dairy business. He wanted to start a family of his own and continue the traditions his parents had put in place in their home. Most of all, he wanted to make a life with Sadie Beiler. He'd grown up loving Sadie as a sister and had spent countless hours teasing, joking around, and talking with her at the Lapp farm. Somehow, as they'd both left childhood behind them, Sam's attachment to Sadie had transformed into a different kind of love, strong and heart-rending.

That morning in the dim light of the milking barn, he'd decided that this would be the day that he'd let Sadie know how he felt about her after years of holding back. Ever since she'd taken up with Mark Miller, he'd chastised himself for not making a move sooner, for expecting her to always be nearby, putting up jam with Essie or wading in Joyful River on a hot summer day. All this time, he'd failed to let her know how he felt. Enough with being angry with himself! What was done was done. But today, being paired up with Sadie in the bridal party, he saw it as Gott giving him one more chance to tell her his secret. Another wedding season was ending and Sadie still hadn't married Mark, so he figured he still had a chance.

Until Sadie got sick. That had slowed him in his tracks.

And now, after hearing Mark claw at her like an angry cat, Sam knew this wasn't the time. She needed rest. Quiet. A warm place to sleep.

He glanced down the road behind him, but Mark was long gone. Straightening his jacket, Sam grasped the basket and walked over to the bench. Not wanting to startle her, he made sure his shoes crunched on the gravel, but

Sadie didn't seem to respond to the noise, and so he called to her, "Sadie? Is that you?"

She turned to him, and despite the darkness, he saw that her cheeks were wet with tears. It hurt him to see her that way. He wished he could take her in his arms and rock her and tell her everything would be all right.

She swiped at her cheeks. "Did you see Mark?"

Sam froze. What could he say? He was tempted to pretend that he'd just arrived, that he'd passed Mark on the driveway, but that would be a lie, a sin, and no good would come of it.

"When I walked up I saw that you and Mark were talking. I thought I'd wait and give you some privacy, but I caught bits of the conversation."

"Oh. Well. He's upset right now." She sniffed. "It must be hard for him to stand by while I have all my duties with the bridal party. Mark doesn't have any close friends in this group."

And whose fault is that? Sam wanted to ask. Mark seemed to spend a lot of time with representatives from other auction houses, some Amish, some not. The Millers were members of this church community, but Mark chose not to mix with the folks here. Among church acquaintances, Mark wasn't the star of the show, the way he was down at the auction house, spouting off the auction bidding in two languages while throwing in little jokes about a man's wife or his lazy mule on the farm. Mark could turn on the charm, and he'd dated before Sadie. There'd been two girls, both older than Sadie. One of them, Lavern Gingerich, was married now, and the other girl, Tootie Frey, had gone off to live with her auntie in another settlement.

Sam knew there were stories there, but he didn't go in for gossip.

Sam did know that Mark loved to be the center of attention, as he was on the auction stage. When Amish folks gathered together, people tried to get along and mix in. But Mark had a way of drawing attention to himself. And if people did not pay him special homage, he stewed for a bit and then usually left early.

"You know, Mark grew up in our church," Sam pointed out. "I wonder why he doesn't have friends."

"He has friends," Sadie said, pressing the backs of her palms to her cheeks. "But most of his friends are people from other auction houses. Business friends. Some of them aren't even Amish." She sighed. "I'm burning hot and cold at the same time. I just want to get home."

He slipped his jacket off and put it around her shoulders. As the back of his rough hand grazed the softness of her cheek, he could feel her burning with fever. "Do you want me to check on the buggy?"

"No, please stay. I don't want to be alone with my thoughts. Maybe it's the fever, but . . . I feel like I'm going crazy."

"You're not." Sam sat beside her, so close that his knee nearly touched hers. "I heard what Mark said, but you're not crazy, Sadie. You're a good and kind person, and you don't deserve to be treated that way. Mark was acting like the crazy one."

"He didn't mean it," she said. "Sometimes he just snaps."

Still defending him.

Sam wanted to let Sadie know that he would accept no excuses for the likes of Mark Miller, but it would be wrong to make her even more upset at this point. She was in so much distress that her eyes were closed, and one hand was pressed to her neck.

"You hang on, there. Your dat is probably having trouble finding the hostlers, but I'm sure your folks will be here soon."

She nodded, her face creased in pain, which undid Sam.

Not caring who might see, he reached around her and rubbed her upper arm. He meant it as a soothing gesture, but it struck him that this just might be the closest he'd ever get to Sadie Beiler.

He felt his own face crease in pain—though not the physical kind. During rumspringa, he'd heard lots of popular music at parties and in Englisch stores, all those Englisch songs about the heartbreak and the agony of love. He'd thought they were silly and overblown.

Until now.

They sat like that for a spell, sharing their pain in the cool, dark night.

When Sam saw the headlights of an approaching buggy, he was sorry for the brief interlude to end. Sadie seemed to have dozed off, her head tipped to the left and resting against Sam's shoulder. Nestled as she was in the nook of his arm and chest, she seemed to have found some peace.

God, bless her heart-shaped face and make her well, Sam prayed.

God, love her.

Sam knew he did.

Chapter 7

Megan didn't want to leave the pond

As the day had faded, folks had begun to leave the pond to head back to the Lapp barn for the singing. The western sky was a wash of rose, orange, and purple as the sun broke through the pewter sky for one last glimpse of the day. Megan took advantage of the emptying pond to skate the perimeter and cut through the center without having to be mindful of others on the ice. When she'd gotten ready for the wedding that morning, she definitely hadn't expected to have a chance to get out on the ice.

Ignoring the inky darkness that filled the sky, she practiced skating backward, pivoting and spinning on the bumpy surface. The rough surface made things more challenging, but she was picking it up, learning to cut the blades of her skates into the ice with more force.

"Looks like you're starting to get the hang of it, Megs." It was a low male voice, a deep baritone.

"Thanks." Megan glanced over and saw a tall, broad-shouldered guy mostly hidden by his black jacket and hockey helmet. They were the only two left on the ice. She watched as he unstrapped the helmet and removed it. He had square-framed black glasses and pale hair. "Isaac? I almost didn't recognize you in your hockey gear."

"Tell the truth. We Amish all look alike."

She laughed. "Not true. Though you definitely dress alike."

He chuckled softly. "That we do. We'd better get going. I've got to get into town." He skated to the edge of the pond, walked to a bench in the frozen grass, and started unlacing his skates. "And you won't want to miss the singing."

"Oh, I'd rather be out here, I think," she said, carving a wide arc in front of him.

"But it's lively. Fast songs, and lots of snacks."

"Trust me," she said. "I'm fine with missing it."

Since singings were such a popular sanctioned event for teens in Amish culture, Aunt Miriam had encouraged Megan and her sisters to attend one and see if they might enjoy it. Megan's favorite part of the evening had been the feeling of adventure and excitement among her Amish cousins on the buggy rides there and back in the dark.

The singing itself—that was another story. Everyone had been nice to them, and Megan had been impressed by the array of snacks, including chips and pretzels, home-made cookies, bars, and Chex mix. But after the social hour, the Amish youth had sat facing one another at long tables, and Megan had felt trapped in a strange world. They'd sung a goofy Wild West ballad called "Shoot the Buffalo" and a rousing song about the abolitionist John Brown. But most of the songs were in German, and friend-ship groups among the Amish seemed to be firmly set. Sitting at the long table amid Amish teens, Megan had re-alized that she was truly a fish out of water here. She loved her Amish family, but she wasn't going to become Amish. Much as she embraced their customs, at large community events like singings, she would always be sort of on the outside looking in.

"I went to a singing a few months ago," she told Isaac, "and it's hardly rock and roll."

"Isn't that a Rolling Stones song?" he asked, pulling on his shoes. "'It's Hardly Rock and Roll'?"

It was her turn to chuckle. "Something like that. You know the Stones? You know rock music?"

"I catch my fair share when I go to work. I'm training at the Joyful River Ambulance Corps. In fact, I've got to leave soon to work an evening shift. And tomorrow morning I have an anatomy class at the community college. Required training for the job."

"I heard you were in school. Community college. My teachers want me to sign up for some classes next semester." She whipped around and stopped in front of Isaac with a spray of ice behind her blades. "I've seen you in the library, and Sam said you were going to college. I thought Amish people weren't allowed to do that."

"You're correct. We finish school after eighth grade and then get a job or work at home, in the family business or on the farm."

"So . . . how are you managing to break the rules?" Megan asked.

"Not very well at all. But they tolerate me around here. Everyone's hoping that I'll give it up and get baptized. Follow the path of my parents and friends and commit to Amish life."

"But you're rebelling." She sat on the bench beside him. "Are you going to leave the Amish?"

"I don't know. Maybe. Probably. Maybe not."

"A very decisive guy."

"It's important for me to make the right choice for the future. And what feels right? Well, that changes every day."

"I can relate to that," Megan said. As she unlaced her skates, she told Isaac how she had been sending out college applications, careful to get them out before the mid-January deadline. When she and her twin sister had arrived here last summer, they'd been determined to get into a college back in Philadelphia so they could get back to their friends. But these days, when Megan considered where she wanted to be next fall, Philly was low on the list. What did she really have in common with her friends and former teammates from the city? "I'm not sure that Philly is home anymore, but I don't really fit in here, either."

"I think you fit in just fine here. Your aunt and uncle, Miriam and Alvin, they accept family with open arms."

"They've been great. But still, I'm not Amish. So no matter how much they love my sisters and me, we'll always be fish out of water here in Joyful River."

"Fish out of water." Isaac nodded. "I know that feeling."

Megan gathered up her skates and nodded at him. "I think you do." As they started walking back toward the farm buildings, she thought of the way Isaac had always seemed quiet and withdrawn whenever he came around. She'd thought he was critical of her and her sisters, but now she saw that he had insecurities of his own.

"You're really taking to the ice," he said. "Did you skate back in Philly?"

"Not much. Soccer was my game."

"Ach, soccer. A good summer sport."

"But lately I've been learning the nuances of hockey. Sam's been a big help. In fact, I was hoping for a pickup game this afternoon, or at least some shots on goal, but Sam never made it out here."

"What happened to Sam?" he asked. "He said he'd meet me out here."

"It probably has something to do with Sadie. Maybe he's helping her get home."

"Hmm."

"It's okay. I know how he feels about Sadie."

"What's that?" Isaac pretended to be confused.

"And I know you know that Sam's been crushing on her for years. You're his best friend, right?"

"That much is true. Though you seem to know a lot of things about Sam."

"I'm his cousin. We spend a lot of time walking the fences together. When you've got a few miles behind you and a few miles to go, things get real. You start to talk about things that really matter."

Isaac nodded. "Hmm."

"Don't be all fake mysterious on me."

He smiled. "I was just thinking that Sam is my cousin, too, though he doesn't tell me much about Sadie."

"You guys are probably too busy discussing farm implements and better ways to milk cows and stuff."

"Not really. I'm afraid the dairy business isn't for me." He gave a shrug. "As you said, a fish out of water."

"Wait, how are you related to Sam again?"

"My father is Vernon Lapp, the brother of Alvin."

"So your dad is Uncle Vernon." Megan nodded, trying to piece the family tree together with people she'd met. "And your mother is Milly?"

"That's right. My dat lived his whole life on a dairy farm. The Joyful River Lapp family has been raising dairy cows in Lancaster County for generations. They expect their sons to take on the work."

"Sounds like a lot of pressure. It must be hard for you.

But you shouldn't go into a career you don't love," she said.

"Amish don't have careers. You work hard till the end of the day. There's no questioning if you like the work. It's what you do."

They had reached the end of the pond trail, but Megan didn't want their conversation to end. Off to her left, light shone from the open doors of the barn, where wedding guests were assembling for the singing. Their animated voices, occasionally punctuated by laughter, sounded warm and welcoming. Her sisters and her Amish family would be there, expecting her, but she would rather stay here and talk to Isaac.

"Are you sure I can't twist your arm and get you to come to the singing?" she asked.

"I need to get to work," he said.

"Got it. So maybe we can talk again sometime."

"Maybe." He looked over toward the house, where a cluster of young people emerged, heading toward the barn. "But it might be good that it was too dark for most folks to see us out by the pond. Chins would be wagging at the prospect of an Englisch girl and an Amish guy spending time together."

"Oh, please." Megan took off her helmet and raked back her short hair with one hand. "I can take it. I've been the subject of a scandal before."

"It sounds like you have an interesting story to tell. Some other time."

"I'll hold you to it," she said, smiling.

Isaac nodded, then turned and strode off toward the house. His broad-shouldered silhouette seemed to command the path as he moved away. Funny how she'd been concerned about feeling weird at the wedding, but instead, she'd made a friend.

"You know," she called after him, "I would have talked to you a long time ago if I knew you were so cool. How come you were so quiet?"

He turned around and shrugged, walking backward. "In your world, I'm a fish out of water."

A fish out of water? Maybe he felt that way, though with his calm demeanor, she suspected that Isaac fit in seamlessly in different environments. More than a little intrigued, she hummed a song as she headed back to the wedding celebration.

Chapter 8

After a day on antibiotics, the cutting pain in Sadie's throat eased and the fever went away. By Sunday afternoon the worst part of strep throat was that she had to stay home and remain isolated from her friends and the girls at the pretzel factory.

"You can't go back to work until Tuesday, at least," Mem told her as she handed Sadie a mug of tea. "They can't have girls with strep throat making pretzels." Joan Beiler clucked her tongue at the prospect. "Think of how you could've damaged Smitty's business. He has a reputation to uphold."

"I didn't mean to get sick," Sadie said as she added a tablespoon of honey to the tea. "They think it started with Eve Schmucker. Hers got so bad, by the time she saw the doctor it was scarlet fever." Eve was one of the Amish girls who worked with Sadie at the pretzel factory.

"Yah, I heard that three in the Schmucker family got strep." Mem sighed. "At least you're on the mend."

"Though you'll probably be docked for a few days' pay." Dat spoke without lifting his gaze from the *Budget*, the local Amish newspaper. Reuben Beiler sat in the rocking chair closest to the wood-burning stove—his usual place in cold weather. In the past few years, since their orchard had failed, he seemed much older than fifty-five. There was just a small sprig of gray in his hair and beard, and yet he seemed to lack the energy to get out and about, leaving the maintenance of the mushrooms and herbs to Sadie and her mem.

"It's a shame, but she can't go to work sick," Mem pointed out.

Dat looked up from the paper, his mouth a stern line. "We sure could use that money."

Fortunately, Mem didn't blame her. "It's Gott's will. She'll go back when she's recovered."

Sadie felt a little guilty about missing work, but she knew her parents would make do without the money. The family budget had been more stable since Dat had sold off most of the failing orchard and scaled the family business down to growing mushrooms and hothouse herbs. In the past few years, many Lancaster County Amish had moved away from farming and turned to smaller specialty crafts and niches to make a living. Sadie knew that dairy farms had been hit especially hard in the face of competition from large companies. Fortunately, most of the milk farmers she knew, like Essie's family, were part of a family operation that ran like a cooperative business. Alvin, Lloyd and Vernon Lapp had been in business together since they'd inherited the acreage and milk cows from their father.

Sadie cradled her mug of tea, staring into the rising curl of steam. This was her life at home: bickering and short-comings all around. Nothing she did seemed to satisfy her parents' expectations. Instead, she was always letting them down in one way or another. Her wage at the pretzel factory wasn't to Dat's liking. She lacked Mem's green thumb in the greenhouse. The money she needed for fabric to replace her threadbare dresses threatened to break Dat's budget. The coffee she brewed didn't taste as good as Mem's.

The list of Sadie's shortcomings went on and on . . .

She took her mug of tea to the corner of the kitchen, where the warmth of the stove eased the winter cold that frosted over the edges of the windowpanes. She had missed the end of the wedding day and the big day of cleanup on Saturday. Not that she was any fan of cleaning, but getting together with friends and neighbors for a big event was always the highlight of Sadie's week. It was an off week, so there'd been no church today. Not that she could have gone, but still, it set her mind to thinking how lonely she was, cooped up in this dreary house. Ordinarily, she could have counted on Essie to stop in, but her good friend was likely wrapped up in post-wedding activities that had to be taken care of before Essie and Harlan began their rounds of visits to the guests.

She sat at the kitchen table and took out her knitting. With Christmas only weeks away, she decided her seclusion was a good time to work on her gift for Mark—a ruby red scarf to keep him warm. Red brought out the color in his face. How handsome he'd look with it wrapped around his neck!

As her needles clicked and the rich red yarn became linked, she tried not to think about the fact that Mark hadn't come by to see her. Maybe he'd stayed away because she was contagious yesterday. She didn't say anything to her parents, but she was hoping that he would stop by this afternoon or evening. It would be a joy to break her seclusion, and now that her fever was gone, she was eager to smooth things over between them.

She had knitted a few more inches of vibrant red scarf when she heard her parents talking in the front room. Mem appeared in the doorway, removing her reading glasses and smoothing the apron of her dress.

"There's a buggy out front," she said. The pink color on her cheeks made her mother seem suddenly cheerful. "Looks like a young man is here to visit you."

Mark!

He had come to see her! Joy rose in her chest like a summer sunrise. Sadie got up from the table, then went back to tuck her knitting away to be sure to keep the surprise gift out of Mark's sight. She smoothed back the sides of her hair and then moved into the front room, trying to ignore the jittery feeling over their last words together. Surely he'd be in a better mood today, especially if he'd come to visit her after her illness.

She took in a deep breath and held it as Mem opened the door and greeted him.

But the man who came in the door was taller and thinner than Mark. He took his hat off to reveal lighter hair . . . a medium brown.

"Come in, Sam, and leave the cold air outside, now."

"Sam." Sadie pressed her lips together and nodded a greeting, hoping that he couldn't see the disappointment seeping in.

Mem pushed the door closed and rubbed her arms. "How's it going with your house now with the commotion of the wedding over?"

As Sam chatted with her mother, Sadie took the time to pull herself together and think of the next step. It was nice to have a visitor, even if it wasn't her heart's desire.

As Sam talked, he squeezed the brim of his black hat, as if wringing it out. Was he nervous? No need for that. They'd known each other for years. She'd been over at the Lapp house so frequently that she hadn't noticed Sam passing the threshold from a boy to a man, but it had happened. He'd once looked so similar to Essie, but now Sadie saw that he had the same strong brow ridge as his father, with dark eyebrows that lifted expressively as he talked. He tended to be serious, like Essie, but when he was happy, his smile lit up a room, the way his mother's always did. She hadn't thought much about Sam during rumspringa, but today it occurred to her that he would make a wonderful good husband for a nice Amish girl.

"Let's go talk in the kitchen," she suggested. "I can make you something warm to drink. The kettle's still steaming. Would you like some tea, or maybe hot chocolate?"

"Hot chocolate would be good." He peered out above the ice crystals on the windows and asked about the structure out back. She explained that this time of year, they often had to light a propane heater to keep the mushrooms and herbs at the right temperature. But Sadie knew he hadn't come to talk about growing plants.

"I'm glad you came to visit," Sadie said as she poured hot water from the kettle into a mug. "I've been cooped up in here like a chicken. Did Essie send you to check up on me? I felt so bad, leaving the wedding, and then missing the cleanup yesterday."

"Everyone was sorry you got sick, but the cleanup went okay." He pressed the brim of the hat, moving it in his hands as if it needed smoothing out. "Scout's mother offered to do the linens and napkins in her washer and dryer, and Mem couldn't believe how quickly the benches were moved out. The house is already back to normal, though

Dat says it might take him weeks to sort out his tools in the buggy barn."

"Oh, your dat doesn't like anyone messing with his tools, I know that." She thought about Sam's family as she spooned Swiss Miss hot chocolate powder into the mug of steaming water. If she hadn't been recovering today, she'd most likely have ended up spending time over at his house, putting up jam or baking with Essie. Actually, since it was Sunday and a day of rest, they would have baked something easy. Maybe those double cocoa cookies that melted in your mouth like warm chocolate. The Lapp farm was a second home to her. "When I think about it, I don't know what I'm going to do with my free time once Essie and Harlan find a place of their own. When I have a day off from the factory, I'm so used to heading over to your house to help with the baking or the laundry."

"You can still come; you know that. Essie and Harlan will be living in the Dawdi House for a while. And Mem wanted me to invite you to come over tomorrow. You're to have dinner with us and then go to the schoolhouse to see the Christmas program."

"I do love seeing the children perform at Christmastime." She thought about it as she stirred some milk into the cocoa—that bit of extra creaminess that improved the mix. "I promised Lizzie I would be there."

"Then I'll tell Mem you'll be there tomorrow." He took the mug from her. "Mem and Essie will be pleased."

"Thank you for being the messenger," she said, adding warm water to her tea. "And thank you for helping me out the night of the wedding. I can't believe I fainted. I don't know what I would have done if you weren't there to catch me."

"I just want you to know that if you ever need a

friend . . ." His warm brown eyes stayed on her as he took a sip of the cocoa. "I mean, I know you have friends, but I just want to say that I'm here if you ever need help."

"Now, why would I need that?" she asked, sitting at the table beside him. She wanted to sound coy, to make light of things, but her tone seemed to make fun of his offer.

"You never know."

"It's kind of you to say that, Sam. Since I don't have any brothers, you've always filled that spot for me. It's as if Gott put you in my life so that I could know a brother's love." How blessed she was to have a kind brother in Sam.

"After all these years you've spent with Essie, I'm surprised you'd even want a brother," he said. "Remember how she used to spy on me and my friends, and I reported her to Mem?" He shook his head. "She got in so much trouble."

"I did, too," she admitted. "We must have been terrible pests."

"Worse than mosquitoes. Isaac and I couldn't get away from you two."

Giggling, she gripped the warm mug as childhood memories came rolling back. "You and your friends gave us something to do. I don't know how you put up with us."

"We let you have it a few times. I remember winning a few snowball fights."

"Yah, but there was that time when we chased the fish away in the river," Sadie said. She and Essie had marched along the riverbank, clapping loudly to disturb the fish. The boys had been so exasperated! Jacob had thrown his hat to the ground.

"Ach! That made us so mad! But I think we had the last laugh. Remember?" He looked to the ceiling and chuckled. "I pushed Essie into the water."

"That's right! And I got soaked, wading in to help her."
She covered her mouth, but it didn't restrain the laughter
that rocked her body. "Oh, Essie was furious with you. But
I have to admit, I thought it was funny."

He nodded, a glimmer in his warm brown eyes as he
chuckled. "And that day, we all walked up the path together.
We got to singing some songs. And by the time we got back
to the farm, we were all friends again."

"We had some wonderful good times, didn't we?" She
smiled, feeling warmed by her tea and the easy laughter
she shared with Sam. It was another reminder of her attachment to Essie's family and the large farmhouse where
she could always find a friendly face.

Now that Essie was married, Sadie wasn't sure how her
relationship with the Lapp family would change, but she
sensed that she'd be invited there less often. That thought
scared her, but she pushed it aside as Sam launched into
another story of their childhood antics.

Sam had ended a tedious day with laughter. For now,
she would enjoy his company and the memories that
bound them.

Chapter 9

"And then Sadie got her coat and we went out back so she could show me their growing operation. Not so much the greenhouse—I've seen plenty of those—but the mushroom shack was what I wanted to see." Sam felt a little silly spilling his guts, but he needed some honest feedback.

On the way home from Sadie's, he'd stopped to pick up Isaac, who'd brought his hockey gear. When they arrived back at the house, they convinced Megan to come out to the pond with them to practice some hockey drills. And once Megan asked about Sadie, the whole story of Sam's afternoon began to trickle out.

"I've heard you can make a good amount of profit selling edible mushrooms," Sam went on. "It's one crop that doesn't rely on the weather so much. No sun or too much rain—it doesn't matter, as long as you keep the shack within a certain temperature and keep the soil moist and dark."

"Are you serious?" Megan swung her stick, sending a puck flying into the goal box with a satisfying *plunk!* "Mushrooms are your idea of a romantic conversation?"

Isaac chuckled as he skated backward, narrowly

cradling a puck with his stick. "You Englisch have strange ideas on dating. Amish folks are more practical. We're happy with a buggy ride or a few goopy looks at a singing."

"A buggy ride could be romantic, but still . . . the mushroom shack?" Megan shuddered. "I guess if you like the smell of dirt and worms."

"There are worse smells than dirt," Isaac said dryly. "Chicken coops. Fertilizer. Have you ever stepped in manure?"

"Unfortunately," Megan said. "But right now we're talking about Sam trying to make an appeal to Sadie. I wish you could have thought of something more appealing than the mushroom shack."

"That part turned out okay. Actually, it's a good thing we went back there to take a look. Turns out the heater ran out of propane, and the shack was cooling off fast. If the temperature had dropped overnight, they might have lost the mushrooms to the overnight freeze." Sam skated up to the wooden box he and Harlan had constructed to simulate a goal guarded by a goalie. There were two slits on either side of the wooden bar in the center for the pucks to slide in to score a goal. Sam had stuck rubber lining onto the wood so that it wouldn't shatter every time the puck went flying into it.

He reached into the goal, picked up the pucks they'd been using for practice, and tossed them out on the ice, where they skittered over toward Megan and Isaac. "Sadie was really grateful that I noticed it," Sam added. "I changed the tank for her and took the empty one home with me. I'll get it filled tomorrow."

"That's a romantic thing to do," Isaac said. He pulled a puck closer with his stick and looked to Megan. "Our Sam saved the day."

"Well, it's certainly helpful," Megan agreed.

"It was nothing." Sam skated away from the goal, found a puck, and nudged it along the ice. "Sadie shouldn't be pushing herself with tasks like that. She's still recovering, and those tanks can be heavy."

"And when you return the tank, you'll get another chance to see her," Megan said.

"Maybe. Either way, she's coming here tomorrow for dinner and the schoolhouse Christmas program."

"Perfect!" Megan lifted her stick in the air, as if victorious. "There's another chance for you to spend more time with her."

"Mmm." Isaac shook his head. "Not here, in front of parents and with Essie around. Sadie and Essie stick together like they've been glued."

"Do you want me to talk to Essie about giving you two some space?" Megan offered.

"No!" the young men answered in unison.

Megan laughed. "I hear you. I'll stay out of it."

Sam pushed away from the goal and scooped up a puck with his stick. "As my dat says: 'If you try to plow through frozen ground, you'll break the plow.'"

Megan stopped skating abruptly, ice chips flying behind her. "You think I'm pushing too hard."

"No," Sam said. "But I can't push like that. Not while Sadie is with Mark Miller."

"I get that," Megan said. "It's tricky. What are you going to do?"

Sam wasn't sure. "Sometimes, there's nothing to do but wait things out." He skated toward the center of the pond, moving his stick rapidly to keep control of the puck. It was a drill all the hockey players did, a bit of repetitive work that paid off over time. Patience and time, they were virtues.

He could wait for Sadie.

Already he'd been waiting years for her.

He could keep waiting if he knew that, one day, she'd finally see Mark's true nature and turn him away. Spending time with her today, laughing and talking so easily, he had been reminded of the special relationship they had. Even if she insisted that she saw Sam as a brother, there was no denying the bond between them. Mark Miller couldn't take that away from them. All the charm and wealth in the world couldn't erase the memories Sam and Sadie shared of river days, snowball fights, Monopoly games, and volleyball out on the wide green lawn in front of the Lapp house.

Even if that was all they ever had between them, Sam thanked Gott for those times. He had learned that you had to recognize your blessings and be grateful for the good things Gott placed in your life.

And Sadie was a good thing.

As she'd taken him through the greenhouse, pinching off dried leaves and explaining the different ways they tended to basil and rosemary, flat parsley and dill, he'd fallen into the cadence of her voice. Words had a different sound when they came from her lips. There was a freshness, like the shimmering of a spring breeze through newly budded leaves on a thick branch. Her moss-green eyes brought a sense of life to everything around her. Looking in Sadie's eyes, he felt special, like more of a man than he'd ever thought possible.

But these were not thoughts he could share. Not with his best friend or cousin or sister.

He couldn't tell them how time flew by when he was

with her. How he had wanted to pin her down about Mark, to warn her that he'd seen Mark's temper fly before, more than once, at a singing, a volleyball game, a campfire gathering of youth. Mark Miller was not one to be trifled with, and if the conversation he'd overheard the night of the wedding was any indication, Sadie wasn't immune from Mark's anger.

He wanted to protect her, keep her safe, but in the short time at her house Sadie had quickly veered away from any mention of Mark, and he hadn't the heart to pin her down. All he could do was wait, watch, and be ready to help.

Her own guardian angel.

Chapter 10

"Isn't it wonderful good that we can have this time together?" Miriam rocked back in her chair as the needles in her hands clicked away in a steady rhythm. The warmth of the potbellied stove made the room cozy, as did the smells of baking that filled the house. Across from her, daughter Essie and her friend Sadie sat on the small sofa, each with a knitting project in her hands. It was a delight to have them here for the day, both having arranged to come over to attend the Christmas program at the schoolhouse after supper.

It was a Monday evening, and Harlan was due home from his job at the Amish furniture factory soon. Essie and Harlan were living here in the Dawdi House, though it was only a temporary arrangement until they got on their feet. Miriam knew that her daughter was looking forward to cooking for her husband in the small cottage, but tonight the new couple would eat with the family and then head off to the school.

Sadie would stay for dinner, too, as the children had asked if she could attend their program. She seemed recuperated from her terrible throat—a strep infection, they had told her at the clinic. Most weekdays Sadie would have had to be at work, but Smitty, the owner of the pretzel factory, had told her to stay home until Tuesday, just to make sure the medication wiped out all the infection.

They had spent the afternoon baking pies with strawberry-rhubarb filling that Essie had canned in the summer months. Miriam was pleased with the success of Essie's new business selling jams and pie fillings. She'd just started it in the summer, and already she'd hundreds of dollars. She and Harlan were saving to buy a house, and Miriam thought it was a fine goal. She could only imagine them living on their own, with children underfoot.

Her grandchildren! Wouldn't that be a thrill?

But she couldn't let herself get ahead like that. One day at a time! What was it that Alvie liked to say? *The man who lives for tomorrow forgets about today.* Right now, she had the joyous treat of a half hour of knitting with these girls, and then off to see her school-age children in a celebration of the season. Life was good!

After baking, Essie and Sadie had cleaned up the kitchen, while Miriam had quickly assembled her hamburger hash casserole and popped it into the oven. Alvin was out milking the cows with help from Sam and Annie. Lizzie was at the dining table doing homework with Grace and Serena. Pete and Paul had begged to spend the last bit of sunlight out on the ice with their cousin Megan, who enjoyed learning hockey moves from them. Miriam had granted them their wish, but she'd sent five-year-old Sarah Rose along with them as a guarantee that they would return home by suppertime. Sarah Rose wouldn't last long out in the cold. Now they were thirty minutes away from a delicious dinner, and Miriam had the joyous treat of getting off her feet for some knitting and conversation.

"Only three days since the wedding, and your house seems to be back to normal," Sadie said.

"We were so lucky to have family and church members help us pack up the songbooks and benches," said Essie. "I don't know what we would have done without our work crew, right, Mem?"

"They were a marvel," Miriam agreed. "They packed up the bench wagon and loaded the dishes into the wedding trailer. Alvin's brother sent back the portable toilets. The day after the wedding, all the rentals were gone, so we could scrub the floors and put the house back together."

"I wish I could have helped," Sadie said as she carefully looped a stitch. "I hated being stuck at home in quarantine."

"We missed you, but those were doctor's orders," Essie said. "I'm grateful to all our helpers. Serena's friend Scout took all the tablecloths and kitchen towels to his mother's house, and things were washed and dried within hours."

"So many people to thank," Miriam said. "Essie and Harlan spent yesterday evening with Harlan's mother and sister, but after tonight, the thank-you visits will begin in earnest."

"One down and about two hundred to go," Essie said, though her tone was light. Miriam was happy to see her oldest daughter moving easily into her role as a wife. Though she was going to miss having Essie, the most responsible of her children, around the house. Old and young, these girls needed to learn their household duties, from bed-making to cooking, and Essie had been so handy to have around.

It was a custom for the newly married Amish couple to visit their guests after the wedding and extend a thank-you in person. On weekends, the new couple set out to visit their local relatives. Once close family were thanked, the couples often linked up with other newlyweds from the same community to pay their thanks in combined visits. The couples usually enjoyed traveling together, and the combined visits cut down on the time and expense of the host families. Such was the Amish honeymoon. Miriam liked the custom, as she believed it prompted the newly-weds to socialize within their community and it seemed to seal the identity of the newlyweds as a couple.

The conversation turned to Christmas. Miriam loved the holiday, but this year she felt a bit sad at the prospect of sending her three nieces home to be with their father for a few weeks. She understood that the girls missed their dat, but after their months under her roof, Miriam was going to miss those girls!

The three women chatted about different holiday recipes, Christmas traditions, and gifts that the girls were consid-ering. Essie hoped to give her aunts some of the special jam that she had put up for the holidays—strawberries, cran-berries, and a bit of orange zest. Sadie had purchased a calendar with flowers of the season for her parents, and she was knitting a scarf for Mark. "I'm not experienced enough to knit him a sweater," Sadie said, "but a scarf I can do."

"That red will look good on Mark," Essie said, leaning closer to admire her friend's handiwork. "A scarf makes a very nice gift. But the big question is, what will Mark be giving *you* for Christmas?"

Sadie winced. "Oh, I don't know . . ."

"Is the gift really that important in this season of Christ's birth?" Miriam asked.

"I know it's the thought that counts," Essie said. "But Mark works in the auction house, Mem. He sees lovely things come in and out all the time. Maybe he's picked out a shiny crystal candy dish. Or a china butter dish. Or a handmade quilt . . ."

"A quilt is too much. It's too dear a gift from a beau you're just courting," Miriam told the girls as her needles clicked away. She had long had a squeamish feeling about this Mark Miller, though it was nothing she could really put into words. Anyone who saw him fast-talking down at the auction house could see he had charm and skill, though Miriam wasn't quite sure if his heart was big enough for a sweet girl like Sadie.

"An expensive gift isn't right for a casual relationship," Miriam said. "Unless there's more there." She lifted her eyes to Sadie, giving the young woman a chance to jump in and expand on her feelings for Mark Miller.

But Sadie simply smiled, her gaze steady on her knitting.

What did it mean? Miriam wondered. She knew the girl wasn't shy around her. Sadie was like another daughter in this house. Hmm. If Sadie hoped to marry Mark, she was keeping it to herself. Did she love him? Truly love him, like the big-heartbeat, warm-hug feeling a woman felt when her man walked into the room? Miriam felt confident that her Essie had found a blessed love for her new husband. But Sadie and Mark . . . Miriam wasn't sure they'd last through the winter, let alone through a lifetime. With all the talk of Mark's access to material things, she hoped Sadie didn't have stars in her eyes over the Miller family's wealth. Reuben Beiler's family had suffered some difficult times, with Sadie's dat having to sell off his orchard, but they were on an even keel again. "A simpler life, with less demands," Sadie's mother Joan had explained recently when Miriam saw her at church. To everyone's surprise, their mushroom business was doing quite well at the local markets.

"Mem, what do you want for Christmas?" Essie asked, distracting Miriam from her thoughts.

Miriam's fingers kept moving deftly as she considered the question. "That's sweet, but what do I need that Gott hasn't provided?" She smiled at her daughter, touched by the question. "You and Harlan work so hard, and I know you're saving for a house. I wouldn't have you spend your money on me."

"But if you could have anything," Sadie said, "what would that be?"

"The happiness of my family . . . that's what makes Christmas a wondrous time for me."

"I don't know that we can find a box big enough for all that!" Sadie teased.

The ding of the windup timer prompted Miriam to put down her knitting and fetch her casserole from the oven. "Dinner is ready," she told the girls in the dining area. "If you want to pack up your books, you can help me set the table."

"It smells delicious!" Serena said.

Grace was rapidly closing books and stuffing them into her backpack. "Just in time. I need a break from algebra."

"You and algebra don't get along well," Lizzie observed as she folded up her notebook.

The savory smells of beef and tomato filled the air as

the back door exploded open and the rest of the family filed in.

First came the boys, their cheeks rosy from the cold.

"I'm starving!" Pete cried.

"Me, too!" Paul agreed. "But I could have played longer."

"How could you see the hockey puck in the dark?" Miriam asked.

"I have very good eyes," Paul insisted.

"Hey, guys, get back here and wash up," Megan called from the mudroom.

Miriam pointed the boys back out the door as Sarah Rose came in. "Megan helped me wash my hands," she said.

"Good." Miriam guided her youngest to the table, wondering how she had managed her brood before her Englisch nieces had arrived from Philly. Oh, the girls had suffered their worries and issues, but they had responded in kind with such fierce love that it seemed they'd always been a part of the close family.

Then came the milking crew. Already three of them had washed up, left their muck boots behind, and stowed their headlamps. Alvin came up behind Miriam and placed a kiss on her cheek.

"That smells like the best dinner you've ever made," he told her, giving her shoulder a squeeze.

Alvie said the same thing nearly every night, and every time Miriam chuckled. "You must be hungry," she said. "The cold takes it out of you."

"It does," he agreed. "But I'm looking to get a second wind for the Christmas program."

"I think you're going to like it, Dat," Lizzie said as she went around the table, setting down forks. "I have some lines in the 'meaning of Christmas' skit, but I can't tell you what. It's a surprise."

Miriam chuckled. The program was always supposed to be a surprise, but bits and pieces always spilled out. She filled the baskets with hot rolls and covered them with the red-checkered napkins. She put out a big bowl of salad, butter, and two serving dishes of pickled beets, and then called everyone to the table.

Harlan came in just as Essie was taking a seat. He kissed her cheek and sat down beside her. Alvie called everyone to pray, and heads were lowered as the family thanked Gott for this generous, bountiful meal.

Closing her eyes, Miriam gave a prayer of thanks for the blessing of having her family together under one roof tonight. How she loved these children, these young folk, this kind and steady man who had been her husband for more than twenty years!

There were two large dishes of the hamburger hash—plenty to go around—which was a good thing, as the boys were not bashful with their portions. The rolls were still steaming hot when broken apart, making the butter melt on contact. It was a hearty meal—just the thing to stick to the ribs and warm everyone up.

For dessert she served Essie's strawberry rhubarb pie to anyone who was interested, and then she went into the kitchen to get the cleanup underway. The girls set up a line of workers to scrape, rinse, wash, dry, and put away the plates and silverware. With a few songs and their efficient system, the dishes were done in no time.

Which was a good thing, as they needed to be on their way to the schoolhouse. Alvin and Sam hitched up two buggies, and Miriam made sure the family bundled up in scarves and hats. Then they were off to the schoolhouse, the hooves of their loyal horse Comet and mule Sunny clip-clopping on the pavement in the dim glow of the headlights.

As they rode along, Sarah Rose pouted that she couldn't sit with her Englisch cousins, who were riding with the young people in Sam's buggy. Miriam assured her that she would see the girls at the schoolhouse. Pete and Paul commented on how Megan had taken to ice hockey "like a boy," which made Alvie chuckle. Her children's fondness for their Englisch cousins brought Miriam great pleasure. She knew her sister Sarah, who had passed from a terrible cancer, would have found joy in the new family ties that had been strengthened of late. It was Gott's way to shine love on a difficult situation. Love could mend all hearts.

The schoolhouse glowed from the distance, alight with kerosene lamps. They were greeted by Teacher Julie, an eighteen-year-old who had been a student herself but a few years ago. She was handing out programs that said "Welcome" and had an illustration of a snowman that had been colored by the students.

There was an air of excitement in the room as the schoolchildren went to the front and the families found seats. Sarah Rose crawled onto Grace's lap and settled in. Lizzie told Serena and Megan about her part in one skit to make sure the girls didn't miss it, before hurrying off to join the class. Seating was tight, so Sam, Sadie, Essie, and Harlan found a spot on the bench in front of them. It gave Miriam a chance to gaze at Essie and her new husband, full of gratitude to Gott for the good life they had ahead of them.

The program started with a song, "O Come, All Ye

Faithful." Miriam smiled at the children assembled in the front of the room as she scanned their bright faces for her own. There was Pete, staring straight at his parents with a bored look that said he'd rather be doing something else. Beside him, Paul tugged at one sleeve of his jacket as he sang. Goodness, was it getting too small already? These boys were growing like weeds in a summer garden. How was a mother to keep up with them?

Miriam found eleven-year-old Lizzie, who kept her eyes on the teacher as she sang every word. Such a dutiful student and a sweetheart. Little Lizzie was a schoolteacher in the making. It made Miriam's heart lift to see her daughter in her happy place.

There was a little skit about winter being the season of snow and ice. The children held up snowflakes that had been cut from white paper—such delicate creations. They spoke clearly, their lines well learned, as they reassured the audience that winter's cold would give way to springtime, with warmer weather and signs of new life in green chutes and budding trees.

Next up was a poem about Christmas that the children recited together. Then one child popped forward with the letter *C* on a decorated card as she explained that *C* stood for Christ's birth, "the most important reason for this very special season!"

As another child stepped forward with the letter *H*, Miriam secretly scanned the crowd, pleased to see so many friends and neighbors in attendance. And it was nice of Sadie to come along. Dear Sadie was a fixture at the house. Once, Sadie's mother asked if her daughter was a bother, coming by all the time, but Miriam had responded, "The more the merrier!" And she'd meant it.

At the front of the room, the spelling of the word *Christmas* was up to the letter *S*, and ten-year-old Davey Fry turned his card to reveal the word *SAVIOR*.

"*S* is for our Savior who came from heaven above. God sent his only son to show his endless love." Davey let out an audible sigh of relief when he was finished, causing Alvie to chuckle beside Miriam.

Next Lizzie stepped forward and turned her card to reveal the word *THOUGHTFULNESS*.

Miriam touched Alvin's sleeve, watching with anticipation.

Lizzie's cheeks were pink, her smile a beacon in the night. "*T* is for Thoughtfulness at this special time of year. Take care of lonely and sad folk; be sure to keep them dear." Lizzie's big, cheerful voice filled the room.

"That-a-girl," Alvin whispered.

Miriam squeezed her husband's arm as a wispy blond angel of a girl stepped forward to talk about the *M* in *Christmas*.

In the row in front of them, Sadie nodded at Essie, who turned to her with a smile. Sam watched them both, lost in a state of wonder. Miriam blinked, her focus now shifted from the presentation to her son. It was as if Sam had tiny, twinkling stars in his eyes—a bit of an overreaction to watching his sister perform in the Christmas program.

Actually, Sam was watching Sadie.

Miriam took in a silent breath and then pressed a hand to her mouth. That was it! Sadie was the one.

That was the look of love in Sam's eyes.

But how could that be, when Sadie was planning to marry Mark Miller?

Miriam pressed a hand to her mouth as all the dangling

clues were tied together in a neat bow. Sam's unhappiness. His reluctance to start courting anyone. Her eldest son wouldn't even take a girl home from a singing. She'd begun to think he wasn't trying hard enough, but now she knew the sad truth.

He was in love with a girl whose heart had been won by someone else.

Chapter 11

Megan put her duffel bag by the door and moved past the fat red holiday candles, burnt down to squat nubs, to look out the window for the car. Still no sign of Dad. All around her, the house seemed like a haven in winter, with warmth emanating from the woodstove, smells of cinnamon and sugar cookies coming from the kitchen, and Christmas cards on display. It would be hard to leave, but their father was picking up the three girls this afternoon for Christmas in Philadelphia.

The Xs that Lizzie drew each day on the wall calendar showed that there were just three days until Christmas. Lizzie and Annie sat at the table, working on a five-hundred-piece jigsaw puzzle of a winter scene, while Serena helped Sarah Rose staple Christmas cards onto a wide green ribbon so that they could hang them up for all to see.

"Any sign of Dad?" Serena asked.

"Not yet." Megan paced across the room to the back window, where she could just make out the dried reeds at the edge of the frozen pond. She wished she could be out there right now with Pete and Paul, practicing some hockey moves. But that would have to wait a few weeks, until they returned.

"I'm going to miss Scout so much," Serena said with a sigh. "That's the downside of leaving."

"What about me?" Lizzie asked. "Aren't you going to miss me?"

"Aw." Serena's brown eyes opened wide as she nodded. "With all my heart and soul!"

"You're going to miss Christmas," Lizzie pointed out.

"We'll be celebrating with our father," Megan said.

"But we can start the celebration now!" Serena got up from the table and started singing. "Deck the halls with balls of holly!" She grabbed Lizzie's hand and danced her around the living room. "Fa-la-la-dee-dah . . ."

"La-la-la-la!" Megan chimed in, lifting little Sarah Rose and twirling her around.

Grace, who stood at the top of the stairs carrying her pink suitcase, quickly descended, dropped the bag, and came over to join the fun.

By the time they finished the verse, crooning at the top of their lungs, Grace, Serena, Annie, and Lizzie collapsed on the couch in giggles as Megan and Sarah Rose cheered.

"Merry Christmas! And God bless us, one and all!" Megan proclaimed as she lowered her little cousin to the ground.

"That was so much fun, I'm going to pretend you had the song lyrics correct, though you didn't," Grace said in her usual wry tone.

"What's wrong with the way I sang?" Serena asked.

"I think the song sounded wonderful good," Lizzie said.

Grace let her head loll closer to her cousin. "Of course you do. You don't have a pessimistic bone in your body."

"Yes, I do," Lizzie insisted. "What's 'pessimistic,' anyway?"

"I love that 'fa-la-la' part," Annie said.

"It was a joyous song." Aunt Miriam appeared from the kitchen. She was wiping her hands on a towel, a few white streaks of flour marking her cooking apron. "I'm so glad to see everyone in high spirits."

"It's Christmastime, Aunt Miriam!" Serena exclaimed.

"Indeed, it is," Miriam agreed. "One of my favorite times of year."

"And we're *finally* going home," Grace added.

Megan wanted to elbow her sister in the ribs for making the comment, but she was too far away. Not that it was bad to go home to Philadelphia for the holidays; it was just that expressing the desire to get away from Lancaster County made Grace sound like an ingrate.

Fortunately, everyone took it in stride, and talk began about other Christmas songs they could sing together.

"But wait," Serena interrupted. "Before Dad gets here, we have some Christmas gifts for you, Aunt Miriam."

"Just small little things to say thank you," Megan explained.

Miriam pressed one palm to her chest. "Good heavens, girls! That warms my heart so."

"Will you open them now?" Serena asked. "Since we won't be here for Christmas."

"Absolutely." Miriam sat on the sofa, and all the girls gathered round as she opened their gifts one by one.

"This one's heavy," Miriam said with a look of curiosity. She unwrapped the white tissue to find three new candles from Grace. Two were white, and one was an emerald green.

"When you brought out the Christmas candles, I noticed that they were burnt down to almost nothing," Grace said. "These are scented with pine, so they smell like Christmas."

"How wonderful!" Miriam passed them around so everyone could have a sniff. "I so enjoy adding a little light to our house in this dark time of year. Denki."

Next she opened a set of holiday cookie cutters. "I saw them at the store and thought how much fun it would be to have wreath and tree shapes," Serena said.

"These will work well for my sugar cookie recipe," Miriam agreed.

Next came Megan's gift. Megan bit her bottom lip as her aunt tore off the wrapping. When picking out the gift, she'd thought long and hard about the love and protection that Aunt Miriam and Uncle Alvin had offered her and her sisters, and she wanted to give her aunt something that afforded her a little bit of warmth and comfort.

"A new pair of slippers!" Miriam held them up for all to see. "How did you know my slippers are falling apart?"

"I noticed," Megan said. "Merry Christmas, Aunt Miriam."

"I'm delighted with these gifts. So thoughtful of you girls to spend your own money and think of me! I'm so grateful." Miriam opened her arms wide. "Merry Christmas to all of you, my dear nieces!"

The well-wishes were followed by a round of hugs that almost brought Megan to happy tears. She took a deep breath to gain control as she hugged Annie. Why was she feeling so weepy? She wasn't the emotional type, but this . . . this was different.

Last summer she had been dumped here feeling lost, alienated, and stressed-out. She took to walking as her therapy—something her counselors had suggested when she was struggling with addiction—but at a certain point, she realized that she was walking to try to escape her life.

And soon after she arrived here, Sam started walking with her. Since he had to check the fences to search for damaged areas to make sure no cows were stuck or escaping, he figured walking with Megan would make the time go faster. In the process, they'd become good friends, and over the months, Megan and her sisters had adjusted to living on an Amish farm. They'd made a few friends at school and found some hobbies, but mostly their life was taken up by their large, lively Amish family.

Aunt Miriam, who seemed to know what they needed before they did, kept them busy and happy. Uncle Alvin, with his jokes and wise sayings, always made them feel as if they belonged here.

And their cousins, each kid with his or her own interests and personality, were united in the way they welcomed their Englisch relatives. Although Megan missed her father, it was hard to say goodbye and spend Christmas away from the Lapp family. She longed to see the kids' faces on Christmas, to watch Lizzie and Sarah Rose open their presents. Plus, she was being pulled away from the ice just as she was mastering some hockey moves.

"That's Dad's car!" Grace cried.

Everyone was talking at once as Dad came in the door with a hearty greeting. His joy at seeing his daughters made Megan feel a little guilty for wishing she could stay here. Uncle Alvin and Sam came in from the barn to say goodbye, and Pete and Paul snuck in wearing their snow pants, much to their mother's dismay. At the last minute, Aunt Miriam rushed out after them with plastic baggies filled with cookies.

"One for each of you, since you probably won't have time to do any baking before the holidays," she said, handing them to Megan.

Megan and Serena exchanged a knowing look. There'd been no baking in their Philadelphia apartment since before their mom died. After Sarah Sullivan was gone, no one had had the heart to go into the kitchen to make a nice meal beyond mac and cheese or a sandwich. The Christmas cookies were like gold bricks in Megan's hand. Precious treasure.

"Yum!" Grace exclaimed. "Yay."

"We'll try not to eat them all in the car," Serena said.

"Thank you, Aunt Miriam," Megan said. "Have a wonderful Christmas."

"You too. Drive safely!" she said, waving. "I hear there are some ice patches by the covered bridge near Joyful Falls."

"Will do," Dad said, starting the engine.

Megan just had time to fasten her seat belt before they were rolling out. When she looked back at her aunt, she seemed small and vulnerable in front of the large farmhouse—definitely an illusion.

Aunt Miriam had amazing powers. Beneath those sparkling eyes and that kind smile, there was a superwoman.

"I'm going to miss this place," Megan said.

"You know, I can't wait to get back to the city," Serena said, "but I'm missing Scout already, so I'm kind of feeling torn. Caught between two places."

"I won't miss it," Grace said. "I'll always be a city girl."

"But it's the people who make a place," Megan said. "I'm glad we've really gotten to know our Amish family. Sam and Essie have become good friends. The twins taught me to play hockey."

"Lizzie's supersmart," Grace said. "And I like hanging out with Annie, although that girl is obsessed with animals.

I think she really understands them, like she can read their thoughts."

"An Amish Doctor Dolittle," Serena said, and they chuckled together.

"Aunt Miriam and Uncle Alvin have put up with a lot from us, but they seem to take it all in stride. I think they kind of like having us around."

"Of course they do," Sully said. Although he kept his eyes on the road, Megan could tell that he hadn't missed a word. His fine cop senses kept him tuned in to what was really going on. He must have understood that his daughters were doing a balancing act between two worlds.

Having been away so long, Megan half expected to find the apartment full of dust and cobwebs, like a haunted mansion. Instead, the place was clean and neat as a pin. It smelled of lemon and detergent, and the carpets had tracks from being freshly vacuumed.

"You got a cleaning lady!" Serena observed. "Awesome!"

"It still doesn't mean you can be a slob," their father said. "You need to pick up after yourselves."

"Will do, Daddy-O," Grace assured him, patting his arm on the way to the fridge.

The couch in the living room seemed to reach out to her like an old friend, and the flat-screen TV would provide hours of entertainment. She had missed that! Grace appeared with a glass of milk, stretched out on the couch, and immediately tuned in to a reality show with young people stuck on some island.

Megan went on down the hall to the room she used to share with her two sisters. The bunk beds, with the single pushed against the wall with the fairy lights strung above it—Serena's doing—seemed a bit empty compared to the big room with three sets of bunks that she shared in the Lapp house. She put her duffel bag by the closet and sank onto the familiar brushed-denim comforter of her bed. This was home, wasn't it? It felt good to be here right now, but thoughts of the coming days were muddled with stress. While there were many good memories of this room, this apartment, there were also the desperate times and bad choices that had led to her addiction to painkillers—the devastating problem that had driven her away from here.

The last time she'd sat on this bed, she'd been trying to figure out what to pack for her move to Lancaster County and what to leave behind. Back then, going to live with her Amish family had seemed crazy and desperate, like jumping off a cliff.

Now she could see that it had not only saved her life; it had redefined her, giving her a new, very different life in the country. Of course, her time with the Lapps was temporary. As was her Christmas vacation here in Philly. She couldn't know where she'd end up, but right now, she had to navigate her old friends and teammates.

She opened her suitcase, pulled out some clothes, and changed from her football jersey to a black sweater, more appropriate attire for meeting her friend Hadley Cribben. In a text conversation on the way home, Hadley had insisted that Megan meet her tonight at a pizza restaurant in the neighborhood before their soccer team assembled for their Christmas party. "I miss you so much, and everyone is dying to see you!" Hadley had insisted.

Megan was reluctant to see everyone, but she couldn't say no to her best friend.

* * *

For Megan, Amerigo's was a blast from the past, with colorful Christmas lights strung up in the window and blinking screens and bonking noises from video games and pinball machines that lined one wall. The smells of pizza—dough, spices, and tomato sauce with cheese bubbling on top as the worker slid it out of the oven—made her mouth water.

"Megsie!" Hadley pushed away from a small table by the window and rushed over to envelop Meg in her arms. "I've missed you so much! I'm so glad you're here. Let me see you." She leaned back and nodded. "Very sophisticated in black. And look at you, with color on your cheeks. Are you actually wearing makeup, or is that a healthy glow?"

"You know it's not makeup," Megan said, and both girls laughed. Megan had always thought that primping in front of a mirror was a waste of time—a notion that had been reinforced by Amish living.

The two girls ordered slices and Cokes and sat at a small table by the front window, where the colored lights inside and out lent a festive mood to the place. They talked about guys and their college plans. Once upon a time they'd planned to go to the same college, but now Hadley admitted that her grades weren't good enough for Penn State or Temple. "I'm planning to stay at home for a while and do community college," Hadley explained. "It'll give me a chance to get my grades up."

Megan nodded as she chewed, trying to appear nonchalant though the news hit her hard. Hadley hadn't mentioned this during any of their conversations in the past few months—but then, living without an Internet connection, Megan hadn't been able to keep in close contact.

"More and more people are starting with community college," Megan said, trying to stay positive.

"How about you?"

"I'm hoping for Penn State, but I've got a few other applications in," Megan said, trying to pretend that it didn't matter, that it hadn't been her main motivation these past few months. A few months ago college had seemed like an escape. It was her way out of Lancaster County, her ticket back to civilization, to cell phones and sports stadiums and like-minded people her age. But as she had adjusted to farm life, she'd come to see that escape wasn't exactly welcome anymore. "I'm signed up for some online college classes next term, so I'll get advanced credit. We'll see."

Their conversation was interrupted by Heather Newell, a pretty girl with scraped-back blond hair and a willowy frame. Hadley introduced Heather as one of the new members of the soccer team.

"Some of the other girls are here," Heather said, pulling a chair over to their table. "They're out in Bailey's car, pregaming."

Megan gave Hadley a curious look that said: *What's that about?* but Hadley shrugged it off.

"Megan used to be one of the stars on our team," Hadley said. "She got us to the championship last year."

"Really?" Heather took out a small metal tube, put it to her lips, and sucked on it.

Vaping? Megan couldn't believe this girl was a serious soccer player. Not to judge, but vaping and drinking were only going to slow an athlete down.

"So how come you left the team?" Heather asked.

"An ACL injury," Megan said.

"And then after that, she had to move to Amish country, where there's no television and no cell phone service," Hadley said.

"That sucks," Heather said. "Aren't you mad at your parents for ruining your life?"

Megan stared at the girl with the bold cheekbones and smoky eyes. Very pretty on the surface. "Actually, moving in with my Amish relatives saved my life," she said. "After I got injured, I got hooked on painkillers."

Heather stared at her as if she'd just sprouted horns and a forked tail. "Wow. Like, Oxy?"

Nowadays, even the slang term for the drug made Megan want to cringe. "The drugs really did a number on me. It happens a lot. When a drug tells your brain to block the pain, you kind of want more of it so you don't have to deal with things."

"Sounds really intense," Heather said.

"It was. I'm really grateful my family helped me pull out of it. Being in a different place, in Lancaster County, that really helped. A change of venue worked for me."

Heather nodded. "But now you're back in civilization, and I bet you're dying to chill a bit." She sucked on the vape pen and paused, and then a cloud billowed from her mouth.

Hadley stopped chewing the end of her straw. "Wait. What?"

"We should go out to Bailey's car before they drink all the White Claws."

"That's not why Megan is here," Hadley said.

"That's okay," Megan said, tucking her cell into the pocket of her jacket. "I need to head out anyway."

"Don't go," Heather ordered. "The rest of the girls will want to see you. This was your team, right?"

Half the team had graduated last year, and the other half—well, Megan was beginning to suspect that they weren't the motivated, driven athletes she'd come to love.

She was trying to slip out the door when some of her former teammates emerged from the car.

"Megan! Oh my gosh, it's you!" There were squeals and hugs and lots of questions.

While Megan was happy to see some familiar faces, she knew she didn't belong here anymore. The team had morphed into some other group, with an atmosphere that was not only strange to her but also dangerous. She chatted for a few minutes, but when they tugged on her to come have a drink in the car, she told them she really had to go. She gave Heather a hug, promised to text soon, and then slipped out of the crowd.

The walk home was cold, but Megan was familiar with the streets of her old neighborhood, Queen Village, an area near downtown Philly that was usually bustling with people. She turned down a side street with brick row houses lining either side, determined to bask in the garlands and Christmas lights strung here and there.

Things had changed here. Her friends weren't necessarily her friends anymore. She pulled her beanie down to cover her ears and held her head high. That was okay. She'd moved on, too, but she wasn't sure what that meant for the holidays. What was Christmas at home if she had no one to hang out with?

Back at the apartment, she found her sisters in the bedroom with a rap song playing from Grace's phone. Grace was kicking back on her bed, while Serena sat at the desk, leaning in toward the mirror to apply makeup.

"Well, that was a bust," Megan said. "I went to hang out with Hadley and almost got sucked into a team party." She told them about how her soccer team had changed. "It's weird to see an athlete vape. I'm just disappointed to see old friends going down that path."

"It's everywhere," Serena said, passing her cell phone. "Look at my Snapchat feed."

Megan took the phone and saw that her twin's social media accounts were full of invitations to a party that night.

"Lexi Moscowitz says it's bound to be a rager," Megan read aloud from her sister's feed.

"Lexi was always a party animal," Serena said, staring into the mirror.

Megan felt anxiety mounting. The party scene had been Serena's downfall when they lived here. Megan looked up at her sister in concern. "So you're going?"

"Are you kidding me?" Serena paused with the mascara wand in front of one eye. "I'm so done with that stuff. Grace and I are going to a movie."

"A Christmas movie," Grace said. "It's animated, probably really corny, but it will get us in the Christmas spirit. You should come with us."

Relief seeped through Megan as she passed the phone back. "I'm not really a movie person," she said. It was hard for her to sit still for long periods of time.

"But this will be fun, the three of us together. And if you get antsy, you can go get us all some popcorn."

"I do love that salty theater popcorn," Megan said, considering it. When she realized the alternative was staying back in the apartment alone, she decided it would be fun to spend some time with her sisters. "Okay. Count me in."

Much to Megan's surprise, the movie held her interest. The story of two sisters who tried to be fair and just rulers in a community threatened by evil invaders took her away from her own problems and reinforced the value of having sisters who had your back through thick and thin.

"When was the last time we did something together?" Grace asked as the girls strode three abreast down a city street that sparkled with Christmas lights. "Just the three of us?"

"It's been forever," Serena said. "Look at that. I can see my breath."

"I love that. Mist puffs." Megan smiled. "Tonight was fun. I just wish there was more to fill my time while I was here."

"We need some Christmas traditions," Serena said. "Living with the Lapps, I realized how little routines and rituals can be soothing. Let's start some Christmas rituals."

"Like what?" Grace asked. "The only thing we do is open one of our gifts on Christmas Eve, and that's kind of lame now that Santa doesn't come anymore."

"Serena's right. We need some new traditions." Megan smiled as a plan formed in her mind. "We used to have traditions when Mom was alive."

"Baking Christmas cookies," Serena said.

"And sending out Christmas cards. And the Advent calendar. I mean, we wouldn't have to do everything the same, but we can begin Christmas traditions of our own, starting this year."

"I like it," Serena said.

"And we can go beyond the cookies and gifts. It's Christmas, and we should be doing some things to help other people. We could volunteer somewhere, or make cookies to give away. Remember how Mom took us to the wishing tree in the mall? We each picked an ornament with a Christmas wish from someone less fortunate, and we bought their present and wrapped it up and put it in the donation bin."

"I remember that." Grace clapped her gloved hands together. "I picked out snuggly pjs for a little girl who loved the color pink."

"And I got a warm sweater for a woman named Nancy." Serena's lips formed a pouty expression. "It felt so good, thinking that my gift might warm someone else up. We should definitely do that again."

Megan stopped walking and let out a whistle. "Okay, girls. The night is young. We're going to turn around, go back to the Fashion District mall, and find that wishing tree. Who's with me?"

Grace and Serena paused and looked back at her curiously.

"But how would we pay for that stuff?" Grace asked.

"With our own money." Megan gave her youngest sister a stern look; sometimes Grace could be a cheapskate. "I thought you've been saving your allowance from Dad."

"I have, but I was planning to use it for Christmas shopping. I already got Aunt Miriam's gift, and I've been looking forward to hitting the stores to shop for you guys and Dad."

Megan held up one hand. "Take the money you were going to use on me and buy a gift for someone in need."

"Me too," Serena said. "I like Megan's idea, and my heart needs a little lift. Good deeds will do that for you. I know that might sound selfish, but that's how I feel."

Grace let out a sigh. "You guys make me sound greedy for wanting to buy you Christmas gifts. I just want Christmas morning to be fun again."

"It will," Megan said. "But in a different way. Trust me."

"Fine," Grace said. "Let's go back to the mall."

"No time like the present to start buying presents," Serena said. "And, you know, shopping is one of my talents!"

"Right behind modesty," Megan teased as they headed back down the street.

Chapter 12

"That's it," Sadie told her little niece, who stood on a stool beside her scrubbing potatoes with the vegetable brush. "Scrub it well, so we can cook it up for dinner."

Three-year-old Lovina's brows drew together as she concentrated on rubbing the skin of a large, uneven potato. "Why potatoes so dirty?"

"They grow in the dirt, underground. But you're doing a good job cleaning them. You're a good helper in the kitchen," said Sadie, who thoroughly enjoyed having Lovina by her side. The little girl had been like Sadie's shadow since Sharon and her husband, Elam Schwartz, had arrived for the holidays. It helped that Lovina slept on a cot in Sadie's room, giving Sadie a chance to tell her stories, tuck her into bed each night, and then greet the smiling, bright-eyed child each morning.

"All done with the potatoes," Sadie said, helping the little girl down from the stool.

"Let Mammi put them on to boil," Joan said, moving the large pot to the stove. The potatoes would be mashed and then spread atop seasoned ground meat for their family favorite, meatloaf casserole. It was to be their dinner, a celebration with all of Sadie's sisters attending. Sharon and Elam had made the trip from York and would be staying for a few days, and sister Polly would be here soon with her five children ranging in age from four to eleven. Tomorrow was Christmas Eve, but a festive holiday spirit had filled the house ever since Sharon and her family had arrived.

"Sadie, do you have a minute?" asked Sharon, who had been nursing the baby in a bedroom. "He's fussing again."

"Maybe it's gas." Sadie took the precious bundle and looked into his shiny eyes. "What's up, little man?"

In the rare moments when Lovina was napping or playing on her own, Sadie soaked up the sweet infant her sister had given birth to just three months ago.

Those baby jowls! Those rosebud lips! Those tiny fingers flexing at the world! How Sadie loved baby Nathan! She loved cuddling him. She loved bathing him and swaddling him in a blanket. She even loved walking him round and round the room when his lips puckered and let out whimpers and wails. "Oh, yah, I know," she told him in a quiet voice. "It's okay. It's all just fine. You're here with people who love you, and you're going to have a very merry Christmas."

"Our Sadie is a natural with the babies," Sharon told their parents. "What I wouldn't give to have her living closer. Ach! She's such a big help."

"You could hire her as a maud," Mem said. "I think they could spare her at the pretzel factory."

"What young girl wants to go off and raise her sister's children?" Sharon said. "She needs to have children of her own."

"Maybe someday," Mem said on a sighing note.

"I can hear you talking about me, and I don't want to be a baby maid," Sadie called as she paced through the main room, patting Nathan's back.

"So then tell us," Sharon said as she pulled Lovina onto her lap, "when are you going to get married and start a family of your own?"

"Only Gott knows the answer to that," Sadie said, wishing that she felt more confident about her relationship with Mark. Every time the subject of marriage came up, he managed to wander over to another subject like a stray calf. Although Sadie longed to know the mysteries of marriage and the blessings of children, she didn't feel comfortable pushing Mark to talk about it. What if it scared him off for good? "Gott knows, and so far, he hasn't given me the answer," she muttered quietly into Nathan's delicate shoulder.

But with a dinner to prepare and a buggy full of family coming to join them, there was no time to moon about being single. While Mem finished preparing the meatloaf casserole, Sadie and Sharon chopped parsley, peppers, onions, and celery for the chow chow and Dutch noodles. They lifted the heavy wooden leaf into the center of the big table, covered it with the special linen tablecloth, and then set out flatware and plates for thirteen people.

Lovina looked up at the table and frowned. "Where's Aunt Polly?" she demanded.

"She'll be here soon," Sadie promised, "along with your uncle and cousins. Do you remember your cousin Ruthie? She's about your age. Maybe you'll want to play together."

Lovina pursed her lips, then nodded. "Okay. I'll play with Roofie."

Sadie and Sharon tamped down their amusement as they finished setting the table.

As Sadie smoothed down a corner of the tablecloth, she wished Mark could be here tonight. How nice it would be for her family to see a simple token of his affection; that would fend off some of the comments from her sisters pushing her toward marriage. But Mark had a family obligation, which everyone had this time of year. He had invited Sadie to dinner with his family tomorrow, on Christmas Eve, and she had set aside her green dress from the wedding to wear for the special occasion. On Christmas Day, Reuben and Joan Beiler would host a dinner for their three daughters and their families. And then on Second Christmas, celebrated on December 26, the family would have dinner at the Lambright house, the home of Polly's in-laws. Emery and Madge Lambright owned and operated the Country Diner in town, and their gatherings always had plenty of space and food. Second Christmas, known as Ztvett Grishtdag, was one of Sadie's favorite days, as the celebrations with large, extended family were always festive and fun.

Such a busy season, but Sadie loved being around her sisters and their families. Every moment spent baking with little Lovina or comforting baby Nathan reminded her of the true desires of her heart—to be a wife and mother. Each night she prayed that tomorrow would be the day that Mark finally came around to planning their marriage, but so far it hadn't happened.

"Patience, dear Sadie," Essie told her when she confided her deepest fears in her best friend. "Gott's plan will be revealed in good time."

Sadie knew her friend was wise and true. Oh, but the waiting was so hard to do!

* * *

The next day Sadie walked Nathan around, cooing softly to settle him, as Lovina trailed behind her. "Where Sadie going?" the little girl asked, dragging her cloth doll beside her. She had asked the question a dozen times, as was her current habit.

"I'm going to visit my friend Mark," Sadie answered.

"No. Sadie, stay here."

"I'll be back. Don't you worry." Sadie adjusted the baby on her shoulder, making sure that the diaper stayed in place to protect her dress. It wouldn't do to appear at Mark's house with a stain on her clothing.

She crossed the room again, glancing at the clock. Mark was late, but it wasn't a problem. The longer Sadie could spend with the children, the longer their mother could help Mem with the baking. And Sadie wanted Mark to see her with the children, to recognize her natural ability to care for them and keep them content. Sadie loved the way little Nathan's head fit into the crook of her neck and shoulder, the way Lovina's little body could straddle her waist and rest on her hip bone as if she were attached there.

"Still no sign of him?" Sharon appeared from the kitchen, wiping her hands on her cooking apron.

"Not yet." Sadie was starting to get antsy about introducing Mark to her sister. Just then, Nathan lifted his head, looked over at his mother, and let out a cry.

"He wants his mem," Sadie said.

Sharon opened her arms. "Come, schatzi."

As Sadie was handing him over, the clip-clop of an approaching buggy came from the road. At last! Sadie straightened her dress and smoothed down her apron before going to the door. "It's him," she told her sister.

"At last. I was beginning to think he was an imaginary friend."

Sadie gave her a pointed look. Although Sharon was five years older and lived in another town, she still had a way of getting under Sadie's skin at times. She waited until the buggy had halted and Mark had emerged before swinging the door open and welcoming him inside.

He looked up at her with a mild smile, his dark eyes looking sleepy—or maybe that was because he was squinting into the winter sun.

"Merry Christmas!" she said brightly.

He nodded. "Are you ready to go?"

"I am, but come on in and meet my sister, Sharon."

He stepped inside and removed his hat. "The sister from York, is that right? I've been hearing of nothing else all month. Sadie's happy to have you here."

Sharon chatted with him a bit as Sadie held back, glad for their easy interaction. When Sadie noticed Lovina peeking out from behind her skirt, she picked the little girl up and swung her onto her hip. "And this little one is my niece, Lovina."

"Another welcome visitor," Mark said. "How old are you, Lovina?"

"This much." She held out three fingers. "Almost four."

"A very good age," Mark said cheerfully. "The hardest thing you have to do is brush your teeth and drink your milk."

Lovina squinted at him. "I like milk."

"Then I guess you have an easy life," he teased.

Lovina reacted by pressing her face against Sadie.

"Suddenly shy," Sadie said.

"We should go," Mark said, his smile a bit forced.

Sadie got the sudden sense that something was not quite right.

Mark's lips curled in an odd way, and his dark eyes, usually smoky and intense, seemed somewhat blank, like chalkboard that had been wiped clean. "Get your coat," he said, taking an awkward step back toward the door. "We need to go, or we're going to be late. My mother doesn't abide latecomers well."

Sadie slipped on her coat, gave Lovina a kiss goodbye, and sent her into the kitchen to distract her while they headed out the door.

"Nice to meet you, Mark," Sharon called after them.

"Yah, it's good," Mark said, not even turning back to spare a look for Sadie's sister.

This was not like Mark. He was usually one of the most charming, cordial people she'd ever met. Something was definitely wrong. Was he still feeling cross from their argument?

Sadie went around the buggy and was surprised to see someone sitting in the front seat, holding the reins.

"It's my cousin Tom," Mark said, opening the door of the buggy for her. "You can sit in the back here. We were just on our way back from . . . from some travels."

As she moved past him to get into the buggy, she caught the sting of that familiar scent. It was something she'd known since she was a girl, catching a whiff of it on her father's breath or sometimes just from being near him.

Alcohol. So Mark had been drinking. He'd probably gone off to share a bottle of whiskey or something with his cousin.

A cold shiver threaded through her body as she settled onto the bench in the back of the buggy. She had to force herself to acknowledge Tom as Mark explained where he lived, how long he was visiting, and how they were related.

You were drinking with Mark, she wanted to say. *He doesn't drink. He never touches it. And now here you are, taking him down that wretched path and ruining our lives . . .*

As the buggy moved down the road Sadie thought of the many times the drink had darkened their home. In the grips of alcohol, her dat had fallen to the floor and passed out in the middle of the day. He'd turned sour and angry, chastising his daughters and scolding their mem. A fine, sunny day would be ruined when Dat plodded in the door with his red eyes and stony face. Sadie and her sisters used to finish their chores quick as a bunny so they could run to their bedroom and huddle quietly until the storm blew over.

In the years since Sharon had married and left Sadie alone with their parents, Dat's drinking bouts had come less frequently. There were times when he went for months, maybe even a year without touching a drop, but then Sadie would come home from the pretzel factory and find Dat with his bloodshot eyes or already gone to bed. Mem made excuses for him, bless her patience. Sadie didn't know how she did it. Sometimes Sadie prayed to Gott to cure Dat of the terrible thing, but then, Gott answered prayers in ways a person couldn't always understand.

Now, riding in the back of the buggy, Sadie knew there would be no lifting the glum cloak that had fallen over her heart. The meal at Mark's house would be torture, knowing that the man she loved was lost to her for now, his mind numbed by drink.

She would have to make the most of it and try to win over Mark's parents. Although she'd met them before and seen them often at church, she'd never been invited into their home, and first visits were so important!

After a miserable buggy ride, Sadie drew in a deep breath and vowed to put on a happy face as she climbed down from the buggy. Inside the house, she straightened her spine, held her head high, and tried to keep things light. Mark introduced her quickly, but then settled in with the other men in rocking chairs in the living room. He seemed to forget she was there as the men chatted about the prices of things and the weather. It was clearly not a place for Sadie to be, even if there were a chair for her.

Which left her trying to make connections with his mother completely on her own, without Mark by her side to grease the pan with easy conversation and his smooth charm. Clutching her homemade package, she pressed on into the kitchen, where Mark's mother, Carol, noticed her right away.

"Sadie, it's good you could join us," she said, stepping away from the stove to come closer.

"I've brought you a fruitcake," Sadie said, handing over the gift wrapped in foil and plastic wrap and a red bow. She explained that it was one of her mother's specialties.

"Denki, I'm sure it's delicious," Carol Miller was a petite woman with tawny brown hair and skin as smooth as cream. She patted Sadie's arm and put the package onto the kitchen table, her movements slow, as if trying not to startle a cat.

That was the moment when Sadie noticed that the table was laden with sweets, nuts, and desserts. There were velvety, plump dried cherries, apricots, and raisins. Pistachios, almonds, and seasoned cashews. Christmas cookies shaped like trees and coated with glimmering green sugar. Shoofly, pumpkin, and fruit pies. Brownies, sugar cookies, molasses snaps, and sand tarts with a perfect pecan at the center of each cookie.

"Such a feast!" Sadie said. "Your table looks wonderful!"

Carol gave a nod. "We like to go all out on Christmas," she said. "It's Wayne's birthday, you know, and he does love to celebrate."

Sadie hadn't realized Mark's father had a birthday, but she felt a fissure of worry that her modest fruitcake lacked excitement among so many delightful desserts. Still, it was a favorite in her family, and Mem always got many compliments when she gave them out as gifts.

The table was set beautifully with sparkling plates and silverware, much fancier than Sadie was used to. She offered to help and was relieved when Mark's aunt Doris handed her a pitcher and asked her to set out water for everyone. Filling glasses at the lovely table, Sadie hoped that Mark would drink his fill to help him sober up. She hated being stranded here, feeling alone in his house.

A minute later a group of women came in from a walk, the cold seeping from their shawls and jackets as they quickly shed their outdoor garments, washed up, and joined in the kitchen work.

The dinner was to be a prime rib roast—not a typical Amish meal, and not something that Sadie had eaten before. When Carol Miller removed it from the oven, Sadie had to bite her tongue to keep from commenting that it looked like a charred log pulled from the fireplace.

"It's perfect," Carol said. "Should be pink inside."

"It smells wonderful," Sadie said, which it truly did.

"We must let the roast sit for five or ten minutes before we carve it up," Carol instructed. "In the meantime, let's open this gift from cousin Mae." She reached past the canisters on the counter and picked up a tall, narrow green bottle.

Wine?

Sadie, leaning against the counter, shifted uncomfortably as the women voiced their approval.

"Wine with dinner," one of the younger women said. "Well, it is Christmas Eve."

"We only have wine on special occasions," Carol said, cutting through the foil seal with a paring knife.

Sadie didn't know any other plain folk who drank as a family. Not that she knew so many families that well, but in her experience, when alcohol appeared at an event, the drinking was usually an activity for men in a back room or shed. Carol took some glasses from a cupboard and started pouring. When the wine was passed out, Sadie was glad to see she wasn't the only one who declined; at least she wouldn't be singled out. But it was one more thing that separated her family from Mark's. Although Dat had his drinking going on behind closed doors, the rest of Sadie's family would never have opened a bottle of wine to share. Not to judge, but Sadie didn't see what good could come of it.

When everyone was assembled at the table, heads bowed in silent prayer, Sadie prayed for the grace to make it through this evening. Although the meal was cordial enough, with some cheerful conversation and so many delicious foods, Sadie chewed methodically and forced herself to swallow. The joyful anticipation she'd felt this morning had faded to disappointment and worry over the man sitting beside her. How could she have fallen in love with a man who drank? Now that she'd chosen Mark, the misery she'd suffered from her dat's drinking was going to follow her for the rest of her life.

She couldn't bear to think of it as the meal went on. Such delicious food, and so much of it! She hated to seem ungrateful, but the festivities were wasted on her when all she could think of was Mark. Her love for him. His callousness. His drinking, and how it threatened to ruin their life together.

Chapter 13

It was Christmas Eve in Philadelphia, and Megan and her sisters had declined a few party invitations for a very special evening volunteering at a local soup kitchen. Megan had made a few calls, and the girls decided that the Welcome Kitchen was the best place to pitch in over the holidays. The volunteer coordinator, an energetic, wiry guy named Donatello, gave them plenty of responsibility and made them feel a part of the mission of providing meals to people who needed them.

"Joy to the world!" Serena sang, tipping her red Santa-capped head back and forth as she lifted a giant slotted spoon of beans and waited for it to drain before placing it on a grizzled man's plate. "There you go. Is that good, or do you want more?"

"That's fine, thanks." The man nodded and moved on to Megan, who used tongs to dole out chicken and fish tacos.

"Let earth receive her King!" Serena sang with cheerful enthusiasm during a lull in the line.

"You're in a good mood," Megan teased her twin.

"I just love feeling like I can make a difference in a

person's life," Serena said. "And I'm so happy that we got to wear Santa caps in lieu of those old-lady hairnets."

Megan adjusted the band of her own cap. "Yeah. Not quite a fashion statement, but 'tis the season. And I'm glad we're here. It feels good to give up the comforts of home to make someone else's Christmas a little better."

"It does. Thank you, sister dear, for pushing us to step out of the bubble. You've made this the *best* Christmas ever!"

"Wow. You're welcome." Megan had come to appreciate her sister's bold theatricality. She could always count on Serena to ratchet up the emotion and drama of a moment. By contrast, Megan tended to be cooler, more low-key, and less impetuous. But with Serena's wild sense of wonder there came a deep honesty that allowed people to know what she was truly feeling. With Serena, you always knew where you stood.

"And I have to admit, I'm pretty psyched that Scout will be here in a few days. Do you know, he's never been to Philly before?"

"I'm sure he'll love the city," said Megan. "He's an adventurous guy."

"I miss him so much." Serena had first met Scout when he'd arrived on his nightly run as a truck driver picking up milk from the Lapps' farm. Scout's earnestness was a far cry from the callousness of the bad boys Serena used to date, but it was a welcome change. He kept Serena's feet on the ground, and for that, Megan liked him.

"So what are you planning to do while he's here?" Megan asked.

"He wants to see the Liberty Bell and Independence Hall. And he definitely wants to run up those stairs that

Rocky climbed in the movie and throw some air punches. Where are those stairs again?"

"They're in front of the Philadelphia Museum of Art. You guys have to do that."

They stopped chatting when two more people came on the line—a young man and woman, both with thick, dark hair, hazel eyes, and similarly shaped noses.

"Are you guys brother and sister?" Serena asked. "You have the same eyes, and they're stunning."

"We are," the young man said. "Fiona's my baby sister."

"Not true," Fiona said. "He always says that because he wants to take care of me, but I'm almost two years older."

"But you're smaller than me, and I'm so much more mature."

"Oh, stop it!" Fiona swatted at him affectionately.

"We're sisters, too," Serena said. "Twins. But not identical, as you can see."

"I definitely see the resemblance," Fiona said, nodding.

"Do you guys want beans?" Serena offered.

"Sure." He held up his plate. "Give us the works."

Grace came over from the dining room, where she'd been wiping down tables. "Give these two the red carpet treatment," she said, folding the wet cloth into a square. "They didn't laugh at me when I wiped out on the floor."

"Of course we wouldn't laugh," Fiona insisted.

"What happened?" Serena asked.

"Someone spilled some water, and I didn't see it. Went barreling through. But Jackson helped me up."

"That was nice," Megan said.

Serena gestured grandly over the steam table. "Well, Jackson and Fiona, we have an excellent assortment of tacos for your dining pleasure tonight."

"Sounds great," Jackson said. "Feliz Navidad!"

* * *

As Megan helped serve people coming in off the streets, she realized how different the city had looked since she'd returned. Her eyes were opening to different aspects of life she hadn't been aware of before. People scurried in the door with cold seeping from their coats and hunger in their eyes. Some people smiled, while others were unwilling to make eye contact. Donatello directed everyone to a big row of sinks in a hallway by the door so that they could wash up before eating.

What would it be like to wonder where your next meal was coming from? Megan felt grateful that she'd never suffered food insecurities. In some ways, her life had been so easy, with her dad and now her aunt and uncle taking care of the big things like food and shelter.

Gratitude—that weighed heavily on her shoulders these days.

She was grateful for the people who took care of her, and happy for the new bond with her sisters, who seemed to want to spend time with her now that they were back in Philly.

Her new vision also showed her parts of the city she hadn't noticed when she lived here. The grime. The glimmering lights that made her feel warm and fuzzy. The person wrapped in a blanket who was trying to make a bed of a stairwell beneath those lights. Such a glorious and tragic city. She would always love it, but she didn't feel completely at home here anymore.

Philly was not the same for her. The apartment seemed stale and empty now that she was used to a houseful of cousins. The noise of the city kept Megan up at night, and she felt tension building inside her when she thought of the direction her life had been going when she lived here. She had resented being dumped in Lancaster County, but now she was grateful for her life in Joyful River.

What was the family doing back there? Were the guys out chasing the puck on the pond? Was Aunt Miriam scooting the young ones off to bed so that she could set out their Christmas treats at their places on the kitchen table? Lizzie had explained the Amish Christmas tradition with such delight that Megan had longed to see it. Maybe some other year.

Was Sam hanging out with Isaac, concocting some way to get Sadie Beiler to see that he was crazy about her? Megan missed hanging out with those two. She'd never had a close male friend before, and when she was with them she got an inside view of the male perspective, as well as Amish life. Sam was like a brother, and Isaac truly intrigued her. Everything about him *looked* Amish, but the guy was definitely different from the rest. She missed hanging out with him. When she was around Isaac, she got the sense that even the most complicated problems would be resolved. It was comforting to think that things were going to work out just fine.

By the time they were getting ready to close the dining room, patrons had stopped coming in.

"You girls need to take a break," Donatello told Megan and Serena, shooing them toward the tables. "Get yourselves something, whatever you want, and chill till it's time to break down the serving station and clean up."

The girls filled cups with water and headed into the dining area, where Grace was already sitting with Fiona and Jackson.

"So how were the tacos?" Serena asked. "You can be

honest; I didn't cook them, but I thought they smelled delicious."

"They were delicious," Fiona said. "We're just grateful for a good meal. Donatello knows our situation, but he always welcomes us here. No judgment."

Megan nodded, wanting to know more, but reluctant to ask.

"Their situation is that they're not homeless. Not technically. Fiona has an apartment and a job, and Jackson is staying with her right now. But things are tight."

"I'm a foster kid. At least, I was," Jackson said. "I just turned eighteen."

"Happy birthday," Serena said.

"Yeah, happy birthday to me," he said, exchanging a look with his sister. "Eighteen years old, and I'm on my own now. That's the thing with being a foster kid. When you turn eighteen, the program gives you the boot. If you don't have foster parents who take a liking to you or want to go above and beyond . . ." He shrugged. "You're out on your own."

"They kicked you out?" Megan was surprised. "Did they at least offer for you to stay until you get a job?"

"Not these folks. They're decent people, but they needed the room for a new foster kid. As they explained, getting payouts for their foster kids is one of their only sources of income."

"That's terrible!" Serena exclaimed.

"It sounds like a really messed-up system," Megan agreed. She found it hard to believe that kids would be dumped out of their foster homes just because they turned eighteen. As Jackson and Fiona explained the situation, she studied their attitudes, their manners, and their behavior. They were well-mannered, and she didn't think they were into alcohol or drugs. Was it possible that Jackson had been kicked out even though he hadn't done anything wrong?

Fiona explained that she had gone through the same thing when she turned eighteen. There'd been a mad scramble to find a job—even a low-paying one—but without a credit rating, no one would rent an apartment to her. She'd gotten lucky when two girls she knew from a group home had offered to let her move into their place. "Right now, Jackson's staying on our couch, but it's kind of tricky, with my roommates. They understand, but it's a tight space. We've got to find him some other place to live."

"In Philadelphia," Jackson said, "so that I can work here and be near Fiona. She's the only family I have."

Fiona held up her hands. "That would be nice, little bro, but beggars can't be choosers."

"Keep the faith, Fiona. I'll find something soon."

Watching them, Megan wished she could do something to help. It seemed overwhelming to have to find a job and a place to live at the age of eighteen. What would she and Serena have done if they'd gotten kicked out of the house on their birthday? It was hard to imagine.

"It sounds like what you're going through is rough," Serena said, "but at least you have each other. That's important."

Fiona agreed with her, and Jackson made a joke about taking care of his "little sister." Megan could tell they understood how important it was. Megan looked to her twin sister, surprised she'd made that comment. Serena had come a long way from the head-in-the-clouds, self-centered girl who had been distraught when they were sent to live in Lancaster County. Over the past few months, she'd begun to see that family really mattered.

As they were talking, Megan saw Sully come in the door and stop to talk with Donatello. He was here to pick them up, mostly because he was worried about the safety of his daughters in this part of town.

"You can volunteer at Welcome Kitchen on one condition," their dad had told them when Megan had shared the plan. "We need to make arrangements so that I can get you girls home when they close the kitchen at night."

"Don't you trust us, Dad?" Megan had asked.

"One hundred percent," Sully had answered. "It's the unsavory characters out there I don't trust. Not everyone in life is on the level."

Megan had poked her dad in the arm. "Seriously, Dad. You know I can take care of myself."

"A father never stops wanting to protect his daughters," he said. "And all my years as a cop have taught me a few things. One is that the missions and soup kitchens in Philadelphia aren't always in the safest neighborhoods. And two, you can't trust the people you meet in those places."

"Dad . . . you're so jaded," Megan had told her father, though she'd gone along with his conditions.

Now she excused herself from the table and went over to greet her father. "Hey, Dad. We haven't started the clean up yet." As this was their third night volunteering, Megan was becoming familiar with the routine.

"I'm a little early," he said. "But I signed out of work so we can spend the rest of Christmas Eve together."

"That's awesome."

"Sounds like a good night for y'all," Donatello said. "Got any special Christmas Eve traditions?"

Megan smiled. "This year, we're creating some new ones." Traditions with meaning, she thought as she waved and called "Merry Christmas" to some of the patrons heading out the door. "How about you?"

"I'm heading over to my mother's in Lansdowne after this. She always makes a special dinner, and then we go to the midnight service at her church."

"I'll bet your mother loves having you visit," Dad said.

"More like she demands it." Donatello chuckled. "With my mom, attendance is not optional. But she's the glue that keeps my siblings and me together."

"Every family needs someone like that," Dad agreed.

"They do. But we need to get this place cleaned up if we're going to get out of here on time." Donatello tasked Megan with storing leftovers in bins in the walk-in fridge, while Grace and Serena were given dishwashing detail.

When Megan had her chore done, she peeked out into the dining room and saw Dad sipping a Coke and talking with Fiona and Jackson, who'd been introduced as "friends" by Grace. They seemed to be getting along well.

The young people might be just what Dad needed to change his impression of the "dangerous" people who frequented soup kitchens. Megan knew it was wise to be cautious, but you had to be willing to give people a chance.

Back in the kitchen, she sprang a new idea on her sisters. "Dad says he has off the rest of the night, and I was thinking we could go to midnight mass, the way we did when we were kids."

Serena's eyes lit up, but Grace made a pouty face.

"But I thought we were going to wrap gifts and make cookies," Grace said.

"We can still do some of that. Wrap the gifts and do one batch of cookies," Megan said, gently pummeling Grace's shoulder. "Come on."

"We have to do mass!" Serena insisted. "It was one of

Mom's favorite things. Remember how she used to tell us that once we got out of the church, it was Christmas morning? I always thought there was something magical about that."

"Am I getting outvoted again?" Grace asked. As the younger sibling of twins, she found herself in that spot more often than not.

"Midnight mass is a great way to get back to our old traditions," Megan pleaded.

"Oh, all right. But if we don't get those cookies done, you guys need to promise you'll help me on Christmas Day."

"You got it," Megan agreed. Now she just had to sell the idea to Dad.

Chapter 14

Sadie was so disappointed, so wounded in her heart, that she kept quiet as Mark helped her into the buggy.

"It's a cold night," Mark said as he took up the reins and opened up the lap blanket. Most of it fell over his thighs, with a loose portion of wool fabric hanging in Sadie's direction.

"I hope you're sharing that," Sadie said, tugging a bit of the blanket over to cover her lap. Most winter nights when she got in the buggy with Mark, the blanket was an excuse to nudge closer to him for warmth and affection. Tonight, though, she fixed the blanket and stayed in place, lips pressed together as she thought of how to approach the difficult topic.

He called to the horse, and they were rolling away from the large house, the dim lights of Mark's buggy illuminating a small space ahead of them. When they reached the end of the lane, he halted the horse and looked over at her. "You're mighty quiet."

She turned so that he could see the sorrow on her face. "I'm disappointed. I know you were drunk when you picked me up."

"Come on, now." He signaled to the horse, and the buggy rolled onto the road. Even in the dim light she could see his slight wince. "'Drunk' is a strong word for it. I just had a few drinks with my cousin Tom. He got a bottle of whiskey. It's something he enjoys, and you know, he only comes to Joyful River once in a blue moon."

"You told me you didn't drink," she said.

"I usually don't, but I wasn't going to stop Tom from enjoying his Christmas."

"You know how I feel about alcohol. Mark, you know what I've gone through with my dat."

"It's too bad your dat is a drunk. That's not me. And I only had a few drinks, anyway."

The words cut through her like a sharp blade. "Mark . . ."

"I mean it. I know you've gone through a lot with him, but I'm a different person. I don't drink every day or every month, and I don't try to hide it when I do."

She shook her head, wishing she could shake off the pain his words caused her. "Don't you see what it does to people? What it does to you? A couple of drinks, and you barely spoke a word to me. It was as if I were a stranger at your family's table."

"I sat next to you at dinner. What did you expect? Weren't you getting to know my mem and cousins in the kitchen?"

"You could have introduced me. You could have stayed by my side."

He shook his head. "I wanted to sit with the fellas. I was tired."

"Because you were drinking. Drink turns a person's heart to stone."

"You don't know what you're talking about."

"We both know you were drinking," she said. "You ruined the night."

He stared straight ahead as the dark, hulking structure of a covered bridge came into view. The narrow Harris Bridge, popular because of its proximity to the interstate, was used by both cars and buggies. In the summer, Sadie enjoyed the cool shade of its darkness as the buggy passed through; but on a dark winter night she worried about Mark plunging into the structure at too high a speed.

"Better slow down. The bridge is ahead." She stared at him hard now, almost daring him to take back his words and slow the buggy down.

To her surprise, he pulled back on the horse and steered to the side of the road. The buggy slowed and rolled to a stop on the clearing just before the bridge. What was he thinking?

Mark took a deep breath, then turned to her. Despite the dim light, she sensed a change in him, a softening in his face.

"I know you think I botched things today." He shifted closer and placed one hand on her cheek, gently turning her to face him. "You don't know what it's like to be a man. You can't know that, and you will never understand my decisions."

His words made him seem a thousand miles away, but his touch brought a warm, tingling sensation that danced on her cheek and ran straight to her heart. She wanted to protest, to tell him that she wanted to understand him as the urge to fight him faded.

He cupped her cheek, and she felt herself succumbing to his touch.

"Sitting here now, looking at you . . . good grief, you're so pretty, Sadie. Your eyes catch all the stars in the sky."

He'd said the star thing before, and she loved it.

"And I wanted you to have a good time today," he added. "I wanted for things to go well, for my family to see how wonderful you are."

"I wanted that, too," she whispered.

"My mem seemed to take to you."

"I hope so." She thought about the fruitcake she'd brought, which didn't get put out with the other desserts. Maybe they just had too much food. But she worried that Carol Miller hadn't been impressed by their family specialty.

And here she was thinking about fruitcake when it was such a small part of a disappointing day. "I wanted things to go well," she said. "But from the moment you picked me up, I felt like I'd lost you. I felt so alone."

"Alone in a crowd of a dozen people?" His dark eyes seemed to be a window to his intense love for her as he leaned closer. "Now, how does that make sense?"

"I just wanted them to like me."

"They do. And so do I." He leaned away momentarily to reach for something on the floor. "That's why I wanted you to have this for Christmas." He held up a small box. The glimmering wrapping paper on the small box caught the scant light in the buggy.

A gift for her? After Mark's behavior today, Sadie hadn't expected a gift from him. The scarf she had knitted for him was finished and wrapped back at home; she had planned to give it to him when they arrived there, not wanting to make a scene of it in front of his family today.

Now, seeing the box wrapped in gold and white paper

with golden speckles, she was glad to have something special for him waiting at home.

She reached for the gift, but he quickly snatched it back. "Not so fast. If you take the gift, you have to promise me you won't be mad at me anymore." He drew his fingertips across her cheek to the sensitive skin in front of her ear. "I can't stand it when a pretty girl is mad at me."

She tilted her head and sighed against his hand. "You act like this is a game."

"You're still mad."

"That's not the point." She wanted to ask him why he drank today, why he acted so far away when she visited his parents' house, why he treated her like a pretty doll instead of a young woman with feelings and ideas. A woman who wanted so much to be his wife.

"Mark," she said. "I'm not mad. I'm just . . . disappointed. I wanted things to go well tonight."

"But they did. Come on, Sadie. Mem liked you, and everyone had a good time. It was a very good Christmas Eve." He smiled, his eyes fixed on her with a look that seemed to say that everything would be fine.

If only she could trust that.

"Here," he said. "Open your gift."

Still tentative, she took the box from him. It was heavier than she'd expected for its small size. Probably a candy dish or serving bowl. Her fingers tore through the pretty paper to a box with a clear plastic lid on it.

She had to squint to see the contents of the box, but when she saw that it was a clock, she gave a slight gasp. It was a beautiful clock, shiny silver, with an old-fashioned clockface and a little chamber beneath in which tiny silver balls rotated to keep the time.

A clock.

It was the traditional engagement gift for an Amish young man to give his intended bride.

A clock. Such a beautiful gift, with a romantic significance.

Sadie's heart started beating a rapid dance in her chest. Did this mean they were engaged?

Chapter 15

The night sky had gone from indigo to black as Sam and Isaac sat by the small fire and talked about anything and everything. Warmed by the flames, Sam felt himself relaxing after such a long day. He'd been up milking the cows before dawn, chasing his chores all day, and then going out a mile to mend a piece of fence that was coming loose. Then, after the evening milking and Mem's special potato soup and pork and sauerkraut dinner, Isaac had joined Sam and his siblings for a skate on the ice. Yah, Sam was weary to the bone, but it was a good feeling to have at night. "Do you think the sky looks different on Christmas Eve?" Sam asked his friend.

Isaac let his head tip back to take in the vaulting darkness above. "You mean, on account of Gott sending a special star to guide the wise men?"

"I just think it's a different color. Darker. Maybe because these are the shortest days of the year."

"And the longest nights," Isaac said, still staring up at the sky. "I've always loved Christmas Eve. Most people enjoy Christmas Day, but I like the day before. The anticipation. The feeling that a very special day is coming."

"I don't understand you, Isaac." Sam stepped forward and poked a long stick into the fire, making red sparks fly. "You know the Bible better than anyone I know, and your faith is strong. But I can't talk you into preparing for baptism with Jacob and me."

"It's not for lack of faith in Gott," Isaac said. "The problem is that many of the things that are important to me would be forbidden in Amish life. I know I complain about college classes, but I do like the challenge up here that school brings." He pointed to his head. "It keeps me thinking, and many of the things I'm learning have practical applications. There's a lot of first aid instructions that could save a person's life. And the anatomy classes—if I continue them, I could one day go on to be a nurse or a physician's assistant."

"That sounds like a pie-in-the-sky dream to me."

"I know that, but I think Gott wants me to make it real. In the Bible, Gott tells us to take care of each other, chide?"

"Right," Sam agreed, wondering if Isaac had slipped into Pennsylvania Dutch to make his argument stronger.

"Well, if I can get through a medical program, I'll have a chance to help Amish folks with their health issues. So many folk suffer from diabetes, and then there are syndromes like dwarfism and metabolic disorders that happen to the Amish. Many Amish can't get to a doctor. Those are people I can help."

He'd lost Sam after diabetes, but Sam got the gist of it. Isaac had a good heart and a good mind. He wanted to use those qualities to help other folks.

"And then there are folks like my mem, who get diagnosed with cancer and never come back from it." Isaac shook his head. "Sometimes I wonder if Mem had gotten to a doctor sooner, maybe she'd be here now. If they'd caught it earlier . . ." He clapped his gloved hands together as the topic seemed to hang in the air between them.

It had been a few years since Isaac had lost his mem. Rose Lapp had been a smart woman, much like her son. A little on the quiet side, but when Sam was younger he'd enjoyed spending time at his cousin's house because of their complete set of encyclopedias and the cookie jar that never seemed to empty. How many hours had they spent reading different volumes of the fat books and sharing words they could barely pronounce? The diagrams of contraptions and stories of great inventions could fill a snowy afternoon with amusement.

When Rose Lapp had died, Mem had sat Sam and Isaac down and told Isaac that she would always be there for him if he needed someone to talk to. "Or maybe you'll find yourself in need of a homemade meal. You must come to us," she'd added. She recognized that their hearts were hurting over the loss of Isaac's mother, but emphasized that Gott didn't make mistakes. "We don't understand why things happen the way they do, but we need to trust Gott in his infinite wisdom. His will be done."

Mem's words had stuck with Sam. Whenever Isaac brought up his mother, Sam reminded Isaac that it wasn't his fault that she hadn't gotten to a doctor sooner. Over the years, Isaac had made some peace with his mother's death. Now Sam could see that the tragedy had brought about something positive.

Sam poked the fire again, hoping to keep it going for just a few more minutes before heading into the quiet house. He figured all the younger ones would be asleep, dreaming of Christmas morning. "It's good that you want to help people," Sam said.

"That's the best way of putting it," Isaac admitted. "The other truth is that I'm not cut out to be a dairy farmer. I grew up on a farm, and I don't have much interest in staying there. An apartment in town would be a better fit for me."

"Lots of plain folk are doing that," Sam said. "Getting day jobs in towns and factories. Living in apartments. The farmland in Lancaster County's been running out for a while now."

"But I want more than a day job. I want to help people stay healthy. The things that give me a lift—the things that promise an exciting and fulfilling future—are outside Amish life. It's like a ray of the sun luring me out of the dark. It's something I've got to do."

"Then you've got to answer the call. Just as sure as I'm going to be a dairy farmer."

Isaac was nodding. "Most folks would say you and I are blessed to be born into a successful farming family. It's not a good fit for me, but you—you're a born dairy man."

"It's something I know well, and for me, I can't imagine leaving Amish life. It's my family, my community." It sounded too corny to say that he wanted an Amish wife and children, but he did. "It's time to talk to the bishop. Start the baptism training in the spring."

"Jacob will be happy to have you along for the ride."

"Yah, but we'll miss you."

Isaac clapped his hands together, then stretched them toward the fire. "But I'll be right here. The fish that got away."

Sam shook his head with a chuckle. "You're going to drive your father crazy."

"Probably. But a man has to do what's right in his heart."

"True." Sam extended his hand, and they shook on it.

"So when are your cousins coming back?" Isaac asked.

Sam shrugged. "Sometime after Christmas. In the new year, I think. Why are you asking?"

"Just wondering about Megan . . . her hockey skills, I mean. If she doesn't get on the ice during the holiday, her skills will slip."

"And you're worried about her hockey skills?" Sam squinted at his friend. Yah, Isaac was obsessed with hockey, but this seemed like something more.

"She's a nice girl," Isaac said.

"An Englisch girl."

"Maybe that's what makes her so much more attractive," Isaac admitted.

Sam felt his jaw drop, but he turned to the fire and closed his mouth. Isaac was interested in Megan? It hadn't occurred to him—especially since she wasn't Amish—but now it made sense. They spent a lot of time together on the ice. They were both salt of the earth, practical people.

"But you're cousins."

"No. You're her cousin, since your mother is her mother's sister. I'm no relation by blood." Isaac stood up and stepped toward the fire. "Forget I said anything. So far, we're just friends."

Which said a lot, as most Amish guys didn't befriend young women unless they wanted to court them. But then, Isaac was no ordinary Amish fellow.

"So. On to the really important matters," said Isaac. "Do you think our team has a chance at the Myers Pond games?"

"With the twins, Jacob, you, and me as our main players? Who could possibly beat us?"

"So humble." Isaac laughed.

"We're a great team," Sam insisted. The hockey tournament hosted at Myers Pond each January was an annual tradition. Since the Myers family was Mennonite, they had lights at the pond so that games could be played late into the night.

"A great team with no depth," Isaac said. "Our three backup players barely know how to skate."

"We'll be fine," Sam insisted. "I have hope for us this year."

"I do, too. Hope is contagious this time of year. We'd better go." Isaac took a stick and spread out the remaining embers in the firepit.

Sam hitched his hockey gear over his shoulder and clapped his friend on the back. "Merry Christmas, my friend." He was grateful to have such a good friend as Isaac.

Isaac slipped an arm over Sam's shoulders and gave him a squeeze—not something they'd do around others, but tonight it was just them and the stars above and the frozen earth beneath their feet. "Merry Christmas."

Sam helped Isaac hitch up his buggy, and then made his way into the house. Everything was quiet as he stored his pads in the mudroom and left his snow pants out to dry. Most likely everyone was asleep already, since it was after nine. His face was so cold from the extended time outside that the warmth of the house made him feel like he was thawing.

He stepped into the kitchen and startled at the sight of his mother sitting at the table, leaning over bags of candy.

"Mem, I thought you'd gone to bed."

"Soon. I just can't help myself from fussing over the Christmas plates," Miriam said, adding a shiny silver-wrapped snack-sized Baby Ruth bar to each plate.

It was an Amish tradition Sam had grown up with. Every year on Christmas Eve, each child set an empty dish at his or her place at the table. After the children went to sleep, parents loaded the plates with different kinds of candies, nuts, and dried fruit. Come Christmas morning, the children were delighted to find their plate filled with delicious treats.

"Let's see." Sam rubbed his chin, examining the table. "Each child gets two mini Baby Ruths, dried apricots, root beer barrels, Chex mix in baggies tied with ribbons, peanuts, and bite-sized Peppermint Patties. I'd say that's a good Christmas treasure."

"Do you think so? I tried to find those sour candies that Lizzie likes so much. Starshines."

"Starbursts?"

"Is that what they're called?" Miriam chuckled. "Well, no wonder none of the stores had them. I was asking for the wrong thing. I hate to disappoint Lizzie."

"She'll be fine," Sam said. "If she isn't, I'll take her Peppermint Patties."

"Oh, you. So practical." She tossed a peppermint candy to him. "I have plenty of those. Why don't you put a plate out?"

"Because I'm not ten years old. I'm over that stuff."

"It's a Christmas tradition," she said, tipping her head to one side to observe him with a thoughtful expression.

"It's a tradition for the children, and you know I'm beyond that." He gestured to the Dawdi House, the small house on the property where Essie and Harlan were living temporarily until they could find a place of their own. "Just because Essie got married first, it doesn't mean I'm clinging to childhood. I'm twenty-one, my hands are calloused, and I'm one of the best workers on this farm."

"Hmm." She nodded. "I understand. In that case . . ." She grabbed a few snack-sized Peppermint Patties and tossed them to him. "You get to share in the setup."

Sam reacted quickly to catch the candies, but one fell to the floor. He picked it up, tore into the wrapper, and took a bite. "Mmm. Peppermint always reminds me of Christmas."

"Me too." Mem unwrapped one for herself. "I'll have to start back on my diet tomorrow."

"Or the next day," Sam said. "Give yourself off for Christmas."

"If you say so," she said with a smile.

"Where's Dat? Doesn't he like setting up for Christmas?"

"He's gone to bed. He helped me pull the treats out from the back of the cupboard, but for him, the real joy is seeing the faces of the children on Christmas morning." She emptied the rest of the candy bars onto Annie's plate and started tucking the smaller empty candy bags into the largest one. Sam knew his mem would try to reuse them for school lunches. Nothing went to waste in her kitchen. "You know, Sam, it won't be long until I'm watching my grandchildren wake up on Christmas morning. God willing, Essie and Harlan will start their family soon. And I'm sure you won't be far behind."

Sam nodded, letting the sweet mint of the candy melt on his tongue for a minute. His mem always meant well, but talking to her about the future was a bit like rubbing against a weathered fence. He never knew when he might encounter a splinter. "I'm behind Essie, that's for sure. But don't worry about me. I'll get you grandchildren someday."

"Oh, Sam, I know it was hard for you, with Essie getting married first."

He shrugged and took another bite of candy.

"You went through it all with grace and good humor. I'm proud of you. And I pray every day that you'll find the wife Gott intends for you. Love is such a wonderful thing. Gott's greatest gift."

"Yah." He put the empty candy wrapper on the table.

"Want another peppermint?"

He shook his head. "This talk has gotten a little too sweet for me."

Miriam laughed. "Oh, Sam! You know how much I enjoy seeing people find each other."

"Matchmaking." He nodded. "I know you mean well, Mem, but that stuff never works out."

"You'd be surprised. Sometimes folks don't know what's good for them. They need a little push in the right direction."

"Not me. I know the right direction, and I don't need a push. I'm going to talk to the bishop about baptism. I want to be in the next group in the spring."

"That's wonderful news!" Her eyes twinkled with delight as she clasped her hands against her chest. "So you'll be eligible to marry come the next wedding season."

Sam let out his breath and looked down at the table.

Mem had a way of hitting the nail so squarely on the head; it was awkward. "That's right."

"Nothing to be embarrassed about. Your dat will be so pleased. It's a good move you're making, Sam."

"It's the right decision for me." He knew that much was true. But once he was baptized, would he be any closer to winning over Sadie? Probably not.

"Oh, Sam." Mem tilted her head to one side. "I wish I could help you right now. Choosing someone to marry— it's such an important part of life."

"Mem . . ." He let out a breath. "I know you mean well, but I'm not desperate."

"I know that."

"And if I trusted myself to a matchmaker, I'd be liable to end up with the likes of June or Dotty Hostetler."

Miriam laughed. "Oh, those two. I can never tell them apart. Which one has the very long neck?"

"Like a goose?" Sam grinned.

"Like a swan. They're not so hard on the eyes, those girls, but their mother can be so disagreeable, and if they're anything like her? With one of those girls around, I'd have to bite my tongue half the day through."

Sam laughed at the image of his mother biting back conversation. "Now, that would be a challenge for you."

"It sure would." She chuckled. "I do love to speak my mind."

"But you do it in a nice way." His mother had a knack for saying the right thing at the right time and turning criticisms into helpful advice. He loved her, but he needed to court Sadie in his own time and place. "I'm sure you're a good matchmaker, Mem." He rose from the table and picked up the empty candy wrappers. "Just not for me."

As he put the wrappers in the trash, he expected a funny retort. But she was silent. He turned back and saw her watching him with a big smile on her face—the cat who lapped up the cream. "What?" he asked.

She shook her head, her eyes shiny with joy. "Merry Christmas, Sam. Now, off you go. See you in the morning."

He wished her a merry Christmas and went up the stairs shaking his head.

Chapter 16

With mixed feelings, Sadie arrived home on Christmas Eve, the box containing Mark's gift held close to her heart. The gift made her feel that he valued her at last. Finally, he was showing her that he loved her, too, and wanted to get married. Finally. How long had she been waiting for Mark to come around? The waiting was behind her now.

But as she entered the house and came upon her parents sitting up late to talk with Sharon and Elam, she held back the announcement.

"What's that in the box?" Sharon asked as she taped down the red and white wrapping paper on a wooden truck for Nathan. "Did you and Mark exchange gifts?"

"It's just something he got for me," Sadie said, realizing that in the excitement she'd forgotten about giving him the scarf. But there would be time later.

"How was the visit with the Wayne Millers?" Mem asked. "Did you meet some of Mark's family?"

"Yah, many from out of town." She talked a little, but left out the disappointing parts of the evening. Best to stay on the sunny side of things.

But as everyone said good night and Mem turned off

the lantern, Sadie pressed the box to her breast and moved down the hall with a feeling of foreboding. How much power did Mark's gift have? Could it unravel the sorrow of a dismal, uncomfortable evening?

She tiptoed into her room, careful not to wake Lovina, and put the clock, still in its box, on the shelf. Inside, the clock was beautiful, its face luminescent, its silvery case shiny and bright. It should have filled her with joy at the prospect of marrying the man she loved. Instead, she felt a painful weight in her chest, a thorn of confusion.

Something was wrong, but she couldn't quite cut to the heart of the matter.

She changed quickly into her nightgown, said her prayers, and slid under the quilt. Despite the whisper of her niece's steady breath, peaceful as a summer breeze, sleep eluded her for a long time.

Christmas Day was a wondrous occasion, a day full of delicious foods, funny stories that had been saved up all year for the occasion, and the joy of watching happy faces when family members opened a gift and realized someone had taken time to think of a present that fulfilled their needs or hobbies.

With the portion of her earnings she'd been able to keep, Sadie had purchased gifts for her sisters and parents. For Sharon she'd found a set of salt and pepper shakers, and for Polly a pretty candy dish with red streaks in the glass that reminded Sadie of peppermint sticks. For Dat she got another year's subscription to the *Connection*, his favorite magazine with Amish contributors. He seemed so very grateful as he showed Elam the stack of magazines he kept in case he wanted to read something again. Watching him,

Sadie realized how much happier he'd seemed lately. With Sharon and her family here, everyone felt a bit more cheerful. Or maybe it was part of the wonder of Christmas.

Mem's gift was pricey, but after seeing Mem suffer cold feet on her trips out to the glass house and mushroom shack, Sadie knew it was worth every penny.

"Boots!" Mem exclaimed, holding them up for everyone to see. "Rubber on the outside, and lined with fleece."

"For when you're working out back, in the cold," Sadie said.

"And would you look at that lining. So fluffy!" Joan wasted no time slipping her feet into the boots to tromp around the house; her dress was lifted just enough to see the fleece cuffs at the top of the boots. "My feet are happy already. Denki, Sadie."

Sadie made her cinnamon rolls for breakfast, and by the time her mem and sister laid out the table with the rolls, eggs, sausage, and homemade applesauce, snow was feathering through the air outside the window.

"It's snowing!" Sadie exclaimed, dancing Lovina around merrily.

"Why you like snow?" the little girl asked.

"It covers the world with a wonderful quiet hush, a blanket of white that makes everything seem clean and bright."

Lovina pressed her face to the glass and pulled back. "Cold!"

"Yah, it is," Sadie said as all the women chuckled.

The snow continued throughout the day as they cleaned up the breakfast dishes and set to work preparing a meal that would include JR and Polly's family this evening. For the most part, Sadie left the cooking to her mother and sister and focused her attention on minding her niece and nephew. How they made her heart glad! Lovina hung on her every word, learning new things by the minute, and Nathan laughed uproariously when she brought her face in close and spurted air into the folds of his neck and jowls.

Sadie tried to imagine Christmases to come. Next Christmas, she and Mark would be married. Would Mark spend the day with her family as Elam did, keeping the fires tended and helping Dat fix a shelf that Lovina had nearly wrenched from the wall? That would be nice. The alternative, spending the day at his parents' home, would be torture. And two Christmases from now, if she and Mark were here with a baby of their own, would Mark lend a hand, minding their baby and bringing her a cup of tea when she finished nursing? Would he tend their children when Sadie wanted to join in the baking with her mother and sisters?

Much as she tried, Sadie couldn't picture Mark here in the house, joining in the family Christmas festivities.

By noon, when Elam brought wood in from the pile outside, a thick sheath of white covered everything. "There must be a foot of snow already," Elam called from the mudroom, clapping his arms to knock off the white flakes.

"I want to see!" Lovina cried.

Sadie ducked into the mudroom, slipping on a pair of rubber boots, and hoisted Lovina onto her hip. "We'll take a quick peek," she told her niece.

The air was surprisingly still, so quiet that Sadie was sure she could hear the tinkling of icy flakes as they settled over the landscape. Snow was caked upon fences, trees, bushes, rooftops, and the ground for as far as the eye could see. The glass of the hothouse seemed to be sugarcoated, as the warmth of the interior gave a melty glaze to the center of each glass panel. The bare trees in the distant orchard were coated with snow, beautiful white angels with their arms lifted to the heavens.

"White!" Lovina declared. "Everything turned white."

"That's right. Isn't it beautiful?" Sadie stepped out from the cover of the eaves, snow squeaking underfoot. "The world is fresh and new again. It's almost the perfect Christmas." The words were out before Sadie realized what she'd said.

Almost.

What was keeping this from being the perfect holiday, surrounded by people she loved?

Sadie wasn't sure, but she knew it had something to do with that clock that sat in its box on the shelf in her room.

Lovina reached one upturned hand out. "I can catch it!" She was delighted as flakes landed in her palm. But when she pulled them close to her face, they turned transparent and started to melt. "What happened?"

"It melted," Sadie said, and tried to explain how snow turned to water when it warmed up.

Lovina listened, but she was far more interested in catching other snowflakes.

Sadie smiled and humored the little girl by whirling her around the yard a bit before hurrying back into the mudroom before the cold got to them.

When Polly and JR arrived with their five children that afternoon, the small house was once again bursting with laughter and life, stories of the trip through the snow and favorite moments of Christmas morning. Dad and Elam, who had disappeared into the buggy shed out back, now emerged with JR's mule hitched to Dawdi's old sled, a lovely open vehicle with gracefully curved runners and green panels along the sides. Someone had attached some bells to it years ago, and now it was befitting of a "Jingle Bells" Christmas sleigh.

"Who wants to go for a ride?" Dat asked, pleased as punch that he'd found something to amuse his daughters and grandchildren alike. Everyone wanted to try a sleigh ride. Dat announced that they would go in two shifts: one before dinner and one after.

Sadie waited for the second shift. She stayed behind with her mem and sister Polly, who kept things moving in the kitchen while Nathan napped in the back room.

"Dat's looking good," Polly said as she transferred beets into a serving dish. "And he seems happier."

"That's because Sharon is visiting," Sadie said. "She's always been his favorite."

"Is that what you think?" Joan frowned.

Sadie nodded. She was sure of it.

"Good grief!" Mem exclaimed. "Your father loves you all just the same. Yah, he's glad to have Sharon and Elam and their little ones here. But that doesn't explain the change in Dat."

"Mem, it's okay," Sadie said. "He's out there doing a sleigh ride for them. When we're here alone, he can barely get out of his chair for dinner, let alone activities outside."

"That's because he's finally begun to take care of himself." Joan Beiler took the oven mitts off and put them on the counter. "Not a word of this in front of your dat, but he got a dire warning from the doctor a few months ago. He's a borderline diabetic, and his blood pressure is too high. The doctor told him he needs to eat healthy and keep an eye on his blood pressure."

"I knew something was up," Polly said. "He seems to have lost some weight already."

Mem nodded. "He's been cutting out desserts, as much as he can. And you know how he loves his shoofly pie."

Sadie could barely believe what she was hearing. This had been going on around her, and she hadn't noticed a thing. "What about drinking?" she asked.

Mem let out her breath, staring down at the floor. "Drinking is no good for him at all. The doctor was clear about that, and God bless him, your dat has been staying away from the liquor since he got the warning." Mem pressed a hand to her forehead as she leaned back against the counter. "It's been weighing on me so much these past weeks, all bottled up inside, but it's good to talk about it."

"It'll be okay, Mem." Polly put a hand on their mother's shoulder. "That's great that he's trying to eat right. I can tell that he's trimmed down."

"He has, and the blood pressure is getting better. When he goes into town, Dat uses that special machine at the pharmacy to check the numbers." Joan turned to Sadie. "So if he seems happier lately, it's because he's feeling better than he has in years."

"That's wonderful news," said Polly.

"It is," Sadie agreed, forcing a smile as she wondered how she could have missed the signs. It would have helped if Mem or Dat had said something before this. "You should have told me," she said. "You know I worry about him with his drinking."

There, she'd said it again—the forbidden topic.

"We all worry about Dat," Polly agreed.

"This doctor's warning may be a blessing in disguise," Joan said. "I think your father is done with the drinking for good. God willing."

"This is good news," Polly said. "More reason to be grateful on this Christmas Day."

The timer dinged, indicating it was time to take out the roasht and put in the dinner rolls. Sadie put the hot pads on, grateful to be able to lean in toward the stove, where no one else could see the mixed emotions on her face.

Could it be that Dat really loved all his daughters all the same? Maybe she wasn't such a terrible burden to him after all. It was good news, for sure, but it made her feel weepy to think that she'd misunderstood his irritation these last few years.

By the time the sleigh riders returned, their cheeks ruddy and their coats covered in snow, Sadie was able to join in the festivities and help finish cooking dinner. With such a large group, they had to do two seatings, so they put the six children at the table first and served up their plates. Lovina sat beside her four-year-old cousin, Kate, and the two of them seemed to have an understanding, though they didn't see each other often.

With the children fed, the adult dinner was more re-laxing, as Polly's eleven-year-old daughter, Elizabeth, corralled the children and kept them busy with some toys. Sadie was able to sit back and observe how pleasant her family could be with Dat in a good mood. People felt free to talk and laugh. Even Dat told a funny story about a friend who'd lost his fishing gear in the hole while ice fishing.

Sadie took note of her brothers-in-law, who had been part of the family for years now. Elam was low-key and patient with the children and attentive to Sharon's needs. It had been hard for them both to move away from Joyful River, but when the factory he'd been working in closed down, they'd found a community with far more employment options. Polly's husband, JR, had a bigger, louder personality. While his booming voice could vibrate through the house, the vibrations were always jovial and kind. He was an asset at his parents' diner in town, where Polly also helped wait tables when they were low on staff.

Elam and JR were different types from Dat, and maybe her sisters had chosen them deliberately. Neither man cared for alcohol, even on special occasions.

Sadie probed a cube of bread stuffing with her fork, wondering about her own choice. Mark was moody, like Dat, but when he was happy, he shone a light on everyone around him. Those were the moments when he melted her heart. The problem was, she could never count on him being in a good place. And after yesterday, she couldn't count on him staying away from alcohol, either.

She had made a poor choice, but there was no changing that now.

After dinner, JR was in charge of the second sleigh ride so that Dat could rest up for a spell. Snow kept falling, filling the air with a shower of white and covering the earth with its blanket of quiet.

"I'm not sure about getting home in the buggy," Polly said as she scanned the white yard.

"You should stay," Mem said. "It'll be tight, but we can accommodate."

"We'll fit you in," Sadie assured them. "And it will be fun for the children to have the night together."

"We'll see," Polly said.

All bundled up in her jacket, scarf, boots, and gloves, Sadie climbed aboard the sleigh and took a spot between Mem and Polly. There was still daylight to be had, but the gray tint of dusk was setting in. JR handed out the head-lamps they used in the herb garden and shed, and Mem held an LED battery lantern so that there'd be enough warning light when they went on the road.

JR called to the horse, and then they were off, gliding into the white expanse. The bells jingled as the sleigh bumped over ridges in the ground, but for the most part, Sadie was surprised at how smoothly they moved along down the lane.

"Oh, this is a fun thing to do on Christmas," Mem called out, laughing as they jogged over a bump on the main road. "Do you remember when you girls were little? Your dat brought the sleigh out almost every year at Christmas."

"I remember," Polly said. "I think that was before Sadie was born. We should do it every year. A new tradition."

"That would be wonderful," Mem agreed. "But you can't always count on snow."

They chatted and then sang the cheery "Jingle Bells" song. Polly started a few other carols in Pennsylvania Dutch, finishing with the reverent "Silent Night."

"If this snow doesn't let up, we'll be riding this sleigh home," JR said as they passed a stand of evergreens painted white.

Polly laughed at the idea. "It would be lovely, but not safe. That's too far to travel in a vehicle without proper lights."

Sadie noticed they were on the road that passed by Alvin Lapp's dairy farm. "You should stay at our house tonight," she told Polly and JR. "If you drop me off here, at Essie's house, I'm sure they'll let me stay. Then you and JR can use my room."

"Mem, what do you think?" Polly asked. She patted Sadie's knee with her gloved hand. "I hate to kick you out on Christmas night."

"Don't worry about me," Sadie insisted. "We've had our

good time together. After this, I'm sure everyone's off to bed." And Sadie knew that Essie, Harlan, and other people her age at the Lapp farm would be staying up much later.

"Then it makes sense," Mem said. "Best for JR and Polly to stay over and keep their family safe. It's hard to know when this snow will let up."

Polly told her husband they'd be making a stop up ahead, and Sadie showed JR where to turn off. The lane leading to the Lapp farm was just a bit hard to find, with snow covering the markings, but Sadie was able to guide her brother-in-law between the two fence posts, making sure to avoid the left side, where the drainage ditch sloped down. As they approached the house, Polly made sure to give the bells a jingle, "To let them know we're coming," she said. Gliding over the smooth snow, Sadie laughed aloud. This was a form of travel she might get used to.

As they approached the house, warm, golden light glowing in the windows downstairs, the front door opened and two people stepped out on the porch. Sadie recognized Miriam, Essie's mem, waving from the porch as JR brought the sleigh in close.

"Merry Christmas!" Miriam called.

Everyone called out a "Merry Christmas!" in return.

"We heard your lovely bells and wondered what on earth it could be," Miriam said. "Can you believe this glorious snow?"

As Sadie brushed snow from the shoulders of her coat and pushed the blanket back from her lap, Mem and Miriam talked about the snowstorm and the possibility of Sadie staying the night here to free up some space.

"Absolutely!" Miriam said. "We'd love to have her, and there's an extra bed in the girls' room."

Sam, wearing muck boots, came down the porch steps to steady the horse and help Sadie out. She smiled, wildly happy to see him, overjoyed to be visiting here, her second home, on Christmas day.

When she went to jump down from the sleigh, she hesitated. It was clear that the snow would be over her shoes. "The snow is so deep, and I didn't wear boots," she said, perched on the edge of the sleigh.

"I'll give you a lift," Sam offered, opening his arms tentatively.

"Denki!" She was grateful when his arms closed around her and he picked her up and held her to his chest. She grasped his shoulders, so pleased to be able to keep her feet dry and warm!

Sam moved slowly through the knee-high snow, carrying her along as if she were no heavier than a baby lamb. For a brief moment she was aware of the solid power in his biceps and the rigid muscles in his belly, and it dawned on her that Sam was truly a man now. The boy she had come to think of as a big brother had moved far into the grown-up world of working men and farmers.

When he climbed the first two steps, then delivered her gently to her feet on the porch, Sadie felt reluctant to let go of him. It surprised her, the way that Sam's solid, steady body had provided the support she needed, and he offered it without a price or a promise.

"There you go."

"Denki," she told him again, straightening a bit unsteadily. Something about Sam took her by surprise, but there was no time to contemplate it, as she was quickly snatched up by Essie's mother.

"God bless you!" Miriam exclaimed, sweeping Sadie

into her arms for a hug. "Such a lovely gift to land on our doorstep!"

The door flew open again, and out popped Essie, Harlan, and Annie—all with Christmas greetings and hugs and exclamations about the snow and the sleigh and the miracle that had brought Sadie to them this Christmas night.

"Look at you, covered in snow!" Essie said, brushing flakes from Sadie's shoulder. "Your coat is soaked through. We need to get you inside."

"But the snow is so beautiful," Sadie said as her friend tugged her toward the front door. "I'm so glad it gave Dat a chance to get the sleigh out after all these years."

"It is a glorious Christmas," Essie said, looking over at her new husband with love in her eyes. "And you've got to tell me everything about your dinner with Mark. His family." She lowered her voice and leaned in to ask: "Any special news? A secret engagement?"

Sadie shook her head quickly. "I can't—I don't think I can be his wife."

"What?" Essie grabbed her hands. "But I thought—"

Sadie glanced back to be sure her family didn't overhear, but they were engaged in conversation with Miriam and Annie. "I'm so confused."

"Come." Essie tugged her toward the door. "We'll hang up your wet things in the mudroom. You have to tell me what happened. Everything."

Chapter 17

Under the guise of checking on the cows, Sam went down the porch steps and traipsed through the snow to get to the back of the house. From the snippet of conversation he'd heard, it was clear that something had happened between Sadie and Mark. Something about getting engaged . . . or not getting married. Sam had to know, and he could tell Sadie was bursting to tell Essie. He would take a listen.

Not proud of eavesdropping, he vowed to make a trip to the barn before coming back in. But for now, he had to hear the conversation the girls were so determined to have in secret.

Snowdrifts loomed against the north side of the house as he slogged through the sticky white powder. When he reached the back, he cut a wide swath in case anyone was looking in the kitchen window, then moved back closer to the house. He ducked down low to avoid the window in the back door, then pressed close to the wood-shingled wall of the mudroom. This extension of the kitchen was an add-on, barely insulated. On a laundry day in the summer, you could hear the noise of the diesel-powered wringer machine for miles.

The night was still and quiet, one thing on his side. As soon as he got close, he could hear the blurred sound of the girls' voices. He went to the big window, thinking that they were probably sitting on the bench Mem used to stack clean clothes. Hunkered under the windowsill, he could hear more clearly.

"It was ruined from the start when he picked me up that way," Sadie was saying. "It came totally out of the blue. I mean, who knew Mark would take up drinking?"

Essie said something about the chance it was a one-time thing, but that didn't seem to reassure Sadie. "He's not the most attentive boyfriend to begin with, but drunk? He was awful. Closed up tight like an Amish business on Sunday. He barely talked to me the entire time! He just sat with the men, in that sort of group where you know a woman's not welcome. It was a terrible time for me, and you know about my dat. Mark knows about the misery drinking has caused our family, and still, he's decided he's going to drink."

Sam couldn't hear Essie's response, but he had a sense of what Sadie was going through. Although it was a sin to gossip, and folks tried not to keep tabs on other people's problems, Reuben Beiler's drinking had been hard to ignore sometimes over the years. As a kid, Sam had seen Sadie's dat going off at weddings with a small group of men who managed to find a spot over the hill or in an outbuilding to drink some bottles of wine. He'd also heard his parents speak, when they thought the children weren't listening, about the difficulties of running a dairy farm or a fruit or-chard when liquor was in the picture. Everyone knew

Reuben Beiler's drinking had harmed his business at times, though it wasn't discussed in public. The Amish had a way of dancing around certain topics and sweeping other issues under the rug.

From the other side of the wall, Sadie lamented that she didn't know what to do, and in the murmurs that followed, Sam could hear his sister cooing softly.

Sadie was crying. Sam could tell.

His heart ached for her, for what she was going through. He hated that Mark treated her this way, and she didn't realize that she deserved better. And sometimes he was annoyed with himself for lacking the nerve to tell Sadie how he really felt about her.

On the other side of the wall, Sadie talked more about her visit to Mark's home. How she felt uncomfortable despite the fine food in the very nice house. Sadie said she would never feel at home there.

Sam listened, sympathetic to Sadie's sorrow and angry with Mark Miller for causing Sadie so much heartache.

Then Sadie talked about the ride home, how Mark's mood changed when he gave her a Christmas present.

"He gave you a clock?" Essie's voice held disbelief.

Had she said a clock? As in an engagement gift? Sam shifted his stance and leaned into the building in an attempt to avoid the onslaught of falling snow.

"So he asked you to marry him?" Essie said.

"Not exactly. He didn't mention marriage, but we both know that the gift of a clock is a marriage proposal."

"So he wants to marry you?"

"I wish I knew. But it's weighing on me like a cape made of stone. I should be so happy! This was everything I wanted, the man I dreamed of marrying. But I don't feel good about it. Whenever I think of the gift sitting in its box on the shelf, I get a bad feeling deep in my heart."

"Oh, Sadie! What are you going to do?"

"I don't know. I just don't know."

"Hey in there!" a different voice called into the mudroom.

Sam suspected it was Annie. Sounded like she was trying to drum up a board game.

He needed to go if he wanted to avoid getting caught. Keeping low, he moved away from the window, then hurried toward the barn, avoiding the deeper drifts as he went to check on the cows.

He'd heard enough to know that Sadie was having doubts. He was sorry for her distress, but the situation gave him hope. Did he have a chance? Gott had given him this opportunity. When every door was closed up tight, Gott had opened a window.

It was up to him to climb through.

Twenty minutes later, when Sam left his coat and boots in the mudroom, it was empty. Once he stepped into the kitchen, he heard the voices of everyone assembled at the big table under the lit lamp.

"Sam, I saved the man on horseback marker for you," Annie called as she lifted the game piece from the Monopoly board.

Essie and Harlan sat beside each other, while Annie and Sadie were seated across the table. It was a calmer, brighter Sadie he saw now. The storm of minutes ago had passed, and she seemed her old self, rolling the dice over and over in the quest for doubles as she waited for the game to start.

"Denki. But how did you know I'd want to play?"

"You're always up for fun, Sam." Sadie smiled across the room at him, and in this light, the green of her dress deepened the color of her eyes. She had always been a beautiful girl; Sam knew that. But it hadn't been until the last few years that he'd realized she was just as beautiful inside.

"I like the sound of that." Sam took a seat at the end of the table so that he was adjacent to Sadie and Harlan. It was not unusual to have such proximity to Sadie. This was the sort of thing they'd done all their lives, gathered round the table to play cards or a game. But tonight—tonight he sensed that so much was at stake between them.

At first, Sam had to force himself not to stare at her. To avoid basking in the light of those green eyes. To appreciate her smile and stop looking for signs that she was hurt or angry with Mark Miller. He kept his tone even and his gaze on the game board, where each player took a turn rolling the dice. Slow and steady. Try not to notice the drape of her green dress over her delicate shoulders and arms. The fine fingers and pink nailbeds of her hands as she swept up the dice to roll.

His approach worked. Once they'd gone round the board, the game in full swing, everyone at the table lost themselves in the jokes and camaraderie that were a rule at the game table in the Lapp home.

"Community Chest," Sadie said, picking a yellow card from the board. "Oh!" she laughed. "It says I've won a prize in a beauty contest. Collect ten dollars."

As Annie—the banker—slapped a bill in front of Sadie, Sam found it fitting that she'd won a beauty contest. Funny how things worked that way. He wished he could tell her how pretty she truly was. Given the chance, he'd tell her every day of her life.

Given the chance . . .

As Monopoly games tend to, the game went on for hours. Harlan lost out fairly early, but he stayed at Essie's side, sharing in the jokes and bringing them servings of leftover pie.

"The game has to end sometime," Essie said, giving up her leftover money to Sadie.

Annie straightened up the real estate cards she'd purchased. "I wish we could leave it set up until tomorrow."

"We need the table for meals and such," Essie reminded her.

"I know," Annie admitted, "but I can't stop when I'm winning!"

Sam and Sadie exchanged a smile at that; they were familiar with Annie's competitive streak.

The game went on until after two a.m., when Sam magnanimously agreed to give the win to Annie.

"Yippee!" Annie thrust her arms in the air, celebrating her victory until Essie shushed her.

"People are sleeping upstairs," Essie said, stern as a schoolteacher.

"Yay . . ." Annie whispered, waving Monopoly money at her sister.

Sam helped put the game away, and then it was over too quickly, with yawns and good nights, and one more slice of pie for Harlan. Essie and Harlan put on boots and coats for the brief trek to the Dawdi House, and Annie led Sadie upstairs to the girls' room, which was half-empty now that Essie and their Englisch cousins had vacated. At least

Megan, Serena, and Grace would be back soon, after New Year's Day. Sam missed them all—especially Megan, who was good at giving him a girl's perspective on things.

Up in the room he shared with the twins, he could hear the quiet breathing of Pete and Paul coming from the bunk beds. They were still on the boyish side of twelve, but it wouldn't be long until they'd be asking Mem and Dat to stay up later and join in late-night Monopoly games. Sam hoped he'd be married and out of the house before that happened. No Amish family wanted to have a lonely bachelor son living at home.

He hung his pants and shirt on hooks, left his long johns on, and slid under the quilt of his double bed. Just a few yards away, Sadie was getting into bed under the same roof. Her presence in the house gave him an advantage over Mark.

There was hope.

Hours later, sounds of awe awakened Sam. His brothers stood at the bedroom window, staring out into the predawn landscape.

"It's still snowing!" Paul exclaimed.

"Look at it come down! Everything is covered!" Pete raked his fingers back through his auburn hair. "We should have brought the cows in! They'll be frozen like Popsicles!"

"The cows will be fine," Sam called from bed. He swept the covers aside and sat up. "Their hair catches the snow and keeps it from their hides. And then a pocket of warmth from their hot bodies forms to keep them comfortable."

"How do you know this?" Pete asked.

"From Dat. And he learned it from his dat. Cows are fine in the snow, unless we get really low temperatures."

"So that's why Dat is always checking the thermometer outside the kitchen window?" Paul said.

Sam joined the boys at the window and patted Paul's shoulder. "That's right." Looking out, Sam marveled at the way something as simple as snow could transform the land. Even in the darkness, their farm glowed white, and the pristine blanket of snow stretched over hill and dale as far as the eye could see. "It's beautiful," he said.

"And it's a holiday." Pete grinned. "We can make a snow fort!"

Chuckling, Sam grabbed his clothes from the hook. "You can get building just as soon as we finish milking the cows. Don't forget to put on snow britches."

The morning chores went quickly. It helped that everything outside the barn resembled a winter wonderland. As Sam grabbed coffee and some of the egg casserole his mother had made, there was talk of the snow affecting their plans for Second Christmas. On this day following Christmas, Amish folk gathered with extended family. This year the extended Lapp family members, including the families of Sam's uncles Vernon and Lloyd, were planning to get together here. Sam was looking forward to seeing Isaac.

"I think they can make it through the snow," Mem said. "It's just down the road apiece."

"But Vern's family needs to get across the river," Dat pointed out, "and the Harris Bridge is bound to be icy."

"That's true, though it is a covered bridge," Mem said, taking a break from chopping celery. "Am I just letting my hopes get in the way? I so want all the family to be together today."

"Uncle Vern knows to shoe the horses with shoes for ice," Sam said. "And horses can make it through three feet of snow."

Dat sipped his coffee, considering. "True. Horses are better than cars in this weather." He put his mug on the table. "I'll go out to the phone shanty and leave messages for my brothers that the gathering is still on."

Just then someone called to Sam from the mudroom. "Sam!" Pete peeked in through the doorway; he knew enough to keep his snowy body out of Mem's kitchen. "Come see our snow fort! Harlan helped us build it, and he made it like a real hut. He's a right good builder."

"That's what carpenters do, son," said Dat with a smile.

"But it's really spectacular! He showed us how to make snow bricks," Pete insisted.

"I'll be out in a minute," Sam promised, finishing off the last of the casserole and a small glass of tomato juice.

"Peter," Mem called, "you and your brother need to come in for breakfast."

"We will, Mem."

"Sooner than later, before it's gone. I don't have time to make a second batch today with so many coming to visit."

"Yes, Mem," Pete said.

Sam put his dishes in the sink and joined his brother in the mudroom.

"Let's go!" Pete insisted, as if they were running to put out a fire.

"Patience is a virtue," Sam said wryly, well aware that Pete was too young to care about such things. His outdoor britches were still damp on the outside as he slipped them on over his pants and grabbed his other gear. "Show me the fort."

They pushed to the whiteness outside, following footsteps in the snow to the field beside the Dawdi House, the small but cozy two-bedroom house where Essie and

Harlan currently lived with Harlan's mem and sister Suzie. Many Amish farms had a Dawdi House where the farmer and his wife could live in retirement after passing the farm on to his son. In this case, Essie's grandmother, Mammi Esther, had offered the little house to Harlan's family in a time of need. "I hate to see it go empty," Mammi had said. "And I can't live there again. Every day in that house is a day that reminds me of my Mervin, Gott rest his soul." Instead, Mammi chose to live down the road with her son Lloyd and his family.

Snowflakes danced in the air, but that didn't make the sight of the fortress any less impressive as they approached. "Look at that! You weren't exaggerating at all!"

"I told you!" Pete said.

Sam trudged faster toward the three-sided structure made up of a main wall that was at least ten feet wide, with two wings to provide cover. Around three feet high, the fort was tall enough to shelter a person sitting or crouching behind it.

Just then Harlan popped up from the other side. "Oh. Hey." He was pouring something from a bucket onto the interior fort wall. "I thought you were Paul, coming up in a sneak attack."

"I like your fort," Sam said.

Harlan nodded. "It's for everyone. We built it together."

"I told you it was good," Pete said, his breath misting before him. "We made bricks out of the small coolers. You just stuff the cooler with snow, pack it in, and then turn it over. Sometimes you have to probe the ice brick out with a spade."

"Are you watering it?" Sam asked, touched that Harlan had spent the morning helping Pete and Paul. It was a really nice thing to do on Second Christmas, when he could have been spending the time with Essie and his family.

Harlan nodded. "You need to douse the walls with water to make an ice coating. It makes the walls stronger, gives them some support."

"Until the spring thaw," Sam said.

Harlan grinned. "That's right. Every snow fort has its expiration date."

Off to his left, Sam spotted Paul sneaking closer and then ducking behind a tree. "I think it's time we tried the new fort out," he said, casually reaching down to scoop up some snow and then running around the wing of the fort to take cover inside.

"Haaaa!" Paul darted out from behind the tree, launching a snowball as he ran. It hit Harlan, smashing on the dark fabric on his shoulder.

"Hey! Don't hit the builder!" Harlan objected.

Paul laughed and chucked another snowball at Harlan.

Sam chuckled as he molded the snow in his hands and called to Pete. "Come on. Take cover over here."

"Nay!" Pete was already shaping a snowball in his hands, packing it tightly, the way Sam had taught him years ago. "It's Paul and me against you two." He punctuated the statement by lobbing the snowball in the air.

Sam dove into the snow near the fort wall, and the incoming snow landed on his legs. "All right," he called to his younger brothers. "Get ready for a snowstorm!"

The snow battle went on for a good fifteen minutes. Sam and Harlan worked together, with Sam molding a pile of snowballs and Harlan popping up over the barrier to toss them at Pete and Paul.

"You built a fine fort," Sam told Harlan as they huddled together during a lull in the attack.

"It's solid, but it's not very fair for them," Harlan admitted. "Maybe we should switch sides."

"You're way too nice," Sam said.

"I try."

Just then they were both hit by two snowballs, followed by hoots from Pete and Paul.

"Yahoo!" the twins hollered as they came running into the U of the fort, having sneaked around the side wings.

"We're surrounded!" Sam shouted. He and Harlan began chucking snowballs at the invaders.

"That's it!" Harlan exclaimed, laughing. "We're done for."

"We surrender," Sam shouted, laughing along as he covered his face in defense.

"We won!" Pete exclaimed. "The fort is ours!"

Paul clapped his brother on the shoulder, and the two younger boys collapsed in the snow near Harlan and Sam.

"That was fun," Pete said. "Next time, I want Harlan on my side."

"That might be a fairer split," Sam agreed.

As Sam rose and brushed snow from his pants, he spotted Essie coming their way, dragging a Radio Flyer sled behind her.

"Pete and Paul," she called, "Mem says you're to get to the house right away and have breakfast."

"Aw." Pete hung his head. "We were just getting started."

"I'm not even hungry," Paul proclaimed.

"Just go, do as Mem says," Sam said. "The snowball fight can continue when you finish."

As the boys plodded off through the snow, Essie motioned to Harlan and Sam to come to the lane. "Come!

I've got the sled, and I thought we could take a few runs down Linden Hill before it's time to prepare for Second Christmas."

This was a new side of Essie, who was forever putting up another batch of jam or scrubbing the kitchen floor. Sam suspected that married life had brought his sister a sense of fun.

"What about Sadie?" Harlan asked.

"She's going to meet us at the hill as soon as she finishes breakfast."

Sadie . . . Just the thought of her lightened Sam's heart. He started heading toward his sister, then stopped. This might be a rare chance to talk with Sadie alone. "You two go ahead," he said. "I'm going to finish putting water on the fort." He picked up the pail that Harlan had tossed aside. "We can't let your creation fall to the ground too soon."

Harlan's lips curved in a slight smile as he walked past Sam. "We'll leave it up to you to get Sadie to the hill."

Sam nodded. He suspected Harlan sensed what was going on, but he was cool about it. Good man.

As the couple went off, Harlan towing a squealing Essie on the sled, Sam went over to the side of the Dawdi House to fill the pail from the outdoor spigot. He traipsed back through the snow to douse the outer walls of the fort, the way he'd seen Harlan do it. The water froze instantly, creating a glossy coating on the wall. Pure ice.

When he looked up, Sadie was coming down the path, a beautiful, dark silhouette against the snow-covered landscape.

"Are you watering that snow fort?" she called.

Sam smiled to hear his own question come back to

him. "It makes the walls stronger," he answered. He tossed the empty bucket to the side and walked toward her, his pulse thumping loudly in his ears. It wasn't nervousness, exactly. He'd known Sadie most of his life. It was excitement coupled with expectation—the way you feel when you're about to jump into a cold lake on the hottest day of the summer.

"Harlan built it with the twins," he said, close enough now to see the rose on her cheeks and the sparkle of her green eyes. "I was just finishing it off for them. Essie and Harlan went off to Linden Hill."

"For sledding," she said. "I'm so glad to see your sister enjoying married life. She does love Harlan so, and he pushes her to stop working so hard and enjoy the moment."

"They're good for each other," he agreed, pausing at the edge of the lane. "I'm finished here, if you want to head over there."

"But I want to see the fort first," she said, lifting her chin to see beyond him. "It looks better than anything we rolled together in the past."

"That's what happens when a carpenter is the master builder. Come on, I'll show you." Sam led the way, thinking of the forts and snowmen they'd built in the past. "Remember the year when we built that family of snow people? Eight of them."

Sadie chuckled, leaping a bit to follow the tracks already made through the deep snow. "That was good fun. We gave each one a carrot nose taken from the stash your mem had put aside for a pot roast."

"That's right." He smiled at the memory. "Later, Mem said she thought she'd lost her marbles when she had to make a second trip to the cellar to fetch more carrots." He was laughing now. So was Sadie.

"Miriam didn't realize what had happened until a week or so later when Lizzie dragged her outside to see the snow people. 'My carrots!'"

He paused and turned back to face her as they laughed together. This was the Sadie he had come to love—carefree and joyous. Not the glum, fearful person she became when Mark was around.

When she started walking again, he noticed she was struggling in the deep sections of snow. "Let me help you." He reached out to her, and she took his hand, but as she continued she slipped and started going down.

"Whoa." He stepped closer and slipped an arm around her waist, bracing her against his body for support.

Suddenly, he was holding her in his arms, and his body thrummed with joy. The light weight of her body, the feel of her flesh and bones, all apportioned as Gott had planned—she was perfection, inside and out. Even in this fleeting moment, to hold her, so precious, in his arms . . . it seemed nothing short of a miracle.

"I'm so awkward," she sputtered.

"It's not you. The snow is slippery. Icy."

"Well, you saved me." She tipped her head back, and suddenly her face was inches from his, so close he could feel her warm breath on his neck.

He tipped his face down, and their gazes locked. Her eyes, green with glimmering bits of gold, didn't hold the hesitancy or apathy he expected.

Instead, he saw a tender curiosity. A longing?

The next thing that happened wasn't planned or even wise, but he couldn't help letting his face drop gently, his nose brushing hers, his lips grazing hers. So tender, so sweet. He realized he was holding his breath, on alert, but he couldn't seem to make himself breathe.

Her small gasp—really, just a slight breath—seemed to say yes. Her eyes encouraged him. Her body, chaste and delicate, seemed willing in his arms.

Maybe he was a fool, but he couldn't pass this chance up.

After a lifetime of waiting, he threw caution to the wind, lowered his lips to hers, and kissed her.

Chapter 18

A kiss. Warm and breathless and wonderful.

Sam was kissing her.

Sadie's eyes closed as the bright white world and the cold snow chilling her feet fell away to the spark of warmth on her lips. The soft pressure of his mouth sent warm-honeyed joy surging through her body, awakening feelings that were sweet yet unfamiliar. In Sam's arms, she felt like a silky, tender rosebud on the verge of blossoming, unfurling its petals, and opening to the world.

It was a spectacular moment. Fireworks! A shooting star! That moment of losing yourself in a torrent of laughter or a cozy nap by the fire on a winter's day.

Part of her wanted the moment to last forever, but then, as if she'd been swimming underwater in a summer lake, she needed to come up for air, to open her eyes and breathe again and know that this was all truly real. When she looked at him through the glaze of emotion, he was more handsome than ever, his brown eyes smoky and soulful.

"Oh, Sam. I—"

"I shouldn't have done that. I'm sorry."

"Don't be sorry. It was wonderful good. But—"

"I know. You've promised to marry Mark."

"I haven't—not really. But we've been dating; everyone knows that."

He looked down in dismay, and she immediately wished she could take it back. The last thing she wanted was to disappoint him! It had been a wonderful kiss . . . a hint of good things to come, she hoped. But she couldn't move ahead right now, not when she was dating someone else. "Sam, you know I need to do the right thing by Mark."

"What if this is the right thing?" he said, his voice clear and steady as a river current. "You and me?"

"Together?" Could this be real? She reached up and pressed a palm to his cheek, smooth and clean-shaven. Nice to touch. Until very recently she'd been blind to Sam's appeal as a man, looking to him as a surrogate big brother, shouldering responsibilities for Essie and her. He was the brother involved in that mysterious world of men with a slightly different language, a different manner, and a very different sense of camaraderie. Now, in this moment, she sensed that world opening to her for the first time in her life.

"Can't you see us together, Sadie? Truth is, when you're around, everything is that much better. We're good together. It may sound daft, but if we started dating, I think you'd see it, too. We belong together. I believe it with all my heart." He slid his arm around her waist and settled one palm on her hip, holding her close.

His words and gesture ignited sparks of joy in her heart, but at the same time, this seemed like the most natural thing in the world—as if they'd always been hooked together, two peas in a pod. She looked into his eyes, and suddenly it was as if she'd never seen him before. His brown eyes held a warmth for her, a loyalty, and the promise of the truest love she'd ever known.

How could she have not seen this before?

Sam knew her well, and he cared for her.

Her heart sang at the discovery. He loved her, this man whom she'd always loved as a brother. A love that Gott, in his infinite wisdom, had expanded in her heart, as if the Almighty had made a beautiful patchwork quilt out of a bag of rags while she'd been fast asleep. Her brotherly love for Sam had come to encompass so much more now, as evidenced by the feelings evoked by the nearness of his body and the gentle pressure of his touch.

"Oh, Sam," she breathed.

"Don't say no." He stared straight ahead, a strained look on his face. "Please. Not now. Just . . . give it a day or two. A week. Think about it."

"I don't need any time." Sadie felt the earth beneath her, now more supportive and solid than she'd known in weeks. And cold—icy cold, but real. Gone was the bad feeling of the clock, the botched proposal, the stressful Christmas Eve. Right now, right here—this was where she was meant to be. "I know the answer."

"Shh! Don't make a decision now. Just give it a few days."

"Sam . . ." She pressed her hand over his, keeping it in place on her hip. She wanted to spill forth the joy she felt, but then, too much too soon might scare him. "I love being with you. I've felt that way for a long time. You know I'm here at your house all the time."

"To see Essie," he said.

"Essie is my friend, but there's been a stronger pull for

me to come here. I was mourning the loss of a reason to visit after Essie and Harlan get their own place. I want to be here, and that's all about you. I was a fool not to know my own heart, but . . . there you have it. So don't be sorry about kissing me."

The strain eased from Sam's face, and a new light shone in his eyes. "For real?"

She nodded. "I'm not sorry at all, Sam."

"Hallelujah!" He swept her close again, this time lifting her off her feet and twirling around in the field of snow as Sadie laughed joyously.

Once he lowered her to her feet, they came together for another kiss. This time, Sadie's concerns melted away to a warm sense of security and pleasure. She was where she belonged in the world, sheltered in Sam's arms. Everything was as it should be.

Well . . . almost everything.

"There's just one problem. Until I can call off things with Mark, we've got to keep things quiet between us. We can't date, and no one can know." She looked off toward the lane and shook her head. "I can't even tell Essie." A laugh slipped out. "Won't Essie be shocked to find out?"

"Knowing Essie, she'll probably be mad at me," Sam said.

"I won't let her be that way." Sadie squeezed his hand extra hard through their gloves. "I can't wait to tell her. But wait we must."

He nodded. "I can be patient, when the prize is worth waiting for."

"So. Are you ready to go sledding and pretend that you're still just my best friend's older brother?"

"Sure. And if you want me to be really convincing as

the older brother, I just might wing a snowball or two your way."

"You wouldn't!" she teased.

He grinned. "Don't push me."

Such a wondrous day! As Sadie and Sam traipsed along the snowy path to Linden Hill, Sadie was quite sure that, as long as she lived, she would remember this Second Christmas as one of the most spectacular days of her life.

And to think that true love had been here all along! For Sadie, it was an astounding and surprising turn of events, as she'd always considered Sam to be more brother than a suitor.

But he wasn't her brother. He was close, a good friend. Loyal and reliable. Wonderful, funny Sam, who enjoyed making her laugh and stayed up all night long to sit beside her at the kitchen table playing cards or a board game.

The once tiny glimmer of possibility had burst open like a window of light, revealing Sam, steadfast and patient. Willing to wait for her to end things with Mark in the proper way.

We belong together, he'd told her. *I believe it with all my heart.*

His confidence in their future together made her love him that much more. Sadie couldn't wait for the time when they could actually start dating, going to singings together, taking long buggy rides in the summer. For now it was lucky that Essie was her best friend and no one would think twice about Sadie spending her free time at the Lapp farm. But soon—as soon as she could get Mark to meet with her—she would straighten things out. Honesty was important to her, and she respected Mark enough to tell him the truth right away, even if it might not be what he wanted to hear. She would tape that clock back into its box and hand it back to him. Probably to be used as a gift for his next intended, and that would be fine. She wished Mark all the happiness she was feeling in this moment.

As they took turns riding the sled down the gentle hill, Sadie could not keep herself from smiling. The snow had stopped falling, but the whiteness in the surrounding hills and pastures was pristine and bright. Something to match her mood.

At one point Sadie and Essie rode the sled downhill together, shrieking at the steep part of the hill and gasping when they went over the little ridge that sent the sled flying momentarily. By the time they slid to a halt at the bottom, Sadie couldn't stop laughing.

"You're just full of giggles today," Essie said. "Did you put extra sugar in your coffee?"

"Maybe that's it." Sadie rose from the sled and extended a hand to help her friend up. "Maybe it's just Christmas cheer. I'm so grateful to have this time to spend here with you and your family."

Essie tilted her head to one side, studying Sadie carefully. "That's sweet, but you know you're always welcome, long as Harlan and I are living here."

And beyond, Sadie thought. *I'll be here to see Sam.* The wonderful secret threatened to burst from her lips. The urge to spill it all was so strong that Sadie had to turn away and reach for the rope tether on the sled. "I'll tug this back up the hill."

"We can each do half," Essie said.

"But I don't mind."

Essie clucked her tongue as they tromped through the snow. "I don't know what's got into you, but I like it."

* * *

Later that day when Sadie's parents arrived in a buggy to pick her up for the dinner at the Lambright home, Sadie felt torn. It was always hard to say goodbye to everyone at the Lapp farm, but now, to leave Sam when they'd just begun to know each other in a new and different way—it was all so bittersweet.

And yet, the joys of Second Christmas with her extended family beckoned her. Sharon and her family were in town but a short time, and Sadie rarely got to see Polly's crew. JR's parents always greeted guests with open arms, and although they were family by marriage, they always made Sadie feel connected and right at home. It was a novel time, not to be missed.

When Sadie settled into the back of the buggy, Mem turned to her with a delighted smile. "Look at you, fresh as a winter rose," Mem said as Dat called to the horse and the buggy started to move along up the snow-slick lane.

Sadie pressed one hand to her mouth, wondering if her lips were pink and swollen from kissing Sam in the snow fort. Could her mother tell?

"I thought you'd be dragging, having stayed up most of the night playing cards and games with the young folks. But no. Your cheeks have a rosy glow, and your eyes are bright and clear." Mem gave her knee a light tap. "Did you actually get some sleep last night?"

"Umm, I did sleep well," Sadie answered, which was partly true. Those few hours in the bunk bed, she'd slept soundly, knowing she was safe and part of the buddy group. She'd been a bit slow starting this morning, as she'd slept only for a few hours. But once she'd run into Sam at the snow fort, she'd been rejuvenated. The joy inside her outshone any weariness.

"I don't know what it is, but you look different." Mem squinted as she took a closer look. "What is it, Sadie?"

I'm in love! Sadie wanted to say. *In love with a wonderful, kind person I've known forever.* How she wished she could share the good news, a revelation that would delight Mem and Dat. But not yet. Out of respect for Mark, she would have to wait.

"It's been a wonderful Christmas," Sadie answered, suddenly wishing Mem weren't so intently staring at her. "You know I love this holiday." She turned toward the snow-covered trees they were passing, noting how the sunlight sparkled on the tops of branches as if someone had dropped diamonds there in time for the late-afternoon sun.

How beautiful was Gott's world.

Pristine and silvery white.

She suspected it had always been that way, only her eyes had not possessed the ability to see such beauty. Now the surrounding landscape had new texture and light. Joy colored the world in magnificent ways.

Once they arrived at the Lambright home, Sadie was happy to be reunited with her sisters and their families once again. As they entered the brightly lit home, simply decorated with fat red candles and holly, Lovina hugged her thigh and clung to her until Sadie picked the little girl up and carried her on her hip as if she were her own daughter. Sadie leaned into the childish jowls and kissed her puffy little cheek repeatedly. Another mother might have been jealous of the affection between Sadie and Lovina, but Sharon was grateful, as her own arms were full of a cranky little boy, his upper lip creased in the perturbed expression that warned there might be a crying fit any moment.

"Is he hungry?" Sadie asked.

"I just fed him on the way over." Sharon rocked him in her arms and leaned down to kiss his forehead, right between the eyebrows raised in anxiety. "Oh, come, little man. Don't be a bupp."

"Ach, don't say that," said Sadie. A "bupp" was a fussy baby who cried at the smallest bit of discomfort and shrieked in full-scale rage at his or her worst. The buppa kept their parents or baby nannies up all night long, resisting sleep and lashing out for no discernible reason. "Nathan is a good baby. He just has a few sour moments."

The baby's face puckered in annoyance at Sadie's words, and both sisters laughed. They moved along through the crowd with their family, greeting acquaintances, friends, and people they knew from church. Emery Lambright welcomed them heartily and made sure that Mem and Dat knew what a great server and part-time manager Polly was at the Country Diner.

"You raised a hard worker," Emery said, his beard bobbing a bit as he nodded. "We've come to rely on Polly, and Madge says she's good in the kitchen in a pinch. So good, Madge might even let her in on the family recipe for fried chicken!"

"Ach, you!" Madge swatted her husband's shoulder affectionately. "Polly is welcome to any recipe she wants, and she knows it." Madge turned her attention to fussing over Lovina and Nathan. "Beautiful babies!" she gasped.

Behind Madge, Mem and Dat looked on with smiles that could not hide their pleasure as their hosts made positive remarks about their families. When Sadie was a child, she had assumed that one of the reasons Dat took to drinking was shame over his family. She'd assumed Reuben Beiler had been disappointed not to have sons and that the activities of his daughters brought him no joy.

But tonight—tonight, joy and love shone bright in his eyes.

Again, Sadie sensed that she was seeing things she'd not noticed before, as if a veil had been removed from her eyes and she was beginning to see the true character of the people in her life. Looking at her parents, her sisters, these kind people around her, she reveled in the lovely sight.

The snack tables held a delicious assortment of popcorn, nuts, candied fruits, and Chex mix. After an hour or so, everyone was moved to a big room in back that had been added for church and large family gatherings. Rows of tables were set with festive green and gold tablecloths. For dinner, there was the traditional roasht—a stuffing dish with chopped chicken, bread cubes, celery, and always lots of butter—as well as the signature dish of the diner, fried chicken. Sadie's eyes marveled over the dishes of corn succotash, mashed potatoes, cranberry sauce, applesauce, green beans, and pickled beets. Such a feast!

After the meal Sadie spent a few minutes socializing, talking mostly with Polly's sisters-in-law, who were near her age. She knew Janine and Kate Lambright the best because they were close to her age, and they'd always been teachers' pets in school. Now they both worked at the family diner and frequented the singings, where young people got to mix. Today, Janine seemed particularly animated and bright-eyed, probably because the guy she'd been dating, Kyle Stevick, was here, talking with her cousins on the other side of the room.

"Did you invite Kyle?" Sadie asked when Janine pointed him out.

Janine nodded sagely. "We've been dating awhile now. At last, a guy my parents approve of."

"And he's really fond of Janine," Kate added. "He comes round all the time. She barely has a minute for a cup of tea or a quilting bee."

Looking over at him, Janine smiled. "He's a good man."

"I'm happy for you," Sadie said. Girls their age were under a lot of pressure to find a suitable match. So much pressure that sometimes people forgot how important love was in the equation.

"What about you?" Janine asked. "Are you still seeing Mark Miller?"

The question took Sadie by surprise. Although she should have expected it, in her mind she had removed herself from the relationship with Mark. "I saw him on Christmas Eve," she said, trying to stay with the truth.

"How's that going for you two?" Kate asked.

"Okay, I guess."

Kate looked at her sister, then squinted at Sadie. "You're not bowling us over with enthusiasm."

A warm flush overtook Sadie's face as she tried to back out gracefully while sticking to the truth. "Mark is just so . . . busy. You know how much time he and his dat put into the auction house."

"Mmm. And I guess it will really pick up when they host the mud sales in the spring."

"I guess it will," Sadie agreed, wishing for the subject to drop before the truth spilled out. She had come so close to revealing that she was ready to end her relationship with Mark the next time she saw him. It would have been the most honest answer; but then, it would have been wrong of her to spread the story before she talked to Mark.

The subject turned to the recent snowfall, which had

come at the perfect time, as most of the Amish businesses, like the Country Diner, closed for Christmas. Sadie chatted with the girls awhile, then noticed Sharon struggling to cope with the children. She excused herself and went over to help.

"Can you amuse Lovina while I feed him?" Sharon asked. "I'd ask Elam, but he's playing Ping-Pong in the rec room, and I hate to end his fun."

"I've got this," Sadie said, hoisting the three-year-old onto her hip. "Did you eat a good dinner?"

Lovina nodded, holding up a hand with a bunch of splayed fingers. "I had this many drumsticks."

"That's a lot for a little girl."

When Lovina rested her head against Sadie's shoulder, Sadie noticed her eyelids were drooping. She decided to follow her sister to a quieter place, away from the commotion. They came upon a small sitting room with a sewing machine, settee, and rocking chair. Sadie closed the door behind her while Sharon settled onto the small couch to begin nursing Nathan. Lovina was already fast asleep in Sadie's arms—a heavy weight—and it felt good to sink into the rocking chair and rest a bit.

They talked about the meal—such a lot of food—and joked that the roasht had more flavor and moisture than Mem's. Then Sharon let out a tired sigh. "I love visiting here with you, coming home. But the holidays are tiring. So much rich food and commotion."

"And you and Elam and the children have to squeeze into one room of the house," said Sadie.

"We don't mind at all." Sharon rubbed the downy hair on Nathan's head. "Whenever we're here, Lovina has her own private maud, her own nanny. And it's good of you to give up your room."

"The house is a happy place when you're visiting. Even Dat brightens up."

"That reminds me—about your room. Last night while you were away, Lovina got into some mischief in your room. She managed to get into that box you had left on the shelf. I know, it was above her head, but she convinced one of Polly's children to get it for her. She opened it up and took the clock out and set it up on the bed, insisting it was hers. When I came in, the cardboard and shredded wrappings were everywhere."

"Ach! Such a little monkey." Sadie didn't usually fret over material things, but she had planned to return the gift to Mark.

"I'm so sorry! I didn't know it was there. I didn't know Mark had given you a clock." Sharon's head tilted to one side, her green eyes opening wide with curiosity. "Are you two secretly engaged?"

"No. At least, I don't think so. He never said the words, and I've felt a weight on my shoulders ever since he gave me that clock. I planned to give it back, but now, I don't know what I'll do."

"You can still give it back," Sharon assured her. "Nothing was broken, and I managed to pack it back into the box."

"That's good. Well, back it goes. And tomorrow, first thing, I'm going to call the Millers' phone and leave a message for Mark."

Sharon's green eyes opened wide with surprise. "You're going to break up with him through a message left in the phone shanty?"

"I may be your younger sister, but I wasn't born yesterday," said Sadie. "I'm going to leave a message for him to call or stop by the house one evening this week. I know I need to talk to him in person."

Sharon nodded. "That sounds like a good plan, but tell me what happened. The last I heard, you were crazy over Mark Miller. I assumed you two would be getting married."

"Oh, Sharon, it was what I wanted most in the world, to marry Mark. And then . . . visiting his home, I realized I barely know him at all, and he was hardly willing to lift a finger to make me comfortable there. We're not in love. I think I just loved the notion of marrying Mark Miller."

Sharon's smile reached her tired eyes. "When did my little sister get so wise?"

"It's not wisdom. Gott intervened."

"Did he?" Sharon stared, unblinking.

"He's opened my eyes. He showed me what a mistake it would be to marry Mark. He also showed me that love has been waiting for me—real love—and I've been too blind to see it."

Sharon lifted the baby to her shoulder and patted his back to burp him. "It sounds like you've been blessed! Who is this real love?"

"Sam Lapp, Essie's brother."

"I remember Sam from school." Sharon nodded. "That Lapp family is a kind and good group. But are you sure this time?"

Sadie nodded. "With Mark, I was always hoping that he would learn to love me. With Sam, the love is there. My heart comes alive when he's near. I want to sing with joy, but I have to keep it a secret for now, until I can tell Mark. So, please, don't say anything to Mem."

"I won't say a word. But I'm so happy for you. You're such a beauty, I always knew you'd marry one day. But to have found a partner you truly want to share your life with—that is truly a marriage blessed by Gott."

Sadie didn't wait until morning. That night, when they'd returned from the Lambright house, she carried Lovina into her bed and then slipped out the kitchen door to walk down to the phone shanty they shared with a few other neighbors. The little hut with a phone and answering machine was not the most efficient setup, but it was certainly quicker than sending a letter through the U.S. Postal Service.

She walked briskly, an extra shawl bundled around her shoulders against the cold. Inside the shanty, the little white switch on the wall turned on an overhead bulb that gave her enough light to dial the number she had written down on a slip of paper.

When it was time to leave a message, she felt no hesitation. She specified that it was for Mark Miller, since the family shared the phone, and she specified that she needed to see him one evening this week. When she replaced the phone in its cradle, she felt tension drain from her stiff shoulders.

This was the right thing to do.

She fairly skipped home, minding to watch out for the icy patches on the driveway.

The next day, she returned from work at the pretzel factory and spent the evening helping Sharon and Mem with a puzzle. When they had most of the border done, she glanced at the old clock on the wall and saw that it was after eight. Would Mark come this late?

"Sadie, stop watching the clock and help me find more blue border for the sky," Mem said.

"I wasn't watching the clock," Sadie said, reaching into the box to search for blue pieces.

"Good. Because one thing you learn by watching the clock is that time passes by keeping its hands busy."

"Ach, Mem." Sharon smiled as she perused the puzzle pieces. "That nugget of wisdom must be a hundred years old."

"Wisdom never goes out of date," Mem insisted.

When it came time for the kerosene lamp to be put out for bed, she was disappointed that there'd been no buggy in the driveway.

Tuesday and Wednesday followed with more of the same. Sadie went gladly to her job at the pretzel factory, grateful for the little jokes and conversation with the other girls. The longer Mark stayed away, the more nervous she was getting about telling him that it was time to end their relationship. As she folded each little pipe of dough into a pretzel shape in three swift moves, she worried he might appear at her house in a bad mood. Well, that wasn't her responsibility. And if he cared about being her boyfriend, why wasn't he answering her message?

On Thursday she awoke early to help see Elam and Sharon and their little ones off.

"I'm going to miss you," she told them as she helped load the baby's Pack 'n Play into the back of the van hired to drive them home. "The house will be so quiet without you."

"Your parents will be grateful for some peace and quiet." With Lovina resting on one hip, Elam put his other arm around Sharon's shoulders and pulled her close for a minute. Sharon smiled, kissed the baby she held against her chest, and then looked at her husband, her eyes full of love.

The sight of the four of them, a loving family, made Sadie's throat grow tight with emotion. She had always dreamed of having a family of her own—partly out of a desire to escape the problems at home, but also because she'd seen how married life had brought joy to her sisters. Now that a relationship with Sam was on the horizon, she realized that love and marriage involved so much more than keeping house and doing laundry for a husband. She would be entering into a lifetime commitment to love, cherish, and honor her husband, and at last, she had found a man who inspired that love.

She was so ready to love him.

"Don't cry, Sadie," Sharon said, leaving her husband's side to give Sadie a hug. "We'll be back to visit soon. This summer, when the weather is better."

Sadie swiped at her eyes and smiled. "They're tears of joy."

"Happy to see us leave?" teased Elam.

"Happy for the future," Sadie said quickly as Mem came rushing out with a bag of sandwiches and fruitcake for the road.

Sharon squeezed her shoulder. "Write me a letter and let me know how everything works out."

Sadie propped herself up and went to work feeling hopeful that all this would be sorted out soon. That evening, she checked the phone shanty. There was no word from Mark, but she'd had two phone calls from Essie, inviting her to come over during her days off for New Year's.

Sadie wanted to spend her long weekend at the Lapp farm, but first she needed to straighten things out with Mark.

Why hadn't he answered her?

Sitting on her bed, she felt trapped. She wanted to move on, but she was constricted by the unspoken promise of a young woman who starts dating a guy. A commitment was implied until someone ended the courtship.

Well, if Mark would not come to her, she would deliver her message to him in writing.

She found the little box of stationery she'd received as a gift years ago, and tested the shiny blue pen before writing: *Dear Mark.*

In her letter, she told him that she had enjoyed the times they'd had together, but believed they were better off going their separate paths. She wished him well and thanked him for all his kindness.

Short and sweet, she thought, reading it over. She put the letter in an envelope, placed it on the box with the clock, and changed into her nightgown.

Tomorrow, after breakfast, she would bring it to Mark at his home. She dreaded the visit, but once she talked with Mark, once she handed him the letter spelling things out in no uncertain terms, it would be over.

And she would be free as a bird to follow her heart.

Chapter 19

Five days.

Sam hadn't seen Sadie for five days, since Second Christmas. It was less than a week, but the days without a call or visit from her seemed to stretch on like the long ribbon of Joyful River that wended its way through miles of the valley.

He missed her. He thought about her when he was prodding the cows in for milking. Riding Comet out along the property line to check the fences. Pulling bales of hay. Eating, drinking and sleeping. He thought about pretty much her all the time, because the notion of Sadie's love lifted his spirits like nothing clsc in his life.

He wondered why she hadn't come round this week. Granted, they'd agreed to keep things between them a secret until she could have "the talk" with Mark. But he couldn't help wondering what was taking her so long to end it with Mark Miller?

Not that he didn't trust Sadie. She wasn't the kind of girl to string two guys along.

"There's got to be a good reason for it," he said as he scraped the shovel along the dirt floor of a stable, mucking it out. The stable was so cold and damp he could see the steam puffs coming from his nostrils. This time of year, they had to come by and break the ice that formed on the top of the water troughs so the horses could drink. Not that the horses minded the cold. Mucking wasn't his favorite job on the farm, but on a cold winter day like this, if he got into a steady rhythm of scooping and tossing, he could warm up, sometimes even get a sweat going.

With the floor of the stall clear now, he leaned his shovel against the wall of the stable and moved the wheelbarrow down to the next stall. The big wheel squealed a bit. Time for some oil. There were days when one task begot another, and then another. It was the nature of life on a farm, a twenty-four-seven lifestyle that suited Sam just fine. He liked being responsible for animals and a broad expanse of Gott's land, and it was a blessing to live and work close to the earth.

He had turned back to get his shovel when his gaze locked upon something moving into a shaft of light from the hayloft window. She stood tall, the light shining over her like a beam from heaven. A black wool cape draped over her swept gracefully as she walked.

"Sadie?" He couldn't believe his eyes, but it sure looked like her. For a moment he wondered if he'd dreamed her up, but the woman at the end of the stable was real, as she pivoted and turned toward him. "Sadie," he called again. He was going to be embarrassed if it turned out to be someone else.

The beautiful figure turned his way and lifted her hand in a wave. "Sam!" The smile that illuminated her face warmed him from head to toe.

They moved toward each other, nearly running. He wanted to reach her before she stepped out of the beam of stark winter sunlight that turned her into an angel. When he caught up with her, she seemed breathless, with high color like the pink of a summer rose on her cheeks. "Have you been running?" he asked.

"I have. To be honest, I told Essie I came to spend the day with her. Which is true, of course, but I had to see *you*. I was helping her make the dough for cookies when I went into the mudroom to chat with Annie, who'd just come in from the cold. It was really a way to try and find you. Annie said you were out here, and I threw on my cape and told her I had a message for you. Do you think she'll blab?"

"Annie's salt of the earth. She doesn't go for gossip."

"I just had to see you, Sam. I really thought everything would be cleared up by now, but . . ." She let out a breath in a huffing sigh. "Nothing's gone as I planned it."

"Are you okay?" For a flicker of a moment he worried that she'd changed her mind, that she'd rethought her decision about Miller. But nay, not Sadie. She wasn't a girl who changed her mind from day to day.

"I'm fine, but . . . missing you."

Sam felt his chest grow tight from the grab of her pretty green eyes.

She looked over her shoulder to make sure no one was around. "I thought we'd be able to spend some time together this week after I told Mark. But the problem is, I haven't—"

Just then the barn door slammed open and one of the twins stomped in. "Sam!" Pete hollered. "Where yah at?"

Sadie looked down at the ground, as if caught doing something wrong, while Sam stepped around her in an attempt to block Pete's view.

"I'm over here, mucking the stables!" he called.

Pete squinted through the shaft of sunlight. "Mem says lunch'll be ready in thirty minutes."

"I'll head in soon," Sam promised.

"Do you know where the ice fishing gear is? Paul and I want to catch some dinner."

Sam scratched his head through the watch cap. "I think it's on the shelf in the buggy shed."

"And where's the ice auger?"

"Everything should be inside the five-gallon bucket. But do you really want to hack through the ice we play hockey on?"

"We're going down to Uncle Lloyd's place. His pond has giant fish, big as a man's head!"

Sam knew that Lloyd Lapp's pond was too small to support much more than turtles and frogs, but the twins could give it a try. "Yah, check the buggy barn for the gear."

The door slammed shut, and Sam returned to Sadie.

"Do you think he saw me?" she asked.

"If he did, I don't think he knows how to connect the dots yet. But sooner or later, my family's going to start to figure things out. I don't care for myself, but I don't want you to be in a jam."

"You're good to try to protect me." She looked up at him pensively. "All I want is for us to be together, Sam, but nothing's as simple as it seems." She looked back toward the door. "Is there somewhere we can talk? So no one sees?"

He led her into one of the clean stalls, where the sweet tang of newly spread hay dominated the rest of the barn smells. He tossed a horse blanket over a bale of hay, and they sat there together.

"This is cozy," she said, lifting her shoulders to ward off a shiver.

"You're freezing."

She looked up at the high rafters as she rubbed her mittens together. "You'd think it would be a little warmer in here, with the wind blocked."

"Here." He undid the hooks on his jacket and started removing it. "Let me warm you." The cold air seeping over his sweater didn't bother him as he draped the jacket over the two of them. At least he could be grateful that this morning he'd put on the sweater without the hole at the neck. He took off his smelly gloves, dropped them to the hay, and then slid one arm around her waist to hold her close. "Is that better?"

She nodded, her face just a whisper away from his. "How do you stay so warm?"

He wanted to admit it was the fire in his heart, the way he felt when she was near, but this was too new and too precious to risk saying things like that just yet. "Just hard work," he said.

Glancing down, he saw that his boots had clods of muck and hay sticking to them. There was a brown stain near the hem of his pants, and a patch on the right knee. His hair needed combing, he was in need of a shower, and he probably stank to high heaven.

"Aw, Sadie, I'm a mess," he confessed. "I've been cleaning the barn all morning, and I'm sure I smell like it. I'd have done differently if I knew you were coming."

"Sam." She turned to him, her eyes full of light. "This is me, Sadie. You don't have to dress fancy or change a thing for me. I know this place. I know you. I wouldn't expect anything else."

"You deserve better, especially if we're just started out dating."

She swept back the hair that hung from the brim of his

watch cap and smoothed a hand over his jaw. "The truth is, you look wonderful to me, Sam. The smells of the farm, the barn, the fields . . . this is a land I've known most of my life. Yah, it's a little different growing up on an orchard, but Lapp Farms has been my second home. So, in my eyes, you're as handsome now as you've ever been, and you're warming me up, right good."

He loved this girl. She was genuine and bright, without the nonsense of other girls who teased and mooned over him at singings and Amish youth events. He touched the hand that rested on his cheek. "So tell me what's happened with Mark Miller."

"Nothing, I'm afraid. And that's the problem." She told him how she had called and left a message on the Millers' answering machine. She'd expected Mark to come by her house every night this week, but he never showed.

"Did he call and leave a message?" Sam asked.

"Nothing, but that's sort of Mark's style. He's not what you would call a good communicator. There've been times when I've had to drag answers out of him. Especially when he's in one of his moods. Anyway." She glanced down. "I'm not here to gossip about other people's problems. I just wanted to let you know that I am trying to straighten things out. Last night, I got so fed up that I wrote Mark a letter, explaining that it's best for us to go our separate ways. Dat let me use the buggy this morning, and I went over to the Miller house to talk with him and give him the clock. I figured if he wasn't at home, I could leave the letter. And that's what ended up happening. When I arrived there, his mem told me Mark went to Lititz, where his uncle is starting a new auction house. He left Monday morning, and she doesn't expect him back for a while. Probably not until the end of January, she said."

"He left town without mentioning it to you?" Sam asked.

"He didn't say a word. I'm guessing he's trying to teach his cousin Tom how to be an auctioneer. When I met Tom on Christmas Eve he was talking about trying it. But that leaves us in a bit of a bind."

"You can't officially end your relationship with Mark until he returns," he said.

She nodded. "I'm not sure what to do. I left the letter and the clock for him, so that should make it clear we're over and done. But I don't feel free to start dating again. Of course, I could. But something is niggling at my conscience, like a cold finger tapping on my shoulder. My mem always says, 'If it feels wrong, it probably is.'"

Sam nodded, taking it all in as he thought back on the long week. Not knowing what was going on had weighed on him. But this delay—Miller being out of town—this was a small obstacle. "So. You and I? We'll need to keep our secret for a bit longer."

She pressed her lips tight together and nodded. "I'm sorry, Sam. I wish I didn't feel that way, but it seems wrong to go out dating while Mark doesn't know."

"Don't be sorry." He touched her chin and gently lifted until her eyes met his. "Your conscience, you wanting to do the right thing, it's one of the things about you that I . . ." He was about to say *I love*, but didn't want to come on too strong. "It's an appealing quality," he finished. "Integrity matters. I'd never ask you to compromise on something like that."

The strain faded from her pale face. "I'm so relieved that you understand."

"I'm on your side, Sadie. I always will be."

"Ach, Sam! Such sweet words! *I'm on your side.* I'm going to embroider that into a sampler!" Her smile was a

burst of light brighter than the sun. It filled him with a
sense of joy in the wonders that Gott had in store for them.
"When the time is right, I can't wait to go off to a singing
in your buggy. But for now . . ."

"For now, we'll keep our secret," he promised, taking
her hands in his. "No word to anyone. No public outings.
But I hope you'll still be spending time here on the farm."

"Every chance I get. It's our secret way to see each
other."

"All right, then." He rose and pulled her to her feet. "If
we're going to keep this a secret, we'd best send you back
to the house without me. Lunch should be about ready,
anyway."

"I'll be watching you over my soup," she said, wiggling
one eyebrow in a gesture that made him chuckle.

Over the next few days, Sam felt a new lift in his step
as Sadie stayed on at the farm. While he was out and about
doing his daily chores, Sadie accompanied Essie and Mem
in the house. Besides the daily meal preparation, there
were cranberries to be turned into jam, cookies to be
baked, and knitting and quilting squares to work on.

It dawned on Sam that Sadie truly belonged here. For
years, she had helped Essie with chores, played games
with their siblings at night, and sought Mem for advice on
knitting and life in general. The sight of Sadie mixing with
his family gave Sam much contentment.

In their free time, he and Sadie stole moments to talk
on their own. After years away from the sport, Sadie laced
up skates borrowed from Essie and let Sam guide her
around the pond. The way she held on to his arm, leaning
into him, made him feel strong and capable. Boyhood

was behind him, and he prayed that his adult life would be filled with Sadie. In his heart, he vowed that he would always support Sadie when she needed him; he would be there for her to lean on, there to steady her when her skate blades wobbled over bumpy ice, there to lift her up and carry her over the deepest snowdrifts.

When Sam's hockey team converged at the frozen pond after lunch on Sunday, Sadie took it upon herself to head inside. "I'll help Essie and Miriam tidy up." No big projects were undertaken on Sunday, the day of rest, though there were always things to tidy and mouths to feed.

Sam came off the ice and bounded awkwardly over the frozen earth in his skates. While Sadie unlaced her skates, they talked of the next week. Sadie had to return to work in the pretzel factory in the morning.

"Our beautiful Christmas interlude is drawing to an end." She stood up, skates dangling from one hand as she stretched close to him, so close that he was sure he could feel the heat from her flushed cheeks. "I'm going to miss seeing you every day, Sam."

She wanted to kiss him, he could tell, but he worried that this wasn't the right place. He touched her shoulder, aware that some of the guys on the ice might be watching. "I wish you didn't have to leave," he said. "Let's walk a bit."

In easy silence, they walked toward the house. It was an awkward waddle for Sam in his skates, but he just wanted to get past a stand of trees. A drift of snow still rose beyond the maples, giving them some cover from the pond. Sam moved behind the fat tree trunks, pulling Sadie with him.

"Where are we going?" she asked, her voice tinkling with light laughter.

"Behind the trees, for a proper goodbye."

"You're a clever one, Sam Lapp." This time when she went onto the toes of her boots, she leaned against him, dropped her skates, and reached up to hold on to his shoulders. Her gaze locked onto his, her green eyes pools of love. "Promise me that you won't drive any other girl home at the singing next week."

"That's an easy one. You know there's only room in my heart for you."

"And that's the right answer."

This time, when she leaned up to kiss him, he held his breath and met her lips with all the tenderness stored up in his heart. It would probably be a week until they could see each other again. This would have to be a kiss to remember.

Chapter 20

"I'm back!" Megan called to her cousins from the edge of the frozen pond. It was the third of January, a bright, blue-sky day, but still down in the twenties. Cold, but Megan wasn't going to let that keep her off the ice.

The group of young men, who'd been huddled in conversation on the ice, turned to her.

She jumped in the air a few times, lifted her new hockey stick, a gift from Dad, and let out a whoop of joy.

Suddenly, the guys soared over to meet her with shouts of welcome.

"Megs!" Sam shouted.

"You got a new stick!" Pete exclaimed.

"Can I try it?" Paul asked.

"Give her a chance to use her own stick," Sam chastised them.

"It's okay," Megan said, handing her stick over to Paul. "Go on, give it a run."

"Denki!" He quickly exchanged sticks, and then took off on the ice.

Megan recognized some of Sam's other friends, Jacob and Micah and Fred. She looked past them to Isaac, who remained quiet but smiling as he and Sam skated all the way over to her. She'd missed them both, but she knew where she stood with Sam. With Isaac, she wasn't quite sure. Had he been thinking about her over the holiday? She wanted to hang out with him, one on one, but a chance of that was unlikely. In Amish society, the only real alone time was for couples who were courting.

"Come join us," Isaac said. "If you haven't forgotten everything you learned."

"Ha! I may have gotten even better over the past two weeks. We skated in an indoor rink a few times in Philly." As she spoke she sat down on an old sawed-off barrel that worked as a bench and changed into her skates. "We got to see a Philadelphia Flyers game, and I watched a lot of hockey on TV. I'm dying to try out some of the things I learned."

"That sounds like quite a Christmas," Isaac teased. "Mistletoe and hockey."

Megan laughed, though Sam just leaned forward on his stick, waiting for her to lace up. "It wasn't the only thing we did," she said. "We volunteered in a soup kitchen a few days a week."

"You girls in the kitchen?" Sam's eyes opened wide. "That's a recipe for disaster."

"We didn't actually have to cook. It was mostly serving and scut work, though we realized we have learned a thing or two from being around Essie and Aunt Miriam."

"What's a soup kitchen?" Sam asked.

She told them about the storefront set up to feed people in need, about how Grace had befriended a brother and sister she'd met there, how it felt good to do something for someone else, and how volunteering had bonded her together with her sisters. "We're going to try to make it a new family tradition at Christmastime." As she spoke, she finished with her skates and launched herself onto the bumpy ice.

"Amish don't have soup kitchens," Isaac said. "When a neighbor needs a meal, we send over a dish."

"Your system works better, I think," Megan said. "At least, it's a lot more personal. So anyway, how was your Christmas?"

"Good," Sam answered. "Great!"

"Glad to hear it. So what did I miss while I was gone?"

"Nothing much." Sam was smiling, his spirits high, but he avoided looking at Megan as he pivoted on the ice and skated off.

"Well, that's weird," Megan said, standing alone with Isaac.

"That's what I've been thinking. Something's going on with Sam." Isaac shook his head, watching his friend in the distance. "He's happy for no good reason. This time of year, with the hockey tournament coming up, he's usually on edge. But not this year. I can't explain it."

"Interesting." Skating backward, she kept her eyes on Sam. "Is it Sadie?"

"He's not saying, but I'd venture it's a good guess."

"I'll see what I can find out," Megan promised, daring a look at Isaac, who moved gracefully on the ice for a tall man. "How was your Christmas?"

"Good," he answered. "But it would have been better if you were here."

Megan felt a glow of pleasure warm her from within. "I missed you, too." She'd thought of him a lot, especially after Scout had arrived to visit Serena. She'd kicked herself for not having invited Isaac. Granted, he was Amish, and most Amish didn't mix with Englisch that way, but he'd been on winter break from classes, and he might have said yes. "Have you ever been to Philadelphia?"

"Only once, when I was eight. I don't remember much besides all the cars honking horns. Is it nice?"

"There's a lot to like about it. You can step outside your door and get coffee and a hot slice of pizza or a sandwich. And you can walk to the movies or a skating rink."

"Do you like it better than Joyful River?"

"You know, when I'm in one place, I feel a little twinge of missing the other."

His hazel eyes opened wide, as if he recognized the feeling. "Maybe you're a fish out of water, like me."

"Maybe I am." She looked around at the pond and shrugged. "Of course I am. I'm the only girl here. The only Englisch person, too. I guess I've just given up fitting in anywhere."

Isaac skated close to her, causing a frisson of awareness in her as he touched her arm. "You may look a bit different, Megs. But once we start a match, if you can keep up, no one will notice."

"If that's a challenge, I accept," she said, raising the stick Paul had handed her in the switch. "Now, if I can get my stick back, I'll show you guys some of the moves I learned over the holidays."

"That I want to see."

After warming up and going through a few practice drills, the skaters split up into teams and started scrimmaging. Megan got a clear shot to a goal at the beginning of the match, bolstering her confidence.

"The power of a new stick!" she claimed, though the guys whooped and nodded in approval. A minute later, she was traveling with the puck when Sam swiped it cleanly away from her. She skated like crazy to catch up with him and get it back. Sam put up a good fight and made off with it, headed to the goal.

Megan circled back to the defender's position, determined to do better next time, but happy that none of these guys went easy on her. Nothing got her blood moving like a challenge. There was also a certain comfort in knowing she was among friends. Her cousins had become like brothers, and Sam's friends had become her own. Megan hadn't realized it until she'd gone off for the holiday, but this group of guys had become her new team.

In minutes, Megan was lost in the game, defending and stealing the puck, racing up and down the pond, cutting her blades into the ice to pivot and stop. The cold, brisk air, the frosty ice, the shouts from other players—all of it faded in her focus on that puck. She appreciated the skills and toughness of the other players, who weren't shy of physical contact, but were not quite as violent as professional players. Some were fiercely competitive, but when a goal was scored, every player cheered.

The group remained on the ice for hours that afternoon. No one thought about taking a break until Annie came out, an LED headlamp shining from her forehead as she hollered for some of the guys to come in. "Jacob Kraybill, your dat is here with the buggy, and he's willing to give a ride to anyone that needs it."

"I'll take a ride," Micah said as the skaters swooped toward the edge of the ice.

"Me too," Fred added, "unless Jerry has a full buggy."

"Dat's always glad to give you guys a ride."

"Wait!" Pete called. "Can't we finish?"

"It's time," Sam said. "It's too dark to see the puck, let

alone any of the defensive skaters barreling toward you. And Mem's probably holding supper for us."

"I don't care about that." With a sigh, Pete joined the scramble on the side of the pond to remove skates and find the right pair of shoes. "I wish we could have lights, the way they do at Myers Pond," Pete said.

Megan kept hearing about the January tournament at Myers Pond, where the frozen pond had lights that stayed on until late at night.

"Simon Myers's family has lights because they're Mennonite," Isaac explained. "It's allowed."

"We should get lights, and then we could practice late," Paul said. "We could play all night."

"And drag yourself off to school in the morning?" Sam said. "Mem wouldn't allow it."

"It's only a few months of the year," Pete said. "The bishop should let us install lights. It's not where we live. It's not even close to the house."

"You're lucky that you don't have lights," Megan said. "They'd shine in your windows and keep you up at night, and they would block your view of the moon and stars."

"If I want to see the stars, I would turn off the lights," Pete said.

Megan smiled, waiting as her cousins walked ahead.

"Pete's a bit too smart for his own good," Isaac said, falling into step beside her.

Megan nodded. "Reminds me of another Amish man I know." She gave him a pointed look, and he adjusted his glasses, trying to hide his smile.

"Am I smart, or just discontent with my lot in life?" he asked.

The question made her feel a twinge of sympathy for

this young man who didn't completely fit in with his family or culture. "Maybe a little of both?"

That brought a full-fledged smile, easily visible in the gathering dusk.

"I know you think you don't belong here, but I'm glad you're back." He switched his skates and hockey gear to his right shoulder and moved closer to her, his left arm grazing hers as they walked. "I think you fit in anywhere you go."

Megan smiled, joy glowing inside her as they walked on, keeping stride. Isaac liked her. He really liked her. And it felt good to be by his side.

Maybe she wasn't such a fish out of water in Joyful River.

The group moved in a line along the path, heading back toward the glow of the house. As they reached the yard of the Lapp home, where warmth and light beckoned, Megan and Isaac paused.

"Do you want to come in for some cocoa?" she offered, nodding toward the mudroom entrance.

He shrugged. "I'd better go. I'm on duty in the morning."

"And I'm back to school." Megan dreaded getting up before dawn to catch the bus, but it was the start of an easy semester. "But we're in two of the same online classes at the CC, right?"

"Englisch comp and history." He gave a nod.

"We can do a study group once classes start," she said.

"I've never done a study group before."

Of course he hadn't. He was an unassuming Amish guy, taking college classes in a town where secondary education wasn't a priority. "You know, you're amazing," she said.

"Well, thank you." Isaac shrugged. "I guess."

As the group continued on to the front of the house, she and Isaac stood outside the entrance to the mudroom, not wanting to separate, but knowing they couldn't linger much longer.

Suddenly, Uncle Alvin came racing around the side of the house, his face strained as he ran on his bad leg. "Jacob! Come!" he called, motioning them forward. "Your dat's not feeling well."

The group separated to let him through as the jovial mood quickly became somber. Everyone followed on his heels as Jacob tossed his gear onto the packed snow and ran forward to the portly, bearded man sitting on the porch. "What is it, Dat? Are you having the pains again?"

The man nodded silently. In the light of the battery lamp, he seemed pale, and Megan could see sweat beaded on his forehead, despite the cold night.

Isaac left Megan's side and came to the porch. "What are you feeling?" he asked, crouching down beside the older Kraybill man. "Is it chest pains?"

"Like something's crushing my chest," Jerry Kraybill gasped, a hand on his sternum.

"Do you have a heart condition?" Isaac asked. When the man didn't answer, Isaac turned to Jacob. "Has this happened before?"

"Not this bad," Jacob said sheepishly. "He always thought it was heartburn. Indigestion. He's got some pills that he takes for it."

"From the doctor?" Isaac asked.

Jacob shook his head. "Nay. Pills he orders from his magazine."

Isaac straightened a bit to speak with Aunt Miriam and Uncle Alvin. "We need to call fire and rescue. Can you get a call out from the phone shanty? Tell them to get here right away."

Miriam nodded. "Annie? There you are. Run to the phone and call 911. Tell them we need an ambulance to come here, fast as they can. Paul, you go with her. Make sure your headlamp is on, Annie. And stay at the main road to wave them in. Hurry, now."

As Annie and Paul took off down the lane, their boots crunching on the snow, Isaac bent over Jerry again to ask him more questions. The man was visibly struggling with pain. Megan wished she could help, but she felt reassured by Isaac's steady demeanor and knowledge of emergency medical care.

"Do you think it's his heart?" Miriam asked.

"It's likely," Isaac answered, then crouched down again to focus on Jerry.

There was talk of moving him inside, but Jerry shook his head no, saying he couldn't make it.

All around Megan, young men stood in wary silence. Cousin Pete watched with the look of an animal about to bolt in fear. Megan moved forward and put an arm around his shoulders.

On Isaac's instruction, Jacob and Alvin helped the ailing man lie down on the porch. Sam went inside the house to fetch blankets, and Aunt Miriam followed him, in search of aspirin. Isaac spoke gently now as he checked Jerry's pulse and seemed to check for a temperature. If the poor man was having a heart attack, Megan imagined Isaac was limited in what he could do without any supplies.

Time was now moving agonizingly slowly. Megan was reminded of dreams she used to have of trying to run down the soccer field and finding her feet weighted down with fat anvils. She wished she had been the one to run to the phone—the person to do something—but there was no questioning the authority of Aunt Miriam.

Little things seemed to help. Jerry was able to chew two aspirin. Sam brought out some quilts and a sleeping bag, and they were able to prop up Jerry's head and bolster him against the cold. The whole time, Isaac crouched on the top step near Jerry, speaking quietly with him and checking his vitals as much as possible. So attentive and reassuring. If Megan hadn't already been falling for Isaac, after tonight, her heart would have been taken by this kind, caring man.

At last, a siren called from a distance. Megan and the others looked toward the main road, but there was nothing in sight yet. And Jerry seemed to be failing rapidly. He patted his chest and reached out for Isaac. Then Jerry cried out, reaching his arms up, before collapsing.

"Are you okay?" Isaac asked the man, tapping his shoulder. When Jerry didn't respond, Isaac checked his pulse. "I think his heart has stopped." He pushed aside the quilts, opened Jerry's coat, pressed his palm against Jerry's sternum, and started doing compressions.

Oh, no! Megan squeezed Pete's arm hard and noticed he had tears in his eyes.

"I need someone to time this," Isaac said, without missing a beat. "Megan. Come. Turn on that stopwatch of yours. We need to know how long his heart has stopped."

With three long steps, Megan was beside Isaac, her fingers deftly working her watch. "Okay. It's on," she said, her own pulse racing in triple time. Her eyes were on Jacob, who was intently watching his father.

"Keep praying," Aunt Miriam said, placing a hand on Jacob's shoulder. "We must keep praying."

Looking down at the fluttering seconds on her stopwatch, Megan thought of the God who had let her mother die young, when the family needed her most. She'd been so angry about that, but now, it seemed so long ago.

Good things had happened since then. Bonds had been forged with her sisters and her Amish family. There'd been happy times, rainbows of hope, moments of sheer joy. Life was good. Life was precious.

Please, God, she prayed silently, *get Jerry Kraybill through this. Help Isaac help this man. Make him well and whole so he can know just how wonderful life can be.*

Chapter 21

Miriam sank into the chair in the hospital waiting room and silently prayed that Gott would restore Jerry's health. As she receded into her thoughts, quiet conversations and silent prayer went on around her. A handful of men filled the seats along one wall, their beards wagging as they talked in low voices. Alvin sat there, along with Doug Kraybill, Jerry's brother, and their church bishop, Aaron Troyer. Normally the bishop meted out equal bits of kindness and severity, but tonight he was completely a man of compassion.

All the young men who had been playing hockey on the pond out back were here now, eager to support Jacob and his family. Netta Kraybill, Jerry's wife, had brought her two daughters who lived at home, as well as the three grandchildren they had been minding tonight. One of the Kraybill girls had thought to bring along a basket of freshly baked corn muffins, which had been a godsend for the hungry hockey players. Sam and Isaac had gone to the hospital cafeteria and returned with a dozen small containers of milk to go with the muffins.

This was the way of the Amish when someone they

knew was hospitalized. Everyone went to the hospital and stayed as long as they could, lending support to the family and cheering on the patient from down the hall.

Now, watching Sam and Isaac talk with Megan in a corner of the waiting room, Miriam tried to take stock on what she'd witnessed in the past few hours. Her family had already eaten dinner, save those out on the frozen pond. Miriam, Annie, and Grace had been in the kitchen doing dishes when Jerry had knocked on the kitchen door. Alvin had invited him in, but Jerry had declined, but asked that they send someone to fetch the boys.

"It's time they knocked off for the night," Alvin had agreed, sending Annie off. He'd stayed out front to talk with the visitor.

Miriam had returned to the kitchen until Alvin had called to her. She'd found Jerry seated on the front steps, looking pale and concerned. The hockey players had returned in the nick of time. Jacob had explained Jerry's heart condition, and Isaac had taken over. That young man was really something. Miriam knew his parents were concerned over his interest in the Englisch world, his dedication to community college, and his volunteer work on the fire and rescue squad. These were the sorts of things that pulled an Amish person away from his community. Miriam knew this was true, but in her heart she saw the merit of such interests, especially after what had happened tonight.

For Jerry Kraybill had died right on their front porch.

His heart had stopped beating. This Isaac was able to confirm when the ambulance had arrived with equipment like monitors and stethoscopes and oxygen. Ach! Poor Jerry had suffered a heart attack, right then and there. But Isaac had kept his heart moving, through CPR, in the two minutes it took for the ambulance to reach them.

And then Isaac and the paramedic from the rescue crew had rushed to use special electric paddles to shock Jerry's heart and bring him back to life. A miracle! If Miriam had ever seen a true act of Gott, that was it!

Jerry had been breathing—even talking again—when they put him into the ambulance and rushed him off to the hospital. That was when Miriam had seen another fine bit of character, as Sam and Isaac had directed their friends to the buggy barn to hitch up two buggies. One would go directly to the hospital, and the other went to the Kraybill home to notify Jerry's family and transport them to the hospital. Sam and Isaac had organized the two groups, preparing the buggies and keeping the other young men in line.

As Alvin drove the buggy directly to the hospital with quite a load of young people in the back, he put a hand on Miriam's knee, tucked snugly under the blanket, and gave a squeeze. "Our oldest son is a man now," he said quietly. "He stayed calm and focused in a crisis."

"He did. Alvie, it was so gratifying to see our Sam in that light. I'm grateful to Gott that he's come into his own. And I pray that Jerry will be okay."

"He came back to life before our eyes," Alvin had said. "That Isaac, he's the one you'd want to have around when you're not feeling well."

"I think he saved a life tonight," Miriam had said as the mule tugged them along the main road, which had been worn dry by cars and sunshine.

Now Miriam sat in the same row as Jerry's daughter and his wife, Netta, who occasionally dabbed at her eyes with a balled-up tissue. Miriam couldn't imagine the concern and anxiety the poor woman must be feeling. Before tonight, Miriam hadn't known the Kraybill family well;

they were just church acquaintances. After tonight, that would be changed.

A woman dressed in blue scrubs and a blue bonnet came in and blinked at the crowd in the waiting room. She was petite—barely five feet tall—but Miriam sensed a powerful presence in her small body. "I'm guessing you're all here for Jerry Kraybill."

"Yes!" Everyone spoke at once, but it was Netta who rose, tugged the hem of her sweater down over her hips, and moved forward. "I'm his wife, Netta."

"Netta, would you like to step into the hall for a moment?"

"Oh, please tell us," Jerry's daughter Leah begged. "Everyone here wants to know, how is he?"

When the doctor hesitated, Netta encouraged her. "You can say it. Everyone here is friend or family."

"Jerry is doing well. We had to put a stent in to open up a blocked artery, and the procedure was a success."

"Thanks be to Gott!" Netta said, her eyes shining with tears of relief. Her joy was followed by a collective sigh as the room filled with relief tinged with joy. Jerry's daughters hugged each other. Jacob dashed away tears.

Jerry had made it.

Miriam let out a breath and closed her eyes. Her silent prayer thanked Gott for allowing Jerry more time in this world. Time to love and know the love of his family and friends.

As conversations began to rumble through the room, the doctor stepped closer to Netta. "Your husband is doing well, but he had a heart attack because of an artery blocked with cholesterol. He's going to need to take a statin drug and change his diet to reduce cholesterol and fats."

"Thank you, Doctor! We'll work on that," Netta agreed.

They talked for a bit more, and then the doctor offered to take Netta to see her husband. "Just one visitor for tonight," she said, holding up one hand when other people approached her. She stepped into the doorway, then turned back to the group.

"I heard CPR was given at the farm." She scanned the waiting room. "By a young Amish man?"

"That was Isaac," Sam said, nudging his friend. "He's a volunteer paramedic, and he's studying medicine."

"Just biology," Isaac said, in a low voice. His gaze met the doctor's, but there was no pride in his stance. Isaac never did like being the center of attention.

"Well, it sounds to me like you did everything right," the doctor said. "It's fortunate you were there to do CPR when his heart stopped. You probably saved his life."

Isaac nodded graciously, his hat in his hands. As if saving someone's life was the kind of thing a man did every day. Such a good egg, that one. A loyal lifelong friend and cousin to Sam.

As Netta left the room with the doctor, Miriam went over to Sam and his buddy group.

"That was a wonderful thing you did, Isaac," Miriam said as Sam and Megan looked on.

"Denki, Aunt Miriam. But it's not like I did something special. I've been trained in CPR. It's one of the big roles of the fire and rescue squad. One of the reasons I like volunteering is to help people."

"And help you did," Miriam said. "I've been around sick people before, but I would not have known what to do or how to do it. You know, Gott doesn't make mistakes. He meant for you to be there tonight, to save Jerry's life."

Isaac looked over toward the line of men—a cautious look. Miriam followed his gaze, knowing he was aware that the bishop was watching. Aaron pretended to listen to the men around him, but his gaze was fixed on Isaac.

"Funny thing about that," Isaac said slowly. "When I'm studying biology or working as a paramedic, I feel like I'm doing the right thing. But if I were to join the church, get baptized, I'd have to give up my job and my studies. It's a quandary."

Miriam patted Isaac's shoulder. "It's a puzzle only you can solve," she told him as she smiled at their bishop, who nodded curtly in return. Aaron was a man of power—that much was true—but he also knew humility. Any sternness that came from the bishop was intended to keep their community together. It was the purpose of rules that kept church members from owning cars or pursuing careers. These were things that could lead them away from the church. Miriam had great respect for Aaron, but he was not to be feared. She and Alvin considered him a friend, too. These things sometimes could go hand in hand.

As far as Isaac was concerned, Miriam sensed that her nephew already had one foot on the other side of the fence. She knew that would cause his dat and stepmother heartache, but there was a silver lining in his dedication to healing and helping people. That was a good thing, certainly blessed by Gott—but still not okay in the rules of the Anabaptist faith. Miriam wished the situation could be easier on Isaac, but wishing didn't make it so.

One of Aaron's daughters came round, offering up some homemade brittle, and Miriam thanked her and took a piece, despite the fact that she'd meant to start her diet January first. Another new year, another new pound? She hoped not. Biting into the sweet, buttery goodness, she figured this little treat wouldn't count too much after the calories she'd burned worrying about poor Jerry. A heart attack on the front porch! It was a traumatic event beyond her wildest imagination, but she thanked Gott that it had ended well.

Chewing on the delicious peanut brittle, she let her gaze wander back to Sam and his friends. Isaac was explaining something, and Megan listened intently, while Sam talked with Fred. Such a commotion for Megan's first night back! But she seemed reassured by what Isaac was saying. Yah, she was truly fascinated.

Megan grinned just then, giving him a playful punch on the shoulder. Isaac's full-bodied laughter rumbled low amid the conversation in the room. He leaned down close to Megan then, speaking something that he wanted only her to hear.

Miriam stopped chewing.

She recognized that bit of sparkle when she saw it. Cupid's arrow had struck! Oh, joy of joys! There was nothing more exciting than the spark of true love in the world. Terrible things happened to good people—only Gott could understand why—but along with the bad came wonderful things like love. And as far as Miriam was concerned, love needed to be celebrated every chance you had.

Was there a possibility of a long-term relationship between Isaac and Megan? Hmm. Only Gott knew. There was little chance of Megan wanting to live like plain folk the rest of her life, but perhaps Isaac would live like the Englisch. School and doctoring were important to him. If he chose that path, maybe Megan would share the journey with him.

In any case, the spark of love was there in this moment. Thanks be to Gott.

So much to be thankful for. Jerry had made it. Megan

and Isaac. And, of course, Sam and Sadie. Dear Sadie, the sweet girl who had suffered some hardships at home, but never lost hope. The girl was like another daughter in Miriam's brood. It would be a joyous day when those two professed their sacred vows before Gott.

Not that they'd announced anything. They were keeping their love a secret, as far as she could tell, except that two young people who loved each other deeply slipped now and again.

She'd been on her way to the Dawdi House this afternoon, bringing a Tupperware of warm casserole over to Harlan's mem, Collette, when she'd seen two young folk romancing under the noble branches of the maple trees.

At first glance, her heart ached in a sweet way at the love she saw in the embrace of that distant couple. It reminded her of her younger days with Alvin—such longing—and of the love she still felt when he took her into his arms and held her as if she were Gott's most precious creation. Diet or no diet.

A moment later, her nostalgia had shifted when she'd recognized that the young man was her own son Sam and the woman was none other than Sadie Beiler. She'd been so caught up in it that she'd dropped the casserole in a mound of snow!

Such a thrill! Those two deserved the love of a kind, bighearted person, and at last, they had found each other.

Miriam had thought she'd caught a few looks of longing and lingering smiles over the past few days. Lo and behold, love had come to Lapp Farms once again. She could barely recover from her joy, but she did regain her senses enough to pick up the Tupperware and brush off a few chips of snow. Good as new.

Now, standing here among so many young and old folks from her community, Miriam said a silent prayer of thanks to Gott. *Thank you for love. The love between a man and a woman. The love among a community that brings us together and keeps us strong and joyful.*

Thank you for love.

Chapter 22

A dreary week went by without Sam. The January doldrums! The thermometer lingered in the thirties, and the sky wallowed from gray to white, not sure if it wanted to snow or simply threaten a storm.

At the pretzel factory, the tourists who sometimes made Sadie's job more interesting had dwindled since Christmas. Smitty had canceled most daily factory tours during the month of January, though he made exceptions Friday and Saturday if there was any interest.

But today was an ordinary Wednesday. With nothing much going on, Sadie tuned into the chatter of her co-workers as she twisted pretzels on the line with Gerta Chupp and Suzie Yoder. She'd gotten to know Suzie in the past year. Suzie was Harlan's little sister, Essie's new sister-in-law, and she lived in the Dawdi House at the Lapp farm. Such a sweet girl—barely sixteen, with pretty blue eyes and high cheekbones that made it seem that she was always on the verge of smiling. Suzie was always kind, but so painfully shy. At work she always wore the optional sanitary mask, though Sadie was convinced that the girl liked to hide behind the blue and white paper filters.

Gerta was older—in her midtwenties—and more forth-right, but the details of her life were mostly unknown, as she came from another Amish church district on the other side of Joyful River. She liked to talk about her boyfriend, Abe, which Sadie didn't mind.

The chatter was about the weather, as the icy roads had made travel a bit treacherous. "I don't mind the cold," Suzie said, "but when the roads get icy, nothing is safe. I can't wait for the spring when I can ride my scooter to work again."

"But the snow is so pretty," Sadie said, trying to stay positive.

"Pretty cold," Gerta insisted. "And once it gets trampled by cars and buggies and horses, it all turns to gray mush."

They worked on in quiet for a bit, rolling and twisting and filling up trays with their pretzel-shaped dough cre-ations, until Suzie asked about Gerta's boyfriend.

"Abe is fine, but he hasn't worked a real job since the RV factory closed, so it's not looking like we'll be making any announcements next wedding season." Gerta's voice was glum. "He won't marry if he can't support a wife."

"But surely you two could live with one of your parents while you save up," Sadie said encouragingly. Lots of Amish couples began their married life living with one set of parents or another until they could afford their own place. "You've got your salary here, and Abe's bound to find work soon. Farmers will be hiring come the spring."

"Abe says he needs something full-time before he'll marry. It's not my rule, but his." Scowling, she lifted a full tray of pretzels and moved it off to the sideboard. "Such a man. He's stubborn as a mule. And here I'm coming up on twenty-two and still not married."

"Don't be sad, Gerta," Suzie said, earnestness in her pretty blue eyes. "Something will work out."

"I'm sure he'll come around," Sadie agreed.

"It's not that easy when you're dating a guy from a poor family." Gerta frowned, her mouth growing taut as if she had tasted something sour. "But you wouldn't know that, Sadie. He's not like your Mark, you know, with a fancy house and a big family business." Her resentment flared, so fierce that Sadie felt it across the narrow work table.

"But . . ." Sadie wanted to say that he wasn't *her* Mark anymore. And the Miller house wasn't that fancy, not really. But it would be like pouring salt on the wound to argue these petty points. Gerta was suffering now, all wrapped up in worry over an unsure future. It would be cruel to argue with her. "I'm going to pray for you, Gerta. For you and Abe. Gott Almighty has a plan for you, and I'm sure that includes a lifetime of love."

Gerta sniffed, trying to blink back tears. "I hope you're right."

"Gott is always right, whatever his will," Sadie said. "We just need to have faith." It seemed like something Miriam would say, and Sadie felt a bit pleased that the encouraging words had come from her, as if Miriam had slid them into her pocket one day when she wasn't looking. Such was the influence of a good Amish woman of faith.

Sadie felt grateful . . . and a little guilty. All the time she'd been dating Mark, had she acted as if she were better because she'd found a young man with wealth? Money didn't matter to her, not really, though she was realistic enough to know that lack of money was a problem. It had caused her parents many sleepless nights when the orchard business had been losing money.

And there had been a certain attraction to Mark's success, knowing that marrying him would guarantee a roof over her head and an escape from her parents' house. Which was what she'd wanted and needed back then.

But no more. Now she didn't need to escape her home. Now she had a plan to marry for love, not desperation.

But when she'd been dating Mark, had she treated others poorly? Had she been focused on the prize, like a horse with blinders on? She bit her lower lip, knowing it was true. Well, no more. Sadie was determined to be a better person, starting now.

"You know," Sadie said, her gaze on the dough rolling between her palm and the table, "I'm going to ask around and see who needs a good worker. There's the furniture factory where Harlan works, and I have friends at the Lapp Dairy. There's got to be something out there for Abe."

"I keep saying that, but he's looked high and low. Still, if you could get the word out for him, it might help," Gerta said. When Sadie looked up, Gerta's eyes had softened. "His name is Abe Peachy, and he's a good man."

Sadie nodded. "I'll do my best."

On Friday, nearly a dozen visitors arrived, and Sadie was chosen to lead the tour.

"This old brick building is where it all started," she told the group. "I know it seems small for a factory, but this is where Henry Smith opened Smitty's Original Pretzels." As people eyed the old-time photos on the brick walls, she explained that most of that building was used as office space now, though you could still see the charred, blacked walls at the back of the building where the ovens used to rest. "Smitty's is one of the few remaining pretzel factories where pretzels are hand rolled and twisted. Mr. Smitty thinks it adds a special, personal touch to an already delicious pretzel." After allowing a moment for the visitors to take in the old building, Sadie led them to a windowed space with a wooden table.

"This is the part of the tour where we teach you to twist your own pretzels," she said, handing out wads of playdough. People loved trying their hand with the fake dough, and Sadie enjoyed watching their efforts at pretzel-twisting.

"First you want to roll your dough into a stick, at least twelve inches long," Sadie instructed as the group, mostly women and children, started working the dough on the long wooden table. "Next you want to make a U shape, and then cross the ends of the U, like so." Sadie demonstrated by setting her example on a cutting board and holding it up so they could see.

"Next you want to cross the ends again, forming a bit of a spiral." Sadie demonstrated and then walked along the table. "Very good job," she told a little girl, who looked to be around eight or nine.

"Oh, she loves to bake," her mother said as the little girl smiled.

"Are we ready?" Sadie asked the group. "The next step is a big one. You're going to flip the crossed ends down to the bottom of the U, like so. Overlap the dough and press it down, and you have a pretzel." She demonstrated, and then everyone tried it.

Sadie went down the line, helping those who tried to twist the wrong way or stretch the dough too far. People rolled their eyes or laughed at their own mistakes, all in good fun.

"Since this is fake dough, you know we won't be baking it," Sadie announced. "But there's a fresh-baked soft pretzel waiting for you if you'll follow me out to the bakery."

People thanked her on their way out. The little girl tugged her apron, gesturing for Sadie to lean down.

"I like your hat," the girl said.

"Thanks." Sadie couldn't help but smile. "We call it a prayer kapp."

As the little girl's mem led her off, Sadie wondered how it would feel to have children of her own. How she adored taking care of her nieces and nephews! But it would be different, truly a blessing to raise children who called her "Mem." Much as she enjoyed parts of her job here, her true joy would be raising a family, keeping house, and loving Sam.

Over the holidays they had talked quietly about their hopes and dreams one night after the others had gone off to bed. Sam hoped to have a large family. When he asked Sadie, she nodded eagerly at the prospect of having a dozen children—hers and Sam's. She marveled over the miracle that could happen, that their union could create flesh and blood. So precious! Sam had described how much he valued his siblings.

"I couldn't imagine life without them. Yah, the kinder drive me a little crazy sometimes, but they all add something special to the day. Do you get along with your sisters?"

She had nodded. "My sister Polly is eleven years older than me, so she's been out of the house a long time. And I miss Sharon every day. It's especially hard since she lives so far away. After she got married, it was just me in the house with my parents." She rolled her eyes. "You're lucky to be the oldest. You don't want to be the last one in the house with two Amish parents."

He'd laughed at that. "No, I couldn't stand to be the center of Miriam and Alvin's attention all the time."

"It's not easy!"

Oh, how she missed Sam! Sadie took comfort in knowing that Sam was just as eager to see her as she was to visit him. Each night after work Sadie had stopped at the phone shanty on the main road and listened for messages from Mark, hoping that this might be resolved without even having to see him again.

Unfortunately, there'd been no messages from him.

Today, Sadie decided to take action. When she left the pretzel factory, she declined the ride home that she usually got from Josie and set out walking toward the Millers' house. If she couldn't reach Mark by phone, she was going to find a way to get a message to him. It was just after four—meaning there was a good hour of sunlight left—and she intended to use the walk to clear her head.

So much had changed in her life. Sadie thought of the quiet that had descended on the house since Sharon's family had left after the holidays. At first a glum feeling of isolation had hung in the air when Sadie had found herself alone in the house. It was so quiet, the only noise coming from the clock ticking outside the kitchen.

She looked to Dat's empty chair, where he usually sat reading his Amish newspapers. Where he used to sit and bark comments at Sadie and Mem.

One evening this week, Sadie had noticed the quiet, and suddenly the question had hit her: Where were they? Where had her parents gone? She had thrown her coat back on and hurried outside, calling their names. It took a moment, but the door to the mushroom shack had popped open, and Dat had poked his head out.

"We're here, daughter." His eyes were intent over the glasses propped low on his nose.

"What are you doing back here, Dat?"

He held up his hands, black with soil. "Harvesting mushrooms. I need to help your mem so she doesn't fall behind."

"You're working in the dark hut?"

"Yah, and I don't mind it so much. With you gone to work and whatnot, as it should be, so much of the responsibility falls on Joan's shoulders. I can carry some of that load."

Sadie had been nearly speechless as Dat had ducked back into the mushroom shack, leaving her to sort through the changes that had transpired in their house. Dat hadn't had a grouchy spell since before Christmas. It had been a while since he'd complained of the pain in his feet, which the doctor said was related to diabetes. She hadn't found any half-empty bottles of liquor in the house while cleaning, so it seemed that he was off the drinking for good. But to see Dat out of his chair and working out back—that was the most eye-popping surprise of all.

Later that night, when Dat went out to check on the horses, Sadie mentioned it to Mem.

"I was surprised to see Dat out back, helping out," she said, rubbing a plate dry and placing it on the stack in the cabinet. They were doing the last of the dinner dishes—a small chore, with only the three of them in the house now.

"Ach, it's wonderful good," Mem said. "I think he's going to take on a lot of the work as we move ahead, and that's a huge burden off my shoulders."

"I can always help you at night and on my days off,"

Sadie insisted. A twinge of guilt stung her as she thought of the hours and nights she'd spent away from home, especially over the holidays. It hadn't occurred to her that she'd been shirking her chores and responsibilities here.

Mem shook her head, a new gleam in her green eyes. Was it weariness? "You're a good worker, Sadie. A huge help. But you're a youngie, and you have things to do, places to go. I'll not deprive you of that. And to be honest, the bit of tending and cultivating out back is good for your dat. A man needs a purpose, and now that your father is feeling good enough to work again, he's got something important to do."

Sadie kept quiet as she soaked this development up. She had assumed that Dat would finish out his life from that rocking chair, squinting and scowling at newsprint. But this news—the notion that he was going back to work, participating in the new family business, this was not something she had seen coming.

"Are you sure he's up to it?" Sadie asked, thinking of the warnings from Dat's doctor.

Mem nodded. "He had a good holiday, and he's feeling better inside and out." Mem rinsed a glass and put it on the drying mat. "Such an effort he made at Christmastime. Didn't you notice that he had no pie? What a sacrifice for him. You know he loves his shoofly pie, any time of year. But the doctor told him that changing his diet is the only way to back out of diabetes, and his blood pressure's a bit high, so he's been cutting back on sweets and foods with cholesterol. Trying to eat healthier foods. And most important, the changes are making him feel better."

"I've noticed how much more cheerful he's seemed," Sadie said. She'd been so wrapped up in her own concerns, she hadn't paid him much mind. "I'm glad he's following the doctor's orders, but, Mem, I'm a little afraid to trust it. Don't you worry that he's going to go back to the drinking?"

Mem frowned. "I don't like to think that way. We have to stay positive."

Sadie turned toward the cupboard so Mem couldn't see her confusion. If only staying positive would have made a difference all those years when Dat had growled mean things to everyone in the family. So lost in drunkenness. A hundred times Sadie had prayed and wished that he would put away the bottle and see the family who loved him. A hundred times, she'd been disappointed. "I don't mean to be negative, Mem," Sadie said. "It just worries me."

"Your father's been trying so hard to keep away from the alcohol. It's hard for a man to lose the only business he's known. 'Twas hard for your father to sell the orchard, but he knew it had to be done." Mem let her breath out in a grateful sigh. "And look how well it's turned out. The mushrooms are bringing money in, enough to care for us all, with far less work than the orchard required of our small family. It's time to count our blessings and look to the future."

Look to the future.

Sadie mulled the words over now as she walked the last stretch to the Miller house.

What would the future look like for her parents? If Sadie married in the next few years, which everyone expected, it would be up to Mem and Dat to run the small mushroom and herb business on their own, or else hire in a young Amish teen to help them keep things moving. It was time for Sadie to move on, time to make a change. There was no need to feel responsible for her dat's behavior or her mem's denial. And gone was the desperation she'd always felt to escape her home and get married. In her heart, she had to admit that it had been one of the reasons she'd latched onto Mark so tightly, hoping for marriage. Now when she married, it would be for love, not escape.

No husband could save her from the sorrows of the past; she knew that now. But with Gott's blessing, her dat would stay on an even keel, and over time she would let go of the worry and pain that had shaped her childhood.

As the Bible said, "To everything there is a season, and a time for every purpose under the heaven." Looking up to the sky, where ribbons of red, orange, and lavender clouds threaded over the setting sun, Sadie had to trust that Gott would guide her to a path of forgiveness and love.

Thy will be done.

Chapter 23

Friday evening, Sam was on his way in from milking the cows when he saw a single light coming up the lane. He paused and squinted into the darkness, wondering what might move so quickly with a single light.

A person with a headlamp on a scooter. An Amish man dressed in black. Isaac.

Sam hurried over to the lane to meet him. "What are you doing here? Kind of brave to take the scooter out on icy roads."

"I had to leave home fast." Isaac adjusted the headlamp so that it wasn't pointing in Sam's face. "I told my family I'm not getting baptized. That I'm joining the Mennonite church. I made the mistake of telling them at dinner."

"And? They couldn't have been surprised."

"Not surprised, but not happy. Dat left the table, and Gloria cried." Isaac peeled off the headlamp and knit cap in frustration. "It's a terrible thing to see your stepmother cry and know it's your own fault."

"It's a heavy burden you're shouldering," Sam said. He knew his friend had struggled with the decision, determined to do what he believed was right. "Your plan, it's all with good intentions." He thumped on the wool coat covering Isaac's chest. "You've a big heart in there, Isaac."

"You know, an enlarged heart is not a good thing in the medical world," Isaac pointed out. "But I get it. You're trying to say nice things about me even though I'm a disappointment to my parents. You're a good friend, Sam."

"I'm trying," Sam said with a shrug. "I'm headed in for dinner. Come. Mem will add a place at the table for you and we'll talk after."

"I don't want to be a bother, and I'm not too hungry anymore. I can wait for you out in the barn."

"Come. Mem will have my head if she finds out you were here and she didn't get a chance to feed you."

They went inside and washed up. Adjustments were made at the table to add another plate, and Sam saw to it that Isaac got to sit close enough to Megan that they could chat. After everyone lowered their heads in silent prayer and then dug into the casserole, conversation rolled out. Megan talked about a quiz she was studying for in AP bio, and Isaac mentioned that he had to learn the name of every bone in the body—hundreds!—for his A and P class. When asked, Isaac explained that A and P stood for "anatomy and physiology." That didn't mean much to Sam, though he had figured it was about the human body.

Since Megan had returned from the city, it had become obvious that she and Isaac had a special relationship. They had begun meeting at the library in town and working on school assignments together, and Isaac had been spending more and more time here at the house, although Sam joked that with all the time Isaac spent with Megan, he was seeing less of his friend. "If it weren't for hockey, I'd never see you," he teased Isaac, who swatted at him and countered that Sam was occupied with his own business.

"What? Milking the cows?" Sam asked.

"I've noticed a certain Amish girl who's spending a lot of time here lately," Isaac had said. "I don't know why you don't talk about her, but I'm onto you."

"Not a word to anyone," Sam had admonished his friend. "When the time is right, we'll talk, you and me."

Isaac had nodded and let the subject drop.

That was one of the things that made Isaac such a good friend; he knew how to give people space, and he didn't blather on about things he knew nothing about. A man of few words, a good man.

After dinner they split some logs, took them out to the firepit beyond the barn, and built a crackling winter blaze. Megan helped them—and she was strong, for a girl. Sam knew her sisters and Annie would join in later, once the fire was going, but for now, it was Isaac's chance to be heard.

"What bothers me most is hurting my father and Gloria," Isaac said when the three of them were settled by the fire. "I want to help people, not hurt them."

He pounded a fist against his chest. "Deep down in my heart, I know that this is the right choice. I'm supposed to continue my studies, keep training with the paramedics. It's the right path for me. But I'll never have the approval of the church, and so I'll always be a disappointment to my family."

"It's a heavy burden," Sam agreed. "But I don't see that there's any way you can undo it."

Megan shook her head. "You guys, that's such a big choice you have to make, but really, Isaac, I think your parents will get over it."

"I don't know, Megs," Sam said, poking at the fire with a stick. "Amish parents have long memories."

"So you're in, Sam?" Megan asked. "You're going to get baptized? When will that happen?"

"The church leaders pick the date, but it will be sometime in the spring. There'll be a group of us, going together." He looked pointedly at Isaac. "Jacob is in the group. We were hoping to get Isaac in, too. But now you've made your choice, I'll do what I can to support you."

Isaac stared into the fire. "I'm going to join the Mennonites here in Joyful River. I went to speak to their pastor just before Christmas, and he said I was welcome."

"Wow." Sam clapped his hands on his thighs. "That makes it seem so final."

"It is." Behind the lenses of his glasses, Isaac's eyes burned with intensity, with decisiveness and courage. "And you know it's not something that came easily. But my classes and my work on the ambulance corps are important to me, and the medical knowledge can help folks, Amish and Englisch alike. That's what I think I'm meant to do. Care for people who need help."

Both Megan and Sam were watching Isaac. The intensity in his voice, his somber dedication, his clarity— everything was combined in a compelling way. Isaac knew his purpose in life, even if it went against the grain of Amish culture. Sam admired his friend's fire, his purpose strengthened by his calm demeanor.

"You're so noble," Megan told him.

Isaac shrugged. "Not really. I think I'm good with science. But I suck at farming."

Megan and Sam burst into laughter. "I've never heard you say that!" Megan said.

"It's true." Isaac grinned. "Sam's the farmer here. I was

always running the tractor into a ditch or botching up the milking. That's why I've thought about it a long time. Prayed about it long and hard. This is Gott's path for me. I just hope that, down the road, the people I care about will forgive me. Especially Gloria, my stepmother."

"There's nothing to be forgiven," Megan insisted. "Children go against their parents all the time, and sometimes that's all for the better. No one else can know what's right for you, Isaac."

"He's going against the path of plain folk," Sam said. "People are going to think that's wrong."

"But you can't let the opinions of people around you stop you from doing what's right for you," Megan said. She held her hands closer to the fire, staring into the flames before she turned back to Isaac. "Believe me, I've been influenced and pushed around by my fair share of people. If rehab taught me anything, it was to stand up for myself and make sure I get what I need to stay healthy."

"The Englisch world is different," Isaac said.

"That's true, but some things are universal. Parents making demands on their children. Expectations. Arguments. You know, over Christmas when we were back in Philly, I got into an argument with my dad. I hated to disappoint him, but I had to be honest with him."

"What did you argue about?" Isaac asked.

Megan tilted her head to one side, thinking back. "My dad assumed that we'd all be coming back at the end of the school year, that Serena and I would attend college in Philadelphia, as we'd planned."

"And you're not going back?" Sam asked.

"I told him it would be a horrible idea. Serena and I have changed a lot since we got booted here last summer.

We've grown, and made adjustments. It's been good for us to be removed from the city environment, the social life there . . . the temptations."

"Pizza on every corner?" Isaac asked.

"That's a small part of it, yes. I'm afraid that if we go to college in Philadelphia, we'll slip back into our old habits in no time. Unhealthy habits." She shook her head and adjusted her wool cap over her ears. "I don't know what Grace wants to do, but Serena and I can't go back. And our dad didn't want to hear that. I think it hurt him when I gave him a blast of reality. I kind of yelled at him. Maybe I should have tempered it a little. I didn't mean to hurt him, but the emotion that puffed up inside me when I was back in Philly, seeing the people I used to trust, walking the streets that once had been home . . . it made me feel weepy and grateful, all at the same time. I like the city, but I can't live there right now. Not until I'm on really steady feet."

"You're making me feel better," Isaac said.

"Good. That was my intention."

"And I didn't blast my father and Gloria. I just spoke the truth."

"Now you make me look like the jerk?" Megan gave Isaac a stern look. "Go ahead. I can take it. I've got thick skin."

"We know that," Sam said, laughing along with his two cousins. Megan's athletic skill and grit had impressed all of the guys on their hockey team. In fact, there had been recent discussions about adding Megan to the team. "The guys on the team know you're tough, too. We've been talking, and we're wondering if you'd fill in for Jacob during the tournament."

"What? Jacob's out?" Megan's mouth dropped open. "He's one of your best players."

"Jacob's got to fill in for his father while Jerry is recovering," Isaac explained. "The family business requires someone to go to Reading Terminal Market to take care of the cheese concession, and Jacob's the one to handle it."

"Wow, I didn't think of that. But you've got Micah and Fred, right? And the twins. That makes six, so one can be a sub."

"Fred and Micah are not so strong with stick skills," Sam said. "And one sub isn't really enough. Come play with us."

"Look, I love the game, but I just really started. And what's everyone going to say when you roll out on the ice with a female on your team? Not just a female, but an Englisch girl?"

Isaac and Sam looked at each other and laughed. "An Englisch girl is probably better," Isaac said. "I think those Amish fellas would fall out of their skates if they saw an Amish girl on the team. But you know, with your helmet and gear on, you look just like any other team member."

"Well, thanks," Megan said, clapping her gloves together to stay warm. "I guess hockey gear can be a great neutralizer."

"No one has to know you're a girl," Sam said. Knowing how Megan loved playing hockey, he hadn't expected her to resist the suggestion. "And there's no rule saying that all players have to be male."

Megan put her hands on her hips. "Has there ever been a female player in the tournament?"

"Not that I can remember," Sam admitted.

"It's traditionally been all men," Isaac said, turning to

her. "But knowing how you enjoy turning tradition on its ear, I thought you'd want to play."

"That much is true." Megan let out a sigh, creating a puff of white. "I think I'm going to pass. Now's not a good time for you to rock the boat, Isaac."

"I'm already flipping the boat over," he said quietly.

"We had a team meeting, and everyone wants you," Sam said. "The twins will be devastated if you don't play. Pete said you have 'mad skills,' and you know how Paul loves to win. Everyone wants you on the team."

"Guys . . . I don't know."

Sam wanted to persuade her, but he kept quiet. She was hedging, but in the end he couldn't imagine Megan giving up a chance to play in the tournament. In her heart, she was just as competitive as any Amish guy he knew.

"I should probably focus on my schoolwork," she said.

"It's just three nights," Isaac said.

Megan got up, circled the fire, then sat down again. "I'll think about it," she said.

Isaac and Sam exchanged a grin. They both knew what she'd decide. Megs was in.

Sam got up from the log he was sitting on, stirred the fire with a poker, and tossed in another piece of wood. That should keep it going for an hour or so.

In the meantime, he had something important on his mind, and he knew his cousins would appreciate some time alone. "I've got some stuff to take care of," he told Megan and Isaac. "I'll see you later."

As his boots crunched on the iced snow on the way back to the house, he heard Isaac's low, rumbling voice and gleeful Megan's voice rise melodically before they both dissolved in laughter.

Sam thought back over his long friendship with cousin

Isaac. Some of the qualities he appreciated in Isaac—his inquisitive nature, his curiosity and love of science—made him stick out in Amish society. But those seemed to be the very things Megs had in common with him. They were well suited, those two. It reminded him of something his mem always said: There's someone for everyone. It looked like Isaac and Megan had found their someone.

Chapter 24

That night, Sadie lay in bed staring at the ceiling and wondered how she could get out of this mess.

She felt trapped—locked into a bad situation, though one she'd gotten herself into.

Her plan hadn't worked out that afternoon. Mark's mother hadn't been very helpful when Sadie arrived. Clearly, Carol had been in the midst of preparing dinner, and her pensive expression and taut mouth had been about as welcoming as a bucket of ice water.

"I don't understand what you want me to do," Carol had said, returning to the stove to stir a pot.

"I'm just wondering if you could give me a way to reach Mark while he's in Lititz. Is there a phone number I can call? Maybe the number for his cousin Tom, where he's staying."

Carol shook her head, rapping the spoon sharply against the pot. "That would not be a good idea."

"Is there an address I can write to?" Sadie persisted. "Or maybe if . . . did you send him my letter?"

Carol let out a huff of breath. "Your letter is upstairs,

with the box you gave me. Mark will see it when he returns at the end of the month. Or in February."

"February." Sadie closed her eyes, trying to rein in her frustration. She had thought Mark's mem would offer some help. "There has to be a way I can reach him in the meantime."

Disapproval was obvious in Carol's dark eyes as she ended the discussion and ushered Sadie out as if she were a squirrel who had scrambled in from the yard.

Oh, it is no use trying anymore! Sadie rolled over, tried to punch some fullness into her pillow, and collapsed on the bed again. She would just have to wait. "Patience is a virtue," Mem used to say. It was a virtue that Sadie had never truly possessed.

A tapping sound made her alert and stiffen. What was that? It sounded like rain on the glass of the window, but the sky had been clear and studded with stars when she went to bed. As she listened, there was another series of taps, like hale hitting the roof, and then a sudden bolt of light was shining at the edge of her window shade.

She jumped up in bed with a burst of delight. Someone had come courting.

Sadie pulled the quilt over her nightgown, went to the window, and opened the shade. Her first-floor bedroom wasn't too challenging to reach, though it sat a good eight feet above the ground. Once he lowered the beam of the flashlight, she made out the details of his handsome face beneath the brim of his black hat. Sam!

The sight of him, standing in the snow with a handful of corn kernels, filled her with a mixture of excitement and joy. How she'd missed him this week! She longed for a time when they would never have to separate.

Quickly, she turned away from the window and pinned on her prayer kapp before turning back to unlock the latch and open it. "I'm so happy to see you tossing corn against my window," she said, her breath a puff of white in the night air, "but I have to ask, what are you doing here?"

"What do you think? I've come to see my favorite girl when everyone else is asleep."

She laughed, filled with delight and a feeling of danger. "My dat would have a fit if he knew you were here."

Hands on his hips, Sam seemed to give it some thought. "I would guess that Reuben tossed grains of corn on a few girls' windows in his younger years. Come out with me, Sadie. Bundle up and we'll go for a buggy ride."

"I want to, but I thought we were keeping a low profile."

"No one else needs to know we went for a late-night buggy ride. Who will see us in the dark? Come on, Sadie girl."

She couldn't say no. As she hurriedly dressed, she thought of the many times she'd wished Mark would come calling for her late at night. She loved the excitement of spontaneous events, but it seemed that Mark poured all his animation and energy into calling auctions. He was a masterful auctioneer, switching quickly back and forth between Englisch and Pennsylvania Dutch. His calls were laced with jokes to the audience, teasing a man that he'd better win an item lest his wife get angry or joking that a bidder was chickenhearted for backing out when the price got steep. At the auction house, Mark knew how to handle a crowd and keep things all in good fun. That was the Mark she had fallen for, unaware that he had a darker side when he was out of the limelight.

It was all for the best that she had realized they weren't a good match. As she crept through the house, mindful not to wake her parents, she said a silent prayer, thanking Gott for leading her down a new path. Just when the sky had seemed dark, he had opened up the clouds to let sunlight stream through.

Outside, Sam greeted her with a joyous laugh, lifted her off her feet, and swung her around. She chuckled along with him, holding on for dear life and not letting go when her feet landed on the frozen earth. They came together for a breathless kiss and then climbed into the buggy. Sam spread out the lap blanket, and Sadie tucked it around them until they were cozy. With a signal to the horses, they were off and ready for a winter ride.

It was a beautiful, icy cold night. The blanket kept them warm for a while, especially in the center of the buggy, where they snuggled close to each other. The rare Amish buggy with heat was fitted with a portable propane heater, which could be dangerous. Most families relied on body heat, blankets, or the occasional hot water bottle.

"I know it's getting cold," Sam admitted after an hour or so. "Are your feet okay?"

"Like Popsicles," she said. "But I don't care, if I can be with you."

"You're really something special. But I can't let you turn into a snowman. Do you want to go back to my house? Everyone will be asleep, so we'll have the downstairs to ourselves."

Sadie agreed, and Sam turned the buggy toward the Lapp farm, where Sadie made them hot cocoa and they talked and snuggled for hours. Most weeks, Sadie would have needed her sleep after working full-time at the factory.

But being with Sam ignited a spark of energy inside her that made each moment a joy. There was so much to say, and scarcely enough hours to be with him.

When Miriam came into the kitchen and found them laughing just after five, a huge smile lit her face. "Well, good morning to you two!" she said brightly.

Sitting close to Sam, his arm over her shoulders, Sadie knew she should have been embarrassed to be caught, but the glow of happiness in her heart overcame any awkwardness. "I guess we chatted the night away," she said.

"I guess so!" Miriam's eyes were soft with joy. "Are your parents going to worry when they discover you missing?"

"I left them a note, so they'll know I'm in capable hands," Sadie said.

Sam removed his arm, but his eyes were ardent, full of loving support. "Do you want me to take you home? I can make a run before it's time for milking."

"Don't be silly." Miriam waved off the idea. "You go up to bed and get some sleep. Your father and Annie can handle the cows, and the twins can step in if need be. You too, Sadie. There's that empty bunk in the girls' room After breakfast, we'll find you a way home."

She thought drifting off to sleep in a cozy bunk of the familiar girls' room would be the perfect end to their special time together. Sweet as the icing on a birthday cake! Sadie thanked Miriam and followed Sam up the stairs.

At the top landing, he took her hand and pulled her into his arms.

"Well, if she didn't suspect before, Mem knows now," he said.

"She wasn't mad."

"Why would she be? She just caught her oldest son cuddling up with the best girl in the world."

"You say the sweetest things," Sadie whispered. "Do you think she'll keep our secret?"

"She will if I explain it to her."

Face-to-face with Sam, she noticed the natural dark shading on his eyelids and the slight stubble on his chin from a day's growth of beard. Usually she liked a clean-shaven jaw, but this reminded her that they were no longer children anymore, palling around in the haymow. Sam was a man, and she was a woman, and everything between them had changed. When their eyes met, she felt a burst of connection, the way a crackling fire pops and sends sparks flying. She knew she should tear herself away, go off to bed, but she couldn't resist the comfort and thrill of being in Sam's arms.

It seemed risky, standing in the hallway, their bodies pressed together as if they were one person. As if they were man and wife, joined and blessed by Gott. Being in his arms was a wondrous thing.

Someday, she prayed.

Anyone could open a bedroom door and discover them, but the brief intimacy was too special to forgo. When he kissed her, he tasted of cocoa with a slight hint of the peppermint stick she had used to stir their hot drinks. She closed her eyes and fell into the kiss, wishing to prolong it indefinitely but needing to come up for air.

Sam pressed his forehead to hers. "Sleep well."

"You too." She turned away and floated down the hall on a cloud of happiness.

* * *

The next morning sunlight flooded the room when Sadie stirred. The smell of sweet cinnamon teased her awake. Something delicious was baking in the kitchen downstairs. What time was it? She turned to the wall clock and saw that most of the bottom bunks were empty. Annie had probably gone off to milk the cows. It looked like Serena was in the bunk by the window, but then, it was Saturday—a day to sleep in. The wall clock said that it was almost eight—still time for breakfast if she got moving. She reached her arms overhead and yawned in bed, feeling like a cat stretching in the sun. What a wonderful good day to awaken at Lapp Farms, just down the hall from Sam!

She was about to throw back the quilt when the door creaked open and Essie bustled into the room. She paused to take a quick look, then bustled over to perch on the bedside of the bunk Sadie had chosen last night.

"So." Essie's caramel-colored hair was swept back neatly under her white prayer kapp. Her white apron seemed clean and crisp over her maroon dress. Sadie didn't know how Essie did it, but she always seemed neat as a pin and well put together. "When were you going to tell me, your best friend in the world?"

"Oh, Essie, please don't be mad at me. I've found love, real love, for the first time in my life, and . . . my heart is bursting with so much joy. It's been hard to contain, and I so wanted to tell you, but I couldn't. It's got to stay a secret. Promise me you'll keep it a secret."

Essie gently stroked a strand of hair away from Sadie's eyes. "You know I will."

Sadie sat content for a moment, then propped herself up on one elbow. "How did you hear it, anyway? Did Sam tell you?"

"No one told me anything about you and Sam. But when I ran into Annie outside the henhouse and she mentioned that you were asleep up here, I knew. Why else would you be here at the house, when I'm now living in the Dawdi House?"

"You've always been a smart one," Sadie told her friend, straightening a fold in Essie's apron, then looking up into her warm brown eyes. "I wanted to tell you. I was about ready to burst. But we can't let anyone know yet. I'm not officially broken up with Mark."

"But you delivered a letter, and returned the clock, too. What more can you do?"

"I just don't want the news to take him by surprise. Mark has a temper, and none of us wants to see it boil over."

"He's a sore loser at volleyball," Essie said. "Probably a sore loser in love, too. I know you loved Mark, but sometimes he's not very mature."

"I was never in love with him," Sadie said thoughtfully. "I thought I was, but that was more wishful thinking. Now that it's hit me . . ." She let out a breath and smiled up at her friend. "Real love is more wondrous than anything I've ever imagined!"

"I'm happy for you. But I'm kicking myself for not figuring it out earlier. I did notice a few looks passed between you and Sam. Like you were both in on a joke. Like you both could barely keep from smiling."

"It's true, Essie. I've never been so happy," Sadie admitted.

Suddenly, the bunk rocked, and Sadie gasped as a bright-eyed head peeped down over the edge. "This is wonderful news to wake up to on a Saturday morning." Eleven-year-old

Lizzie's upside-down face grinned from the edge of the bunk. "Hurray!"

"Oh, Lizzie, come down!" Essie ordered, pressing a hand to her chest. "My heart just leaped out of my chest with your face popping down."

"I didn't mean to startle you." Lizzie climbed down from the top bunk and perched on the bottom bunk near Sadie's feet. "But I heard everything, and I'm so happy for you and Sam, and I'll keep your secret, for sure. Though I don't really know why it's a big secret when grown-ups fall in love all the time."

"Just keep it to yourself for now," Essie warned her.

"I will." Lizzie grabbed hold of Sadie's feet under the quilt and gave them a wiggle. "This is good news! I've noticed the change in Sam since Christmas. He used to be mopey most of the time, but I can tell he's happy when you're around, Sadie. When he looks at you, he has stars in his eyes!"

Essie held up her hand. "You're imagining that, Lizzie. Have you been reading Mem's romance novels?"

"I like to read everything," Lizzie said defensively.

"Hold on, Essie." Serena popped her head out from under the covers and rolled over to face them. "Lizzie is right. I've seen the way Sam and Sadie look at each other. Megan and I figured it out a while back."

"You did?" Sadie let out a sigh. "I thought we were doing such a good job of keeping it a secret."

"No worries." Serena sat up and scraped back her long, toffee-brown hair. "We won't say anything until you guys are ready to go public. Right, Lizzie?"

"That's a deal," Lizzie agreed.

Looking at the bright, sympathetic faces around her, Sadie felt the security of being surrounded by love. Despite her impatience to set things right with Mark, she was grateful for the comfort and support she'd always found in this family.

Lizzie rose and stretched toward the ceiling. "Who wants breakfast? I smell cinnamon rolls!"

Chapter 25

Sunday was a church day, hosted at the house of Len and Linda Hostetler. Not long ago, Sadie would have dreaded the day, partly because of the flirtations between June Hostetler and Mark, and partly because of the fear that Dat might sneak off after church for a bit of wine or whiskey. But now she had no more worries on those fronts! Funny how things that had once been such a bother had lost their power to hurt her. Time could heal many wounds, she thought as Dat steered their buggy toward the outskirts of town.

The Hostetlers ran a successful harness business in town and thus lived in a more suburban home, close to the business. Mem liked the Hostetler house because it was one level and had plenty of space, with walls that could be removed from the main living area to make room for the church benches. "It's such an open, airy space," Mem said now.

Sadie smiled, realizing that Mem said this every time the Hostetlers hosted, which was about once a year or so as the rotation went around. Speaking of the Hostetlers, Dat was reminded that they might need a new harness come the spring. He'd make his way into town to talk to Len later this week.

"And, Dat, I wonder if you could do some asking around for me," Sadie said. "One of my coworkers at the factory, Gerta, her beau is looking for work. The name's Abe Peachy, and he's a hard worker, she says. He had a job at the RV factory until they closed down."

"No harm in asking around," Dat said as he tugged gently on the left rein to turn the horse into the parking area, where young Amish men in the community worked as hostlers on church day. Old Gray remained steady as Sadie and her mem climbed down from the buggy. Dat took a bit longer, wincing as he bent his legs and then landed on the ground.

"Dat, are you all right?" Sadie asked.

"Just a little stiff. All the bending and lifting in the hothouse is giving me some twinges in the hinges," he answered, rubbing his lower back as he straightened.

Sadie smiled, pleased by his newfound good nature. They greeted friends and then separated, Sadie staying with Mem, and Dat going off to join the menfolk, who would sit on the other side of the room during the church meeting.

Across the room Sadie was glad to see Essie filing in between Miriam and Collette, Harlan's mem. A married woman now, Essie would be sitting with the other wives, while Sadie filed into the room with the other unmarried females. She found a seat next to the Lambright girls, who didn't grate on her nerves the way those Hostetlers did. But not much conversation went on during church. There would be time for socializing and a light meal after church, and then, in the evening, Sadie would be back for the singing, one of the most popular events for Amish youth.

During the service, Sadie's gaze kept drifting to the section where the single men sat. There was Sam, his light brown hair framing his handsome face, his smoky brown eyes shining with strength and faith and love.

She had to keep from craning her neck to peek. It wouldn't do to be caught staring at him across the crowded room. Restraint was needed. She kept trying to stare down at her lap, as if in prayer.

But then, minutes later, she slipped again and dared herself a look. Ach, but he was handsome, and so wonderful. A heart of gold.

Once he turned and met her gaze, and she was sure a fire was going to spark right then and there in the church meeting! She soaked it all up for a moment, starved for that connection with him, but then tore herself away before everyone in the congregation grew wise to their union.

After the service Sadie and Essie stood in line to get some food. After church, folks divided into male and female groups—a comfortable tradition, but one that made sure Sadie wouldn't have much chance to talk to Sam this afternoon. No matter. Guys and girls would be allowed to mix at the singing tonight.

Sadie and Essie made sandwiches with Amish peanut butter that had been sweetened with marshmallow, and helped themselves to cups of coffee. As they sat down on a bench, the women chatting nearby were talking fervently.

"Men need their independence," one woman said. "It's their nature. Bullheaded, they can be. That's why we lose more men than women when it comes time for baptism. Car ownership and alcohol . . . they lure the men away."

"But Isaac's not a drinker," another woman said. "He's leaving for the education, and he wants a job in medicine. That's his reason."

Sadie gave a quick glance and saw that the woman speaking was Isaac's stepmother, Gloria Lapp. Heads were nodding as the older women soaked up the information. Sadie leaned close to her friend and whispered: "They're talking about Isaac."

Essie nodded, staring forward as she swallowed a bite of sandwich. "I thought so," Essie said in a quiet voice. "He didn't come to church today. That's the first time. I think he's really gone and joined the Mennonites."

"I guess we saw it coming, but still . . ." Sadie frowned. "Poor Sam. He's worried. It's hard, losing Isaac that way."

"Isaac will always be Sam's friend, always our cousin," Essie said. "There'll just have to be some changes if he leaves the Amish for good."

Sadie nodded, knowing that even the most rebellious teens found it hard to leave the Amish forever. It wasn't so much a matter of faith as a fear of leaving behind the way of life and the people and lifestyle you've always known. "I can't imagine leaving the Amish ways," Sadie said, "though Isaac has his reasons. He's such a help to folks. Remember at your wedding when I fainted? He knew exactly what to do."

"Once, after church, he stopped a little child from choking on a grape," Essie added. "And he saved Jerry Kraybill's life. That was amazing."

From what Sadie had heard, it was nothing short of a miracle. Isaac was a special person, for sure, but his choice made Sadie uncomfortable. "I can't imagine leaving the Amish. My family. You." She lowered her voice and added, "Sam."

Essie nodded. "You and I, we weren't much for rumspringa parties or nighttime frolics. We're good Amish girls," she said with a chuckle.

"Who become good Amish wives," Sadie added, prompting her friend to gasp and cover her mouth.

"Have you and Sam talked about it . . . getting married?" Essie asked.

Sadie grinned, her head bobbing up and down. "A little bit."

"Ach my! That's wonderful good news." Essie pushed her plate aside so that she could give Sadie a hug. "At last, my brother has stepped up. Gott has truly blessed us, Sadie. Blessed us with love."

"Love and friendship. We've had such good times, haven't we, Essie?" Sadie couldn't imagine how she'd have made it through the difficult years without her best friend.

"And Gott willing, there'll be more good times to come," Essie said.

"Gott willing."

That night Dat hitched Old Gray to the buggy and gave Sadie a ride to the Hostetler home. It was customary for an Amish girl to get a ride home from a suitor, and though Dat understood this, he didn't question the details. On the way, Sadie asked if Dat had gotten any employment leads for her coworker's beau.

"Nothing that a man could hang his hat on," Dat said as he steered the buggy toward town. "Plenty of farmers will be looking for day workers in the spring, but most

Amish have sons to do the heavy lifting, so they don't need anyone full-time."

"Well, you tried," Sadie said, staring out as they passed a field covered in snow with indigo shadows of trees cast by the moon in the evening dusk. "But I do feel sorry for Gerta and Abe. They're getting past marriage age, with no chance in sight if Abe can't find a job."

"It doesn't take money to get wed," Reuben said.

"It's a requirement for Abe. He knows he has to be a provider. Gerta says he's hardheaded that way."

"Some men are like that. It's not a bad quality." Dat lifted his free hand to adjust his hat. "You know, I've been thinking. We could use a good worker to take the lead with the new business."

"Cultivating the mushrooms and herbs?" Sadie swung round to face her dat. "I'm sorry, Dat. I should be helping more."

"You have your job at the pretzel factory, and you're a big help to your mem around the house. The truth is, the business is turning a good profit now, but it's hard to keep up. I thought I could pick up the slack, but since I've been working out back, I've had some dizziness. And I don't like what I see on that new blood pressure cuff your mem got me for Christmas."

"Dat! If your blood pressure's up, you need to pay attention. Stop working and take care of yourself."

"I know that, daughter. That's why it would be good to have a hired hand for the business. It would ease the burden on my shoulders, and give your mem a break, too."

"That sounds like a wonderful good plan," Sadie said. "So you'll meet with Abe to see if he fits the bill?"

"We will. I hope the young man's got a green thumb."

"You can teach him what he needs to know, and Mem will be a good boss. She's been bossing me around since I was a baby," she added with a chuckle.

Back at the Hostetler house, Sadie entered to find that, once again, the expansive common space had been transformed, this time with long tables and the hard wooden church benches for young people to sit on. The main feature of a singing was the relentless stream of songs, fast and slow, that were sung in German as everyone gathered round the table. The inclusion of some church songs made it a sanctioned activity. But for most Amish teens like Sadie, the socializing before and after were the big draw.

Immediately, Sadie searched the crowd for Sam. Most of the young folks were clumped together by gender, though there were some "couples" chatting, too. She saw that his sister Annie was here, so Sam had to be close by. They'd devised a plan for Sadie to leave with Annie so that no one would be wise to Sam and her. Sadie wished she could find Sam and stay by his side all night, but that couldn't happen just yet. At least the need for secrecy was becoming a game that added excitement to things.

Looking around the room for her buddy bunch, Sadie quickly remembered that dear Essie wouldn't be here, as now that she was married, she'd moved into a different phase of Amish life. It seemed strange to be socializing without Essie, but then it felt good to know her friend was at home with her true love, a man who was the perfect match for her.

"Sadie! Come!" Laura Kauffman called, waving from behind a pillar.

Sadie hurried over to join the conversation with Laura, Sam's sister Annie, and Suzie Yoder. Although Sadie worked with Suzie most days at the pretzel factory, it was unusual to see Suzie out and about socializing. Essie always explained that Suzie was still recovering from the buggy accident that had injured Suzie and her mother last year. Sadie didn't know the details of the injuries, but she gave Suzie lots of credit for making it to work day after day.

Annie gave Sadie a meaningful smile as she approached. Sadie linked arms with her and leaned close to whisper, "Where's Sam?"

With a glance around the room, Annie shrugged. "Outside, I guess."

"We were just talking about how we're sick of the snow," Laura said. "So beautiful, but it's so hard to get around."

"I always worry about traveling in bad weather," Suzie said. "It can be dangerous on the road." Ever since last year's buggy accident, Suzie was a nervous traveler any time of year.

"But when the snow makes everything smooth and white, it's such a sight," Sadie said. "It lifts my heart."

"I like it," Annie said. "If it's going to be cold, it might as well be pretty, too. And from what I saw today, it looks like we're in for more snow. All the cows were sitting down. That's how they keep warm. But everyone says it's a sign that a storm is coming."

"Is it true?" Suzie's eyes opened wide. "The cows tell you when it's going to snow?" She started to giggle. "That's the funniest thing I've heard in a long time. Cows giving you a message."

Laura laughed along, but Annie didn't see the humor in it. "Not so funny when you grow up on a farm. I'm going to get some punch."

"Me too," Laura said.

"Here's some good news for you, Suzie. I talked with

my dat, and he's looking to hire someone to cultivate our herbs and mushrooms. He said he'd interview Gerta's Abe first and give him a try."

"What? Is it a full-time job?"

Sadie nodded. "If Abe comes with a good recommendation, I'm sure Dat will take him on. I can't wait to tell Gerta."

"That's wonderful good news!" Suzie's eyes were bright with pleasure as she gave Sadie a quick hug. "You really came through on a promise, Sadie. Good on you!"

"I told Gerta I'd try. Just so happens Dat needs a hand with the business."

"But you did the asking, and Gott made it happen. That's the power of prayer!" As Suzie spoke, she flattened one hand against her face, cupping her cheek as if it ached. "You know I pray for all the girls at work every night. You're like my family, and I so want you all to be happy and have good things happen in your lives."

"You're such a good friend, Suzie." Sadie leaned in close to tuck tiny gold *schtruvvell*—stray hairs—in place behind Suzie's ear. Seeing the girl's face up close, Sadie was reminded that Suzie always wore a mask at work, and now her hand wouldn't leave her cheek. Was she trying to cover the small scar there? It was barely noticeable, but Sadie understood that folks saw things with different eyes. Maybe, to Suzie, it marred her face. Sadie knew no scar could detract from the sweet goodness of a young girl like Suzie, but then, when it came to courtship, all sorts of obstacles went into the odd mix between guys and girls.

"I'm glad to see you here tonight, Suzie. You know, I'm a pretty good matchmaker." Sadie stepped closer, lowering her voice confidentially. "Is there someone you're keeping an eye on? Someone you want to talk with? Maybe I could help break the ice."

Suzie's eyes grew round as quarters. "Oh, no. No, denki. I just like to come out for the music part. It's so much fun when everyone sings together."

As Suzie talked on, Sadie saw that Sam was in the room, grabbing some chips and pretzels. She was about to make her way over to him when she saw two young women dip over to chat with him.

Sadie tried to listen to Suzie while studying the exchange. Lily Myers said something with a brisk nod. All business.

Then June Hostetler moved in with that moony look in her eyes as she pretended Sam was the funniest person on earth. Her tinkling laugh was like fingernails on a chalkboard. Sam replied and then turned away, grabbing a drink.

Good, she thought with a sigh of relief.

But June struck again. She stalked him like a red fox trying to capture a rabbit. She followed him over to the drinks table and literally pounced on him, grabbing his arm. It was a wonder that Sam's drink didn't spill when she touched his sleeve.

Jealousy was a bitter taste in the back of her throat. *Don't be a jealous fool,* she told herself. At the end of the night, she would be in a buggy with Sam. Right now Sadie had to put it out of her mind and focus on sweet Suzie, who truly deserved her attention.

When it came time to sit at the long table, she planned to sit across from Sam, and she was moving in that direction until Annie gently whisked her aside and took the chair she wanted, forcing Sadie to sit farther away from Sam and gaze diagonally across the table at him. Well, that was for the best, as Sadie's feelings would surely slip out in two hours of sitting opposite Sam. And the chair Annie took gave her closer proximity to Zachary Coblentz, whom Annie seemed to like.

The singing went quick as lightning, with everyone singing along, often laughing and commenting between songs. It was one of the few times in Amish life when teenaged boys and girls could share a few joyful hours without the elders peering down on them. The songs always cheered Sadie up, but today there was the added thrill of a cat and mouse game with Sam, peering over at him, smiling, and then turning away before anyone else noticed.

When it was time to leave, Sam immediately left to head outside and start hitching up buggies. Sadie was one of the first young women to get up from the table and tell Annie it was time to go.

"I'll meet you out back," Annie told Sadie, who noticed Zachary waiting nearby to talk with Annie.

As Sadie let them be and went outside, she wondered if Zachary might ask to take Annie home in his buggy. She hoped Annie wasn't pushing him off just to take care of her.

As they were waiting, Kate Lambright emerged from the house and made a beeline over to her. Kate's golden hair and white prayer kapp were a halo that caught the glow of the moon. "I thought that was you, Sadie. I didn't expect to see you all alone tonight. Did you and Mark stop dating?"

Yes, it's over, Sadie wanted to answer. *And if you're interested in Mark Miller, please, pursue him.* Sadie longed to say those words, to make it all official and move on with her life. But it wouldn't be right. "Mark is away on business. He's helping his uncle open an auction house in Lititz."

"Is that right? That explains why he hasn't been in the diner for weeks." Kate's face was animated, her eyes bright. "You know, he loves our fried chicken. He makes it a point to stop in for lunch at least once a week, but he hasn't been in since before Christmas, I think."

"That explains it," Sadie agreed. She couldn't tell if Kate had a bit of a crush on Mark or if she was just one of those friendly people who liked everyone. Just talking about Mark felt odd now, as if she were discussing a stranger. "When he returns, I'm sure he'll be back in line at the diner."

"I hope so." Kate's enthusiasm was so genuine, so earnest. Sadie felt a little sorry for her. The girl seemed to believe that Mark's outgoing, charming personality was there all the time. She'd probably never seen the dark side Sadie had come to know.

Just then Jacob called to them. Their buggy was ready. Sadie climbed into the buggy and watched Kate go off to talk with another cluster of young women. Kate reminded Sadie of herself a few years ago. At the end of every singing, when guys and gals paired off to ride home together, Sadie used to feel such a longing to have someone special to ride home with. It was the dream of most young Amish women to meet their mate—a single man who would be a good husband and partner through life. Sadie's desire for a beau had been so strong, she'd been willing to overlook Mark's bad moods.

She wished the best for Kate. Dating could be such a difficult, twisted path for Amish girls, and yet it was one of the most important things—finding a husband who was a good match. When she thought of Sam, Sadie knew she'd been blessed by Gott.

Sadie and Annie shared the lap blanket during the

peaceful ride. Annie was a girl of few words, a quality that used to make Sadie a bit uncomfortable until she realized that Annie spoke when necessary but seemed to like the quiet spaces in between. It had been a lesson to Sadie about understanding other people. She now realized that people were largely in their own worlds and that just because someone didn't reach out to her didn't mean that they disliked her.

For a while there was a line of slow-moving buggies behind them. One by one, they turned off until there was just one set of buggy lights following them on the road. A few cars passed, but that buggy stayed with them. Sam's buggy. Sadie hugged her coat tighter round her, secure in the knowledge that they'd be together soon.

At last they reached Harris Bridge, the river crossing that always signaled to Sadie that they'd reached the edge of town. Inside the bridge, Sadie held her breath as the buggy lights cast long shadows on the wooden walls. The horse's hooves clacked loudly on the wood-planked roadway. They quickly emerged into the winter night again, and Sadie drew in a breath of cold air. At last, it was time.

Annie worked the reins, expertly guiding the horse off the road to the little parking area where the snow had been cleared. A minute later, Sam's buggy was clunking over the bridge.

"Denki, Annie," Sadie said as she removed the lap blanket. "Maybe next singing you'll be getting a ride home with Zachary."

"We just like to talk," Annie claimed. "I'm not going to date him or anything."

"And why not? This is the time to get to know a guy better. If you like to talk, that means you like to spend time with him."

Annie shook her head. "Nay."

Sadie smiled, realizing she had some work ahead of her if her friends were going to find their matches in life. "Well, thanks for helping Sam and me keep our secret." Sadie climbed down from the buggy and turned toward the road. She could hear Annie's buggy leaving behind her, but her eyes were on the light of the approaching buggy.

All the sacrifice aside, it was incredibly romantic to be meeting Sam by the bridge after dark. All her life, Sadie had never lived beyond the norm of a typical Amish girl, but now, her life and love were wrapped in this bit of mystery, a special secret that they shared.

Her pulse raced a bit as Sam halted the buggy and jumped down. "Hurry, Sadie. Before a dozen buggies happen along and catch us on their way home from the singing!"

She raced through the cold night and climbed in before anyone could see. Sam was suddenly beside her, his face inches from hers as he settled his arms around her.

"I thought we'd never be together again," she whispered.

"But now I've got you at last!" His arms brought her close to his warm body, igniting a heat inside her that was comforting and exciting. Gazing up at him, she had just a brief moment to see the spark of love in his eyes before she closed hers and lost herself in his kiss.

The heavenly moment ended too soon, as a wind gust whistled through the crevices of the buggy, causing her to shudder.

"Okay, let's get you warm." He pulled the lap blanket over them, leaving a generous amount on Sadie's side for her to tuck around her legs.

She thanked him, and he called to the horse and got the buggy moving as they saw lights approaching from the distance. "Maybe next singing we should do the switch in a more out-of-the-way place," he said.

"If Mark isn't back by the next singing, I think I'm going to have to stay home," she told him. "It's hard for me to be in the same room with you and not let on that I'm head over heels in love with you."

Sam smiled as he put an arm around her shoulders and pulled her close. "So you saw June Hostetler make a move."

"I did, indeed. I was about to part the crowd, run straight through, and let her know you aren't eligible anymore."

Sam chuckled. "That's a sight I'd like to see."

"It wouldn't have been my best moment," Sadie admitted. "But somehow, I held back."

"Willpower," he said. "It's a good thing."

"It may be good, but I've barely got a drop left."

"Then I'll just have to loan you some of mine," he teased, and they laughed together as the horse took their buggy off into the winter night.

Chapter 26

"This is a great essay," Megan said. "You focused on your goal to help people, and you gave a little bit of your background growing up Amish." Isaac had scratched out the essay on a yellow pad of paper, and Megan had helped him add it into the online college application on the library computer. "It's just the sort of thing people enjoy reading, a true slice-of-life story," Megan added.

Isaac looked back at the monitor, rubbing his knuckles against his chin. "Personally, I'd rather have a slice of pie than a slice of life."

Megan chuckled. "You're just being modest. Trust me on this. Between your grades and your unusual background, the university will recognize your potential as a student who can make great contributions."

"So . . ." He scrolled through the application on the screen, his fingers surprisingly adroit on the keyboard. "Is it ready to send?"

"It's a go." They'd worked on the application together, proofreading and making corrections a few times. "Go on and click Send."

"Here goes. One click, and I'm off to college." He clicked

the mouse, and the screen indicated that the application was submitted.

Megan took in a breath, giddy at the prospect of the two of them going to college together. When she thought of other guys she'd dated, the idea of doing college together would have cloyed at her sense of independence, but this felt right. She and Isaac worked well together. As a twin, Megan had always understood the value of teamwork.

He frowned at the screen. "It seems too easy. What if they don't receive my application on the college computer?"

"They will," Megan assured him, though she was always intrigued by his vision of the Internet. "You'll get a confirmation on that email account we set up. And if you don't hear from them for a while, you can always send them an email message to check in."

"Thanks for helping me, Megs. If you hadn't suggested this, I would never have applied."

"I'm glad you did. But if you get in, do you think you'll go for it? Would you really leave your family and friends in Joyful River and go to East Stroudsburg?"

"Since I'm not joining the church, it would probably be best for me to leave here for a while. Not that I wouldn't come back. There's a lot to love in Joyful River. But since I'm going against what folks expect, I'd rather be out of the way while my friends are getting baptized. It might ease the embarrassment for my dat and stepmother."

Studying his handsome face, Megan was intrigued by his quiet confidence—the conviction in his vision, the peace in his demeanor. He knew what direction his life should take, and he was willing to face obstacles to get there. He had the heart of a rebel wrapped in a nerdy, handsome exterior, and she was a sucker for the combination.

They exchanged essays they were working on for the

composition class they had together, then Isaac got up to leave. "I'm on duty tonight with the ambulance corps," he said. "But I'll see you in class tomorrow. And don't forget—the tournament at Myers Pond starts Friday."

"Can't wait," Megan said, watching him go.

As Isaac passed the main desk, two heads popped up over the divider.

Serena and Grace giggled, their faces bright with smiles.

"You guys! I didn't see you come in. And you were listening all this time?"

"Well, we weren't going to sit right beside you and Isaac," Serena said, grabbing her books and coming around to take the seat Isaac had vacated. "Besides, we don't have any secrets."

"Secrets are one thing," Megan said. "Privacy is another. I don't snoop on you and Scout."

"You can't snoop in a public place," Grace pointed out, landing in the cubicle beside Megan. "Besides, we know you're planning to attend East Stroudsburg. No reason to explain that. Though Isaac is a surprise."

"How did you convince an Amish guy to go to college?" Serena asked.

"I didn't. He's been attending for a while."

"But a four-year college," Grace said, "Sounds like a big deal to me."

"And he's going with you," Serena said. "Sounds to me like a boyfriend."

Megan tilted her head and met her sister's eyes. "He is."

"I thought so," Grace said.

"Holy cow! I didn't know." Serena's eyes opened wide in surprise. "Are you going to turn Amish for him? You'll have to grow your hair out really long and start wearing dresses."

Megan rolled her eyes. "I don't think it's quite as simple as flipping a switch or growing out my hair."

Serena giggled. "You'll look adorable in one of those thin white prayer caps with the thin stringy things."

"Stop, already. I'm not going to become Amish, though I'd like to stay in Lancaster County. I think rural, small-town life is good for me. Living here in Joyful River forced me to reprioritize things. Figure out what really mattered." She looked up at her sisters. "You guys and Dad are numero uno, of course. And Aunt Miriam and Uncle Alvie and our Amish cousins. We'll never be Amish, but they love us just as we are. That's a really special gift."

"We're so lucky." The light twinkled in Serena's eyes, and Megan realized there were tears there. "Our Amish family saved us when we needed a home. I'm getting all misty just thinking about it, but I know what you mean," Serena said. "Living here, I feel like there's more time and space to experience life. People are earnest—sometimes so honest it's embarrassing. Aunt Miriam makes me feel so good about myself, and I feel like Scout has become my North Star. If I move too far away, I'm afraid I'll lose all sense of direction. I know that probably sounds crazy."

"It's not crazy at all," Grace said. "Love is never crazy. You should make a plan that won't take you too far away from Scout."

Megan rubbed her sister's shoulder. "I wish you'd apply to East Stroudsburg, too. We could room together."

"I think it's time that I did my own thing, though I don't know what that is," said Serena. "I wish I could stay here and go to college, but there's nothing nearby."

"You could do online community college," Megan suggested. "That way, you can be near Scout, and keep your business going." Serena seemed to find comfort in restoring old furniture, and so far her hobby had been lucrative, too.

"That might work." Serena shook her head. "Right now I'm more concerned about getting this history assignment done."

"I'll proofread it for you when you're finished," Megan offered as they settled in and logged onto the computers.

Grace was digging for a book in her backpack when she asked why Isaac was allowed to go to college, when other Amish students finished school after eighth grade.

"Isaac is leaving the Amish faith—he's bucking the system. He believes in God, but he's made the decision to forgo baptism in the Amish church and continue his education."

"Wow. He's leaving? So he's going to be shunned. That's so awful." Grace shook her head, disapproval apparent in her stern expression. "I've heard about shunning. Isaac won't be able to have dinner with his family anymore. They can't eat the same food."

"It's not like that." Megan had made the same assumption early on, but Isaac had set her straight on the consequences of declining to get baptized. "Shunning happens to Amish people who have joined the church. If he doesn't choose baptism, he's not violating his faith by leaving the community. So he won't be banned, and his parents don't need to kick him out of the house or the family."

"Oh. So wait, they won't be mad at him?" Serena asked.

Megan shrugged. "Sounds like some people are going to be upset. Amish parents want their kids to follow in their footsteps and stay in the religious community. But it's Isaac's choice. His parents might be disappointed, but they don't have to disown him."

"That sounds scary," Grace said.

"It can't be an easy choice," Megan agreed. But having seen Isaac in action during more than one medical emergency, she understood that deep-seated motivations guided his decision. He had a vocation—a conviction that he'd been called by God to take care of people.

The day of the tournament dawned clear and bright, though temperatures still lingered in the thirties. Myers Pond was much busier and better organized than Megan had expected. On the way down the hill from the parking lot they passed a building with restrooms, an outdoor pavilion with picnic tables, and a firepit, where a few people were currently huddled, seeking warmth. Sam explained that the picnic areas were often crowded in the summer months, when the pond was a popular swimming spot. The pond itself was huge, doglegging in a Z shape beyond tall, majestic pine trees. The front section of the pond that was visible from the entrance was open to regular ice-skaters, while the back areas of the pond—space for two hockey arenas—were marked off with orange traffic cones for hockey players only.

At the moment the ice in the hockey section was empty but for ice-tenders who skated the pond pushing wide brooms to clear the ice of snow and debris. A cute little snack booth sold hot cocoa, tea, hot pretzels, and hotdogs— which seemed to be a hit with the skaters.

"They set up a snack booth just for the tournament?" Meg asked.

"Nay," Sam answered as they laced up their skates on a bench. "The pond is open to skaters all winter, for a fee. Folks like it, especially with the lights. You can skate at night."

"But we skate at the Lapp pond, where the price is right," Isaac added.

As they were lacing up their skates, a bearded guy with a clipboard came over and talked with Sam about the schedule. Isaac explained that Zach was the tournament organizer, and a skilled hockey player himself. Their game was next on the back pond, as soon as the current match ended.

With skates laced and helmets and pads strapped on, Megan, Sam, and Isaac set out to warm up on the ice. As she stretched her muscles and got her ice bearings, Megan observed the local kids goofing around on the ice. A line of girls skated together, holding hands, while a small group of boys whipped one another around, sending their friends off with crazy speed. Some couples skated together, and over by the rails at the snack bar, new skaters tried to keep their balance, stiff-legged as their arms flailed in the air. Megan enjoyed watching the skaters, especially the antics of the boys, who reminded her of her own behavior at that age. The festive scene showed just how eager people were to get outside after the big snow.

Once they were warmed up, they crossed the orange cones and then walked along the snowpack on the side of the pond to watch the last part of the match. Megan appreciated the skills of the players, but she had long ago realized she was a terrible spectator. After her ACL injury, she'd been unable to attend her team's matches to root them on—not because of her injury, but because of her frustration over being forced to sit on the sidelines and watch the action from afar. Megan moved from foot to foot, digging her skates into the hardpack and itching to get on the ice and start the match. The nervous jitters in her chest would melt away once the game started. She was a competitor at heart, but she was relatively new to this sport. Pounding her feet, she said a silent prayer that she didn't let her team down.

At last, the previous match ended and Megan's team took to the ice, ready to start their match against the Maple Run team, who looked impressive.

"They've got uniforms," Isaac pointed out as the Maple Run team skated a lap around them. "Pretty fancy."

"They've also got a name," Megan said with a grin. "I mean, what are we called? Sam's team?"

Isaac smiled. "Doesn't matter. Pretty looks only get you so far. The proof is in the playing."

Megan gave him a nod, then got in position as the ref blew his whistle to start the game.

When the final whistle blew, Sam's Joyful River team was ahead by one goal.

"Yes!" Megan shouted, her arms up in the air. The adrenaline rush was pumping through her body over the thrill of victory. They'd won their first game!

The competition had been stiff; the Maple Run players had played hard and put up a good fight. Megan had heard that one of the Englisch players had flooded his backyard and made a hockey rink for team practices. Well, their hard work had shown, but in the end an assist from Megan and a goal by Isaac had won the game.

"Good game!" Isaac called to one of the Maple Run players.

"Nice one," Sam said, slapping an opponent a high five.

Megan joined in the handshakes with opposing players.

Although Megan had played with her team for a few weeks, it had taken the game against outsiders to crystallize a few observations. Although the Amish played with great zeal—especially Pete and Paul, who had the fervor of youth in their favor—they didn't attach huge importance to winning. Yes, they enjoyed being in the thick of a good game, but the act of playing held the joy for them—not the win. The Amish respected the referees and didn't argue about outcomes—unlike the Englisch guys who were mixed in on the opposing team.

There was one Maple Run player who'd kept arguing the referee's calls. Megan assumed he wasn't Amish, as his attitude sucked, and the back of his jersey was emblazoned with the name "Blondie."

"Mad skills out there," Megan said as he skated by her. "You kept us on our toes, Blondie."

He turned, stared at her, and continued skating away.

"Oh, well," she said to herself. Someone was not happy.

Just then one of the other Maple Run players skated up to her and stared with a curious expression. "Wait a minute. You're a girl."

Megan smiled as she unstrapped her helmet and ran a hand through her short hair. "I am."

Blondie did a U-turn and skated back to the center of the ice. With his helmet off, the blond player was clearly not Amish. His hair was trimmed short on the sides, with a pile of golden locks on top of his head, and his left ear was pierced with diamond studs. "That's not fair, guys," he said. "You didn't tell us you had a girl on your team." Blondie squinted as he sniped at her. "They kept calling you Max."

"Megs," she said. "Short for Megan. I'm a girl, all right, but I've come to love the game. My cousins taught me."

"And she's a good player," Paul said, skating into the center of the group.

"She's been practicing with us for weeks. She's part of our team," Sam said.

"Megs can skate circles around most guys," Peter insisted.

The blond player tipped his helmet back and put a hand on one hip. "I'm just saying that girls aren't supposed to be in the tournament. There are rules about things like that."

An awkward silence fell on the group as heads turned toward Megan. Suddenly, the heat of the dispute was on her. Part of her wanted to snap back at Blondie, tell him that she had the same right to play in the tournament as any man here. Which she did. But she honestly didn't know if there was a rule about gender. And she definitely didn't want to jeopardize her team's ranking in the tournament.

"Let's calm down now," Isaac said. "To be honest, I've checked the rules, and there's no mention of gender. Nothing that says the players have to be male."

"It's a tradition," Blondie said.

"Ach, come on, Chip." One of Blondie's teammates elbowed him. "Don't be a sore loser."

"I'm just calling out what's not fair," Chip insisted.

Just then the organizer skated over to the group. "Good game," Zach said. "Right now, I need you all to move to the other side of the orange cones, as we've got another game starting here. Over there."

"Come on, guys." Isaac waved everyone over. "Let's go."

The group obeyed promptly, skating beyond the cones and reassembling on the public part of the pond.

"Thanks for that!" Zach said, looking at his clipboard. "So . . . Sam, your team will play one more game tonight, and then if you win, another in the morning. Good game!" He skated off.

"Wait up! Hold on, Zach," Chip called after him. "We've got a cheating issue here." Chip held up one hand and pointed at Megan. "They've got a girl on their team."

Zach nodded at Megan. "I noticed. And a skilled player. It was a close match, but your team toughed it out there."

"Thanks," Megan said.

"But isn't there a rule against girls playing?" Chip raised his chin, making it more of a statement than a question. "We don't allow girls."

"Our tournament rules are focused on good sportsmanship. We accept players as they are, as long as they behave out on the ice." Zach patted Chip on the back. "You know, I have a younger sister who grew up playing hockey. She's never played in a tournament, but maybe now she'll consider it."

As Zach skated off, Megan extended a hand to Chip. "Good game, Chip. You guys pushed us to a new level."

There was a tense silence as Chip stared hard at her, still not happy. Then he let out a breath and took her hand. "Yeah, good game."

"All right!" Isaac said as the guys on the ice started talking and laughing.

Tension drained from Megan's shoulders. As she turned to Sam and Isaac, she felt like she could finally breathe again.

"You look like you're in shock," Isaac said.

"I was scared that you guys would get disqualified because of me," she said under her breath.

"You worry too much, Megs," Sam said.

Just then, Pete and Paul skated over with the announcement that they wanted to get food from the snack shack, and that Annie and Sadie were here, and they'd watched the last period of the match, and they wanted food, too.

"They're here? Where?" Sam looked up and skated off to join them.

Megan looked over to the edge of the ice and gave a wave to the girls. She expected her own sisters to come by, and Essie and Harlan, too, but not until the evening. Serena and Scout figured that ice skating and a bonfire might be the highlight of their weekend. Such a change from the party girl Serena had once been. A good change. Sometimes Megan found it hard to fathom that she and her twin would be attending different schools come September, but since they'd arrived here they had ventured in different directions. Not that they didn't have each other's backs. Their bond ran deep. But much of Serena's world involved Scout and her new business. Megan wasn't sure what her sister would do after high school graduation, but she felt grateful for one thing: Serena had met a guy who got her, who laughed at her jokes and appreciated her scattered bursts of energy and enthusiasm. In the world of love, Serena had met her match.

Megan stowed her equipment in her big duffel bag and pulled a fluffy wool cap onto her head—a hat knitted with love by Aunt Miriam. So many things had changed in the past few months. Megan still dealt with waves of anxiety at times, but mostly she felt a new freedom here.

Like a bird trapped in a cage and flapping its wings but getting nowhere, she'd been stuck in a prison of her own making, her own bad habits. But here in Joyful River, she was able to spread her wings and soar.

"Do you want to get a hotdog?" Isaac asked. "My treat."

Suddenly, she realized she was starving. "I would love that," she said, falling into step beside him.

Chapter 27

Sadie took in the happy, apple-cheeked faces gathered round the bonfire as they ate hotdogs, soft pretzels, and slices of pizza. These were good friends, and her heart sang with joy at the merriment of their jokes and laughter. Having just arrived, Essie and Harlan were soaking up the highlights of the team's first game. Sam and Megan were expounding on the small moments in their victory, while Isaac, ever the sage voice of reason, kept their drama in check. Pete and Paul added a few poignant details, but mostly they concentrated on feeding a voracious appetite that an entire pizza pie barely quenched. Annie was joining in the fun, which delighted Sadie, who believed Sam's teenage sister needed to socialize more and join in the fun activities now that she was in her rumspringa.

Such a good group of people!

But the shining star in her sky was Sam, who sat beside her, his thigh touching hers on the bench in the most subtle way. No one else seemed to notice, thank goodness, but Sadie savored the glow of warmth passing from Sam to her, a beam of love that went straight to her heart.

She still longed for the day when she would be free to

be Sam's girl in public, but she had come to be grateful that they had time together—quiet time alone, too—and their relationship was progressing, even as they kept it out of the public eye.

"When does our next match start?" Peter asked, holding a half-eaten hotdog in midair.

"Probably an hour or so." Sam squinted at his brother. "So you might want to stop eating soon. You don't want a lead belly weighing you down on the ice."

"But I'm still hungry," Pete protested.

"And that's your third hotdog? You'll survive for a few more hours," Essie told her younger brother. "Really Peter, this isn't your last meal. I'm sure Mem will have dinner waiting when you get home."

Paul stood up and stretched with a growl. "You have to sacrifice to be a top athlete."

"All right," Pete said, wrapping the hotdog back in its paper and handing it to Essie. "Hold this for me until after the game."

Essie gingerly accepted it, shaking her head. "The things we do for family . . ."

Sadie and Sam were chuckling as the group started to rise and tidy up the area. Sam and the team were headed back to the pond to do some practice drills before the game. Essie and Harlan were going to take a walk and explore, and Annie decided to go back to the snack bar to get another hot cocoa. Sadie chose to stay by the bonfire for a bit.

"We'll all meet back here in a few minutes," Essie said.

As Sadie settled in by the fire, she felt grateful to be here on a Friday afternoon. Smitty had been generous enough to let her leave work early, though he teased her that never before had she asked for a day off. She'd replied that she wouldn't want to be away from a job that she loved so much, and though they'd both laughed at her joke, Sadie knew there was a grain of truth to it.

She enjoyed her job, and spending time with her co-workers made the days go quickly. It was hardly a chore to chat with folks, give tours, or twist dough into pretzel shapes as she talked with the other girls. Sometimes they helped each other through bad patches, and other times they laughed until their bellies ached. Just this week Dat had told Sadie that he wanted to hire Abe Peachy, and since then Gerta had been walking on air. She told the girls they'd certainly be invited to her wedding, and she didn't know if she'd return to the pretzel factory once she was a wife.

Sadie wondered about that for herself now, as the sun faded and a pearly winter sky brought a new chill. She decided it would be good to stay on at work after she married. She and Sam could use the money, of course, and it would bring joy to her days to see her friends. Of course, the factory job would be fine until a baby came along . . .

"Sadie?" The familiar voice pulled her from her thoughts even as it chilled her. She looked up and saw him looming closer, his eyes dark as his black hat.

"Mark!" Sadie put a gloved hand up to cover her surprise. She'd been so wrapped up in Sam's game and the winter festivities that the last thing she had expected was to see Mark back in town—and here, of all places, attending the tournament. She glanced around quickly, searching for a friendly face she could use as an excuse to escape him quickly, but all her friends had dispersed.

"Sadie." He took a seat near her on the bench, sitting close to the spot where Sam had been. "I've been looking for you."

"It's good to see you." Sadie gave him a friendly smile. "When did you return from Lititz?"

"Earlier today. I stopped by your house, and your mem told me you were here."

"Did she?" Sadie could imagine Mem's awkwardness, trying to field questions from Mark. "She must have been surprised to see you. You got my note, right? And the clock?"

He turned away from her and gestured toward the outdoor ice rink. "I thought I'd come watch the tournament, come reacquaint with all my friends. I've been gone so long. Lititz is nice, but I've missed this place. I've missed you." When he turned back to her, she saw sorrow in his eyes.

Compassion stabbed at her heart. "It has been such a long time," Sadie agreed. An eternity, during which she'd fallen head over heels in love and had started planning a life with Sam. She couldn't begin to explain that to Mark. "How's the new auction house?" she asked, trying to find a safe topic. "Will they be up and running for the spring season?"

"Seems like it. It's really up to Cousin Tom and Uncle Noland now. I taught them what I know as fast as I could, so that I could get back here . . . back to you, Sadie."

She tilted her head to one side, feeling sorry not for loving Sam but for disrupting Mark's plans. "Did your mem tell you I stopped by to ask about you?" she asked. When he gave a pronounced nod, she added, "She gave you my note, right? And the clock?"

"She did. When I saw them, I set out to find you. I knew we would need to talk."

"Okay." She glanced at the ground and swallowed, trying to get past the tightness in her throat. She hated this awkwardness, hated seeing the sadness in his eyes.

She felt sorry for him, but the sooner he accepted things and moved on, the sooner he'd come to find happiness. "What did you want to say?"

"I can't say it here." Drawing his scarf closer around his neck, he gestured to the people sitting near the bonfire. The boys grouped there were eating their lunches and poking at one another, but there were a few big-shouldered hockey players in padded uniforms who seemed a bit curious. "Can't we go for a ride? I have a horse and buggy here."

"I don't know." She couldn't admit that she didn't want to miss Sam's next game. "Maybe we could find a quiet place here?"

"Where?" He gestured to the pond. "There are people everywhere."

She looked beyond him, taking in the activity of ice skaters, the line at the snack shack, the children chasing each other on the frozen pond, the people heading up to the firepit and restrooms. Was that Annie coming up the path, holding two steaming cups in her hands? Sadie waved at her, but Annie's head was down as she made her way, and she didn't respond.

"Who are you waving to?" he asked.

"It's just Annie Lapp. We came here together, and she might be looking for me. But you're right. It's crowded here."

"Come. We'll take a ride."

Reluctantly, Sadie nodded, falling into step beside Mark.

He was silent as they walked the path to the buggy park. Once they reached the head of the path and she saw his horse tied to a post, still hitched to the buggy, a thorn of wariness pierced her. Mark hadn't planned to stay. Had he come here to join in the activities, or simply to fetch her?

"See?" Mark taunted the hostlers who had been minding his horse for him. "I told you I wouldn't be long."

"Yah, that's what you said," one of the teenage boys called, walking away from the horse as if he didn't want to be involved.

Tension knotted in Sadie's throat. Although she had stopped dead in her tracks, it took Mark a moment to notice and turn back to her. "What are you waiting for?"

"I think it's better if we talk right here." She folded her arms and tried to stop shivering, knowing that her body was quaking not from the cold but from a rising fear.

He stepped closer and lowered his voice as a group of young men jumped down from their buggy and handed it off to the hostlers. "You want to talk here, in front of everyone? I think that would be a might embarrassing for both you and me."

Looking around at the young people still arriving, Sadie knew he was right. This had to be put to rest. She would simply do her best to soothe Mark's hurt feelings and try to keep their conversation short. "I guess you're right," she said.

"I always am," he said, his sorrow melding into the hardened edges she had come to dread.

She climbed onto the front bench of the buggy and noted that the seats had been covered in a new rich, velvety upholstery. Only the best for the Miller family.

When he reached over to put her half of the blanket on her lap, Sadie felt a tinge of shame. Maybe she shouldn't be doing this. Was Mark mistaking her cooperation for interest? She just wanted to do the right thing, but suddenly that wasn't clear in her mind.

Worrying the edges of the blanket with her fingertips, she turned to the Plexiglas window and searched for signs of normalcy, something reassuring to let her know that she'd made the right choice.

Instead, she saw Sam coming up the path. He was running as best he could in his skates, running and scanning the buggy park. Searching for her; she knew that.

Something cracked inside her as Sam looked up and recognized her in the buggy. She pressed her hands to the window, wishing she could reach for him. Suddenly it was clear that she'd made the wrong decision. This wasn't a good idea. "Mark, stop," she said with a voice of firm resolve. "Stop the buggy."

"Not yet."

She turned to him, confused. "I'm getting out. Put the brake on."

With a cruel, cold laugh, Mark turned from her and urged the horse to a gallop.

Chapter 28

"Sadie!" Sam shouted after her. "Sadie, wait!"

He burst into the parking lot and ran along after them, as much as he could run in his hockey skates, but Miller only increased in speed, and the buggy raced ahead.

Sam was left behind, forced to stand back as the buggy bounced over icy mounds on the frozen ground. His heart hammered in his chest, pounding with the urgency he'd seen in Sadie's face. Something was wrong. He sensed that she was in danger, which seemed to align with Mark Miller's way of playing things fast and loose. Sam had witnessed his small cruelties, underlining the need to get to Sadie—and fast.

It had been Annie who'd tipped him off that there was trouble brewing. She'd seen Mark Miller approach Sadie at the bonfire, a dark purpose in his demeanor. "Maybe it's nothing, Sam," Annie had told him, "but something about him scares me. I'm worried about Sadie. Why did she leave with him?"

Sam couldn't answer. He'd had only questions as he'd struggled up the path in his skates and made it to the parking lot just in time to see Miller's buggy heading off. He hadn't been sure what to think, until Sadie appeared in the Plexiglas window. Spotting him, she gave a frantic wave, as if reaching for him through the transparent shield.

"Sadie . . ."

Something was wrong. He had to go after her.

Knowing there was no time to hitch up his own buggy, Sam scanned the parking lot and saw two girls who were leaving—two girls that he knew—the bishop's daughters.

He made quick work of begging their help, and they welcomed him in.

"If you've got a mind to catch Mark Miller's buggy, you'd best get in the front seat and drive," Amy Troyer told him. "Tess and I aren't speedy drivers like you fellas."

"Denki." Sam climbed into the front seat and took the reins.

Amy gave him an odd look as he urged the horse forward. "You're still wearing your skates."

"Yah. I left in a hurry," he said. "I'm worried about my friend."

"What are you worried about?" Tess asked from the back.

"The young man she's gone off with, he has a dark side. A temper." Had he said too much? This wasn't something that Amish folk discussed.

"Mmm." Tess's response showed concern and discomfort. As the bishop's daughter, she probably hadn't crossed too many people like Mark Miller.

"That sounds serious," Amy said, turning back to look at her sister in the second seat. "If we're going to catch them, you'd best have Star let loose."

"Heeyah!" Sam shouted at the horse, taking her advice. He appreciated their help, as well as their relative silence as they pursued the buggy down the country road. The last thing he needed right now, when he was concerned about Sadie, was a couple of chatterboxes with a million questions. He had seen Mark's bad behavior in the past—his cruelty—and Sadie had mentioned a few disturbing incidents that had happened during Mark's dark moods.

Sam felt sick at the prospect that Mark was in a foul mood right now. From the way Mark's buggy had torn out of the parking lot, Sam had reason to be concerned.

That Sadie might be the target of his fury.

"We just need to catch up with them," he muttered tensely under his breath. He was going to stop the buggy, have a civil talk with Mark, and take Sadie home. Actually, maybe there was a silver lining to this. Mark had returned, and once Sadie set things straight with him, she would be free to appear with Sam in public.

A simple plan—as long as he could catch them.

Chapter 29

"Mark! Please, slow down." Teeth rattling, bones jarring, Sadie held fast to the edge of the seat as the buggy throttled at full speed down the road.

He'd done this to her once before, after a singing where she'd chatted for a while with Jacob Kraybill. Since everyone at that time knew that Jacob was in love with his girl and that Sadie was dating Mark, Sadie hadn't thought it would be an issue at all. But Mark had been afire with jealousy, as if it had burned away his humor and common sense.

There was a similar blaze of fury in his eyes now as he glared at her. He was trying to scare her, and though it was working, she didn't want to admit it. She met his anger with a scolding look of her own, which seemed to register, as he slowed the horse to a reasonable pace. It was still brisk, but at least the jolting had eased.

"What's the problem, Mark?" Sadie tried to keep her cool, but a shrill note seeped into her voice. "You're driving like a wild man, and you know there's still ice on the roads."

"Always so reasonable," he muttered. "Simple Sadie.

Your type is the salt of the earth, except when a man leaves town for a bit. I never figured you to be a two-timer, seeing someone else behind my back."

"That's not what happened, Mark, and you know it. As I explained in the note, we're better off apart. Your time in Lititz proved that, don't you think? I mean, you went away without saying goodbye or even telling me you were going, and you didn't call or write a lick while you were gone."

"I gave you that clock. I trusted you to be here for me when I came back."

"The clock was returned, and really, Mark, we didn't have much going on between us before you left. It's better off this way."

"We were engaged." There was a grinding sound in his dark voice, like metal gears grinding on a tractor. "We were going to get married."

"That was the dream, maybe, but never a reality. You didn't ask me to marry you."

"I gave you a clock."

"It was a gesture, but there was no agreement. You're upset," she said cautiously, "but you've no need to be, Mark. Don't be cross about this."

"Don't tell me what I should and shouldn't be," he growled. "I'm not the one who took up with someone else while we were engaged. I've heard the stories about you and Sam. How you're at that farm all the time. I know you spend some nights there. You always have. How long has this been going on behind my back?"

"It's not that way. I wasn't involved with Sam when you and I were dating."

"But you nearly live at the Lapp farm. You always have."

His accusations hurt her, but even worse, it made her sad to realize he hadn't understood her need to escape her own home when they'd first started dating. So many of the times when she'd stayed at the Lapp farm, she'd been dodging her dat's bad mood or her parents' arguments. "You know Essie's my best friend. She's the one I stayed with."

"Until you got your hooks in Sam." His eyes glittered, dark and menacing. "I never expected you to cheat on me, Sadie. Not you. But you made a fool of me, and you've ruined your own reputation."

His full-blown anger struck her like a physical blow. How could he think such things? She lowered her voice, hoping to calm him. "Mark . . . no. None of that is true." She noticed the countryside still rushing past: frozen fields, mile markers, snow-covered barns. "Please, slow the poor horse and turn around. Take me back to Myers Pond and we'll finish talking there."

"I'm not taking you back to your friends and Sam and those meathead hockey players. Don't you see that I'm better than all of them? Hayseeds. They don't understand about business. They don't know what it takes to sell to the Englisch, to increase profits and sell smart. Some of them live hand to mouth."

"And what's wrong with that? We're plain folk."

"Do you know that some of the Englisch think Amish folks are stupid? Thick in the head. And you know why they think that? Because Amish don't understand the value of things in this world."

"But we know who we are, and we're secure in that knowledge." Sadie suspected that Mark's business dealings had shifted his values. "The Bible says we should store up our treasures not on earth, but in heaven, where they're safe from moths and thieves and vermin." It was a Bible verse in Matthew that Amish children were taught when plain living was discussed, a notion that Sadie had latched onto as a child. "'For where your treasure is, there your heart will be also.'"

"Ach! Don't preach at me." He waved her off as if she were a pesky fly. "You're just like the rest of them. No appreciation for nice things. And now you've gone and ruined things for both of us. You think you can break up with me? I can't have people thinking that."

"No one has to know."

"They know already, thanks to you. Spending all your time at the Lapp farm so everyone knew what you were up to."

"I went to work every day, and I live with my parents," she argued. "I have fallen for Sam, but we didn't go out together in public. I did everything I could to wait. I wanted you to know where we stood first."

"Everyone knows. That's why you give me no choice."

There was no reasoning with him; Sadie could see that now. As they passed a historic river house that used to be a cider mill for apples, she could see that they were approaching Joyful River. "Where are we going?" she asked.

"Stop talking," he said. "I can't take one more word from you."

When she turned to him, he stared ahead with gritted teeth as the cider mill faded behind them and Harris Bridge appeared. Its bright red paint was a cheerful beacon on the otherwise glum winter landscape of snow and frozen muck, but nothing could ease the tension in the buggy at this moment.

Hugging herself against the cold and fear, Sadie stared at the winter landscape, desperate to reach Mark but afraid that further conversation would aggravate him more. When he slowed the buggy, it gave her hope. "We're stopping?"

she asked, her mind racing ahead with a plan. She would get out and walk—leave—at least she'd be free and safe on her own. She might get help from a passing buggy, and if not, she could certainly make it home. She had walked miles before; she could do it again.

"The covered bridge," he said. "The place where I gave you the clock. Or have you forgotten that, along with your promise to me?"

"There was no promise made," she said firmly.

"That's what you plain folk don't understand. The implied promise in a deal." He steered the horse into the small parking field beside the bridge, coaxed the horse to halt, and jumped down. "We're going up to the covered bridge," he said as he secured the reins to a post.

Sadie stood her ground. "I'm not going anywhere with you." Once he was out of sight, she would leave.

"Don't you want to witness the last breath of a dead man?" The sky had turned pearly gray and opaque, and the air was damp enough to produce a puff of steam with each breath as he headed briskly across the parking lot. "This is my time, Sadie. I'm going to jump in the river. End it now. You've driven me to it, and you've earned the right to see it."

"Don't talk that way, Mark." She climbed out of the buggy, staring after him. "Even as a joke. It's not funny at all."

"I wasn't laughing when I heard you'd left me for Sam Lapp," he shouted, already at the footing of the bridge.

"That's not true!" she called after him, but he had disappeared behind the red wooden siding of the bridge. Sadie waited a second, wondering if his threat was real. It seemed crazy, but then, much of what Mark had said had been twisted and off-kilter.

She looked toward the road—longing to get away and run free—but it wouldn't be right. Not if Mark was truly going to hurt himself. Setting her jaw, she hurried up the road to the bridge. The churning of the river was the only sound as she tried frantically to think of a way to bring Mark back to reason.

She saw him before she even entered—a dark figure in the opening of the wall. The window-sized cutout was designed to let some light into the dark space and give drivers a chance to peer out for oncoming traffic on the single-lane bridge. Mark had climbed into the space, his black boots posed on the ledge as he stared out over the icy river. The look on his face reminded Sadie of a stormy night, dark and angry, with gusts of wind and thunder to shake the earth. What terrible thing had brought him to this place?

Quickly, she rounded the wall and entered the bridge. "You need to come down," she called, her voice echoing slightly in the dim space as she approached him. "Stop this now, Mark. You've made your point. You're angry, and I'm sorry. But nothing good will come of you teetering over the river."

Gripping the wall with one hand, he turned back to shoot her a look and then hopped down. "You're right." With two long strides to close the distance between them, he was face-to-face with her, a cruel gleam in his eyes. "I'm not going to jump. You are."

"No, I'm not." She started to back away from his ridiculous notion, but he grabbed hold of her upper arms. His fingers closed over her sleeves, compressing flesh and bone as he pulled her to him. "It's a much better plan. I'll tell everyone that I broke it off with you, and you were so distraught that you jumped into the river."

"What fool would jump into a river in winter? And with those rocks below." She knew it was a crazy thing for him to say, but he was acting crazy now. His steely grip and wild eyes scared her. He seemed to be serious, on the verge of hurting her.

"I'm glad you didn't jump," she said, trying to get him off the topic, wishing he would let her squirm away. "The fall would have injured you. And the water is icy cold. You'd be sick for sure."

"Simple Sadie." He shook his head in disdain. "Don't you know the fall will probably kill you? And if not, the water will freeze the life out of you."

"You need to let go." Sadie's arms ached in the spot where Mark's hands were clamped on like an iron vise. "You're hurting me."

"You're the one who keeps pulling away! Just stop squirming and it won't hurt so much. Or better yet, go on and climb up on the ledge. Time to be obedient. A good wife obeys her husband."

"You're not my husband." He kept slipping from reality, lapsing into another world.

"Don't be scared now. It will happen quickly."

"Leave me alone!" She wrenched her right arm back, but his fingers remained clamped onto the left arm, digging into the flesh beneath her coat. Writhing frantically, she managed to break free.

Run. Run!

The voice in her head was shrill over the thudding of her heart in her chest as she darted toward the buggy. Her boots pounded the plank floor of the bridge as she ran, flying forward. Focused on the light at the opening of the bridge, she wasn't watching the roadbed. When an uneven plank caught her boot, she went down hard like a kite crashing to the ground.

"No," she breathed. She gathered her skirts and picked herself up as heavy footsteps pounded behind her, closer, closer. She had risen to her feet when he came at her. A tower of strength, blinded by anger, he locked his arms around her waist and dragged her toward the cutout in the old bridge.

Sadie screamed, her frantic voice echoing in the chamber of the covered bridge as she fought back, arms flailing, body bucking, heels grinding into the wooden planks of the bridge to try to get a foothold. "No!"

He had dragged her a few feet along when the clip-clopping of a horse's hooves rose from the distance. A buggy was coming.

Sadie pressed her feet to the ground and pulled away to look toward the road, sure that this was her chance to get away.

Mark followed her gaze toward the mouth of the bridge, then glanced back at her in disgust. Sadie felt sure he must have seen hope in her eyes. That hope swelled inside her, new and powerful. She struggled with renewed strength, flailing against his vise-like grip.

But he held her tight. "You can't get away," he growled in her ear. "Don't you know that? I'll never let you go. Never!"

Chapter 30

Sam's jaw ached from gritting his teeth. In his desperation to find Sadie, every muscle was taut, every nerve on edge.

"Over there." Amy Troyer pointed toward the covered bridge, where a gray buggy was tied to a post in the small parking area beside the river. "Could that be Mark's buggy?"

Pushing the Troyers' horse as fast as he dared, Sam was already steering toward the garnet-colored covered bridge that sat like a small toy house on a model train platform surrounded by cotton puffs of fake snow. Despite the picturesque scene, he could tell something was wrong. He knew it in his gut: Sadie was in danger.

He'd been frustrated by the chase. They'd lost sight of Mark's buggy when a slow-moving delivery van had pulled onto the road in front of them. The van driver appeared to be lost, slowing to a near stop at every driveway and side road. The snail's pace had been maddening, as it meant Sam had had to guess at Miller's destination.

They had headed into town, thinking Mark and Sadie might be found at the auction house, but the place was dark and closed up tight. From there, Sam had turned the buggy out of town, heading toward the Miller home on the other side of the river. His mind still reeled with urgency as they approached the buggy that had been tied to a post.

"It looks empty," Amy said, staring at the buggy.

"But it's definitely the Millers' buggy," Sam said, slowing the horse to a trot. Although Amish buggies in Lancaster County were uniform in size and gray color, young Amish men had a way of discerning who owned what— sometimes by the horse, other times by the condition of the buggy. Ever since his rumspringa, Mark Miller had kept special spokes on his wheels, wheels that irked Sam. They weren't shiny or glittery, but they were a bit fancy, a notch above typical wheels. "He's here with Sadie . . . somewhere."

"But where are they?" Tess asked. "They wouldn't go far in this cold."

A flash of movement in the shadows of the bridge caught his eye.

At the same time, Amy pointed to the bridge, where there was a flurry of activity in the dark tunnel within. "There they are. Good grief! What's happening?"

Sam was equally startled by the sight of Mark holding Sadie by the waist while she squirmed and flailed. Everything was happening so quickly, but Sam would never forget the high flush of color on Sadie's face and the stern glaze over Mark's demeanor.

The image was branded in Sam's mind as he stopped the buggy, jumped out, and ran along the snowy path to the bridge. "Sadie!"

The sound of his voice prompted Miller to release her. Mark's head snapped up, his face puckered, mired in anger.

At the same time, the anguish on Sadie's face turned to relief as she escaped from the shadows and ran straight to Sam. He was never so happy to see anyone in his life.

He ran to her, taking in every inch of her as she drew closer. Her coat was torn at the shoulder and her cheeks were streaked with tears, but her eyes—those moss-green eyes—were full of light and love for him.

"Sam!" she called to him through her tears. "I knew it was you. I prayed it was you!"

"Sadie . . ." When he finally reached her, he worried that she was too fragile to pick up and hug close. He touched her forehead, the way Mem once did when he was feverish, then pressed one palm to her cheek, feeling the tinge of cold mixed with the warmth of her tears. In that moment he was overwhelmed with love for Sadie Beiler. From this day forward, he would always love, cherish, and protect her. "Are you all right?" He clasped her hands and brought them to his chest. "Did he hurt you?"

"He tried to . . ." She looked away and shook her head. "He's not making sense, not all the time. There's something wrong with him. And though he scared me, I'm worried about him. We can't leave him here, Sam. At one point, he threatened to kill himself."

Sam looked up at the bridge as Mark emerged, striding toward them. "I'll talk to him. Are you okay to go wait in the Troyers' buggy?"

Nodding, she seemed suddenly overcome with relief and exhaustion.

"Go. Try to get warm," he told her, before turning to face the approaching young man, who strutted down the bridge ramp like a proud rooster strolling the barnyard. Revulsion was thick as tar in the back of Sam's throat when he thought of the way Mark Miller had treated Sadie. Although Sam didn't go in for gossip, he'd heard some murmurings of a similar altercation between Mark and his previous girl, Lavern Gingerich. This abuse of others, it went on in secret, in the dark, but it wouldn't be tolerated in the light of day.

"What's going on, Mark?" Sam stood tall, getting right to the point.

Mark shrugged. "Nothing."

The answer of a ten-year-old boy.

"We saw you pushing Sadie around. It looked like you were hurting her." Sam noticed the way Mark adjusted his hat, tilting it so that it covered part of his face. The gesture was clear to Sam—Mark had something to hide.

"We were just joking around," Mark said as he paused in front of Sam. "Sadie will tell you that. I was teasing her, that's all. No reason to get all high-and-mighty with me."

"It didn't look like a joke." Sam moved closer, trying to make eye contact, but Mark was staring down now. "You can't go hurting people, Mark."

"You should mind your own business and leave me be. Judge ye not."

Mark started walking away, but Sam put a hand on his chest to stop him. "I'll mind my business, but I won't look away when someone needs help. And I can't abide a man putting his hands on a woman. I wonder what folks would say about that. Your father, and Bishop Aaron."

Mark looked down at Sam's hand, then made eye contact. "It was a joke, that's all. And I'll thank you not to gossip about me to all of Joyful River."

Face-to-face with Miller, Sam searched for a hint of decency in the man's eyes. Respect. Grace. But all he saw was anger.

Sam let his hand fall away, knowing it was no use trying to talk logic with Mark. Their conversation dried up, Mark walked down the ramp toward his buggy.

Walking a few lengths behind him, Sam noticed that Mark passed the Troyer buggy as if it weren't even there. It was a cold gesture, but then, Sam sensed that Sadie was right: Mark Miller's emotions seemed to seesaw constantly. It was hard to imagine what it was like to walk in his shoes, though he had crossed the line one too many times. Laying a hand on a woman could not be tolerated.

Mark's buggy was back on the road, rolling toward town, when Sam rejoined the women. Sadie was in the back seat, and the Troyer girls were doting on and trying to console her.

"I saw him dragging you along," Amy said. "Are you all right?"

"I'll be fine." Sadie nodded, huddling under the buggy blanket for warmth in the second seat. Sam's heart ached for her. Beneath the bristly wool, she looked weary and fragile as a porcelain teacup.

"Goodness, you're shaking like a leaf!" Seated on the bench beside her, Tess moved closer and put an arm around her. "Let me warm you up. Mem used to say I run hot as a potbellied stove."

Sam suspected Sadie was shaking more from shock than from the cold.

"Denki," Sadie said, "but I'm worried about Mark. He's not in his right mind. He's upset that we've broken up.

First, he threatened to jump from the bridge. Then he was going to push me."

"Oh." Tess let out a stunned breath. "How awful. How could he even think such a thing?"

"Mark has a dark side that we can't begin to understand," Sam said. "I think it's like a disease that you suffer from. He can't help it. But his behavior has to be checked. Violence is never okay."

"Dat will need to hear of this," Amy said, staring ahead at the road as she processed the event. "And the other church leaders."

"Oh, no," Sadie objected. "I don't want to make any trouble for Mark."

"They have to be told." Amy turned to the back seat, her eyes shadowed with sympathy. "It's not about you, Sadie, but Mark. You said yourself that he needs help."

Exhaling a heavy sigh, Sadie agreed.

With Sadie safe in the back seat, the buggy ride went quickly. The girls passed the time in conversation about their plans for summer gardens and a quilting they all planned to attend soon. When the question of where to go next came up, Sam insisted that Sadie be taken home immediately. He would figure out how to get his buggy back from Myers Pond later.

"The tournament!" Sadie exclaimed, remembering. "Sam, you have to go back. Your team needs you for the night game."

Sam shook his head. "It's only hockey," he said. "And they have enough players. There'll be other games to play. Right now, I want to stay with you."

Twenty minutes later, as Sam steered the buggy into the drive of Sadie's house, he was grateful to the Troyer sisters for their generosity and kindness toward Sadie after she'd suffered a difficult trauma. He hadn't really known them before today, but he appreciated Amy's practical, down-to-earth demeanor, as well as Tess's genuine enthusiasm.

Inside the house, Reuben was dozing over a recent copy of the *Budget*, while Joan was at the sink doing supper dishes. They both reacted to the sight of Sadie, looking worn-out and fragile. Seated in the kitchen, Sam and Sadie were served cups of hot tea as they recounted the incident. Sam watched the beautiful, sad face of the woman he loved as she spoke quietly.

Mark had wanted to talk over their breakup, and she had agreed to the buggy ride. Along the way, it had become clear that he was angry with her, but he refused to take her back or even let her out. At the bridge, Mark had vacillated between threatening to kill himself and threatening to push Sadie off the bridge. "Some of the terrible things he said, I know it's because he's unstable— mentally ill. He was crushed that I would damage his reputation by breaking up with him. When he stopped making sense, that's when I got really scared. In the nick of time, Sam came along and saved me."

Sadie's mother hugged her, while her dat expressed concern and told her she'd been brave.

"I know it's been hard on you, daughter. Scary and dangerous. But you've come through it with courage," said Reuben. "I'm sorry to say it, but the difficult times shape who we are as much as the good times. There's that saying: 'If the river had no rocks, it would not have a song.'"

Sadie nodded sagely.

Sam wanted to take her into his arms and cradle her,

warm her, soothe her through the night, but he knew now was not the time. In this moment, he just needed to be here for Sadie. In a few months, come September, they would be charged with caring for each other, in sickness and in health, for the rest of their lives.

He was so ready for that.

Chapter 31

After Sam left, Sadie soaked in a tub scented with "relaxing lavender" baby soap and tried to wash the image of Mark from her mind. The hot water warmed the bone-chilling cold from her and the sweet scent made it easier to breathe, but they did nothing to ease the fear that haunted her. Would her life be forever shadowed by Mark's anger and disappointment? Would he always blame her for his wild swings of emotion, his temper tantrums, his dark moods?

In her logical mind, she knew he would eventually fade from her life. But in the near future, wouldn't she have to worry about Mark lingering around every tree and hay-stack?

After her bath, Mem made her tea and offered to heat up some casserole, but Sadie couldn't eat. For tonight, tea and honey would have to be enough. For now, she was grateful for the love and comfort of home.

Saturday morning, Essie came by bearing a basket with a jar of peach jam and half a dozen biscuits baked that morning by Miriam. "Jam and biscuits make the day a tiny bit better," Essie said as she fetched a plate and placed a biscuit and knife in front of Sadie. Dat was working with his new hire, Abe, out in the hothouse, and Mem went off to tidy the rest of the house, leaving Essie and Sadie alone to talk.

In the abbreviated language of two women who had been friends for decades, Sadie recalled the events of the day before while Essie sipped coffee and asked pointed questions.

"I came away feeling a dread that this isn't over—that Mark still has the wrong idea about me, that he owns me in some way. I thought I'd be up all night worrying, but when my head touched the pillow, I was asleep."

"That's a blessing," Essie said, warming her hands on her coffee mug. "But I'd say it's not over, especially since the Troyer girls saw Mark at his worst."

"I thought of that," Sadie said. "They have to tell their dat. I hope the bishop understands that Mark suffers from emotional issues."

"The bishop needs to know." Essie reached across the table and squeezed her friend's hand. "You're not the first one to have trouble with Mark. There's the story about Lavern Gingerich a while back, how her father forbade him to come around. And then that girl Tootie left town."

"We don't know those stories are true."

"We know Mark needs help," Essie said, her eyes round with concern. "The bishop needs to know that."

"I don't want Mark to be in trouble on account of me."

"If there's a consequence, it's because of his behavior, not because of you," Essie assured her. "You didn't do anything wrong."

Sadie hoped that was true. Glad to be done with her account, she took a bite of the biscuit slathered with tart jam. The buttery morsel melted in her mouth. She tore off a second bite, glad to feel her appetite returning.

Essie warned that she couldn't stay too long—it was to be a baking day—but she helped herself to a biscuit and tried to help Sadie by focusing on the good things ahead. Now Sadie and Sam could go to singings together. There was that quilting coming up—all women and girls—and those long afternoons together were always filled with funny stories, joy, and laughter. "And before you know it," Essie said, "the weather will be warming up, and we'll be able to stow away our coats and shoes. We'll be picnicking and wading through the river."

"That's a ways off," Sadie said. She had a shawl drawn over her shoulders, mostly to cover her nightgown. When she awoke today she'd given herself permission to have a lazy morning and lounge in her pajamas for a bit.

As they were talking, there was a stir in the front of the house and the sound of the clip-clop of a horse in the driveway they shared with the orchard. A moment later, Mem came into the kitchen and motioned nervously at Sadie.

"You need to get out of your pajamas," Mem said. "There's a buggy out there. The bishop. I reckon he's here to talk to you."

Within minutes, Essie headed home, Sadie got dressed, and Dat and Mem joined her in the front parlor to meet with Bishop Aaron.

"Amy and Tess were very upset by what they saw on the

bridge," the bishop said. "I spoke to Mark Miller last night. The girls were so concerned, I felt I had to act immediately. But you, Sadie, I wanted to give you a chance to rest." He spoke slowly, as if choosing his words carefully, and though he acknowledged Sadie and her parents, he kept his eyes trained on the wall between them, as if trying to see something happening on a distant hillside.

At least he wasn't staring at Sadie. The very act of speaking in front of the bishop was intimidating, but Sadie steeled herself, hoping that the truth would lead the bishop to understand what was haunting Mark. It had been hard enough to tell her story to her parents, who offered tenderness and support. Now, speaking in front of the bishop, Sadie was filled with fear as she knew he had heard Mark's side of the story and was here to administer Gott's justice as prescribed in the Bible. Sadie knew that Bishop Aaron's rules did not always seem fair, but they had to be followed as an act of Amish faith.

Sadie did her best to tell the story of dating Mark, his sudden departure, her attempt to end their relationship, his sudden appearance at Myers Pond, and the incident at the bridge.

"I kept telling him we weren't getting married, that I wasn't his wife, but he was so riled up, he couldn't seem to hear it." Sadie tried to recount the memory without thinking too much about the anger in Mark's eyes or the fear and bone-chilling terror she'd experienced.

She sat twisting a handkerchief in a stiff wooden chair opposite her parents, who sat on the small couch. Dat had handed her the handkerchief earlier, when tears had sprung from her eyes, and now it gave her comfort as she squeezed it between her fingers, as if her tears could be wrung out and gone forever. Beside her, in Dat's rocker, Bishop Aaron sat still and stone-faced. He seemed neither disapproving nor friendly as she answered his questions and told her story. Sometimes she felt as if he had faded off, his gaze a mile away, until he murmured a "Hmm!" or stroked his beard in a slow, deliberate motion.

Mem leaned over from the loveseat, nodding to Sadie. "Go on . . ."

"Sorry." Sadie snapped back into the moment, trying to pick up her story. "So, the whole time, Mark kept saying—"

The bishop raised his hand, putting a pause to her words. "One question. I know wedding season is a ways off, but had you and Mark Miller made plans to marry?"

"Not really." Sadie wrapped the hankie around one thumb, pensive. "It used to be my intention at one time. It was what I wanted. But then I got to know Mark better, and I realized we wouldn't make a good couple. I told him as much in a letter."

"And what did he say to that?"

Nothing, she wanted to say, thinking of the weeks she'd waited for an acknowledgment. "When I asked him about it, he said I was a fool to think I could break things off with him."

"Hmm." Again, that low grumble as Aaron Troyer's eyes nearly closed in contemplation. The bishop always had a sleepy look, like a man squinting into the sun, which Sadie had attributed to his need to retreat from the details of everyday life and know Gott's will.

Waiting on him now, Sadie considered his longish, graying hair, nearly white in the beard along his cheeks and peppered with gray under his chin. With a strong brow ridge and those thoughtful eyes, he exuded quiet power. A small farmer who had been chosen to lead, he was a careful man who seemed to know he carried the weight of their Amish community on his back.

"This is a danger, Bishop," Dat spoke up. "We can't have a youngie so aggressive toward women in our community."

Sadie held the handkerchief to her breast as her dat sought to protect her. She hadn't expected him to defend her so, but tonight he seemed clear-eyed and firm in his conviction. He was looking after his daughter in a way he never had before, and Sadie's heart swelled with a new love for him.

The bishop nodded sagely. "This is why I'm here." He turned to Sadie. "Go on, please."

"It went on for a while. We went back and forth in all manner of argument, with him wanting me to agree to keep dating and marry him, and me insisting that it was over. He'd been out of town for weeks without a word. I took that to mean he wasn't much attached to me, either."

"So . . . back to the incident on the bridge," Bishop Aaron prodded.

Sadie nodded, wishing that she could dissolve the fear from her memory. "He said he was going to jump from the bridge, that I'd driven him to it, because of breaking up. When I tried to stop him, he grabbed me and tried to force me to the opening of the bridge. That way he could lie to folks and say that I'd jumped when he broke up with me."

The bishop shook his head. "This part is new to me. Mark didn't mention any of this."

Sadie tried to smooth the handkerchief in one long strip without looking at it. "He said that a wife must submit to her husband, and that meant I had to follow his order, which was . . . He wanted me to jump from the bridge."

"Harris Bridge. He ordered her to jump," Dat said, emphasizing Mark's ludicrous order. "Bishop, that shows you the man must be daft. If the fall didn't kill you, the plunge into the icy water would. Mark Miller is a danger, Bishop. Our Sadie got away, just barely, this time. But the next time, another young woman might not be so lucky."

"Is this true?" The bishop tipped his head to one side, staring at her hard. "Do you think Mark Miller would have actually hurt you, Sadie?"

She wove the kerchief between her fingers, considering. She didn't want to get Mark in trouble, and any whiff of violence in Amish society was frowned upon. On the other hand, she knew that Gott didn't abide liars. And the truth was the only thing that might stop Mark from hurting someone else. "It's the truth. He felt embarrassed—his pride hurt, I think—to be rejected. I don't think it mattered that it was me. It was the rejection that bothered him. And yah, he was willing to hurt me."

The air in the room was thick with sorrow. Mark's heart and mind were in a very dark place, and it gave Sadie no joy to testify to his actions. She only hoped that the bishop and church leaders would recognize that Mark Miller needed help.

"Well, Sadie, I'm glad to see that you're all right now," the bishop said somberly. "It's clear that Mark Miller has some confusion over the proper roles of men and women under the Ordnung." The Ordnung is a set of rules that guide daily living, based on the Amish interpretation of the Bible. Like most Amish folk, Sadie and her family had a deep respect for the Ordnung, and they looked to leaders like the bishop to help them make sure they followed the rules.

Aaron sat back in the chair and continued. "It's true that a husband is the head of a family and a wife must submit to her husband. In the Bible, the book of Ephesians tells women to be helpers and supporters of their husbands. And the husbands—" He lifted a hand to gesture to Dat. "Husbands are to love their wives as Christ loved the church, which we know is a sacred bond."

This was a familiar doctrine for Sadie, as all Amish girls and boys were brought up adhering to these roles.

"There are two things here that show how Mark is off the path," said Bishop Aaron. "First, you two are not married, and it sounds like that won't be happening. Second, Mark has not treated you as Christ treated the church, with love and devotion."

Sadie nodded, following the bishop's logic, but wondering if he would recognize the heart of Mark's problem: mental illness. It was not something folks liked to address or even name. Maybe because no one knew quite what to do about it. Sadie felt sure that there was something wrong with Mark, something driving his erratic behavior. Deep down inside, he wasn't a bad person, but sometimes he did cruel and mean things.

"What's to be done, Aaron?" Mem asked, her hands still resting protectively on Sadie's shoulders. "Our Sadie will keep her distance from Mark. You can count on that. But there's no guarantee he won't hurt someone else."

The bishop nodded, stroking the side of his beard. "I'll need to speak with the other church leaders. We'll consider everything and pray on it. It doesn't make it any easier that the two stories are so different."

"So Mark didn't confess to trying to force Sadie off the bridge?" Dat asked, confusion in his voice.

Bishop Aaron shook his head. "Mark told a very different story of Sadie being upset over their breakup, saying that she tried to jump from the opening in the covered bridge. He said if he hadn't been there to stop her, she surely would have jumped in the river. He says he saved her life."

"That's not true." Sadie tried to keep the bitterness from her voice, but the audacity of Mark's lie cut like a thorny vine.

"To think that he's lying on top of trying to hurt Sadie." Dat shook his head. "That's a sad state of affairs."

"In the end, I have two different accounts to go on, and not much else," said the bishop. "Sam and my daughters witnessed some of the conflict, but only the tail end, apparently."

"But Mark is a danger to other people," Sadie said. "Maybe to himself, too."

The bishop stroked his beard with the knuckles of one hand. "But he didn't hurt you physically, did he?"

Sadie only had to think for a second. "He left these bruises from dragging me on the bridge." She pushed back the bulky sleeves of her sweater to reveal black smudges along her lower arms, just above the wrists. There were also a few red scratches where his fingernails had dug in and scraped her skin.

Bishop Aaron let out his breath in another low grumble, undecipherable to Sadie.

Mem gasped, catching Sadie's attention. All this time, Sadie had thought her mother had been listening intently, but from her puffy eyes and the streaks down her cheeks, it was clear she'd been crying. "He hurt you!" Mem cried, leaving her chair to come round behind Sadie and place her hands gently on Sadie's shoulders. "Ach, my Sadie," she whispered in her ear, as if Sadie were a child again.

The gesture of affection made Sadie melt inside. How long had it been since she'd felt this sense of comfort at home, this sense of belonging? Granted, her parents had made mistakes in the past, but now it was abundantly clear that those days were long gone and Sadie was blessed with two parents who truly loved her.

She put her hand over Mem's, soaking up the rare moment of mutual love.

"Those marks on Sadie's arms, I'm sure that accounts for something," Dat said.

"It means he laid a hand on her, yah," the bishop agreed, "but he'll say it was to stop her from jumping."

"But our Sadie wouldn't make this up," Mem pointed out.

"Such a difficult situation." The bishop rose and shrugged on his coat, his lips pressed tight in consternation. "A matter of he said, she said."

"But your daughters were there," Sadie said softly, not daring to be disrespectful.

"Ach. I wish they'd seen more."

Sadie could tell that he found no joy in his role of mediator in such a volatile situation. He was trying to be impartial and fair, but that meant he had to consider what he'd heard from Mark, too.

As the bishop prepared to leave, Sadie prayed that Gott would guide the decision of the church leaders. That Gott above would help them to know the truth and act with wisdom. She held tight to Gott's promise in the Bible: "And the truth shall set you free . . ."

* * *

That night, Dat was called to a meeting with Bishop Aaron, the deacons, and Mark's father—a meeting to discuss the decision of the church leaders. Sadie sent her father off with a hot water bottle for the buggy ride, confident that he would advocate for her in any way possible. Still, she and Mem waited restlessly, so on edge over the difficult situation that they could focus only on deep scrubbing the floor and walls of the kitchen. As she worked, Sadie thought of how her future was now in the hands of these men. Such was the tradition of Amish folk; women had a say in things, but men were the ones who made the big decisions.

It was late, nearly nine o'clock, when Dat returned. Sadie finished washing a section of wall and then took the bucket and rag into the mudroom sink. She started to put a kettle on for tea, but when Dat came in the door, the paleness of his face gave her a fright.

"Dat! Are you dizzy? Maybe your blood sugar is off."

"It's not the diabetes, Sadie. It's this . . ." He shook his head. "It's not good. I'm sorry."

"Come. Sit." A knot of worry grew in Sadie's throat, but she had to take care of Dat over any other concerns. She fetched a small glass of orange juice, just in case he needed it. Mem was already in the kitchen, rubbing the tension from Dat's shoulders.

"You're stiff as a board, Reuben."

"It's cold out there, and I've just sat through some of the worst hours of my life."

Sadie sat utterly frozen beside Dat to listen as he recounted the meeting.

The bishop had suggested that the two young people must be separated immediately until a solution became clear. If nothing was done, the sort of turmoil that bubbled between Sadie and Mark could ripple through their peaceful community and create a divide.

Deacon Seth agreed, but he thought the solution could be found in the time of separation. "A period of three years should diffuse the tension," Seth said. "Mark should go off to another settlement for a time, move in with family, and give them time to get on the right path."

The church leaders were in agreement on this decision.

"But Mark has an important duty here in Joyful River," said Wayne Miller, "and Sadie has none." Mark's father argued that he had a business to run—they needed Mark at the auction house. "You can't expect a man to walk away from his line of work," Wayne Miller had said in defense of his son. "He's young yet, but he'll need to be head of his own household soon."

The men agreed on that fact—everyone except Reuben Beiler, who would lose his daughter in this process.

And so the onus was on Sadie to leave their community. The decision stung for so many reasons. Mostly, it hurt her to leave her family, her home, her community. Essie and Miriam and her second family at the Lapp Dairy farm.

And Sam. Dear Sam.

In one fell swoop, she would lose everything.

Chapter 32

News of the church leaders' decision spread through the tightly woven Amish community like a ripple on a pond. On Monday morning when Sadie went into the pretzel factory to tell Mr. Smitty she had to leave, many of the girls waved to her. Some came off the line to give her a hug goodbye and wish her luck.

"Promise you'll write us letters and tell us everything you're doing," Gerta said, her eyes tender with sympathy.

Sadie hadn't realized she had so many friends, but then they'd always had fun times working together. It had taken this terrible thing to make her appreciate the cheerful, kind girls who had made her smile nearly every day.

In a series of phone calls to York, arrangements were made for Sadie to move in with Sharon, Elam, and their children "for as long as you can put up with us," Sharon told Sadie. "Lovina is going to be happy as a lark! If you don't mind having your little niece shadow you day and night."

Tears filled Sadie's eyes at the bittersweet dichotomy of emotions. So brokenhearted to leave her family and Sam, and yet brimming over with affection for her niece and nephew. "You know I have a special love for Lovina and Nathan." Her voice cracked on the words, and suddenly, she was unable to speak.

"Dear Sadie, I know it must be hard." Leave it to Sharon to understand. "We'll talk about it when you get here."

Then I'll have all the time in the world, thought Sadie. *Nowhere to go. No friends, no job.* It would take years to make friends there and be accepted at youth gatherings in Elam and Sharon's community, and she was too old for that anyway. A baptized woman, who'd been ready to marry. She might as well be going off to live alone on the big silver moon in the sky.

By the middle of the week, she was packed and ready to go. The van had been ordered for Thursday morning, and Mem had decided to come along and stay with her middle daughter for a few days. "It will be good to spend some time there. We so rarely get to see Sharon's family," Mem said wistfully.

I'll be seeing a lot of them, Sadie thought glumly, though she kept her thoughts to herself as she finished loading apple strudel muffins into a basket to take over to the Lapp farm, where she planned to say her goodbyes and spend a little time with Sam.

Mem had offered to drop Sadie off at the farm on her way to town. Their horse didn't seem to mind the cold, but Sadie and Joan shivered beside each other in the boxy vehicle. As they passed the frozen winter fields, the low afternoon sun casting a golden glaze over everything, Sadie knew she would miss this place, this stark land where generations of Amish families had made their homes.

Mem stopped Old Gray in the wide drive in front of

the Lapp house. "I'll swing by after I finish my errands in town."

Sadie grabbed her basket, stepped down, and then carefully made her way to the side door between patches of ice on the frozen ground.

The kitchen was warm and welcoming, the air laced with the scent of cinnamon from cookies that had just come out of the oven. "Sadie's here!" Sarah Rose called from the table, where she was coloring.

"I brought apple strudel muffins," Sadie said, unwinding her scarf.

"My favorite! Come in, come in!" Miriam wrapped her arms around Sadie for a big, soft hug. "Ach! I can feel the cold seeping from your coat. Come, sit by the stove and warm up." She wore her cooking apron, and there was a dash of flour on her cheek. "It's so good to see you before you go. I just can't imagine what we're going to do without you to brighten our days. Where are you off to again?"

"York." Sadie had made the trip once before for a visit. It required a hired car, and you had to take the bridge over the wide Susquehanna River. Only forty miles from here, York seemed to be worlds away.

"I told you, Mem. That's where her sister Sharon lives with Elam Schwartz," Essie said from the sink, where she was rinsing a mixing bowl.

"Ach, yes. I know Elam's mother. A nice family. But tell me, how are you doing, Sadie? It must be hard for you."

"It is." Sadie swallowed, her throat thick with sorrow. She had promised herself she wouldn't cry; she'd had enough tears in the past few days to last a lifetime. But Miriam's genuine concern probed at that sensitive spot in her heart. "I'm trying to make the most of it. I get on well with my sister, and her children will keep me busy."

"Look at you, staying positive." Miriam patted her arm. "Gott loves a joyful heart."

Sadie nodded. There would be no joy now or tomorrow or the next day, but Miriam was not the kind of person you admitted that to.

"We'll want to hear everything about your new adventures. I hope you'll write. And I have a feeling that things will go better than any of us expect. You just keep busy, and everything will work out just fine. You know that expression about luggage, right?"

"Suitcases," Essie said, wiping her hands on the kitchen towel.

"That's right." Miriam's eyes were bright with hope as she went on. "Days are like suitcases. They're all the same size. But some people pack more into them than others. So you need to pack your day with joyous activities."

"I'll try," Sadie promised. Standing here, with Essie's mem, Sadie could almost believe that everything *would* work out happily.

"Come," Essie said, taking Sadie's hand. "We can talk."

They went into the big front room, the scene of so many happy memories for Sadie as she'd gathered with the Lapps to play games at the big table or make puzzles or play cards. Years earlier, when she'd attended the one-room schoolhouse with Essie, they'd sometimes sat at the big table with cookies and milk to do their writing assignments or drill each other on the times tables.

They sat side by side on the tiny sofa and talked about everything and nothing as only best friends can. Eventually, the conversation turned to Sadie's departure.

"I can't imagine what I'll do without you," Essie said. "I wish there was a way to undo the decision."

"Me too," Sadie agreed. They both knew there was no way around what the church leaders had decided, so it seemed useless to talk about it. She changed the subject to invite Essie and Harlan to come to York to visit, and Essie promised to discuss it with Harlan and come up with a date in the spring, after the weather cleared.

"I don't mean to pry," Essie said, "but three years is such a long time to be away. What does this mean for you and Sam?"

Sadie shook her head and clamped her lips tight together in an attempt to stave off tears. "You know I love Sam with all my heart. Right now I'm trying to stay positive and think that good things will happen, but I know . . . three years seems like an eternity. Who knows what Gott has planned for us?"

They were interrupted by a ruckus at the side door: the children returning from school. Lizzie reported that Teacher Julie had made the day fun by teaching them math with a game, and the twins dropped their lunch pails and demanded sandwiches so they could get out on the pond before dark.

"Boys . . ." Essie rolled her eyes, heading into the kitchen to help her mother.

When Lizzie stacked her books on the side table, Sadie went to her. "I've come to say goodbye. I'm leaving in the morning."

"Oh, Sadie." Lizzie threw her arms around her in a wholehearted embrace. "Why are you going away? I don't understand." Even her new glasses didn't hide the stormy emotion in Lizzie's eyes.

"It's hard to explain," Sadie said. "But I'll miss you so."

"I'll write you letters and tell you everything that's going on around here," Lizzie promised. "I love writing. We could be pen pals."

"I would enjoy that," Sadie said, though she wondered what she might write about in a place where she had no friends and didn't even know how to get to the general store. Well, she would find interesting things in Gott's world. And she would learn her way around.

Sadie went into the kitchen to help. She was slicing apples for the children's snack when Megan came in, having ridden the bus home from the Englisch school.

"Grace and Serena went to the library," Megan reported. "I decided to come straight home and use the quiet time to study for my trig test."

Sadie didn't know what trig was, but she was glad Megan was here. She would have liked the chance to say goodbye to all the Englisch cousins, including bubbly Serena and the very practical Grace, but in the last month she had become closest to Megan, who had spent so many hours in their little social group with Isaac, Sam, and Sadie. Isaac had endless questions about how it was to live Englisch, and Megan had many stories of life in the city, some of them sad, many of them causing them all to laugh. Megan had become a good friend to Sam, supportive and spirited, and Sadie appreciated the special relationship between the cousins.

Knowing this was Sadie's final visit, Megan motioned her upstairs to the girls' room. They sat on the single bed by the window. Megan took Sadie's hands and held them in a reassuring way, as if she'd never let go. Her short, boyish haircut had been styled a bit differently of late, with wispy bangs that emphasized her big brown eyes. "Sadie." She tilted her head to one side, and Sadie felt warmed by her sympathy. "I can't believe you're going. It's just not fair."

Sadie gave a nod as she tried to keep the sorrow from rising from the knot in her throat. "I can barely believe it myself."

"What will Sam do without you?"

"And I without him?" Sadie's voice cracked. Her throat felt so tight. "I can't imagine what it's going to be like without Sam. But he enjoys your company, Megan, and he listens to you. Please, don't let him be sad. We can't lose hope."

"I'll do what I can," Megan said. "Every trick in the book. But this is crazy. Isn't there a way you can stay?"

Sadie shook her head. "It's the order of the church leaders."

"Can't you and Sam get them to change their minds? I mean, you didn't do anything wrong. Why should you be punished?"

Sadie sucked in a tight breath as Megan hit a tender spot. "It sure feels like a punishment," she admitted. In her mind, she had couched such an argument many times, going through the logic of her staying in Joyful River, her home, while the leaders came up with some other course of action to address Mark's problems. But in the end, the decision of the leaders was final. "The bishop and the other men have ruled on what's to be done. Their word is law."

"But it's so unfair," Megan said. "And I know you love Sam. How can you just pick up and leave him?"

"I do love him." Sadie closed her eyes as she recalled a song her mother used to sing to her sisters and her when they were little. It described a love that flowed longer than a river, a love that was sweeter and silkier than roses, a love that was bluer than the sky and brighter than the sun.

That was the big love she felt for Sam. The one true love of her life.

"Leaving Sam behind is like . . . like turning away from the sun and living in endless night," Sadie said in a near whisper. "But I couldn't think about disobeying the church leaders. These are the rules we live by, the backbone of Amish life. Our families and communities live in peace because we respect our church and our elders." Sadie shook her head. "We live by the Ordnung. I have to go."

"I'm so, so sorry," Megan said.

They hugged, both of them lingering, holding on for a long moment to share comfort and pain. It was the first time Sadie had hugged an Englisch person, and she measured the sensation. No different. Not in any way that mattered. Megan's hair was shorter than that of any Amish woman Sadie knew, but she certainly smelled sweet and clean.

"Sadie?" a small voice called.

The two girls broke from their embrace. Sarah Rose stood at their side, holding up a cookie sparkling with cinnamon and sugar. "You're sad, so I brought you a cookie."

"Denki." Sadie squatted down and accepted the cinnamon-covered cookie. "A snickerdoodle. Did you get that from your mem?"

Sarah Rose nodded, her eyes impossibly round, her button nose and glib expression barely affected by the emotion in the room. "Why are you sad?"

Sadie broke the cookie in half and gave a piece to Sarah Rose. "I have to leave Joyful River, and I'm going to miss everyone I love."

"Aw." Sarah Rose opened her arms wide. "I don't want you to go."

They hugged, and Sadie savored the weight of the little arms on her shoulders. "I love you, sweet girl," she murmured.

So many hugs! Sadie would have been happy to prolong her goodbyes indefinitely, but Mem would be heading back soon, and the most important goodbye was yet to come. Sadie wished Megan good luck with her studies, then headed back downstairs.

Annie was in the kitchen now, eating a slice of apple slathered with peanut butter. "Sam's out in the stable, taking care of Chester," she said between bites. "I'm heading back, so I'll walk with you."

Sadie buttoned up her coat and tied a crocheted scarf around her neck as Annie filled a large pot with hot water from the sink and lifted it in her arms. "Okay, here we go."

"Bring my pot back," Miriam called after them.

"Yes, Mem." Steam rose from the pot as Annie led the way at her usual brisk pace. "Sam's worried about old Chester being dehydrated. Sometimes horses don't drink enough in the winter, when the water in their trough gets too cold. Or maybe it's a touch of arthritis. That horse has been acting weird."

"So you're bringing the horse warm water?"

Annie nodded. "I'll mix it in with what's there. And Sam wrapped some insulation around the trough to keep it from freezing over."

Sadie nodded. "That should help. I hope Chester's okay."

"Sam'll bring him out of it. He's got the knack."

"Everyone says you're the one who's good with animals," Sadie said.

Annie shrugged. "Sam taught me everything I know."

Sadie knew she was being modest. And how did she move so fast with that heavy pot of water? Sadie worked to keep up, trying to avoid the icy sections of the path. It had only been recently that she had gotten to know Annie better. "You know, all these years I was close friends with Essie, you've always been a good egg. I appreciate your help in the past few weeks, especially when it was tricky for me to spend time with Sam."

"Well, sure. When you find someone you like, nothing should keep you apart."

Sadie walked along digesting that—words of wisdom from the girl of few words.

"Nobody asked me, but I think what they're doing to you really sucks."

"It does," Sadie agreed, appreciating Annie's plain language as she followed her in through the small door of the stable. Inside, Annie went to dump water into the trough, while Sadie moved farther into a stall where Sam was rubbing the flank of a chestnut gelding. "How's Chester doing?" Sadie's voice was strained and low, as if someone else had spoken.

"I'm just rubbing a salve into his muscles and joints. I think he's been feeling the cold this winter." Sam looked up from the horse and nodded to Annie. "Thanks for the hot water."

"I'm taking Mem's pot back to the kitchen," she called on her way out of the stable.

And then it was just the two of them for one last brief goodbye.

"I'm so sorry for the way everything worked out," she said.

"What?" He replaced the cap on the balm and wiped

his hands on a rag. "Don't be sorry. Falling in love with you is the best thing that ever happened to me."

It was the same for Sadie. "But I never thought it would end this way. That I'd be sent away and . . ." She couldn't form the words over the knot in her throat.

"No one could have guessed Miller would blow up like that. Sadie, it's not your fault."

She wanted to believe that. She wanted to tell him that she loved him, that she would love him from afar, but Megan's words had sunk in, and the message was harsh. If she really loved Sam, she needed to let him go. Let him be free to find happiness. "Three years is a long time," she said. "When it's all over, you'll be twenty-four, and I'll be twenty-two." Nearly an old maid. It seemed unrealistic for two people to wait and marry so late.

"Don't think of it that way. We'll find a way to be together." Sam curled one arm over her shoulders, pulling her to him. His hand trailed warmth through her coat. "Promise me you'll write. We can't lose touch."

"I'll be writing up a storm, it seems," she murmured.

"And I'm planning to visit. Dat promised that we could work out a day here and there that I can take off from the farm and go visiting in York."

The prospect of a visit from Sam was like that of a drink of water in the desert, but she knew it was unwise to hang her hope on that. "You're always welcome, but I don't think you'll be coming. You're so busy here."

"Are you kidding me? I'll make time."

"You'll want to, but things will come up. Obstacles. Commitments. We'll both be lonely and so far away. I've seen other girls eyeing you at the singings, Sam. Maybe you'll meet someone else. Maybe you'll—"

"Never," Sam answered before she could finish the

sentence. "We'll be far apart, but that's not going to change my love for you. Come on, Sadie." He put his arms around her and pulled her close. "Tell me you love me. Tell me you'll wait for me."

The emotions she'd kept bottled up during her visit now broke through in a roaring wind. "I will always love you," she said fervently in the quiet of the stables.

"That's all I need to hear." His words melted her heart.

When he bent down to kiss her, the flicker of sensation from his lips stole her breath away. Their embrace wasn't as sweet as before; this time the desperation that consumed them both added a boldness and an edge to the moment. In Sam's kiss, Sadie found the passion of sorrow and the bittersweet longing of love melded into complex emotion.

When the kiss ended, she gasped for air and felt on the verge of sobbing.

"Shh . . ." he tried to comfort her. "It'll be okay. We'll get through this."

"I do love you, Sam, you know I do. But I can't ask you to ruin your life and wait for an eternity."

"Shh. Knowing you love me, that's all I need. Those words will last me for months and years."

Sadie shook her head. "I've never been away from home for more than a few nights. I'm scared, Sam. I'll be gone, and all of the world will keep turning without me."

"But you'll find joy there, Sadie. You always find the silver lining. And you won't be so far. We'll still be under the same moon and stars, the same sun, the same Gott. So when you wake up in the morning or look out at the rising moon, you can always know that we're under the same sky. And that I'm thinking about you."

"The same sky," she whispered, trying to memorize his dark eyes, his strong jawline, the sweep of his hair over his brows. This was one of the moments she would need to remember and cherish, a stanchion to grasp during the lonely time ahead.

They held on to each other in the quiet of the stables, her head notched in the crook of his neck, their arms entwined. The only sounds were the shifting of the horses, the occasional whir of the wind, and the creaking of wood in the hayloft. Sadie breathed deep the scents of Sam— soap and woodsmoke—and the sweet tang of the salve. The periodic puff of his breath in the cold air mesmerized her the way a ticking clock could lull a person to sleep. There was a thrilling comfort in Sam's arms, tempered only by the fact that they both knew it would end soon.

The ring of the bell from the back of the house was the signal. "Is that the supper bell?" Sadie asked.

Sam shook his head. "Must mean your mem is here to pick you up."

She allowed herself one last indulgent look at her beautiful Sam, and then, lest she break apart in front of everyone, she had to shut down her feelings. Eyes straight ahead, she walked stiffly back to the house, where the buggy was indeed waiting. There was another round of hugs; a tin of homemade cookies from Miriam; a jar of berry jam from Essie; a drawing of a flower from Sarah Rose.

Sadie's head felt far too heavy for her neck as she climbed into the buggy—a difficult climb, like scaling a mountain. Fortunately, Mem seemed to sense her distress and did not linger. The clip-clop of Gray's hooves took them away. One last look back at the house, where golden lantern light illuminated the windows behind the people who filled her heart with joy and love. They stood out in the cold waving.

She loved them so.

And then she turned and settled against the stiff backing of the seat.

"How was it?" Mem asked.

"Harder than I expected. Saying goodbye is exhausting." She tried to breathe, but her throat was so tight, the air didn't seem to come. "I know Gott doesn't make mistakes," said Sadie. "I know this is his plan, and I'm trying to stay positive. But I feel so . . . so broken inside."

"Give it time, daughter," Mem said. "I know your heart is hurting, but Gott heals all wounds with time. Down the road, when you least expect it, you'll find another young man."

Another love? Sadie turned away from her mother stiffly, as if the cloth of Mem's coat sleeve had singed her arm. The thought was horrifying.

There would be no other young man. Her heart was so full of love for Sam—joyful, radiant love! If she couldn't be with Sam, she would live a life of solitude and thank Gott every day for the memory of a love that was real and true.

Chapter 33

In the beginning, Sam woke up each morning believing that all was well, that Sadie was still at her parents' house just down the road a piece, and that they need only wait until next wedding season to begin their lives as husband and wife.

In the beginning, he woke up with a smile on his face—until he remembered.

The bishop's decision. The shame. The ruling that would keep him separated from Sadie. The days and months of the calendar stretching ahead without her. Each morning as he tended the cows for milking, he questioned whether it could be true. Maybe it was just temporary, or maybe the bishop would change his mind. Sam struggled with the fact that he and Sadie could be torn apart for something neither of them did wrong.

Each day, as the hours wore on, the ugly truth set in. By lunchtime, he started feeling a pain in his gut. By the evening, dismay crept in around him with the gray cover of twilight.

Sadie was gone. She wouldn't be stopping in after work or leaving the next singing in his buggy. She was miles beyond the purple hills on the horizon, and she wasn't coming back.

When he finally shed his denial, it was replaced by a painful wrench in his chest, as if he'd been kicked in the rib cage by a horse and was destined to walk the rest of his life with the horseshoe embedded there. To his surprise, the pain didn't ease much when he got a letter from her every few days. Sadie's letters were cheerful and full of love and concern, but he could read the longing between the lines, and the pain in his heart worsened when he was reminded how much she was hurting, too.

The handmade valentine that arrived in February only made the pain worse. Night after night he stared at the beautiful note card of snow-white paper that Sadie had stenciled hearts on—hearts floating like bubbles in the air. In the center was a large heart with red ribbon woven through it.

It was beautiful and sweet—just like Sadie. He thanked her for it in his next letter, told her she had the talent of an artist. He didn't mention that the card brought home the hopelessness of their situation. All those floating hearts— each one alone.

How was this going to work out if they couldn't be together?

Three years. Might as well have been thirty.

Sam stopped going to singings and other social events. He tried to avoid trips to town, where the likes of June Hostetler would run over to chat with him at the feed store or the bishop's daughter Amy would give him a pitying wave as their buggies passed on the road. He didn't need a new girl, and he didn't want anyone's pity.

Sadie was his past, present, and future.

He just needed to figure out how to make that future happen.

One Saturday night at the house, he talked with Isaac while Megan and Essie set up the Monopoly board.

"What are you going to do, my friend?" Isaac's glasses magnified the seriousness in his eyes.

"I'm not sure." Sam glanced from the main room to the kitchen to make sure no one was listening. "Leave, maybe. I reckon I might get hired on at a farm in York."

"Ach, I can't believe it's come to this." Isaac stared down at the floor as he shook his head. "We both love Joyful River, but there are many paths to follow. I might be leaving, too."

"You?" Sam was surprised.

"For college. At a four-year university in East Strouds-burg. Megan helped me apply."

Sam straightened and clapped his friend on the back. "That's good news. Not that I want you to leave, but this takes you a step closer to what you want to do. You'll be a doctor yet!"

"A physician's assistant," Isaac said, giving his charac-teristic shrug. "We'll see if they accept me. One step at a time."

Footsteps came from the kitchen—a smiling Megan. "I'm sure he'll get in," she told Sam. "Do you know that this guy is a straight-A student?"

"I had some help. Megan is a good study partner," Isaac said.

"You had good grades before we even met," she said. "Anyway, I've been accepted there, so fingers crossed we can get in the same dorm."

"That's good," Sam said. "Good news." It was one bit of light in the night.

"It wouldn't happen until August," Isaac said. "What are you thinking, Sam? Would you stay here for the spring planting, or leave sooner than that?"

"Wait. What?" Megan turned to Sam. "You're leaving? You can't go. You're Uncle Alvie's right-hand man around here."

Sam shushed her, staring toward the kitchen to make sure no one was paying them any mind. "I'm thinking about moving to York to be with Sadie, but nothing's decided yet. So not a word."

She pressed a palm to her chest. "Your secret's safe with me, but I can't believe it. I mean, I know you love Sadie, but I can't imagine this place without you."

Sam shrugged. The truth was, he couldn't imagine his days being spent away from this farm. But he also couldn't picture his future without Sadie. There was no easy solution.

Finally, in the end of February on an off-Sunday—a day when there was no church meeting—he hired a car and went to see Sadie for the day.

After so long apart, so much tension and misery, the ice was broken immediately when she ran out to greet him as the car pulled up.

"You're still young and handsome," she teased, once they were out of range of the driver. "It feels like we've been apart for years." She touched his jaw with her fingertips. "I thought you might have grown wrinkled and gray, as that's how I feel."

He laughed, the first good laugh in a long while. She smiled, obviously pleased to have landed her joke.

"Ah, Sadie, you're more beautiful than ever." When the laughter subsided, he took her strong but delicate hand and held it between his. "Inside, I've died a thousand deaths over missing you."

"Sam . . ." She pursed her lips to hold back tears, but they filled her eyes nonetheless. "You have such a way with pretty words, but they cut to the heart because I know you're sincere. I've missed you so!"

They hugged, a wholehearted embrace that had to dissolve when Sam heard someone coming out the door behind them—Sadie's sister Sharon and her husband, Elam. They ushered him into their home. Sam felt welcome there, but Sadie was the bright light that filled every room and warmed his heart.

Their time together rushed by too quickly, but Sam's spirits were lifted by the knowledge that the separation had only strengthened the bond between them. When the hired car rolled up to the house after dark, Sam promised to return soon—in two weeks.

"I'll be counting the days," Sadie told him.

As he dozed in the back of the car, Sam eked out a plan—a means of survival. He would visit Sadie every two weeks, on the off-Sundays. He could last two weeks without seeing her. For now, that was the best he could do.

A week later, Sam booked the car to bring him back to York the following Sunday.

Four days after that, a cold front blew in, bringing blizzard winds, blinding snow, and a bleak white sky. Although Sam bundled up and wore a headlamp, it was a treacherous walk to the phone shanty to make his calls. He canceled the hired car, then called Elam Schwartz's number to leave a message for Sadie. He would not make it to York this week.

Numbed by bitter cold and loneliness, he headed back to the house. Ice chips battered his face, and he had to pull his scarf up to ward off the onslaught.

What can I do? he prayed silently. *What do you want of me, Gott?*

The only answer was the fierce howl of wind and the rattling of the icy tree branches. It was no answer at all; Sam knew that. Gott worked in mysterious ways, and most times people were hard-pressed to make any sense of it.

Blinking against the spray of snow, he focused on the blur of golden light coming from the house. The dark sky and raging storm blurred the edges of his view, but the warm, welcome light of home grew stronger as he approached.

This was where he was supposed to be, for now, and he was lucky to have a good home and family. He would have to endure missing Sadie until spring thawed this deep freeze.

The storm, an unexpected burst of winter weather in March, shut down schools and made many local roads impassable. When one of the neighbors needed help getting supplies, Sam was glad for the distraction. He and Dat put winter shoes on Comet, hooked up a buggy, and loaded up boxes and jars of rations to bring to Ezra Graber's house. Mem came along, as she was friends with Rose Graber.

When they arrived, Sam recalled the property. A fire last fall had severely damaged the barn, burning clear through the roof to collapse the top story. Sam and Dat had joined other men from the community to help the Graber family replace the building. It was a traditional barn raising, with a master carpenter directing nearly a hundred Amish men. "This is how plain folk take care of one another," Dat had told him at the time. "Love your neighbor as yourself."

Dat brought the buggy close to the house, where he and Sam loaded items in through the side door, stacking boxes in the mudroom so as not to track snow and muck into the house. When they were done, Rose insisted they come in for something hot to drink and pie, while her boys pulled jars and frozen meats from the boxes and ran them inside like wild, stampeding horses.

"Boys! Please! No running inside," Rose begged them as she lit the fire under the kettle and tucked some stray hairs behind her ear. "Ach! They never listen."

"I bet they've got lots of energy," Miriam said, "what with being stuck inside during these bitter, cold days."

Sam watched as his mother cajoled the boys into taking one can at a time downstairs to the storage cellar. "It'll be a game to see if you can get everything downstairs before we have to go," she said.

Taking a seat at the kitchen table, Sam grinned at his mother's tactics. It was probably the way she'd handled him when he'd been a wild one.

As Rose served them tea and pie, she thanked them over and over again for coming to the rescue. Her husband had been visiting a sick uncle up near Erie when the storm had swept in, and he couldn't make the trip home until the roads cleared. That had left Rose stranded, with a bare pantry to boot. She laughed that they were fresh out of staples—no meat, corn, eggs, beans, or soup—but there was flour and filling to make pie. So the children had eaten pie for breakfast.

"I'm glad you reached out to us," Miriam said. "With Essie doing the canning business, we put up plenty of extra fruits and vegetables during the season."

"And we were having a bit of cabin fever ourselves," Dat said, lifting his mug. "It was good to hitch up the buggy and get out for a bit."

Although Sam nodded and ate his pie in silence, he knew his father wasn't telling the entire truth. Dat had expressed concern over the slipperiness of the icy roads as they'd been changing the shoes on the horse, but there was no mention of that to Rose.

As Sam took a sip of warm tea, he saw the good, kind nature of his parents. Dat always said you could measure a person not by their words, but by their actions. By those standards, Miriam and Alvin were a hundred feet tall.

It made Sam's troubles seem small by comparison. Here was a woman worried about feeding her children, and Sam was suffering from heartache. It was time to man up and find a solution.

On the way home, Sam swallowed his pride and told his parents what was on his mind. "I'm not set on anything, but I'm wondering how it would go for you to manage the farm without me. If I went away for a while."

Dat turned his head slightly, though Sam couldn't see his expression from the back seat. "Where would you go?"

"Alvin . . ." Mem nudged Dat with her elbow. "To York, of course."

Sam wanted to laugh and cry. It was typical of Mem to know exactly where his heart was, while Dat was more in line with practical matters.

Dat gave a grunt, his thinking response. "You're a fine

dairyman, Sam, and I know you enjoy the work. No one is that dedicated when their heart isn't in it. Are you sure you want to go?"

"Not sure," Sam admitted. "Just figuring out my options."

"Well, let's see. Truth is, you'd be hard to replace. Annie's great with the animals, but we need more than two for the daily milking."

"Pete and Paul could help out with that," Sam said. "They've both got it down pat."

"But they'll be in school for a few more years," Mem said. "It's a lot to drag them out of bed hours earlier for the morning milking, on top of schooling."

Sam knew this was true. Although all the children helped out on the farm, they weren't assigned major tasks until they finished eighth grade.

"And I'd probably have to hire on someone to maintain the fences," Dat said. "We can't afford to have our herd breaking out."

"I forgot about the fences," Sam said. It was one of his major tasks. Somehow the cows seemed to find the weakest spots in the barrier, where they'd press in and get trapped or escape into the pastures owned by their neighbor, Dennis Schrock. The worst-case scenario was that one of the cows could wander into the road, where the big animals could injure a driver or get killed.

"There's a lot to think about," Dat said. "You're a big part of our farm, Sam."

"But we could hire a helper, couldn't we, Alvie?" Mem's voice was full of concern, that intuition that sensed when one of her children truly needed something.

Sam closed his eyes, touched by her concern. "That would cost us," Sam said. "A regular salary. Not sure you want to get into that."

"We could make that work," Dat said. "But what about you, Sam? How will you make your way?"

"I'd have to find something over in York." Sam shifted in his seat. "I'd like to work on another dairy farm, but I wouldn't be choosy."

"You're a good worker," Mem said. "I'm sure you'd find something once the spring thaw sets in."

"Yah," Dat agreed. "Have you asked Elam if he knows anyone there who's hiring?"

"Not yet. I know Sadie will ask for me when the time comes. But I wanted to talk to you first."

"Well, I'd hate to lose you," Dat said. "I've always thought you and your Amish bride would settle in nearby so you could keep tending the milk cows. You're a natural here, Sam, but it's a decision you have to make on your own."

"I know that," Sam said.

Just then Mem turned all the way around to face him, and even in the darkness Sam saw a fiery look in her eyes. A sort of determination. Courage. "Gott will guide you in your choice," she said.

Sam nodded, knowing she was right. He didn't feel Gott's hand in everything he did, but he held fast to his faith, trusting that Gott would show him the way.

That night, alone in his room, Sam looked at the red-ribboned valentine Sadie had made and pictured his own heart, cracked down the center. Without Sadie he was broken inside. Broken already. He worried that it might be just as bad if he left this place, his home.

Lapp Farms.

He'd never considered himself to be a material person, but he was attached to this place, this land. Yah, he loved his family and appreciated the community here in Joyful

River. Nearly every hour of each day was filled with the sights, sounds, and smells of this farm. The glittering dust rising in a shaft of sunlight in the haymow. Snow slanting from the roof of the chicken coop. The wide, brown eyes of a cow, eyes that told him they were peaceful and content with their day on this farm, that held the same satisfaction he felt each morning and night. The call of the rooster, and the lowing of the cows, and the chorus of frogs from the summer pond.

These were the sounds of his life on this farm.

Without them, the silence in his life would be deafening.

Chapter 34

"Two more clothespins, and we're done," Miriam said as she hung a pair of boy's underwear on the back of the clothesline near the glazed window.

"One, two," Sarah Rose counted out, then handed the clips up to her mother.

"Denki." The little girl had become such a good helper, especially during the quiet times when the others were off at work or school.

The steady patter of rain on the tin awning over the door reinforced Miriam's decision to hang her laundry inside today. She had started by hanging the bedsheets nearest the kitchen and back door, where people coming in and out would see as they passed by. The center of the room was for dresses, shirts, and pants. And the very back, near the diesel generator–powered washing machine and the small window, was reserved to hang underwear. It was the clothesline order that Miriam's own mem had taught her, one of the many things she had carried into her own routines.

Today, the laundry load was light. Essie took care of the laundry for Harlan and herself, as well as that of his mother and his sister Suzie. Most likely Miriam would find that batch hanging in here later in the week. And since Sadie had left, there'd been few clothes to wash for Sam. Day after day, he wore the same shirt and pants, changing out of them but once in a fortnight when he donned his church clothes. Miriam had prodded him to let her wash them, even knocking on his door last night to try to wrest them away. She'd found him asleep on his bed, facedown and still wearing the old pants and wrinkled shirt.

What was a mother to do? A grown son was not to be consoled by his mem, and Sam was certainly mature enough to manage such things on his own. But Miriam had made sure, over the past two months, to make Sam's favorite meal—Amish pork chops—as often as the budget allowed, and she'd kept the cookie jar full by baking every other day. Food couldn't cure a broken heart, but delicious food could make anyone feel a little bit better.

Food and sleep were so important. She and Alvie had been lacking sleep since the night that Sam had talked about moving to York. Miriam felt sick about the prospect, though Alvie waxed philosophical. "On the one hand, it would be a huge mistake to let Sam go right now. He can be replaced, that's true, but it'll take a while to bring a new worker up to speed, and it'll be hard to make do. But if we don't let him go, will he always resent this farm?"

"Dear Alvie, it's not ours to worry over. It's Sam's choice."

"You say that, but you haven't been sleeping well since our talk."

"You're right. But he didn't actually say he was leaving," Miriam had reminded her husband. "He's trying to figure out his options."

So far, they hadn't heard any more about moving, but

Miriam knew Sam could not go on this way for much longer.

She clamped her jaw tight and lifted the empty clothes basket from the floor. Sam was hurting, that was for sure, but as a young man he did a good job of wrapping himself in the constant work of the farm and the pretension that nothing really mattered. Early to bed, early to rise, and you clench your teeth through the pain in the middle.

It was no way to live, but Miriam knew these were desperate times for her eldest son.

"Come, little rosebud." Miriam put a hand on her little girl's shoulder. "Are you ready for a snack, or maybe some reading time?"

"I can read a book," Sarah Rose said.

Miriam wasn't sure whether the five-year-old could actually read or if she'd memorized every book in their collection. No matter. While the little girl was engrossed in her books, Miriam was often able to get many of her chores done.

Inside the kitchen, Miriam checked the wall calendar once again to make sure she had the date right. There it was, in her own handwriting: the initials "CM." She had made her own little code, knowing that the name "Miller" on the calendar would have raised questions from Sam and Alvie, at the very least. The Miller name wasn't a popular one in their house these days.

The savory smells from the stove were reassuring. Miriam closed the door to the mudroom, hoping to ward off the cold and damp. April showers had washed away any snow left on the ground, but chilly air lingered, and the night frosts were not yet hospitable to putting any plants in the ground. The old stove glowed with a modicum of heat, enough to lure Miriam closer to stir the vegetable beef soup she'd put on to simmer that morning. Soup and a sandwich—that would make a nice lunch for Miriam and Mrs. Wayne Miller.

"Carol," Miriam had called her in the letter she'd written toward the end of March. She'd chosen to be casual, because that was the only way she knew—relaxed, upfront, and personal.

> *"I'd be most grateful if you'd stop by our home to discuss some matters dear to our hearts," she'd written. "Weekdays are a good time for me, as the children are either off to school or working, so we'd have some time for a light lunch and conversation. Would you please call at the number below and leave a message? Let me know a date that works well for you—the sooner the better!"*

After signing the letter, Miriam had folded it, stuffed it into the envelope, and walked it to the mailbox at the road before she could suffer regret and change her mind. She was sticking her neck out, but she liked to think that was one of her gifts: getting involved. Righting wrongs. Healing wounds. Nothing warmed her heart like the glimmer of joy in someone else's eyes.

So she'd mailed the letter, and then put it out of her mind for a few days. It wouldn't surprise her if Carol couldn't make it for a visit, but she did expect an answer. Although she didn't know Carol and Wayne Miller well, they were part of the same church community—which meant they encountered Miriam and the Lapp family every other Sunday. Ignoring her invitation would be rude and might cause awkwardness.

As Miriam had expected, Carol had replied with a phone message, saying she could come by on this date in April. Hence the calendar was marked in Miriam's somewhat abbreviated code. Alvie knew a church acquaintance was coming today, but he hadn't made the connection to Mark's mother. Sam, who was far more observant and would have protested her plan, had been sent off to town on a wild goose chase of errands. As she opened a can of tuna, Miriam bit back a smile. She had given her son a list of hard-to-find items to pick up at the dry goods store and the general store. Cumin and cinnamon sticks. Pineapple rings and shredded coconut. Avocado oil and WD-40. As Sam was not a seasoned shopper and men hated to ask questions, that list would keep him busy.

Miriam chopped celery, onion, and two boiled eggs for her special tuna salad recipe and wondered if Carol Miller was a picky eater. Miriam didn't know Carol or Wayne well. Everyone knew they owned the auction house, which dazzled some folks, who thought the business a success because of the money it made.

Not Miriam. She was glad the Millers had done well, but money was no substitute for a happy life with family, friends, and community. Sarah Rose brought her book into the kitchen, and Miriam made half of a peanut butter sandwich cut into two small squares, the way her little girl liked it. When she heard the buggy coming down the lane, Miriam took off her cooking apron and went out to welcome Carol.

"Let me help you with that," Miriam said, taking the reins from the woman's hands. "We usually just tie off the horses here for short stays." Carol was more petite than Miriam recalled, and from her slow movements it appeared that the woman suffered from stiff joints or some mild illness.

"That's fine," Carol said, heading toward the stairs. "I won't be long."

Miriam took that as a desire to make a quick exit, but she had a few things to discuss before she let Carol go. Inside, Carol sat at the kitchen table while Miriam put the kettle on for tea and served up two bowls of soup. The platter of sandwiches was placed between them on the table, and Sarah Rose seemed content to go through the books on the low shelf in the front room for the time being.

Up close, Miriam noticed Carol's creamy, pale skin, lovely as a child's. There were no wrinkles or freckles there. So far, Carol was also proving to be quiet as a mouse, though that might have been on account of her eating. Either way, it was up to Miriam to break the ice.

"Thank you for coming," Miriam said. She knew that if she was going to reach this woman, a stranger in many ways, she was going to have to find their common ground. "We see each other at church, but never really got acquainted. I have seven children, aged five to twenty-one. Have you others besides Mark?"

"Two others," Carol said. "All boys, all much older. He's been the only one in our household for years now. And the only one to do so well at the family business. My other sons, Trent and William, they help with the bookkeeping and such, but Mark is the only one to become an auctioneer. And so good at it, he is. Have you ever seen him in action?"

"I have! He's so very impressive. My children tease me about being a chatterbox and a fast talker, but your Mark speaks faster than lightning itself! I don't know how he does it."

"Practice, they say. It was his father's skill first. Wayne is so pleased Mark learned it. Pleased to have one son to follow in his footsteps."

Miriam took down two of her wedding cups and saucers—white china with a cloverleaf pattern that she rarely got a chance to use, though it made her smile. As she poured out two cups of tea, Miriam nodded, realizing this might be harder than she thought, with Mark being the favored son. Well, she had to try.

"I have to confess, one of the reasons I invited you here was to talk about the situation with your son Mark and Sadie Beiler." Miriam tossed the last bite of her sandwich in as she watched Carol's expression sour. In for a penny, in for a pound. "You see, Sadie is a good friend of my daughter Essie. She's like a daughter to me. And she's been dating my son Sam. Apparently, they were getting serious, so it's a difficult thing, having Sadie off in York."

"The church leaders made their decision, and we're following it." Carol folded her hands on the table, as if the matter were closed.

"Yah, your family is following the rules. But I think there's more to the situation than the church leaders know. Maybe more than you're aware of. It's sort of like in the summertime when you look at the river and it's churning blue and white. It all seems so simple and clear. But when you wade in and look closely, you see there's so much going on there. The minnows, the crappie and bass. The little plants growing underwater. Water insects and frogs. The river is much more complex and busy than you realize at a distant glance."

Carol squinted at her, losing patience.

Perhaps it was a bad example. Carol Miller did not look like the sort of woman who waded into the river and soaked the hem of her dress on a carefree summer afternoon.

"I don't see your point," Carol said, toying with the teaspoon.

"I'm not speaking to you as a friend, simply because I don't presume to know you well, and for that I'm sorry. I'm speaking to you as a mother, one mother to another."

There was a glint of interest—or maybe it was fear—in Carol's eyes as she lowered her cup of tea to the saucer and leaned forward. "All right."

"I have a few points to make. First, the bishop's decision to keep Sam and Sadie apart is torturing those two lovebirds. They're young, and they deserve happiness. My second point is going to be a bitter pill to swallow, but I have to be honest with you. Your Mark needs help. He suffers dark moods, and he has a temper that he's taken out on the girls he's dated."

"That's not true!" Carol's mouth opened in a round O of disbelief. "He wouldn't hurt a fly."

"He's done worse. I had a long talk with Sadie before she left town, and Sam and the Troyer girls witnessed part of Mark's outburst."

"He was joking around with Sadie, and people took it the wrong way. It was a one-time thing."

"There were similar incidents with other girls. Lavern Gingerich and Tootie Frey." When Carol shook her head, Miriam felt a rush of sympathy. "Carol, I know it's hard to hear difficult things about our children. I'm not telling you this to lay trouble on your doorstep. I say this because Mark needs help."

"Nay." Carol shook her head. "There's never been a problem before."

"There has. It just wasn't brought to anyone's attention."

"It's just rumors, that's all. Folks are jealous of our Mark, and they make up stories."

"No." Miriam kept her voice low, trying to deliver the difficult information with compassion. "I've talked to the girls themselves. Young women, now. Lavern has a family of her own, and Tootie married a year ago. They were victims of Mark's dark moods. His bad temper. And some violence."

"They said that?"

Miriam's heart ached for the woman across from her. "They did."

Carol leaned back in the kitchen chair, the stiffness seeping from her backbone as the truth overcame her. "Dear Gott in heaven, I didn't know."

"Those girls have moved on," Miriam said. "They both told me they put Mark out of their minds; they've forgiven him. But even with forgiveness, Mark's behavior continues. There's a pattern of abuse."

"It's so much to take in. Such a terrible thing. My own son . . ." For a long moment, Carol rested her face in her hands, looking as if she might hide there indefinitely. When her hands fell away, her cheekbones were wet. "He told me he never intended to hurt Sadie, and I believed him. I've never heard anything of these girls from the past, but three young women with the same story . . . I have to accept that they're telling the truth and my son is the one who's troubled." She pushed away her teacup as the edges of her mouth turned down, her face puckered in pain. "I should have known. How did you get these girls to open up to you? I mean, how did you even find them after all this time?"

"Their mothers." Miriam had asked around about Mark, starting with Sadie, and over time she'd begun to piece together the sad tales of his previous girlfriends. Essie had heard a few accounts, which she reluctantly shared, reminding Miriam that she couldn't verify whether they were rumor or truth.

No one dared to barter in gossip. But in Miriam's experience, when bits of detail kept popping up over and again, there tended to be a grain of truth in the story.

Miriam told Carol that she had decided to go to the source. Of course, she couldn't just reach out to Lavern and Tootie and expect them to spill the beans. So she'd tapped her friendship network at church, starting with Lavern's mother, Vera, who invited Miriam over for coffee and conversation with Lavern one glum winter day. How they'd enjoyed chatting and giggling by the fire as the little ones played with the chalkboard on the wall and the pots and pans. The afternoon had been a delight, dampened only by Lavern's brief recollection of Mark's abuses.

A conversation with Tootie had proven to be more of a challenge, but when Tootie came to town to spend Easter week with her family, her mother, Myrna, had made arrangements for Miriam to visit. It had been a quiet afternoon, and to Miriam's delight, Tootie was pregnant, expecting a baby in July. Myrna had been putting up a batch of pickled radishes, and Miriam had shared her recipe, adding a teaspoon of sugar to the apple cider vinegar. The pickling had gone quickly, and afterward, during a short walk, Tootie had shared the difficult details about her relationship with Mark. "I don't mean to cause him any trouble, but in a way, I'm happy to get this off my chest.

When it happened, I was so scared that I told Mem. Dat stepped in and told Mark I wasn't allowed to see him anymore."

"And did that fix the situation?" Miriam had asked.

"It made Mark stay away, but it scared off all the other boys, too. Eventually I realized I needed to make a fresh start somewhere else. That's when my parents made arrangements for me to move in with my aunt Julie in Bird-in-Hand. That's where I met my husband, my Jeff, and I've been very happy there."

"And now you're starting a family of your own." Miriam had patted the girl's shoulder, so warmed by the glow on Tootie's face. Gott made his people resilient, and Tootie was an example of how forgiveness could free a person to move on in life.

Miriam's conversations with Lavern and Tootie had convinced her that going to Mark's mother was the right thing to do. Funny, but she had started her bit of digging to try to find a way for Sadie and Sam to be together. But once she learned about the trail of cruelty Mark had left in his wake, Miriam knew she had to do more. "I'm concerned for Mark," Miriam told Carol. "He needs help; he needs to learn that successful relationships are based not on fear, but love. And the bad behavior has to end."

"I don't know what to do." Carol tipped her face down as a new wave of tears came over her. "I know that Mark's temper is real. I have seen him blow up a few times. But his behavior is well beyond my control. He's a grown man now, free to do as he pleases."

"I'm sure he respects you," Miriam said, handing her a tissue. "And we know he'll respect and follow what the church leaders decide."

Carol shook her head. "I don't know where to begin."

"What about your husband?" Miriam asked. "Will he be willing to support you in getting Mark help?"

"Wayne will be devastated, but I know he'll want to do what's right. He'll want the best for Mark."

"Then you start by talking with your husband. Pray on it, as I will, too."

Carol sniffed and nodded.

"And if you need anything, moral support or just someone to talk to, I'm your gal." Miriam winked. "My husband thinks I'm a bit nosy, but I love being involved, solving problems. Some nights I can't rest until everyone has what they need."

"I'm sure I'll be asking your advice."

"You bet." Miriam took a sip of tea and smiled.

A mother's work was never done.

Chapter 35

Smells of lilac wafted over on the breeze as Sadie hung laundry out in the backyard. The light wind lifted white sheets in the air, and they floated there, suspended, until Lovina ducked under one, giggling. Although Sadie had tried to enlist her niece in helping with chores on this beautiful spring day, Lovina preferred to run circles around her and pick a bouquet of dandelions. No matter. As long as she kept occupied, Lovina was free to enjoy the playtime of a three-year-old.

As a puffy white cloud shifted and sunlight warmed Sadie's back and arms, she thought of Sam, miles away, under the same bright sun. Maybe he was fixing a fence, or tending to a sick cow, or helping his dat plough one of the hayfields. It helped her to think of him sharing Gott's big blue sky and spring sunshine. There was still pain and loneliness—sorrow that sometimes ached from head to toe, as real as any pain or fever. But Sadie had learned to put it aside and get on with her day.

As Sharon had advised her, "Put your sorrow in a box, tie it off with a ribbon, and go on with your day. It will be there waiting for you, and someday you'll find that the box is just a bit lighter."

So far, the box hadn't gotten much lighter, but Sharon was a source of good advice. In their long winter hours together, her older sister had taught her the importance of forgiveness. "Sometimes healing is a matter of forgiving the people who hurt you," Sharon had told her. Sharon counseled that Sadie wouldn't be free to move on until she forgave Mark and even Dat for causing her pain.

Over many hours, they had shared their experiences and fears of Dat's drinking during their childhood. "Why didn't you tell me it was a problem when you were a teen?" Sadie asked her sister. "I thought it started when I was the only daughter left in the house. I thought it was my fault."

"Ach, nay. Polly remembers Dat drinking even before you were born. But she doesn't like to talk about it, and it's one of those things we tamp down and keep secret. Maybe because it's so uncomfortable to talk about it."

"I used to cower under the covers, listening to him yell at Mem," Sadie admitted. "I was so afraid."

"Me too. It didn't happen all the time, but it was often enough to drive me to find a husband and get out of the house as quick as possible. But lately he seems to be doing better."

"Much better," Sadie agreed. "And it's not a secret to be swept under the rug anymore. It helps to be able to talk about it."

Sadie felt secure in the fact that her relationship with Dat had been mended. She was happy for his attention to his health. He'd stopped drinking, and that was a blessing. And most recently, he'd come to her aid as never before.

Mark was another story. Some days she wanted to shout at him for putting her miles away from most of the people she loved. But in the past few weeks, she'd come to realize that her anger with Mark was only draining her. It required a bit of energy to fan the flames of resentment and anger. So . . . enough with him!

Sadie looked forward to Sam's visit next week, and she was often able to lose herself in time spent with her young niece and nephew. She loved playing games with Lovina, and it was a labor of love to feed the children or give them baths. Nathan had now progressed to all sorts of mashed foods, from peas to bananas, which he seemed to enjoy wearing more than eating. And it was a joy to watch him muster all his strength and coordination to pull himself up on the edge of a low table.

But time spent with the children reminded her of the dreams she had of motherhood. The plan to start a family and have babies with Sam. Now it was hard to see how that might happen. Although Sam had talked of moving here and finding a job, she knew it would break his heart in a different way to leave his family and the Lapp farm behind. He belonged in Joyful River; they both knew that.

But then Sadie belonged in Joyful River, too, and here she was . . .

"A flower for you," Lovina said, presenting a dandelion with a giggle.

"You're so kind," Sadie teased, tucking the golden weed into her apron and hanging up the last of the laundry. "Come." She lifted the basket. "Let's help your mem in the garden."

The sweet smell of sun-warm clover reminded Sadie of home. Lovina held the bunch of dandelions out to one side as she followed Sadie across the lawn, greened by their recent rain, and into the house. In her search for distractions, Sadie had found sweet pockets of joy in her moments with her niece. A true gift from Gott.

After dropping the laundry basket by the door, Sadie opened the gate to the garden, where Sharon was working at thinning out the row of carrots.

"Such a beautiful day," Sharon said.

"I brought you flowers, Mem." Lovina presented a bouquet of dandelions.

"Denki. That's almost enough to make dandelion tea." Sharon straightened at a sound coming from the house. A healthy cry came from the open window. "Nathan is awake from his nap. I'll be right back."

Lovina followed her mother inside as Sadie knelt to finish the carrots. She couldn't wait for Sam to see the garden when he came. The straight rows of beans and peas and red beets amid the dark, tilled soil brought Sadie a sense of pleasure she'd never experienced back home in the hothouse—maybe because she'd had an active hand in the planting here.

If there was a silver lining to the last few months, it was that Sadie had been pushed to grow up and be a true adult. Gardening, childcare, cooking and cleaning—she was becoming good at juggling all the things a woman needed to do to keep a household running. And she was grateful to Gott for showing her what true love was before she'd made a terrible mistake with Mark. She'd come very close to a lifetime of marriage with the wrong person!

The noise of an automobile on the main road caught her attention as it turned into the Schwartz driveway.

She stood up and craned her neck for a better look. A visitor?

The back door of the small red car opened, and out

came a handsome Amish man in a deep blue shirt with black pants and suspenders.

Not just any Amish man. "Sam!"

Sadie dropped the garden tool in her hand and flew out the gate. "It *is* you! What are you doing here?" The thought that something might be wrong at home was dismissed by the wide smile illuminating his face.

They ran to each other, and Sadie closed her eyes as he swept her into his arms. He was here—a few days early, but all the better. Her fingers smoothed over the soft cotton of his shirt as she savored feeling protected in his embrace.

"I thought I'd surprise you," he said. "I've got news, Sadie. Great news."

Sadie couldn't imagine what could make Sam so happy. "What is it?"

He leaned back and held on to her arms so that he was looking directly into her eyes. "I've come to take you home."

Sadie shook her head, wishing she could believe him, but still painfully aware of her dread sentence here. Was this a joke? "How could that be?" she asked.

Sam's caramel-colored eyes were impossibly round and serious. "There's been a change. Mark Miller is moving to Lititz for the next few years. He's going to help his uncle and cousin get the auction house running there, and his dat can do without him in Joyful River for the time being."

"So he won't be in Joyful River?" Hope blossomed in her heart as the news washed over her. "If I go back, he won't be there. And then . . . what about the church leaders? They need to approve . . ."

"Bishop Aaron and the others agree that it's a good plan. In fact, they think it's a better plan than before. They said that their original decision was never designed to punish you." The joy returned to his face. "You can come home, Sadie. The hired driver will take us both back this afternoon, if you want."

"I can come home?" Her voice quivered, tentative.

Sam nodded yes, the love in his eyes telling her that it was also his wildest dream, his greatest desire, coming true in a single day.

Sadie looked from Sam's handsome face to the clothes-line, to the garden, and then back to Sam again. All this—her penance at Sharon's house—all this would end today? Her head fairly thrummed with excitement, and tears filled her eyes as she considered the sweetness of returning to Joyful River. The people, the land, the house she'd grown up in . . . it was her home. Her past. And now, with this miracle from out of the blue, it would be her present and future, too.

The driver of the hired car started the engine, causing Sadie to step away from Sam, turning toward the car. "Should we tell the driver to wait?" She didn't want to miss her chance.

She was going home!

"He's going to grab some lunch in town and then swing back to pick us up." Sam smiled. "But I like your enthusiasm."

"That's putting it mildly," she said, turning back to the man she loved. "I'm overjoyed. Thrilled. I didn't think anything could top the joy of seeing you, but now you've done it." She took his hand. "I can barely believe it. I've missed you so much."

"Now you'll get to see me all the time." He pulled her back, closer to him. "You might get sick of me."

"That will never happen." Her voice was a near whisper as his arms went around her and she rose onto her toes to kiss him. The tingling sensations, the fireworks, the delight blossoming like a flower . . . all the facets of love could be found in Sam's kiss.

When Sadie lowered herself to the earth again, a new happiness surged through her. "I must be the happiest person alive," she exclaimed.

"Besides me," Sam teased. He lowered his chin, studying her for a moment. "Sadie, I was going to wait, but I don't want to take any chances after we've come so far. You know I love you. You know Gott means us to be together. Please, will you marry me and be my wife?"

She gasped, then patted his shoulder affectionately. "I thought you'd never ask."

Right then and there he lifted her into his arms, and they laughed together as he spun her around on the wide green lawn.

When her feet landed back on the ground, Sam kept his arms around her waist. "Are we going to keep this a secret until wedding season comes around and the minister can publish our announcement at church?"

"We've kept things a secret far too long," Sadie said, holding back a smile. "Though maybe not so well."

"Yah. Everyone in my family already knows."

"They recognized our love long ago," Sadie said, "because they know what it's like to live each day with a heart full of love. But I say no secrets. We'll go with the new trend and send a 'save the date' announcement so that all our friends and family can attend. We're so blessed!"

Sam nodded. "I've been blessed with a loving family. And now, a beautiful Amish bride." Sadie recognized the love glimmering in his eyes. "A double blessing."

Behind them, a screen door slammed and Lovina skipped out, Sharon following with Nathan squirming in her arms. She bent down to set him on the grass. When she looked up and caught sight of Sadie with Sam, she let out a whoop of delight.

"Sam! What a wonderful surprise!" She hurried over, quickly registering the joy of the moment. "You two look positively giddy."

"Giddy with happiness," Sadie said. "Sam's come to take me home. You've made me feel welcome here, but . . ."

"Back to Joyful River?" Sharon's hands flew to her face. "That's the answer to our prayers! Nothing personal, sis, but we know where your heart is. But how can all this happen?"

They stood in the garden and talked of the many things that had changed so quickly in the past day. Sam mentioned that the church leaders were also insisting that Mark work on anger management with a church leader in his new settlement.

Anger management? Sadie was astounded at the development, though it reinforced the hand of Gott in this matter. Gott, in his infinite wisdom, was making sure everyone got what they needed.

As Sam recounted the events, Sadie handed her niece a spade and her nephew a pail so they could play in the garden. Listening to Sam, Sadie wondered about the abrupt change.

"It's curious, isn't it?" she asked. "Mark changing his mind so suddenly and moving to Lititz?"

Sam nodded. "I don't know for sure, but I think he had a little prodding. Mem seems to know a lot about the situation, and I found out through Dat that Mark's mother had lunch at our house last week."

"Miriam!" Sadie's eyes opened wide. "Leave it to Miriam to get involved. I know she loves matchmaking."

"And miracle working," Sharon said.

"She's a wonder," Sadie agreed. "I don't know how your mem did it, but she managed to change a lot of minds."

"That's my mem for you," Sam said.

As they talked, a cloud veered off toward the east, and sunlight showered them all with a warm glow. Sadie kept smiling, basking in the light.

The same sun, Sadie thought, but this time, she and Sam were together.

Now and for always.